Behind the Ranges, Book III

THE DUCHESS OF OPHIR CREEK

By

Judith B. Glad

*Something hidden. Go and find it.
Go and look behind the ranges—
Something lost behind the Ranges.
Lost and waiting for you. Go.*
Rudyard Kipling: *The Explorer*

This is a work of fiction. Names, characters, places and events described herein are products of the author's imagination or are used fictitiously and are not to be construed as real. Any resemblance to actual events, locations, organizations, or persons, living or dead, is entirely coincidental.

ISBN: 978-1493713509
1493713507

The Duchess of Ophir Creek
Copyright © 2001, 2013 by Judith B. Glad

Cover design and background photo © Judith B. Glad
Bag of gold photo © tmchen

Electronically Published by Uncial Press,
http://www.uncialpress.com

All rights reserved. Except for use in review, the reproduction or utilization of this work in whole or in part in any form by any electronic, mechanical or other means now known or hereafter invented, is forbidden without the written permission of the author or publisher.

This book is dedicated to the memory of so many
young Chinese women who,
in the 19th Century, came to America unwillingly
and found little but slavery when they got here.

And to Neil, of course.

Chapter One

Idaho Territory, 1862

THE TRAIL SPLIT WHERE THE CANYON OPENED UP INTO THE BOISE Basin. Silas Dewitt pulled his horse to a halt, wondering if he'd somehow lost his way.

My God. It's all gone...all changed. How will I ever find it? Dimly remembered landmarks weren't going to help him now. The hills were the same, but everything else was different.

Fifteen years ago tall pines had marched down the steep hillsides and into the valley, taller than anything he'd ever seen. One step off the narrow game trails and he'd been snarled in huckleberry and mock orange that grew higher than his head. The forest had given way to dense willow thickets along the several branches of a creek that tumbled down out of the narrow valley to the northeast, braiding and weaving its way across the meadow, until it plunged down the canyon whence he'd come.

Now the lower hillsides were raw with skid roads and freckled with fresh stumps. The creek banks were bare, scarred with trenches, littered with broken sluice boxes and discarded tools.

He'd heard there were already more than two thousand men in this valley alone. And more were arriving every day.

"Well, hell," he muttered, nudging his horse into a walk. "This looks like it's going to take more time than I'd planned."

Just on the edge of town was a half-finished barn bearing a freshly painted sign. *Livry Stabel*. He arranged to board his two horses and to leave his gear in an empty stall until he found a place to stay.

"Not likely you'll find one, though," the hostler said past the wad of snoose in his cheek. "This here town's growin' like a jimson weed in a manure heap."

"Any notion where a letter might be left? There ought to be one waiting for me."

"Tilly's is the most likely place. Most folks stop in there sooner or later."

Silas listened to the hum of a town in the making as he strode up the rutted, not-quite-straight street. Hammers pounded and saws screeched through green wood, all to the rhythm of rockers thumping along the creek. Tents and shanties and raw, rough-cut pine structures sprouted on every side, slapped together and hurriedly roofed against the coming winter. Of all the places Silas had seen, Bannock City was the newest, the crudest, the ugliest. Here was a town of men with only one thing on their minds.

Gold.

Past the third saloon, he saw miners clustered like iron filings around a magnet. *A fight, I reckon.* He'd guess that not many days went by here without one. Not wanting to get embroiled in the melee, he angled across to the other side of the street. The less notice folks took of him hereabouts, the better he'd like it.

Silas dodged among the oncoming miners, staying on the edge of the crowd. Then a high-pitched shriek made him pause.

A woman? Or a child?

As he hesitated, a rough voice cut across the laughter.

"Git a torch!"

"Yeah, scorch the little varmits!"

For a moment there was taut silence.

"Damn right," a miner yelled. "Filthy slant-eyed heathen."

"Comin' in and takin' work from white men," another cried.

Just then a small, black-clad figure scooted between two men. Before he could escape, a big-bellied miner caught him by his queue. The child screamed as he was snatched off his feet to dangle, kicking wildly.

"Lookee here what I cotched!" the miner crowed, holding him high.

"Hand him here," another shouted. The Chinese boy was passed from hand to hand, until Silas lost sight of him. His shrieks were drowned in the hullabaloo.

"This ain't fitten," a man beside him muttered. "Somebody ought to put a stop to it."

Silas agreed. From their expressions, a few others were of the same mind, but no one looked overly eager to interfere. Well, neither was he.

Another terror-filled shriek from the center of the mob triggered old, unwelcome memories. He shouldered through the circle.

So much for playing least in sight.

Once again Soomey was helpless in the hands of men who were bigger and stronger than she.

She knew the miners were merely amusing themselves. Their laughter was teasing, not threatening. Knowing did nothing to lessen her rage.

Her fear.

Kicking and clawing, she fought as she was shoved back against Tao Ni. A sharp jerk on her queue shot tingles down her neck, across her shoulders.

"You reckon them pigtails is strong as rope?" her captor said.

More laughter.

"Tie 'em good, Eli," someone called.

She leaned into the pull on her scalp. As long as some were

still laughing, perhaps she and Tao Ni would escape serious harm.

"There ye go. Give your'n a poke," the crooked man who held her said. "See which'n pulls the hardest."

Tao Ni yelped. Soomey was jerked off her feet. The men had tied their queues together!

The shouts grew louder, the voices more excited. "Half an ounce on the leetle one!"

"I'll take that. He ain't got a chance."

"Be still, Tao Ni," Soomey cried. "They want us to struggle. Stop pulling!"

Her words were lost in the raucous laughter.

Someone slapped her across the bottom and she sprawled on her face. Moisture seeped through her cotton trousers, icy cold against her belly. Lunging, she tried to catch Tao Ni by the ankle, but as she grabbed, he was pulled out of her reach.

I will not weep she vowed, lifting herself out of the puddle. Her soaked clothing clung to her body like a layer of ice.

Tao Ni was doing his best to escape. Each time he lunged toward an opening in the barrier of booted feet, he jerked her off balance. She threw herself on top of him, gasping when one flailing hand caught her across the nose. Hot blood trickled down her upper lip as she held the child. "Be still, small one," she murmured, over and over. "Be calm"

Fear made him strong. She almost lost her grip.

"Be still. I will not let them harm you," she promised, wondering if she lied.

The circle around her and Tao Ni narrowed as the miners pressed closer, their faces filled with menace. Then the crowd broke apart as a wide-shouldered, yellow-bearded man shoved his way inside. He paused and turned in a circle, as if daring anyone to challenge him.

"Hold on there!" His voice was commanding. The miners seemed to shrink back.

Soomey caught Tao Ni by the wrist and tensed, ready to

run the instant she saw an opening. Too late. With a hand at the back of her coat, Yellow-beard lifted her to her feet.

"You, boy," he said, "what you do here? Why you not work? You think I pay you for makee play in street?" Tao Ni dangled from his other hand.

"Them Chinee yours?" one of the men said before Soomey could answer.

"What does it look like?" the stranger snapped. He set Tao Ni down, released Soomey.

Her legs gave way under her.

"Thought they worked for Harding," another miner commented.

Soomey reached for Tao Ni, wrapping her arms around him, forcing him to be still. The buckets she had been carrying lay empty, rice strewn like pellets of snow on the mud. One stood upside down in a still-steaming puddle of cooling tea.

Li Ching's work gang would not receive their noonday meal. And she and Tao Ni would go hungry today.

"Damn theivin' Chinks," one of their tormentors said. "I saw 'em down there in Californy, gettin' rich whilst us honest men worked our arses off."

There was a wave of agreement. She held Tao Ni against her, felt the shivers that wracked him. For now she was content to let the big man be their defender. But as soon as he turned his back...

"Untie our queues, little one," she whispered.

Tao Ni nodded. His shaking fingers began picking clumsily at the tight knot.

"Did the boys take gold from you?" Yellow-beard said to the miners. "From your claim?"

"Well, no, but..."

"Pick your pocket?"

"Well, no..."

"Steal your dog?"

A few reluctant chuckles sounded.

"Shit!" A miner spat, narrowly missing the big man's foot. "You want to trust them slanty-eyed devils, you go right ahead, mister! Just be careful they don't slit your throat whilst you sleep, y'hear?"

A deep, ringing voice came from the back of the mob. "I have seen their graven images and they are an abomination!"

Soomey saw suspicion flare again in a few faces, saw once more a slow shift away from humor.

Yellow-beard laughed.

"Graven images?" he said, his face showing complete disbelief. "Paper dragons made of scraps of foil and bamboo sticks!"

Tao Ni, not understanding one word in fifty, clutched at her wrist. "What does the one say, Elder Sister?"

"Hush, child," Soomey breathed. "The danger is not yet past."

"We was jest havin' a little fun," said the crooked man who'd first waylaid her. "Ain't done no harm."

"So you say." Yellow-beard's lip curled in contempt. "Well, next time pick on someone big enough to fight back." He turned away and motioned to Soomey. "Let's go, boy. Time you were earning your keep."

She bristled but knew that she dared not refuse to follow him. Most of the miners had lost interest in their sport and were drifting away. But if she refused to obey Yellow-beard, they would be back quickly. Leaving the broken carry-pole, she snatched up the two buckets.

"What did he say to make the miners laugh?" Tao Ni asked, once they were away from the disintegrating crowd.

Still shaking inside, Soomey sought words to reassure him. "He told them we were not worth their while, weak and defenseless."

"Are you angry with him, Elder Sister? He said no more than the truth."

Soomey did not reply, for she knew just how weak and

defenseless they had been. And how fortunate. The miners had merely been amusing themselves today. Their laughter had been teasing, not threatening. But what of tomorrow?

In the future she must be ready to defend herself and Tao Ni. Today the miners had taken her by surprise, seeing only two defenseless children ripe for tormenting.

She dressed as a man, worked like one. She must learn to fight like one, so that no man would rule her. Never again.

Tao Ni still picked at the knot, making little progress. He stumbled, and Yellow-beard looked back. He pulled an enormous knife from its sheath at his belt. "Come here," he said, motioning Tao Ni forward. "I'll fix that."

The child cowered behind Soomey.

She glared at Yellow-beard. "You no cut hair! You not Boss of us!"

He looked down at her with eyes as cold and pale as a winter sky. "Hurry up, then. I've got things to do." He strode off.

Soomey grabbed Tao Ni's hand and trotted after him. She would be patient and see what advantage she might gain.

They followed Yellow-beard to the livery stable. He halted at the door of a stall where saddlebags and a well-stuffed burlap bag were piled. "You two wait here," he told them. "I'll be back in a while."

Soomey had been thinking furiously. The Chinese camp was on the other side of town. Could she and Tao Ni reach it safely, or would the miners catch them again? And was she ready to tell Li Ching of her failure? He was becoming impatient with her. She must give him no excuse to forget their agreement. He would profit greatly by exploiting her. Perhaps they were better off with Yellow-beard.

Knowing they needed him could give him power over them, however. This she would not tolerate. "Why we wait?" she challenged. "We no work you."

Silas scratched his chin. The only sensible thing to do was give these brats a dollar each and send them on their way. But his conscience wouldn't let him. Not until he was sure they had someone to look after them.

The younger lad's fingers still worked at the knotted pigtails. The older stood stiffly before Silas, not yielding an inch, his chin set stubbornly as he all but dared Silas to issue another order.

"Who's your boss?" he said.

A shrug. "Work here one day, there one day. No boss."

"Where do you live?" Surely there was a Chinese community here. "Where are your parents?"

Silence.

Silas said, "Your mother? Your father? Who do you live with?"

"We live over there." The boy's arm waved in the direction of the creek. "No mother. No father." He made motions of digging. "We work. Work good. You want China boy work for you?"

Silas almost said no.

Then he paused. It was like looking into a mirror at his own past. These two might 'work good' but he'd bet they hadn't eaten good in a long time. Neither boy looked old enough to swing a shovel, yet hadn't Silas followed behind a plow when he was barely shoulder high to the plowhorses? Hadn't he been grateful to have food in his belly and a place to sleep? Gratitude, he reflected, often bought strong loyalty.

"I'm not a miner. I don't need anyone to dig." He saw hope start to fade in the older boy's eyes. "What else can you do?"

"We good China boy, work hard. No...no..." He shrugged, made a gesture so obscene that Silas had no doubt that this boy had seen far more than his share of the world's evil.

"How old are you?"

The boy shrugged. "Old enough," he said, face expressionless. "But him, he too little. He no do..." Again the gesture.

"Neither do I." What was he doing? The last thing he needed was two Chinese brats hanging on his coattails. Yet they were so young. So thin and bedraggled. What else could he do with them?

On the other hand, they might be just what the doctor ordered. He and Emmet would need to make sure they weren't followed as they went about their business. One hint of why they were here and they wouldn't be able to take a step without being dogged by half a hundred hungry miners.

He said, "I want...I could use...well, someone who can keep his eyes and ears open. And his mouth shut."

Again the narrow-eyed look, suspicious and calculating. "You want two China boy? Do two times as much look, listen?"

Silas nodded, certain now the boy understood far more English than he would admit. "Yes. I'll hire you both. A dollar a week and found."

The boy shook his head. "Two dolla' him, two dolla' me."

Silas didn't know the going rate for Chinese boys in Bannock City, but he'd wager it was far less than two dollars a week, even if coffee was selling for six bits a pound. Still, he couldn't fault the lad for wanting a decent wage. "Okay. A dollar a week each."

"Two dolla' me, one dolla' him." A thumb jerked in the direction of the smaller. "He no work so hard."

Silas pretended to think it over. "Two dollars a week for you, six bits for him. And found."

"You wait." The boy jabbered at his smaller companion.

Not for the first time, Silas wished he had a better ear for language. He'd never learned to understand more than a few words of Cantonese, even though he'd spent years in the Orient trade. Waiting while the boys talked back and forth, he smiled wryly. Two 'China boys' wasn't what he'd had in mind when he came to Bannock City.

The older boy held out his hand. "We do," he said. "Two dolla' six bits a week and found." A pause. "What this 'found' Boss?"

Silas chuckled. "Food and shelter." He took the outstretched hand, finding it small and delicate, but strong. "You'll do the cooking, but I'll pay for the food and a place to stay."

He wondered if he'd be able to keep his part of the bargain. No hotel—if you could call a tent full of cots a hotel—would let him bring in a couple of Chinese boys. A vacant shack was too much to hope for. Was there a spare tent to be found in this whole valley?

The older boy interrupted his thoughts.

"Is good. I Soomey, he Tao Ni. You Boss. Now come. We find food."

"No, you won't. I want you to stay in the livery stable until I get back."

"You listen me, Boss! We go tell Li Ching we work for you now."

"Li Ching? You worked for him?"

Soomey shook his head vigorously. "Get stuff. Maybe food."

The afternoon was already half gone. "All right, but this hadn't better take long."

"We go fast."

Silas had to stretch his legs to keep up. The streets teemed with bearded, rough-clad men, all hurrying somewhere. Except around the doors of the saloons, where a few loitered. Time was golden, with winter on its way. Tomorrow was the first of November.

Beyond the creek and through a fringe of woods, they came upon a second town, smaller and poorer than Bannock City. Shabby tents and makeshift shelters were set closely together, as if for mutual protection. Here and there steaming containers swung over economical fires, tended by squatting men who all looked alike in their loose black garments and round, brimless hats. Silas wondered how a person managed to navigate among the shelters, so crowded together were they.

Before he could enter the clearing, Soomey stopped him. "You wait here. This China people place. I get food, then we go."

The boy disappeared into one of the tents, carrying the buckets. A few minutes later he reappeared, arms clutching an angular bundle. He was followed by a shouting, gesturing Chinese man. Soomey turned and faced him, yelling back.

The man grabbed Soomey's shoulder.

Silas tensed.

Tao Ni, silent until now, caught at his coattail and chattered at him. The only words Silas understood were "Li Ching."

Soomey pulled a lacquered box from the bundle and threw it at Li Ching's feet. He spat a short phrase and shook his head violently.

Li Ching snatched at the bundle.

The boy jumped back out of reach. He yelled some more and stamped his foot.

Li Ching shrugged.

Soomey looked toward Silas. "You give him two bits, Boss. Then we go."

"Two bits? What for?"

"I spill food, must pay. Or work one day for Li Ching."

Silas dug in his pocket and pulled out a coin, paying no attention to its denomination. He tossed it to the Chinese man. "You got everything?" he said to Soomey.

The boy nodded. "You give him too much, Boss."

"Never mind. Let's go." He ignored the smiling, bowing Celestial. With a hand on Tao Ni's shoulder, he pushed the boy toward the path to town. The cloth under his fingers was wet and slimy. Looking closer, Silas saw how blue Tao Ni's lips were. He glanced back at Soomey, whose clothes were even wetter.

Damn! Both children were half frozen.

He ran them back to the livery stable, figuring that the exercise would warm them as well as a fire. Once there he opened his bedroll and handed Soomey the warm Hudson's Bay blanket. "I'll be back in an hour or so," he said. "You wrap up and get warm."

Seeing mutiny in Soomey's face, he knelt and dug into his

saddlebag. "Here," he said, handing them each a strip of dried meat. "This'll tide you over 'til supper."

The boy opened his mouth to refuse. Silas silenced him with a gesture. "If you're not waiting when I get back, I'll figure you don't want to work for me."

Narrowed black eyes stared back at him, as if Soomey were wondering just how far to push. Once again Silas wondered how big a mistake he was making. "I'll be back before long," he repeated.

Soomey watched Boss out of sight. "You wait here. I will return before he does."

"Where are you going?" His words were blurred by the food in his mouth.

"To watch his back, as he hired me to," she said. Biting off one stringy chunk of the dried meat, she held out the rest. "Eat. I am not hungry." She untangled herself from the blanket and tucked it closely around Tao Ni.

The afternoon was only a little bit cold, and her clothing would dry soon.

Chapter Two

So far the few wooden buildings in town stood along a single street, with tents serving as dining halls and boarding houses. But the bank already had a concrete-and-cobble vault and two guards at its door.

There were three saloons in the first two hundred yards of the street, one lawyer's office in a building little larger than a ship's cabin, and a well-built wooden structure with lacy curtains fluttering at one upstairs window. Silas imagined that, come nightfall, the front door would stand open and feminine laughter would lure the lonely miners inside.

So this is Tilly's!

A bell jingled as he entered. The small foyer looked like a hotel's, complete with register. He leaned on the counter, waiting. After a few moments, a small but voluptuous woman came through the curtained doorway opposite him.

She was past her prime, but still beautiful. She looked respectable, too, except for the ornate scarlet-and-yellow gown. Her smile was welcoming. "What'll it be?"

"Information, for now." Silas smiled. He'd been too busy to bother with women these past few months. Coming in here reminded him just how long it had been.

"Well, now, not many fellows come looking for that. Sure

we can't accommodate you otherwise?" Her voice was deep, rich, like ruby port, and held more than a hint of a Southern accent.

"Maybe later. Right now I'm looking for word from an Emmet Lachlan. Fellow down at the stable said here would be the likely place to get a message."

In a few weeks there would be a central location for mail and shipments, but in a town this new, most businesses were apt to come and go. If the strike was a good one, shopkeepers might decide they'd get rich faster in the gold fields. A whorehouse was likely to stay put, at least until the gold played out.

"Who's the message for?"

"Me. Silas Dewitt."

She lifted a wooden box from under the counter and sifted through its contents. "Smith. Lots of them in places like this. Ambrose. Walters. Holmes. Dewitt." She held the folded paper out to him. "That'll be a dollar."

Silas paid her with one of his smaller gold coins. "Keep the change. Appreciate the favor." One thing he'd learned long since was that madams and bartenders were good people to have on your side. He unfolded the letter.

> Silas,
> Emmet broke his leg last week, so he can't come to help you. Buff wants to come down there. I'm doing my best to convince Emmet otherwise. Buff's too young and too thirsty for adventure. William's helping us get in the last of the harvest and the hay, so don't worry about us. I just hope you can get the...

Here she'd scratched out a word, and Silas was pretty sure he knew what it was.

> ...cache without Emmet's help. If you can't, don't worry. He should be up and around by spring. That'll have to be soon enough.
>
> Love,
> Hattie

Damn! Hattie and Emmet are having more troubles than enough. He'd better get that cache located. The sooner he did, the sooner they could move to a town and start taking life a little easier.

Closing the letter, he stuck it into a back pocket. "You Tilly?"

"I sure am." Her smile was inviting. "And I've got the best whorehouse between the Salmon River and San Francisco. Sure you ain't interested?"

"Interested, but there's something else I have to do first." Tilly was all woman. And she smelled good. Again he leaned on the counter, making himself comfortable. "You been here long?"

"A couple of weeks," Tilly said. "We were in a tent the first few days, until the men got tired of having walls so thin they could almost see through them." Her smile invited Silas's understanding. "It didn't take them long to raise this roof. They had plenty of cause."

She moved the curtain behind her and gestured.

Silas craned his neck until he could see inside the parlor. "Nice place," he said, looking at the rough board walls on which hung artfully draped, colorful shawls and silk flowers. Two upholstered settees and an assortment of chairs filled the room. All the lamps had fancy fringed shades. He wondered how they'd brought the piano up the trail.

"I've got five girls working here, and we keep real busy," Tilly told him, pulling the door shut again. "I rent rooms, too, if you're looking for a place to sleep. The girls are extra, of course, but they'll give you a discount if you rent by the week."

"I'll remember that. I may be looking for something better than a tent if the weather turns off cold any time soon." A thought struck him. "Have you got a safe?"

"With all the dust that comes in here? I surely do, a good, big one, too heavy to cart away easily."

He nodded in understanding. There was probably as much gold dust going through Tilly's hands in a week as through the banker's. Or close, anyhow. "I wonder if you'd have room in it for this." He pulled out his pocketbook and showed her. "I'm camping until I can get a cabin built, and I don't want to risk it getting wet." Not to mention having someone riffling it. There was information in his papers he would need if he stayed here long.

"Why, the safe's not so packed that I can't find a corner in there to put it. How long will you want me to keep it?" Tilly leaned on the counter so that her forearms pushed her round, white breasts nearly out of her bodice.

Silas swallowed. He was getting more interested all the time. "I'm not sure..." He cleared his throat. "Probably a couple of months. I figure my business here won't take any longer than that."

"Come on back." Tilly again swept the red velvet curtain aside. "To my office."

He followed, noticing the rug as he did so. It was a rich purple in a complex pattern of the sort common in the Middle East. He hadn't seen one like that for a while, not since that cargo of Turkish goods he'd delivered to Macao back in '57.

Silas saw his pocketbook safely stowed. He offered Tilly another coin for the service, but she refused.

"I don't charge friends for favors," she said, smiling suggestively, "and I have a feeling you and I are going to be good friends."

When Boss went into the whorehouse, Soomey found a hiding place across the street and waited. Perhaps he was picking up a letter, she told herself.

After she'd crouched beside the saloon wall for a while, she gradually began to feel as if she were being watched. Moving only her eyes, she looked up and down the street. A few miners were squelching through the puddle-filled ruts. An unhitched freight wagon stood empty in front of the general store.

No one seemed to pay her any attention, but the feeling persisted. The back of her neck prickled.

She wished Boss would reappear.

But he was in there a long time.

Too long.

She was furious with him. He had told her he had business to transact in town, and all he had done was visit the whorehouse. When he emerged at last, she ducked behind the saloon and ran all the way to the stable.

Anger still bubbled within her when Boss returned. She kept her eyes tightly closed, hoping he'd think her asleep, huddled with Tao Ni inside the thick blanket. Shivers shook her with distressing regularity, for she'd become chilled through while watching outside the whorehouse.

"Wake up." He nudged her foot. "Time to go."

With a great show of yawning, Soomey opened her eyes. "Go where?" She reluctantly crawled from under the blanket. It had been so warm. And her coat was still damp.

"Damned if I know. We'll look for a campsite up in the hills."

What a foolish man! He needed her far more than she needed him. "I know good place. We go there." Before he could argue, she had the blanket folded and was rolling it with the rest of his bedroll. "Not see from town."

Saying nothing, Boss looked at her. His fingers absently scratched at his bearded cheek.

Soomey stared back, hiding the residual anger, doing her best to look as if she had his welfare at heart. Had she not been told many times that she looked young and innocent?

After a few moments, Boss nodded. "We'll give it a try tonight. Can you carry the bedroll?"

Nodding, she picked it up. Boss had already slung his saddlebags over his shoulder and taken the gunnysack in one big hand. "I carry," Soomey said, reaching.

"It's too heavy for you. Just show us the way." Without another word, he walked out of the stall, followed by Tao Ni.

Soomey led them up a faint trail northeast of town.

Walking in front of the others gave her an excuse not to speak. A good thing, for her tongue was already sore from having words bitten from its tip. The hot fire of her anger had died into a dull smolder of resentment by the time they reached the rocky outcrop of crumbling granite.

"We sleep here," Soomey said. "Is safe place."

Silas stared in disbelief. *This* was the only home these children had?

Fallen pine branches had been dragged to partially roof an opening among enormous, rounded boulders, giving some shelter from the coming winter. A ragged canvas pack was pushed back against one wall and weighted with a sharp rock. Beside a circle of blackened cobbles lay a small pile of kindling.

Soomey squatted next to the fire ring and opened the lacquered boxes. From one he took two lopsided wooden bowls. The other box held cooked rice, of which he put about a third into each of the bowls. One he handed to Tao Ni, another to Silas, along with chopsticks.

"Eat." Soomey began devouring the rice left in the box as fast as the chopsticks could carry it to his mouth. Tao Ni followed suit.

Silas watched. When Soomey picked up the last grain of rice, he held out his bowl and said, "Here, I'm not hungry."

Again that suspicious, under-the-eyebrows stare. "You not want?"

"I ate this morning."

Soomey sat, unmoving.

Silas offered the bowl to Tao Ni. The younger boy hesitated, and then took it.

"Go ahead," Silas told him. "It's all yours."

After a quick nod from Soomey, Tao Ni dug into the rice.

The silence was broken only by the faint scrape of chopsticks on wood for a long moment. Tao Ni ate as if it was the last meal he'd get. Silas had a feeling these boys had eaten little but rice for a long time.

THE DUCHESS OF OPHIR CREEK

No wonder they look half-starved. Silas lowered himself to the cold ground and dug out his moccasins. The mud and rocks had played hell with the finish on his new boots.

"Soomey?" he said.

The boy met his eyes with a black, unrevealing stare.

"You don't trust me much," Silas said, finally, "but you brought me here. Why?"

Soomey shrugged. "Miners not like China boy, want to hurt. You different. You save me, Tao Ni."

Silas knew that many of the Chinese who had come to American shores in the past fifteen years or so were contract labor, bound to unscrupulous masters for periods varying from five to ten years, little better than slaves. Did the labor contractors take children so young as these? Soomey looked to be in his early teens, Tao Ni no more than half that age.

"How'd you get here, to Bannock City?"

"Come with Li Ching, other China boy. Pay Li Ching many dolla' bring us this place."

"Is Tao Ni your brother?"

At the mention of his name, Tao Ni shrank back against the rock. Soomey said something to him, but he looked only slightly less apprehensive.

"We stop in one gold camp. Big fire. Tao Ni master die, other China boy die. Tao Ni run, hide. Soomey catch, bring 'long me." He shrugged again. "Tao Ni stay with Soomey. Work hard."

"You paid a labor contractor to bring you to Idaho Territory so you could glean the gold fields?"

"No. Pay to take to Portland. Sunnabitch cheat. Bring here. No work but dig. Dig, dig, dig, all day long. Soomey want go Portland, catch work cook, clean for rich people. Save money. You pay two dolla' six bits a week, pretty soon Soomey, Tao Ni go Portland."

"You've got it all thought out, haven't you?" Silas did his best not to show his amusement, as well as his admiration. There weren't any flies on Soomey, that was for sure. "But you're working for me now."

"Soomey work you," he agreed. "Look. Listen. No dig."

"No dig," Silas agreed, thinking that any digging to be done would be by him. What he had to unearth wasn't to be trusted to anyone else.

Boss pulled more dried meat from his saddlebags and handed it around after their rice bowls were empty. Tao Ni refused it. Although it tasted like salty leather to Soomey, she accepted the hard strip. She had eaten worse.

She studied Boss as she chewed. He was not a tall man, but his shoulders were wide and his big hands work-hardened. Both his short coat and the billed cap he wore were dark blue wool. He had the look of a seafaring man, yet he walked the land as if his feet knew its feel.

She didn't trust him much, no more than she trusted any man. Still, as long as he was doing what she said, rather than the other way around, she was content. Americans were such fools.

He would not last long here in the gold camp, this soft-spoken man. He was too gentle, too mild. This afternoon he had succeeded in breaking up the mob only because they had grown tired of their play. A truly angry crowd would chew him up and spit him in the mud.

Still, he could be useful. Today's experience had shown that she alone could not care for Tao Ni. Nor would any of the other Chinese laborers accept responsibility for the boy. He was too young, too small. Useless.

Just as she was useless to them, except as a female body, available for relieving a man's needs. Li Ching had protected her so far, but only because she had paid him. If one who desired her offered him more, would not she once again become a commodity?

Soomey would die before she allowed that to happen again.

His voice interrupted her thoughts. "So what do we do now? You got any ideas on how to find a decent place for us to sleep?"

"We sleep here," she told him again, wondering if all men only heard what they chose to hear. "This place quiet. No see fire from down there." She gestured toward the valley where each day more miners came. Soon, perhaps before winter settled in, even this would be a dangerous place to live.

He looked at the thick branches she'd dragged to form a partial roof, so low even she could not stand upright, shook his head. Soomey bristled. She and Tao Ni had worked hard to build their refuge.

"Good thing it's not raining," was all he said as he stood. He stepped out of the circle of firelight and walked away. Soomey felt unaccountably forsaken. *He will be back,* she assured herself. *His saddlebags are here.*

He was, in a short while. He carried pine branches which he dropped beside Tao Ni, who was already asleep, curled up in their ragged blanket on the bare soil. "Make a bed," he ordered. "I'll fetch more." And he was gone again.

Why had she not thought of this? The branches would insulate them from the cold ground. She went to work.

That night she and Tao Ni slept warmer and more soundly than they had for weeks. Just knowing that someone else was keeping vigilance made a great difference.

For breakfast Boss cooked bacon and hard lumps of cornmeal he called dodgers. Tao Ni made a face at his first taste, but obeyed Soomey's frown and ate it all. Soomey washed hers down with tea, as she had many other strange meals. As soon as she could get to town, she would buy rice.

"We need a better roof, and that's my responsibility," Boss told them after they'd eaten. "I'm going to town and I want you to stay here. I'll see what I can find and be back before sundown."

"We go with you," Soomey told him, reaching for her coat.

"No you won't. I haven't got time to get you out of trouble again." He slipped his arms into his coat and crawled to the entrance. Looking back, he said, "If you want to work for me, you'll have to learn not to argue with every damn thing I say."

"How we watch for you when we not with you?" she demanded.

"Are you arguing again?" His voice was mild, but Soomey heard steel within it.

She shook her head, knowing better than to let words escape her mouth.

"Good. I'll see you later." He got to his feet and walked away.

Soomey glared after him. Tomorrow she would obey. Today they needed rice.

She waited until he was out of sight among the trees, and then told Tao Ni why their boss had left them here. The boy spoke practically no English, and understood only a little more.

"He is a good man, our new master," Tao Ni said when he'd listened to all she had to say. "He will see that we eat well."

"You think of nothing but your belly, child. More important, he will protect us from the miners. Some Americans are like that. Kind. And weak."

"I do not think he is weak, elder sister. His mouth is strong and his face holds no evil."

"Perhaps. We shall see." She hoped Boss would find something for them to eat besides the cornmeal that all Americans seemed to like so well. Dried apples would be nice. She had acquired a taste for them in her years aboard the *Gilded Gull*. And meat. Tao Ni needed meat if he was to grow tall and strong.

She wondered if she would have been so ready to work for Boss had she not been so hungry.

If only she could believe Tao Ni saw truly. Boss was a handsome man, perhaps a dangerous man. His skin was the deep, ancient bronze of one who lived outdoors, his eyes a pale, cold gray, and his hair so fair it seemed to be made of molten silver. But could she trust him?

Nothing in her life had ever given her reason to believe that any man cared for anything more than his own comfort and pleasure.

She just wondered what it was that Boss wanted them to watch and listen for. Something highly profitable, she suspected. And most certainly illegal.

For that reason he must not learn just how fluently she spoke English, nor that she was female and fully grown.

"Here comes that stranger made a fool of you boys yesterday," Vester said.

Wilf lifted himself from the section of log he was sitting on and peered down the street. "Sure enough. Damn Chink-lover."

"Keep an eye on him. I want to know what brought him here, why he don't seem in any hurry to stake a claim."

"Reckon I could git him to tell me 'thout much trouble."

"Not yet. I got me a feeling about him. Just keep your eye on him, see what he's up to."

Wilf trailed along behind the stranger. Whatever Vester had in mind, it was bound bring a profit. This time Wilf was going to make sure he got his fair share.

"He must be sleeping up the mountain somewhere," he mused. "Coming into town from t'other end like he did."

Yesterday afternoon the stranger had been to Tilly's. Wilf had first noticed the older Chinee brat squatting alongside the White Top Saloon, then he'd seen the stranger come out of the whorehouse.

The brat had been up to devilment, sure enough. Instead of meeting up with the man who claimed to be his boss, he'd slunk away behind the saloon.

Treacherous little shit! Dewitt had saved his life and now he was sneaking around, looking to do harm.

Wilf spat. Damn, but he hated them slanty-eyed devils. Back in Californy, he'd seen 'em find gold where no white man could. And they'd work for practic'ly nothing, leaving honest men to starve.

Chapter Three

There were still a few gold pieces in her hidden purse. Soomey hated to use even the smallest of them, but Tao Ni would become ill if he had nothing to eat but the cornmeal. In time he would learn the taste of strange foods—had she not, when it was that or starve?—but until then he must have rice to sustain him.

Boss could not possibly return until late in the day, but she must be here when he did. "I will be gone only a little while, child," she told Tao Ni. "You must stay here. And if Boss returns, tell him I have gone into the forest to seek mushrooms."

For a moment the boy's chin trembled, and then he nodded. She feared he had been badly frightened by yesterday's events, even though he had lived through far worse. She tucked Boss's warm blanket about him. "Perhaps I will bring you a sweet. You are very brave."

Lower lip caught between his teeth, he tried to smile. Soomey ducked out the entrance before she was tempted to stay and comfort him.

Each time she came to town, she took a different route, so that no one would suspect where their shelter was located. This time she discovered a small clearing on her way down the mountain. In it was a tiny spring-fed pond, surrounded by the tall, narrow-leaved plant she had learned to dig for its crisp, delicious roots. She gathered enough for supper.

Now she must hurry. Boss could be in trouble and he was unprotected. She ran the rest of the way to town.

"Ye there! Chink-lover!"

Silas looked toward the voice. A group of loiterers stood around the entrance to a tent-saloon. In their midst was a bullish bruiser who'd been part of the mob tormenting Soomey and Tao Ni. His beard might have once been blond; now it was stained with tobacco and God only knew what else.

Silas ignored him.

"I'm talking to ye, mister."

Silas kept walking.

"By God, ye'll hear what I've got to say." The bully lowered his head and charged, clearly intending to knock Silas off his feet.

Using a trick he'd picked up in the Orient, Silas grabbed a coatsleeve, used the man's momentum to help him along.

The charge turned into a headlong slide, ending with the bruiser jammed against an open barrel full of water. Silas stood and watched his attacker, paying little attention to the comments from the crowd.

Groggily the man rolled over, wiped wet sand from his face. He glared up at Silas and swore colorfully. His curses expanded to include his companions, who stood by the tent, watching, saying little. A number of sideways looks were aimed at a broad fellow who sat quietly on a section of log, smoking a long-stemmed pipe. The smoker observed Silas silently, bright blue eyes peering from under bushy red brows. From the way everyone else seemed to be waiting, Silas recognized the man who would decide whether there was going to be a brawl or not.

At last he removed the pipe from between a bristling red mustache and beard. "Afternoon," he said. "New in town?"

"I am," Silas replied.

"Planning to stay a while?"

"I am."

"Chink lovers ain't too popular in these here parts."

Casually Silas laid a hand on the hilt of his belt knife. "I take care of whoever's working for me," he said.

A nod. "I'll keep that in mind." He pointed at Silas with the stem of his pipe. "Folks call me Vester. I got a finger in most of the pies around here."

Silas nodded. "Silas Dewitt," he said, and jerked his chin toward the mud-smeared bruiser who'd finally managed to struggle to his feet. "Is he one of your boys?"

"Piss-poor specimen, ain't he? He's got a sight more sense when he's sober."

"Well, tell him to stay sober or stay out of my way." Touching a finger to the bill of his cap, Silas turned to continue his exploration of the town.

He'd met men like Vester before. Slicker than greased eels, honest only when it suited their purposes, and strong enough to command the respect of local ruffians and thugs. Not someone to make an enemy of.

The faint scent of fresh coffee drifted from one of the restaurant tents, reminding Silas that he'd come to pick up supplies. His grub sack was almost empty, only a little bacon and some dried beef left. He'd get molasses, a fresh flitch of bacon, and some cornmeal and coffee. Tonight he'd show Soomey and Tao Ni how good plain American food could be.

Good thing he still remembered how to cook over an open fire.

When he paid the storekeeper for the supplies, Silas watched him bite each coin, before peering at them all with a peculiar expression. "Something wrong?"

"Wrong? No. No, of course not." He examined one coin. "Funny lookin' things. Where'd you get 'em?"

Silas shrugged. "I don't know. I get around a lot."

The shopkeeper eyed the coin, turning it around and

around. "10 SCVDI, 1837. What's that mean?"

"Hell, I don't know. It's gold. Just weigh it up like you would dust."

Mumbling and muttering, the shopkeeper did so, shoving a couple of silver coins back at Silas. "You probably oughta' get those changed into good old American money, if you want to spend 'em here."

"Thanks, I'll give it some thought." Silas helped the clerk pack his supplies into a gunnysack, thinking how far he'd come from the boy who'd first come to these parts long ago. Back then he'd scarcely had a few pennies in his pocket. Now it was full of coinage from all over the world, just like any seafaring man's.

Relieved that Boss had been able to protect himself, Soomey cut through the woods to the Chinese town. She had much to think about, but for now she must hurry.

Her coin bought much rice and some dried fish at the Chinese grocer's. The storekeeper looked at her suspiciously when she tendered it, but said nothing. By now the whole community must know that she and Tao Ni were working for the yellow-bearded stranger.

As she accepted the pennies the storekeeper gave her in change, she remembered her promise. "And two of the sweets," she said, pushing back one. She had also been very brave.

Bowing her way out of the store, she glanced up at the sky. The sun was low in the western sky. She had intended to be back with Tao Ni by now. Boss would take the trail, so she must return by a roundabout route.

Eli Jenkins kept track of Dewitt as he went from mercantile to livery stable, to freight office. The afternoon was all but gone when he finally headed out of town. Keeping a fair reach behind, Eli followed Dewitt up the trail for a mile and more, until the rain worsened. There was no seein' beyond a few yards then, so he turned and headed back to town.

He'd just keep his eye on that trail. Sooner or later he'd find where Dewitt and the Chinee brats was a'hidin'.

Sometimes Wilf used his fists instead of his head. Eli figured he'd show Vester and the boys he was smarter than Wilf. Then they'd be sorry how they'd laughed at him.

Soomey ran as fast as she could. To her great relief, only Tao Ni awaited her in the shelter. Her heart still pounded in her chest when Boss leaned under the crude roof a few moments later and tossed a heavy roll of canvas, a coil of rope and another well-filled gunnysack to the floor.

"Starting to rain," he said, before she could greet him. "Let's get this tarp strung up so we'll stay dry."

Soomey helped, and so did Tao Ni. Soon they had a roof of sorts, far better than before, and rainproof—she hoped. It had rained the last night she and Tao Ni had slept here alone. They had been soaked and cold clear through.

Boss coaxed flames from a handful of slivers and some dry moss. As it caught, he carefully fed larger slivers, then twigs, until he had a small fire burning cheerfully. Soomey watched as he pulled a coffeepot and a heavy, lidded iron kettle from the bag. The kettle had three legs.

He looked up at her. "Can you cook?"

"I good cook." Silently she accepted the bacon, the coffee. Somehow now that they had a roof, the shelter seemed closer, more intimate. Sooner or later Boss would notice her modesty. And then he would ask difficult questions. Should she tell him first?

Boss held up a sack. "Cornmeal," he said. "Do you know what to do with it?"

Soomey didn't like anything made with the harsh yellow meal. She had never cooked it. She shook her head. "I cook rice. Better for belly." Suiting action to words, she pulled out her small cooking pot and headed for the stream.

Tao Ni slipped back into the shelter and dropped an armful of wood beside the fire. He said something Silas couldn't understand, and Soomey replied with a smile.

"He speak any English?" Silas said, thinking it was going to be damned inconvenient if he needed Soomey around all the time to translate.

"Small bit," Soomey said. "He understand more than he speak. He will learn quick." Nodding rapidly, he spoke again to the younger boy.

"I good boy, Boss," Tao Ni said, bowing low. "Work hard." His words were plain but heavily accented. His smile was ingratiating.

"Damnittohell! I'm your boss, not your master. You don't have to make me happy. Just do a good day's work, and we'll get along fine."

Eyes huge with fear, Tao Ni cowered back against the rocky wall, his forearms protecting his face.

"Shit! Soomey, tell him I'm not going to hit him." Silas took a deep breath, lowered his voice. "Tell him I will never beat him, no matter what he does. I may yell at him, I may fire him, but I will never, never beat him. Tell him that. Make sure he understands."

Soomey talked to the boy, argued with him, but still he cringed into the wall.

Cursing under his breath, Silas crabbed his way across the space, narrowly missing putting one foot in the fire. *Damnation!* Tomorrow he was going to look for a cabin site, see if he wasn't.

He hunkered down beside Tao Ni and wrapped an arm around him. Under his black pajamas, the child was scrawny, almost fragile. Just the feel of him, underfed, shaking with fear, reminded Silas again of a time he'd rather forget. He lifted Tao Ni, pulled him into his lap, and wrapped his arms around him closely.

Soomey watched suspiciously.

Silas stroked Tao Ni's head, feeling the stiff greasiness of his queue, the prickle of the shaved scalp surrounding it. His skin felt scaly, as if it had been months since he'd bathed. Smelled it, too.

Another task for tomorrow. Baths all around.

Tao Ni held himself stiffly, not yielding to Silas's embrace. Continuing to stroke his hand gently across the boy's head, Silas began to hum and to rock his body back and forth. Just so had Hattie once shown an abandoned child that he had a safe place in the world.

"It's okay, little one," he murmured, only loud enough for the boy to hear. "You're safe now. I'll take care of you. No more begging in the streets, no more stealing food, no more sleeping under houses. You're safe now." He went on, sometimes talking nonsense, knowing that it wasn't so much what he said but how he said it. Knowing, also, that it would take a long time to show Tao Ni that he meant what he said, that he would take care of this tiny bit of human flotsam, and give him a secure harbor.

The aroma of coffee filled the shelter. Silas ignored it. Finally Tao Ni relaxed into sleep. Silas laid him on the thin blanket Soomey spread for him, close enough to the fire for some warmth, not so close that the boy was in danger if his sleep was restless.

Had that meager scrap of wool been all these two children had to keep themselves warm? With winter coming?

Silas wondered what they would have done had he not come to their rescue. He had, indeed, taken upon himself the legendary Chinese obligation. He'd saved their lives. Now he was responsible for them.

He moved back to his seat against the wall, hoping there was a decent laundry in Bannock City. All this crawling around in the dirt wasn't doing his clothes any good. "Supper ready?" he asked, when he was settled again.

"Supper ready," Soomey agreed. He scooped rice and some

sliced vegetables onto the tin plate Silas held out, and then piled plenty of bacon over everything.

Silas waited while Soomey dished up a bowl for himself, crumbled a single slice of bacon over it.

The round slices of creamy white vegetable were crisp, yet tender enough that Silas's fork penetrated readily. It didn't look like anything he'd ever eaten, and he'd eaten some pretty strange foods. Taking a small bite, he chewed carefully.

It tasted of...of fresh air and cool water. Bland, but not unpleasant. He took the rest of the slice and chewed it. Soomey still watched and waited.

Silas took a small portion of the rice and tasted it as well. "Not bad. Needs butter, though." He made a long arm and picked up the skillet, pouring a good dollop of the grease over the rice. He stirred and tasted. "Better." He took another bite.

Soomey didn't move.

"Well, what's holding you up? Eat your supper."

"You like?"

"Oh, for Pete's...! Yeah, I like. Now eat your supper."

He waited until the boy had eaten to say, "You only had a little rice last night. Where'd you get more?"

Soomey jumped to his feet. "I get water for wash."

Silas kept his voice low, but put a snap into it. "Sit down."

"But Boss—"

Pointing to the ground at his feet, Silas waited while Soomey challenged him silently. At last the boy squatted before him, chin high and shoulders back.

"The rice, Soomey? Where'd you get it?"

"I go to Chinese store."

Scratching his jaw, Silas considered. Strictly speaking, the Chinese settlement wasn't in town, but it was right next door. "I told you to stay here, Soomey."

He waited for the boy to reply.

"Well?" he said after a full minute's silence.

"Tao Ni not eat cornmeal. Need rice. Vegetable. Tomorrow

I stay here."

He wouldn't have taken insubordination like this from any man who worked for him. Silas wondered why he was being so patient with Soomey. "You won't get another chance, Soomey. Next time you don't obey me, you'll be looking for another boss. Understand?"

"Oh, yes, Boss. Understand good." Nodding, Soomey grabbed the bailed pot he'd cooked rice in. "Now get water, wash pots."

Feeling suddenly very tired, Silas stared across the shelter at Tao Ni who still slept, his small body making not much more than a big wrinkle in the Hudson's Bay blanket that Silas had tucked around him. These children needed more than he could give them. By rights he should send them to Hattie, to let her work her motherly magic on them. But she had her hands full, with Emmet being laid up. Besides, as soon as the thought occurred to him, Silas felt an instant resistance to it.

There was something about these boys, especially Soomey...

"I've got things to do, today. You two lay low while I'm gone."

Soomey frowned. "'Lay low?' What is this?"

"That means keep out of sight. No need to ask for trouble." He paused as Soomey poured the last of the coffee into his cup. "I'll be back by sundown."

"You do not want us to work for you, Boss?" The boy sounded like a pup somebody had kicked.

Silas closed his eyes and reached for patience. "Yes, Soomey, I want you to work for me. Just not now. Not yet." He wanted them to stay out of town for a while yet. No need asking for more trouble. It would be damned hard to play least in sight if he was always protecting these two.

"When?" Soomey's chin was set. "We are not worth pay if 'lay low,' do nothing."

Well hell! "O.K. Here's what you'll do. You and Tao Ni can watch my back trail, make sure nobody's following me." He didn't want a witness to his searches, especially if he should get lucky and find the cave right off. "If you see anybody—can you whistle?"

"Whistle? I do not know that word."

"Like this." Pursing his lips, Silas gave out with a good imitation of a bosun's pipe.

Soomey imitated his expression and blew. All that came out was a faint, high-pitched tone.

Silas showed him again, this time with fingers between his lips.

Soomey's eyes widened. "How you do that?"

Again he demonstrated. And yet again, as Soomey tried and failed to produce anything approaching a whistle. Silas resolutely suppressed his laughter at the puckered up face.

Finally, his chin quivered as he said, "I am sorry, Boss. I cannot do this thing. Perhaps if I try more—"

Instantly Silas was sorry. "Hey, Soomey, whistling's not important. You can do other things," he said heartily. "Lots of other things."

"You are not angry?"

"Of course not. Can Tao Ni whistle?"

All this time the smaller boy had been sitting quietly against the wall, watching. Now he grinned widely. "I do." His whistle was complex, melodious—and loud.

"Good lad," Silas said. "Soomey, can you explain to him what I want? Tell him to whistle like that if he sees anyone on my trail."

Soomey gabbled to Tao Ni. His answering grin was ear-to-ear.

All day she and Tao Ni followed Boss through the woods. He did not break off shards of rock as other prospectors did. His interest seemed to be greatest in the rounded outcrops that were like enormous Wei Qi stones tumbled together. Perhaps there was something Boss knew that other prospectors did not. He was a very smart man. Sometimes.

Tonight she would tell him the truth. But how? What could she say?

And would he be angry?

No, he would not. What man would refuse a willing woman's services?

After these few precious months of freedom, she must accept another master, something she had sworn never to do.

How else could she bind Boss to herself and Tao Ni?

Soomey cooked cornmeal that night, hoping to ensure that Boss's mood would be favorable. Tao Ni again refused to touch the doughy yellow bread, and so Soomey ate his portion, giving him her rice. When no food remained in his dish, she said, "We need more wood, little one. Will you gather some before it grows dark?"

He scrambled to his feet, but she caught him before he could leave the shelter. "There are words I must have with Boss," she said in Cantonese. "Can you take a long time?"

He agreed. In a moment he was slipping off into the shadowy woods. And Boss was there, relaxed against the rocks, his eyes pale in the firelight.

Soomey knelt beside the fire and set water to boil for tea. If only she could read what was in his heart. He seemed a just man. He had bargained with her honorably, had not tried to cheat her as so many did the Chinese. His treatment of Tao Ni had been gentle and kind, surprisingly so, given that he was a man, and an American. Even when she had disobeyed him, he had not beaten her, although she knew his patience had been strained. His face showed no signs of dissipation, his body no softness.

Best of all, he had shown that while he was quiet, he was neither weak nor conciliating with those who would take advantage of weakness. The Vester man, who was very powerful, had treated Boss with respect.

Travel to Portland was out of the question until the passes

opened in spring. While she might survive the journey in winter, Tao Ni almost certainly would not.

Until the day Boss had saved them, she had not worried that she would be seen as a woman by the Americans. Didn't all Chinese look alike to them? But her shirt had ripped a little bit when the pole was dragged from her shoulder. What if it had torn open? The men would have seen that she was female, despite the band that bound her breasts.

She and Tao Ni needed a protector—an American. None of the Chinese would accept responsibility for them, particularly knowing she was female, yet not available. If Li Ching had not forbidden it, the men she'd traveled with would have raped her without hesitation. Unfortunately, his power and prestige did not extend outside the Chinese community.

Soomey looked at Boss from under her lashes, wondering if her assessment of his character was correct. Her life and Tao Ni's depended on it.

She still had a few gold coins left from the sale of her beautiful clothes, but she doubted even a great fortune could buy this man's trust and loyalty. Despite her vow that she would never again be a man's toy, there was only one thing she had that Boss might value.

So. She would not be a possession. What she would offer Boss in exchange for his protection would be freely given, not taken. The difference between him and Captain Watkins was that Boss would not own her.

She sat back on her heels. "There is something you must know," she said, dropping the broken English she had hidden behind.

He said nothing for a moment, just stared at her with speculation in his eyes. Finally he said, "Well?"

Licking her lips, she said, "I am not what I seem. I speak good English. I can read and write. What you see..." She made a gesture that took in her black clothing, the rude shelter. "What you see is because I...because it was necessary for me to travel with

other Chinese, until I reach Portland, find a job as houseboy."
She paused. "You know barracoons in San Francisco?"
"The cribs in Chinatown?" He nodded. "Yes, but...?"
"I would be there by now, if I had not escaped," she said, willing him to understand.

Was this her fate, to always warm an American's bed? At least this time, she reminded herself, it would be her own choice. "You go...went to whorehouse. You are a man. You need a woman."

She bowed her head. "I am woman."

Boss stared at her in the gloom of the shelter for long moments.

"Well, hell!" he said at last.

Chapter Four

POLE-AXED. Silas stared at Soomey. The little devil! She'd fooled him, sure enough.

Damn! He rubbed his upper lip, wondering what the hell he was going to do now. Without Emmet, he really did need eyes and ears about town, and these Chinese kids had seemed perfect.

"Boss?"

She sat on her heels, head bent, a position he'd seen a hundred Chinese women assume—passive, obedient, patient. The queue, with its carefully shaved edge, looked incongruous, now that he knew she was a girl.

Her head lifted and lowered quickly, like a little bird's, snatching at a seed. "You mad with me, Boss?"

Sighing, he said, "No, I'm not mad with you, Soomey. It's just that, well, this changes everything."

She looked up and almost smiled. "Yes, I know. Now I can take care of you. I have much experience."

"Yeah, well, you can start by keeping quiet. I need to think." He leaned as far back against the rocky wall as he could, wriggling against a sharp edge that seemed determined to skewer him. *Double damn.*

Snagging his saddlebags with one foot, Silas dragged them toward him. He dug around and pulled out his tobacco pouch and pipe. Soomey glanced at him as he stuck a splinter into the fire, wrinkled her nose as he applied it to the moist, fragrant tobacco. He raised his eyebrow, but she said nothing.

He inhaled, tamping the tobacco down. A pipe was a handy thing. You could hide behind it while you thought. There was something about a man fussing with a pipe that inclined folks to patience.

So what was he going to do with Soomey? She was his responsibility; he accepted that, albeit reluctantly. But he had to stay here in the Boise Basin until he achieved the goal that had brought him here. Gold camps were no places for a girl, be she Chinese or white. Or maybe especially be she Chinese.

Maybe he would send her to Hattie, after all. Her and Tao Ni. Nobody was better at mothering than Hattie. And in the spring, he'd send her to Portland, if that's what she still wanted to do.

She waited on her knees before him, outwardly patient.

Her eyes were darkly mysterious. Wise. With not a hint of entreaty in their black depths. She would never beg. Not Soomey.

Her lips were sweetly full, pouting. Ripe.

Her body was slim and lithe. A child's body!

He wanted her.

Again he cursed, this time at himself. What kind of monster was he, feeling desire for a little girl? Why, she couldn't be a day over twelve. "You can't stay here," he said.

"Why not? This was my place before I work for you."

"I mean you can't stay in Bannock City. It's not safe."

"I have been in worse places. No other miners know I am woman. And you will keep me safe."

"Don't argue." A thought struck him. "How the dickens did you fool all those men you traveled with?"

She shrugged. "I did not fool them. Li Ching was boss and he said I belonged to him. They did not bother me."

The Duchess of Ophir Creek

That might have worked with the Celestials. Silas had long thought they were more civilized in some ways than his own countrymen. But if just one miner suspected...

Even disguised as a boy, Soomey was in danger. A white girl might be left alone, as along as she behaved like a lady. A Chinese girl would be considered fair game by every horny miner in the basin.

Soomey's disguise had worked simply because all Chinese looked the same to most Americans. Look how she'd fooled him, and he'd been trading in the Orient for years. So she might get away with it—a chance Silas wasn't willing to take.

Her sex wasn't the only problem he foresaw. Prejudice against the Chinese was strong here. He didn't want her caught in the middle of the violence that was sure to break out sooner or later.

Once more he retreated behind his pipe, watching her as he smoked. She stared back, and he could almost see the arguments pushing against her closed lips.

How was he going to get her to Cherry Vale? He couldn't afford to take her. Winter was almost here, and once snow lay deep on the hillsides, he'd be forever finding the cave. She'd not go willingly, so he'd have to send her with someone he could depend on to deliver her safely to Hattie and Emmet.

He didn't know a soul in this whole basin he'd trust.

Caught between a rock and a hard place, and hating to capitulate, Silas said, "All right. You can stay. But only if you promise you won't set foot in either the Chinese settlement or Bannock City without me."

For a long moment she regarded him suspiciously. At last she nodded. "But you will not leave me behind when you go to town. I will not stay in this cave."

"You'll do as you're told, damn it!"

Her long lashes fanned across her cheek as she bowed her head in agreement. "You are Boss."

Tao Ni returned just then, much to Soomey's relief. She

did not want to argue with Boss. He was being very foolish, and very stubborn. Tomorrow she would convince him that she would be much better able to guard him with no restrictions on her movements.

He would be in a far better mood in the morning. She would see to that.

When Boss stepped out of the shelter, Soomey prepared their beds. Earlier she had gathered fresh branches to spread under his blankets, first smoothing the ground beneath and making sure there were no rocks to give him discomfort. Tao Ni was snuggled into his warm blanket and asleep before Boss returned.

She lit a candle, enjoying its steady light. The nights she and Tao Ni had slept here, they had nothing to relieve the dark, except for the fire, which they had kept small and inconspicuous.

With unsteady hands, she set water to heat for tea, using a few shreds of her precious store to steep a single cup. Boss would need the strength it would give him.

At last all was prepared. She sat back upon her heels, fed the fire just enough to keep it alive, and waited.

Her heart beat faster as she contemplated the night ahead. Captain Watkins had sometimes been kind, in his own way, but Captain Slye had not. He had caused her great pain, and had beat her when she wept.

Soomey had learned her lesson well, and had not wept since.

The one unbreakable vow she had made to herself was never to submit to one like Captain Slye again, but that did not worry her tonight. She believed Boss would be kind.

But would she please him?

At last he returned, smelling of rain and tobacco.

"Your tea is ready," she said, pouring it into his tin cup.

He crouched down against the wall and sipped. She watched him, speculating about how his big hands would feel against her skin. They were the callused hands of a man who knew the meaning of labor. But he had been gentle as he stroked Tao Ni, so perhaps he would not hurt her.

"Aren't you having any?"

"Perhaps a little," she said. Something stirred in Soomey's midsection, as if a thousand bees swarmed. Silently she accepted the cup when he handed it to her. Sipped, but found she could not swallow. She caught up the rag she'd used to protect her hands from the skillet's heat and spat the tea into it.

"Your bed is ready."

"Thanks." He stood, hunched over beneath the cloth that kept out the rain. Quickly he removed his coat and folded it, slipped his suspenders down, to hang alongside his legs. Then he sat on the blankets and removed his boots. When his feet were bare, he looked across at her. "Blow out the candle."

Soomey did so. And waited, listening to the rustle of his clothing, the soft rasp of his wool pants against his legs. She knew when he slipped between the blankets, heard his soft mutters as he settled into place.

She gathered her courage, jumped when his voice came out of the dark.

"You going to bed or not?"

"Yes...I will...please, just one while." She slipped into the night, took care of her personal needs. At the doorway to their makeshift home, she paused, taking several deep breaths.

She was a free woman, she told herself. This was her choice. Boss was a decent, honest man who would not seek to own her. And there was nothing he would do...could do to her that had not been done before.

With that thought firmly in mind, Soomey stepped inside. Quickly she loosened her queue, once again regretting the loss of so much of her hair. Captain Watkins had often told her it reminded him of the finest silk. She removed her shirt and trousers, thinking that she must wash them.

Tomorrow.

When she unwound the band that bound her breasts, she

breathed a sigh of relief. Perhaps she would not need to wear it again.

Naked, covered with goose pimples that were not due to the chill in the air, she slipped into Boss' bed.

Silas dreamt of womanly texture, sleek and silky, fragrant with the scent of exotic flowers. His fingers touched breasts white as snow, his hands cradled their richness, as nipples flowered against his palms.

Her fingers danced across his unshaven cheek, lightly, quickly, delicate as the kiss of a moth's wing. Her hands explored his chest, smoothed across his belly, found his already straining manhood and traced erotic patterns from base to tip.

He woke, aching and hard.

And it was no dream.

Her hot mouth was on him. Her tongue licked his belly button, her teeth delicately teased the head of his shaft, before he realized who she was.

"Get out!"

Her hands clung, even as she cried out in surprise and pain.

"What the hell is going on?" He pushed her entirely away from him, held her until she no longer resisted. Groping in his pack, he found the matches. His hand was shaking so much that it took him three tries to get one lit.

God! He'd been on the verge of taking her, of mindlessly slamming into her like any rutting beast.

"Candle."

She stretched for it, handed it to him. Silas lit it and wedged it between two rocks.

Soomey sat in the dirt, huddled into herself. She was naked, her long hair falling across her shoulders and almost to the ground. Pale golden skin gleamed in the flickering light. Her body was taut and the knuckles of her hands, where they were clasped around her knees, were white.

She was so small!

Silas forced himself to relax, willed the remains of lust

away. His anger was less easy to control. It boiled just beneath the surface, threatening to overwhelm his better sense.

"Suppose you," he said, when at last he felt his voice steady, "tell me just what the hell you thought you were doing."

"I already tell...told you. I can take care of you. No need you go to whorehouse."

He was speechless.

"I have much experience," she said, her voice quavering a little. "I can shave you, bathe you. I cook good, will even learn to cook the cornmeal, no matter how bad it tastes. I am hard worker, can do laundry, dig gravel. Even work rocker. I say I do not dig, but I will, for you."

She looked up, peering between two strands of that long, black hair. "I am clean, Boss. No sickness. And I can do what you want. Anything."

Still unable to find words, Silas glared at her. She moved and the silken fall of her hair flowed across her shoulder and back, revealing the sweet upper curve of a breast. He closed his eyes, groped for the shirt he was using for a pillow.

"Put that on."

Even the sounds of her donning his shirt were erotic. His mind's eye pictured her rising to her knees, watched as she twisted her hair out of the way, revealing her slim, tempting body. When she arched back to slip her arms in to the sleeves, her nipples pouted at him, inviting his tongue.

Tarnation! Silas waited until there were no more sounds. Cautiously opening his eyes, he saw her kneeling between him and the fire, sitting back on her heels, head bent, hands lying quiet on her knees. The very picture of patient, obedient woman, submissively awaiting his command.

He cleared his throat. "Soomey, look at me."

She raised her head, but not her eyes.

"Look at me, damn you!"

Her eyes gleamed in the firelight, blank of emotion. A child? Or ageless, oriental wisdom, inscrutable and mysterious?

"Why did you think I wanted you in my bed?"

"You need a woman, go to whorehouse." She sounded as if she were explaining something perfectly obvious to a small child. "I am woman. I give you pleasure, no need you go to whorehouse again."

"You thought...what the hell business is it of yours if I go... my God, girl! Look, I went to Tilly's to pick up a letter, if it's any of your business."

"You stay too long to get a letter. I wait outside, see you go with Tilly, not come back for a long time." She nodded, as if in agreement with herself. "Whores give good time, but I give better." There was definite pride in her voice.

"Soomey, you aren't giving anybody a good time, you hear." Frustrated, Silas threaded fingers through his hair. "You're just a kid. I can't—"

"I am not 'kid.' I am woman." She jerked the shirt open, baring her body. "Does this look like child?"

"No, but—"

Before he could stop her, she came to him and kissed him, using tongue and teeth until it was all Silas could do to keep his hands from her warm, sleek body.

"Is that kiss of child?" she said, as he thrust her from him, forcing her back to the floor.

"Stay there," he commanded. When she started forward, he held a hand to warn her back. "I mean it, Soomey. Stay right there. Don't move."

She eyed him speculatively as he attempted to pull his thoughts into some semblance of order.

"Maybe you like boys?" she suggested.

Silas ground his teeth. "No, damn it, I do not like boys. You just don't understand."

"Explain to me, then."

"You may have the body of a woman, Soomey, but you're just a child. I can't...no gentleman would take advantage. No matter how willing you might seem. You're just too young to know what you're offering."

She opened her mouth to protest, but he stopped her with a gesture.

"Look, if you know what the barracoons are, if you know what you escaped, you must know what goes on between a man and a woman. But you're too young to understand. There are men who use children, but I'm not one of them. And you shouldn't have to submit to that kind of abuse. It's...well, there just aren't words to describe what kind of animal would treat an innocent child like that."

"Boss?"

"Be quiet. Let me finish. Soomey, when I hired you, I didn't know you were a girl, but I did take on responsibility for you. A decent man doesn't hire a child without being willing to protect him...her." Admitting the temptation, he added, as an afterthought, "Even from himself."

"Boss?"

"Don't try to change my mind," he warned.

She shrugged. "You are stubborn man, but if you wish to sleep in cold, empty bed, so be it. Just do not go to whorehouse again. There is no need."

"You let me decide what my need is, you hear?"

"I hear, but Boss?"

God, but he was tired of this conversation. "You can say one thing, and then you're going to crawl in that other bed and I'm blowing out the candle." He tossed her his blanket, knowing a cold bed was what he needed tonight.

"Those men you call animals, the ones who like children?"

Silas reached for the candle. She quickly scooted in next to Tao Ni, but stayed propped on an elbow, looking across the glowing coals of the fire.

"You do not need to protect me from them. I have already belonged to one."

Chapter Five

SILAS HAD SEEN BETTER MORNINGS. HE'D SLEPT LITTLE, HIS MIND worrying the problem of Soomey.

Had she known what she was saying, with her last remark before he blew out the candle? Could she have been used by a base pervert of the sort every decent person must despise? The very thought sickened him.

Hell and damnation! What was he going to do with a girl child in a mining town? Especially a girl child who seemed determined to get into his bed.

Whatever Soomey's past—and Silas was determined not to believe it had been as bad as she'd implied—she was his responsibility now. Until he could get away to take her to Hattie, she was going to be a handful. He'd bet his last dollar on that.

The subject of his ruminations herself broke into them.

"Breakfast ready."

Lowering the towel, he looked over at her. She stood upright in the low doorway of the shelter. So small! She probably didn't weigh a hundred pounds. Skinny, too. That's what came of eating rice all the time. It didn't put any flesh on a body. What she needed was some good beef, twice a day.

He ducked under the sagging tarp. She'd cooked bacon, anyhow. And rice. Again. At least, he thought, sniffing, she made a decent pot of coffee.

Silas sure wished he knew something about mining. As far as he was concerned, if you couldn't pick gold up out of the creek, it wasn't worth looking for. There were better, easier ways to get rich. He'd face a typhoon sooner than grub in the dirt.

Just to be convincing, he'd decided to act like he was seeking the mother lode—wasn't that what all miners dreamed of? He was pretty sure he hadn't fooled Soomey yesterday, but then she watched him a lot closer than anybody else was likely to.

Damn! Why didn't I make a map?

Yesterday had showed him how poor his memory was. Seemed like on every hillside he'd seen a familiar looking pile of rocks. And none had been the right one.

When he'd sealed the cave, he'd taken a long look around, trying to fix its location in his mind. Now all he could remember was the afternoon sun in his eyes and the glint of water far below. After sixteen years, each pine-covered mountain looked just like the next.

What was it Emmet had told him once? "Do what you kin do, and if by chance you lose your pants, you make your skin do."

He just hoped somebody wouldn't stumble on the cave before he found it. He didn't want to get caught with his pants down.

For the better part of a week the three of them searched the hills around Bannock City, checking every rocky outcrop and talus slope. Rain fell every day, a light drizzle. Just enough to leave every pine needle in the forest ready to drip. At last Silas decided he'd had enough. "I'm about to call it quits," he said to Soomey, who squatted beside the fire. "We've been up and down every hillside in this drainage."

She stirred the pot in which a thick stew simmered. "Before you come to Bannock City I hear of good place. Over hill that way—" she pointed to the west—"is another creek, not so many miners."

The Duchess of Ophir Creek

"What's east of here?"

Soomey looked confused. And cute as a bug's ear.

Cursing his horniness, Silas pointed east. "That way. Another creek?"

"No, only this one creek. It goes that way a long time."

"You've been up there?" He was inclined to believe her. In his memory, Emmet spoke of a hellaciously high divide to the northeast. What Silas remembered was lower passes, more gentle valleys.

"Not me, no. But I listen, hear men talk. No gold up that way, Boss."

The cave could be over in the Grimes Creek drainage, or even farther west. He sure as hell hadn't found it anywhere around Bannock City. "We'll see." He thought a moment. "I want Tao Ni to keep a good eye out tomorrow. Somebody may be a little too interested in what we're doing. I saw tracks on the trail yesterday and the day before."

The boy didn't seem to understand, until Soomey spoke. Then he smiled. "I watch, Boss. I watch good," he said, nodding vigorously.

"I will watch, too," Soomey said.

"Not today. I want you to stay close. Keep your eyes open for anybody snooping about our camp. But if you hear anyone coming, you get inside and crawl in behind that stack of firewood." The tracks he'd seen had ended scarcely a quarter mile from the shelter.

"I go with you," she insisted.

"You'll stay here." She'd be better off alone in the shelter than anywhere close to town. With the shortage of women in the basin, Soomey was about as tempting as a five pound nugget.

Her eyes narrowed and her glare was enough to scorch the hide off an elephant. "No. I will go with you, make sure nobody follows you. You pay me to watch and listen, so I will watch and listen. You do not pay me to sit here and do nothing."

"The hell I—" Silas drew a deep breath, but decided not

to tell her how close to the shelter he'd seen the tracks. "Look, Soomey, you're at risk here. Many of these miners wouldn't think twice about raping you, and if there were a pack of them, you wouldn't have a chance."

"You are crazy man. To them I am boy, not girl. Or will you tell them?"

"No, I won't tell them. In fact, I hope they never have occasion to find out you're female. But I don't want you chancing it. That's an order."

Her glare grew hotter, but she said, curtly, "You are Boss."

"See that you remember it." He picked up his pea jacket. The weather was getting colder. "Let's go, Tao Ni."

Soomey waited until they were gone, and then crept along the almost indiscernible trail behind them. Boss worried too much. She had successfully pretended to be a boy for many months now, working briefly as a laundry coolie in San Francisco, and then as a laborer in several gold camps. She smiled. Had she not revealed herself to him, he would still see her as a Chinese boy, looking just like all other Celestials.

When she saw Boss and Tao Ni standing in the fork of the trail, she paused, wishing she could hear what instructions he was giving the boy. Ah, well, Tao Ni would tell her.

Or perhaps she would not tell Tao Ni she was here. Instead she would creep past him silently and go down to the Chinese store to replenish her tea supply. Now that she was making two dollars a week, she could reward herself with more than the scent of good tea in her cup. How Boss could drink the bitter, black coffee she could not understand.

There were still cat-tail in the pond she had found. Perhaps she would dig some of the crisp roots.

Several hours later, feet still numb from immersion in the icy pond, she reached the trail. Ahead of her she saw movement. Boss and Tao Ni?

Not wanting to be seen, she stepped aside and followed a route parallel to the trail but far enough away to be hidden by the undergrowth. She disarmed the snare she had made to catch anyone who entered the shelter and placed her packages inside.

Silently, so the surprise would be greater, she crept back down the trail. Neither Boss nor Tao Ni was anywhere to be seen, so she flitted from tree to tree, seeking them. Instead she spied a man, hunched over behind a tree, watching the trail to their camp.

He was a lean, crooked man, all bone and sinew, with thin hair straggling from under a misshapen hat, a dark cloth coat shiny with grease, and too-long black denim trousers rolled over worn boots. She recognized him as the one called Eli, one of the Vester man's followers.

Soomey stood still, watching him as he seemed to be watching the trail. After a while she saw movement lower down the slope, so she slipped between trees until she could meet whoever was coming uphill.

It was Boss. Wide-shouldered and strong, a beautiful man, and a good one. A man who could protect her and Tao Ni. A stubborn man, too. He would be angry that she had not obeyed him.

But the crooked man might mean harm to him.

Soomey ran to a large tree just off the trail and stood beside it so that she was visible to Boss but not to the crooked man.

"Hssst!"

Boss reacted immediately, moving into concealment with the speed of a striking snake. Soomey smiled. A warrior, indeed. She waved, beckoning him toward her.

In a moment he was beside her. "Didn't I tell you—"

Soomey gestured him to silence. "There is one watching," she whispered, a bare breath of sound. "Up there. See?"

He peered carefully around the tree trunk, and then nodded.

"He waits for someone," she said, still very softly. "You, I think."

"Tao Ni?"

"I did not see him."

"Damn!" Boss looked about. Laying a hand on her shoulder, he mouthed, "Stay here."

Soomey shook her head. If he was going into danger, she would be with him, to watch his back.

"You want me to tie you up and leave you here?"

Knowing he would do it, she agreed. He was a fool to refuse her help, but he would learn.

He moved through the woods like a wild animal, never making a sound, without stirring so much as a branch. Soon he was lost in the undergrowth. Soomey watched the crooked man, sure that Boss would appear behind him.

But he did not. After a little while she heard whistling from a distance, growing louder. Then Boss came from the direction of their camp, walking along the hillside with purpose. He walked right up to the crooked man and said something to him. The crooked man shook his head and pointed down toward town. Boss said something else, and the crooked man shook his head again. Then they both walked downhill, following the trail.

Soomey shrank back behind her tree trunk as they passed her.

"...ran away, I think. If I catch him, I'll show him who's boss," Boss was saying.

"Dam' Chinee," the crooked man replied. "Can't trust 'em nohow. They oughta' be sent back where they came from."

Boss made a sound that might have been agreement. Then she could hear no more as they passed out of sight.

Was the crooked man a friend to Boss? Or was Boss being clever?

And where was Tao Ni, if Boss did not know?

Silas walked Eli Jenkins to the edge of town, still wondering why he'd been watching the trail. He'd said he was tracking a deer, but Silas had seen no deer sign. He hadn't left the tracks Silas had seen yesterday, though. Not with that one turned-in foot.

Jenkins seemed harmless, even though he was one of

The Duchess of Ophir Creek

Vester's men. Silas had seen his sort before. Powerless, cowardly, unable to make friends, they clung to bullies like courtiers did to kings, basking in reflected power, always ready to do their master's bidding.

But they could be dangerous, simply because they were willing to do whatever they were told. Their allegiance and obedience was usually unquestioning and total.

Rapidly Silas strode back up the trail. Where was Tao Ni?

He couldn't imagine the boy leaving his post without a good reason. Unless he'd followed someone. There had been a puppy-like expression of total devotion on the boy's face ever since the night Silas had soothed him to sleep. That could be a problem. Tao Ni would die for Silas now.

An unwelcome responsibility, but one Silas could not refuse.

When he reached the place he'd left Tao Ni, he squatted and studied the ground. The boy's footprints were faint but plain. Tao Ni had stood here, as instructed, for some time, moving a little as a child would, but faithful to his task. Once he'd slipped into the woods to answer nature's call. Another time he'd hidden behind the tree.

Eli Jenkins boot prints were on the trail too, although they did not approach Tao Ni's hiding place. He seemed to have stopped at the place where he'd hidden, so maybe his tale of a deer was true.

Silas turned and walked slowly back toward Tao Ni's tree, examining the edges of the well-packed trail.

There. What was that?

He looked more closely, turning over the damp chunk of bark, studying its underside. Something had scraped against it, dislodging it from its resting place, leaving it upside down.

And there, a bit further on. Something—someone?—had dragged an object across the mat of pine needles that carpeted the forest floor. He followed, seeing occasional subtle disturbances in the forest floor.

An old tree, fully six feet across, had fallen and lay rotting, blocking his way. Around it, taking nourishment from its decaying carcass, seedling pines and firs grew, making an almost impenetrable thicket. The drag-marks led into it, and one seedling was bent and torn.

Silas pushed into the thicket, fearing what he would find.

Tao Ni lay crumpled against the deadfall. His head was bloody, one arm twisted at an unnatural angle. Silas's breath caught as he knelt at the boy's side.

His fingers sought a pulse. Yes! Faint, irregular, but unmistakably there. The boy lived, thank God!

He felt of the small limbs, not moving Tao Ni. But for the one arm, they seemed intact. Knowing what he risked, he lifted the boy carefully, doing his best not to let the head loll. When he reached the trail, Soomey was waiting. "Run ahead," he told her. "We need hot water."

She ran.

They were less than a mile from the shelter, but Silas had seldom walked a longer distance. Tao Ni lay like dead in his arms, cold and limp. Only the flutter of his delicate nostrils showed that he breathed.

Soomey had spread blankets so that Silas could lay Tao Ni beside the fire. Water was already steaming in her rice pot.

"Who did this?" The intensity of her voice spoke of vengeance.

"Don't know." Silas eased the boy's black pajamas from him, laid the pitiful scraps of black cotton aside. His skinny body was black and blue, covered with the evidence of a savage beating.

"His arm's broken. We'll need a splint."

"Yes. I will cut wood." She ripped the shirt Silas handed her into strips, and took a big square knife—where had that come from?—and split off long, fat slivers from a chunk of firewood. "Do you need board for his neck?"

Silas looked at her, momentarily taken aback. "Yeah, we'd

better. I don't think it's damaged, but we'd better be safe."

She disappeared. In a few minutes she was back, carrying a flat piece of yellowpine bark. It was better than an inch thick, and about a foot square. "I could find nothing better," she said.

"It's perfect." Silas eased it under the boy's head and used it to immobilize him, with strips of cloth tied across his forehead and shoulders. Then he went back to sponging the deep split in Tao Ni's scalp.

"This wants stitching," he muttered, wishing he'd not left his medical kit behind. But he'd wanted to travel light and had brought only the barest necessities.

"I can do," Soomey said. "I have done before."

"You're sure?" He looked at her. She was pale, but she hadn't fainted or flinched.

She dug into her small bundle and triumphantly pulled out a needle with a length of black thread, which she dropped into the now boiling water. "I fix many broken heads, sew many cuts. You do not worry."

Silas was doubtful, but let her go ahead. And was convinced.

One thing that surprised him was her cleanliness. She washed her hands and Tao Ni's head before beginning. "Dirty cuts fester," she said, when he mentioned it. "I see many times."

Her tongue caught between her teeth in total concentration, she stitched the long cut carefully. Tiny stitches, as fine as on a linen shirt. The scar would be all but invisible, he'd bet.

When she was finally done, she washed the needle and remaining thread and carefully put them away. Sitting back on her heels, she looked him straight in the eye. None of the submissive Chinese about her now.

"Who did this?" she demanded again.

"I don't know," Silas repeated, "but I'll sure as hell find out."

"You will kill him." It was not a question.

"No, but maybe he'll wish he was dead."

She smiled fiercely. "Good! Now I must go and fetch

willow bark. It will make his sleep easier."

"I've got laudanum."

"No. It is bad thing. Willow bark is better. You watch, do not let him move. I will be back soon."

Before she could squeeze past him, Silas caught her wrist. "You're not goin' anywhere. I'll get the bark. And anything else you need."

She muttered something, uncomplimentary he was certain. But she told him where to find willow bark nearby.

As Silas returned with the bark, he looked up at the sun, almost behind the mountains to the west. *Damn!* He'd hoped to move on tomorrow, now that he was satisfied that his cave wasn't in this drainage.

Now it would be several days before Tao Ni could be moved that far, even on horseback.

Only then could he renew his search for the cave.

The knife had been in his hand when he'd heard the squirrel's sharp warning. For a moment he had hesitated, but then he'd slid the blade back into its sheath. As Dewitt approached, he'd half-hid himself behind a big old pine and waited, knowing that he could not escape silently.

Perhaps it was a good thing Dewitt had come along. Killing the Chinee brat would have been a mistake. It would'a got Dewitt's hackles up, sure enough. Probably made him more cautious, too.

After the better part of a week's watching, he was certain sure that Dewitt was looking for something more than a claim. He was powerful interested in rock outcrops up high on hillsides. The Mother Lode, maybe? There was lots of folks who believed it was out here somewheres in these hills.

He knelt beside a narrow trickle of water and immersed his hand. The icy water stung as it seeped into the deep wound at the base of his thumb.

He'd be dam' lucky if he didn't end up with hydrophoby

or somethin'. Them Chinee was probably worse than mad dogs when they bit.

Chapter Six

SILAS SAT BY THE DYING FIRE AND CHEWED ON HIS PIPESTEM. THE tobacco had been consumed almost an hour ago, but his thoughts still twisted and knotted themselves within his head.

He owed Hattie and Emmet for everything he had—for who he was. Had Hattie not mothered a lonely boy, had Emmet not given that boy a start in the world, Silas Dewitt would still be nobody—a farm hand with only a few copper pennies to rub together.

Now they needed help, and the only help he could give them was to find the cave and the treasure it contained.

Finding it would have been easy had the basin been as empty as it was when he closed up the cave, sixteen years ago. As it would have been only a year ago, when Hattie wrote the first letter. But the letter had followed him from Honolulu to Delhi, thence to Batavia where he had been delayed by storm damage to his ship and cargo. It had taken him several weeks to arrange his affairs so that he could leave them, more weeks to reach San Francisco and then Portland.

And now he had yet another obligation, equally strong.

Tao Ni roused as they were finishing their meal—rice again! Soomey dosed the boy with willow bark tea, and soothed him as he tossed and moaned.

"Ask him if he knows who hurt him," Silas told her.

She said something in Chinese. The boy's head moved, fighting the scraps that held it to the board. Disjointed sounds came from his mouth, interspersed with grunts of pain.

"He say one put something over his head so he could not see and hit him many times."

Tao Ni whispered something more.

Soomey's eyes narrowed, her mouth tightened. "One said he would kill Tao Ni, Soomey, teach you lesson. But first, he say tell him what you look for." She paused, listened to the broken whisper. "Some words one said were strange to Tao Ni. But he was frightened very much. One was very angry, and he seemed to enjoy hurting Tao Ni."

She raised wide, frightened eyes to Silas. "A very wicked man, I think, Boss."

"I'll find him," Silas vowed. "Tell the boy that, Soomey. I'll find whoever did this, and he'll pay."

She spoke to Tao Ni, who seemed to relax. Soomey's voice softened, became a wordless croon. Her hand smoothed Tao Ni's brow, over and over, until the boy fell into deep sleep.

After Soomey went to her bed, Silas smoked and thought, but came to no decision, for there was none he could accept. He had to find the cave and figure out a way to remove its contents without being seen, and he had to take care of the two children he'd saddled himself with.

Soomey stirred in her sleep, and he turned his head to watch her. She slept wrapped in her threadbare blanket, having insisted that Tao Ni have the thick, warm one Silas had given her. Her hand, small, delicate, marked with a smudge of soot, lay outside the blanket. Seeing it now, Silas wondered how he'd ever seen her as a boy. Her face was a perfect oval, pale with a golden tint. Her lips were full, rosy, expressive. And her dark eyes, wide for an Oriental's, were set at a saucy slant in her face, so that whenever she looked up at him, she seemed to be flirting.

She moved again, and the blanket shifted, so that her

upper body was revealed, covered only by the thin cotton shirt she wore. The shape of her breasts showed clearly, breasts he remembered being crowned with bold nipples only a shade darker than her mouth.

His body tightened and he swore beneath his breath. Good thing she hadn't realized how she'd affected him the other night, or she'd not have given up. God! He'd wanted her like he'd never wanted a woman.

And the wanting shamed him. He'd thought himself a decent man.

What a predicament he was in. He supposed he should look for a respectable woman in Bannock City to care for these children. God knows, Tao Ni would be better off in a house, with a woman skilled in nursing to care for him. And Soomey should not have to be living in this hovel—half tent, half cave.

But where was he to find such a woman in a gold town, one who would not see the children as potential servants, because of their yellow skins and slanted eyes?

Having spent the past decade and more of his life in the Orient, Silas found himself unable to share his fellow Americans' prejudice against the Chinese. Far from the lazy, ignorant heathen most thought them, many were energetic, intelligent and often well educated, and certainly far more ethical than some of his countrymen, for all their profession of Christian behavior.

Silas snorted. Yes, he'd seen Christian behavior, all right, in brothels and opium dens and gambling hells from Honolulu to Macao, from Singapore to Bombay. In his opinion, the color of a man's skin or the tilt of his eyes made little difference to his goodness. That seemed to come from within.

He'd bet his bottom dollar that no Chinese had beaten Tao Ni so savagely.

The hour was late. He tapped his pipe on a stone by the fire and shook the dottle loose. None of his problems was going to be solved tonight.

Soomey woke in the night and saw Boss slumped against

the wall, his pipe fallen from his lax hand. Tao Ni was hot to her touch and did not rouse. She forced another dose of the willow bark tea into him, stroking his throat to force him to swallow. Then she tucked the blanket more closely around him and added several more small sticks to the fire. It was warm enough in the shelter, but outside a chill wind blew.

She watched the man for a while. He slept soundly, but she was sure he dreamed. His lips moved in soundless speech and his hands clenched and unclenched.

Silently she crept across to him and tucked his blanket about his shoulders. The fine dark blue wool of his trousers was damp and his shirt, no longer white, stuck to his body, clammy and cold.

Why was Boss being so kind to her and Tao Ni if he did not want her as a man wants a woman? In her admittedly small experience, she had never before met a man who thought anything more important than satisfying his body's urgent needs. Boss did not lack a man's hungers. She had felt the strength of his manhood when she had tried to pleasure him.

Indeed, Boss was a very unusual man. Perhaps, she thought, a very good man.

Would he become disgusted with her when he learned of her past? She suspected he would, for Americans were strange people, full of peculiar morals and odd and contradictory beliefs.

Not that she believed she had done anything so terrible. One could not be held responsible for what she was forced to do. And certainly a child could not be blamed for doing whatever was necessary to avoid pain.

Damn! The fire was out, the morning wind carried the scent of snow, and his clothes were still damp. Silas made his awkward way from the cave and stood outside the entrance, forcing his body erect, stretching arms and legs to work out the stiffness. In a moment he would go back in and start coffee, before the children woke.

"Coffee soon, Boss."

He turned as she slipped out of the entrance, the bucket in her hand. "Soomey! I thought you were sleeping."

She shrugged. "I hear you go, I follow. We must talk."

"Later. First I want to check on Tao—"

"Tao Ni fine. No fever, sleeping well. I gave him willow bark early, at first light. He will sleep a while yet."

Feeling vaguely irritated at her assumption of responsibility, he took the bucket from her hand. "I'll fetch the water. You start some bacon."

Later, his belly full of yet more rice flavored with bacon, Silas vowed again that he would teach her to make biscuits. He poured himself another cup of coffee and hunkered down against the wall. "You wanted to talk? So talk."

Soomey regarded him patiently. "It is time for us to go. The crooked man followed. Others will also."

"The crooked man?"

"The one who hurt Tao Ni. He followed you—"

"Soomey, we don't know he did it. I know it looks that way but we can't be sure." But if he ever was sure, Silas would see that Eli Jenkins never hurt another helpless child.

"He hurt Tao Ni," she said, something dark and savage in her voice. "I am sure."

"Well, I'm not. Now what did you want to say to me?"

"It is time for us to go," she repeated. "Over the hill is better place, not so many miners. We can find good claim before more come. We can build strong cabin to keep out snow. I will help you. When he is stronger, Tao Ni will help you too."

Catching the hand that gestured widely, Silas pushed her sleeve back. On her slender wrist was a wide scar, completely circling it. "You've been chained," he said, remembering other, similar marks on sailors who'd escaped the slavery so common in the Orient.

Her head lowered, so that all he saw was the sweet curve of her jaw. "I was only a child," she whispered, "a long time past."

She sounded ashamed. Apologetic.

He let his fingers drift across the ridged skin. It spoke of years of captivity. She must have been little more than a baby when the manacle was first locked on her wrist.

Cursing under his breath, Silas released her. She clutched her wrist to her chest, her fingers rubbing the scar. A familiar gesture, something he'd seen her do before but not really noted.

Now he understood it.

"We go, Boss? Soon?"

He considered. "I wonder why," he mused, more to himself then to her, "you're in such an all-fired hurry to move. Is there something you're not telling me?"

"I not tell you many things, Boss. None of your business. But this I do tell you. If we stay here, that Vester with the red beard, he will try to kill you. I know. I watch him before. To him only one strong man can be at this place. It is like two dogs. One must—I maybe do not know the words—one must kowtow to the other, to let him think he is boss."

Silas couldn't contain his smile. "Soomey, there's a lot of ways to say it, but kowtow is probably the politest."

"Ah, so. Weak dog must kowtow to strong one, or there be many dog fights."

"And you think Vester McGonigle and I are a couple of dogs, do you?" He was amused, but also impressed with her insightful summation of the situation.

She nodded, not quite smiling. "Men often like dogs, always wanting to be boss."

"You know, Soomey, if I didn't know you were just a kid, I'd think you were a wise old woman. But be damned if I want you to think I've got no more brains than a dog marking his territory."

"I am woman. You are stupid if you cannot see it."

He reached out and patted her head. "You've got plenty of time to be a woman, girl, so relax and let yourself be young while you can. Believe me, growin' up isn't all it's cracked up to be." And didn't he know that truth? He'd been forced out of his own childhood at a tender age and he'd be hanged if he'd do it to this delightful child.

"I think, Boss, you want me to be child so you will not have to be troubled with woman." She ducked her head, giving him a bright glance from those expressive dark eyes. "But I will not fight with you about this. Not if you will listen to me when I tell you we must move to other valley."

A wise old woman, indeed! Or maybe it was something all females were born with, this ability to get to the heart of things. Hattie had done it, too.

And they were all stubborn, too. He chuckled. She was sure a determined little thing, wanting to convince him she was older than she was.

Come to think of it, he didn't know how old she was. Twelve? Thirteen? No more than that, he was sure. He turned to ask her, but she had ducked back inside to answer Tao Ni's querulous cry.

It wouldn't make any difference, anyhow. She was a child, and he had no doubt about it. During his years in the Orient, he'd become accepting of the custom that many men took what he thought of as children into their beds. Of course, the fact that so many oriental women were small and delicate-appearing only added to the impression of their youth.

The custom was not one he had accepted, mostly because he was repelled by the notion of bedding a child. He wanted a woman in his bed, and she'd damn well better look and feel like a woman.

Savagely he clamped down on the memory of just how much like a woman Soomey had felt, before he'd thrown her out of his bed.

He bent down to poke his head into the shelter. "We'll move tomorrow. That suit you?"

Her smile was brilliant. "You are wise man. I will prepare today and we can go at first light."

He hated to move Tao Ni so soon, but the boy would be better off under a real roof, even a canvas one. "I'm going to town. Will you be all right here alone?"

She looked worried. "You will be careful, Boss? Stay out of trouble?"

Raising his hand, Silas swore, "I will be careful. You stick close here and take good care of Tao Ni. I'll see you this evening."

"Bring meat. I make soup. Good for what ails him."

He nodded, chuckling again. Bossy little thing. But she was right handy with a cookpot and a dab hand with a needle. He still didn't know what that white vegetable she fixed the other night was, but it sure had been tasty. A little sweet and nicely crisp. Some Chinese root, no doubt.

"Meat for supper. Yes ma'am."

Joe DiCastro figured Bannock City was a good place to stay for a while, especially since his Uncle Vester ran the Golden Eagle Saloon. The town was growing so fast a man wouldn't know most of the people he met from one day to the next. Even if they got themselves a sheriff or marshall anytime soon, it'd likely be spring before any wanted posters made their way here. He'd find himself a shanty and hole up 'til spring, snug as a bear in his den. And keep his gun in its holster.

Yep, he'd get himself a woman too, a soft, sweet smelling woman to keep him happy. Maybe he'd even do a little job now and then for Vester.

He smiled as he picked up the cards. Pair of queens. "I'm in," he said, nudging a couple of chips from the pile before him.

He was raking in his winnings when Eli Jenkins pushed in beside him. Joe's nose twitched at the sour smell of the turkey-necked bootlicker.

He didn't trust Eli, no matter how harmless Vester said he was. He never looked a man straight in the eye, and he was always slinking around the edges of the crowd, like a rat in a barn.

"Dewitt looks to be moving on," Eli told them. "Any of you hear anything?"

"There was a tent and supplies at the freight depot with his name on 'em," Henry said. "I heard him say he was gonna try his luck over in Centerville."

"Good riddance," Wilf said. "I purely don't like that Chinee-lovin' bastard."

Vester had come out from behind the bar and was standing behind Joe. "Dewitt could give us trouble, that's for certain," he said now. "He strikes me as the kind of man that's hard to make a deal with."

"An honest man, in other words," DiCastro drawled.

"Ain't a man born that don't have his price," Vester said. Laughter rang around the table.

"Somebody oughta teach him a lesson," Wilf said. The big man slouched across from Joe, overflowing his chair.

"What ye waitin' for, Wilf?" Vester inquired in a tone that doubted Wilf's strength and determination.

"You're twice as big as him," DiCastro said. "Why don't you do the teachin'?"

"Yeah, Wilf," Eli urged. His face was twisted in a hungry leer. "Let's go teach that damn Dewitt a lesson."

"Hesh up, Eli. When I want to hear from you, I'll let you know." Wilf picked up his mug and drained it. "As for Dewitt, I'll take care of him in my own time. He'll wish he'd never laid eye on me." Carefully he rose from his chair and wove his way to the door.

Looking back, he said, "And when I take care of Dewitt, I'll do for them little yellow bastards, too." He staggered out into the street.

"I do believe he's riled," Vester observed, before leaning forward and lowering his voice. "Now boys, let's talk about what we're gonna do with those claims we took over. They ain't doing no good just settin' there."

Late that afternoon, Silas stood at the end of town and looked out over the gold field. Despite the backbreaking labor, men were getting rich. Just this morning he had listened to a fellow tell of taking better than two ounces of fine gold from his claim in an hour. Remembering a day when he himself had picked up a nugget, water smoothed and gleaming, as big as the end of his thumb, Silas smiled to himself.

These days gravel was being carried from claims as distant as a hundred feet from the creek to be washed through the rockers. This made claims close to the stream more valuable than ever, for they gave access to the precious water.

Several of the early claims were being worked by Chinese, their original owners having abandoned them as played out. According to Soomey, her countrymen were finding enough gold to make it worth their while. To Silas, reworking the spoils looked only a little less work than sailing through a typhoon in a dinghy.

He turned and walked back to the livery stable. The tent he'd purchased had been delivered there, as had the other supplies. Now that he was moving on, there was no more need for secrecy, so he would take everything up to the shelter tonight. Tao Ni could ride his saddle horse in the morning. He and Soomey would walk.

There was a town growing over in the next valley, and still another in the drainage beyond that. He'd settle for a while in Centerville, move on if he had to. In one of those drainages, there had to be a distinctive rock formation sitting high on a hillside, pointing the way to his objective.

"They tell me there's nuggets big as your fist over on Grimes Creek," the hostler told him, as they were loading the pack saddle. "That where you're headin'?"

"That direction, anyhow," Silas admitted. "Looks to me like there's no decent claims left around here."

"Well, now, I wouldn't say that, not for them as ain't afraid of hard work. Come spring, when there's water a'plenty, some of them draws might just pan out. I hear tell of a fellow takin' five hundred dollars out of the hillside, just in a few buckets full of gravel."

"Do tell." Silas smiled. He'd heard that story and more, all of a kind. And some could be true. There was gold here, and once it had lined every streambed, glittering through the clear water. He had seen it. He had felt the rich weight of it in his own two hands.

If only he could remember where he'd hidden it.

Chapter Seven

Up the hill from Dewitt's camp, Eli crouched alongside a tumble of boulders. He'd been there since before dawn, waiting to see where Dewitt was headed. And whether he'd take his Chinee pets along with him.

Just like Dewitt to pick a cold day like today to pack up and go. Eli shivered when fingers of icy wind found their way inside his coat. He pulled his collar higher up around his neck. How he wished he could find himself a better hiding place. But the huge pines here were far apart, with not much growin' underneath 'em. Not like lower down, where he'd found plenty of cover on other days.

It sure looked like they was movin' out for good. The dun packhorse was loaded heavy. Now the older Chinee brat was tying on a coffeepot, just where it was bound to hook itself on a branch and pull loose.

Eli snickered to himself, thinking about tonight when they set up camp. Dewitt wouldn't like it one bit, nosiree! Not after a few hours packing down the trail in this cold wind, only to find himself with no coffee.

Yep, they were loading the whole shebang. He sure wished they'd forget the tarp they were using for a roof, though. Once they were gone, this'd make him a nice little hidey-hole, if he ever needed one.

Sometimes a man needed a private place, where nobody watched him. He'd learned long ago that some things he did was best hid from other folks. It was that or move on.

Well, this time wasn't nobody going to make him move on. Vester needed him, even if he didn't know he did. Why some of them other fellas, they never worked harder'n they had to.

He'd show 'em, when he found out what it was Dewitt was lookin' for.

Consarn it! Dewitt fixed the coffeepot. And he didn't even swat the Chinee kid for tying it on wrong.

Soomey made one last inspection of the shelter. It had served her well, on those occasional nights when roving, drunken miners had come too close to the drafty lean-to in which she and Tao Ni had usually slept, down near the creek.

A quick peek outside showed her that Boss was busy tightening lines on the pack. Now was her chance. She crawled between two boulders, into a space far too small for anyone but a child, or a slender woman. There, covered with rock fragments and a thin layer of soil, was the leather drawstring bag holding her last few gold coins. She looked again toward the opening before she slipped it inside her trousers and fastened it to them.

She trusted Boss, as much as she would trust any man. But not with her gold. It was all that stood between her and the life she had led since she was a child, many years ago. With gold, she could escape him if she had to, could pay someone to guide her to Portland. Safely there, she would never again be at any man's beck.

"Hey, Soomey, you ready to go?"

She crawled out and quickly dusted herself off. "I am ready. Is Tao Ni comfortable?"

"Ask him," Boss said. "He still hasn't much to say to me."

"He will learn quickly." He must, for she could not always be there to translate, and Tao Ni needed Boss's strength and power as much as she did. More, perhaps, for he was yet young and inexperienced in the evils of the world.

"Are you well, small one?" she asked in Chinese. "Do you need more willow bark?"

"Boss has made me a seat fit for a mandarin," he replied, patting the padded saddle into which he was strapped. "See. The wool of his blanket cushions me. And I feel well, only a little pain in my arm." He lifted his splinted arm, wincing a bit as he did so.

"Perhaps you will sleep, while we travel. That will be good for you." Smiling, she squeezed his ankle, relieved that Boss took such good care of an insignificant child. Of course, Tao Ni was a boy, and therefore of greater value than a mere female.

Boss led their little caravan, the lead strap of his riding horse looped about his forearm. The packhorse followed on a line. Soomey wished to walk beside Boss, so she could ask him questions, but knew that her place was behind him.

A ring of silence surrounded them as they traversed the main street of Bannock City. Boss's beard shone in the sunlight, so pale that it was closer to silver than gold. His stride was long and confident, his bearing as noble as any warlord's. He cordially greeted several people—the hostler, the grocer, and the big red-bearded Vester man. Soomey approved his actions. Only a fool showed his enemies an angry face.

At the whorehouse, he stopped and tied the horses to the porch post.

"Stay here. I'll not be long."

Soomey glared at him, but said nothing. When he had entered the front door, she put one foot in a dangling stirrup and pulled herself up to feel Tao Ni's face. He was warmer than she liked, although his sleepy smile was cheerful enough. She tipped Boss's canteen to his mouth and told him to swallow twice. The willow bark infusion she had prepared this morning was strong, and should keep him drowsy.

Boss was inside a long time, long enough that Soomey was

certain he was taking his pleasure. She fumed, wondering what she could do to convince him that she was woman enough for him. Should she try again, when they were settled?

What if she angered him enough that he drove her away?

Now that Tao Ni was injured, she needed Boss more than ever. Perhaps she would be wise to allow him to patronize the whorehouse, until she could convince him to welcome her to his bed.

She supposed she must learn to cook the bad-tasting cornmeal for him. And whatever other barbarous foods he wished. If only he would not ask her for those vile red roots that Captain Slye had often eaten. Surely they would poison him.

At last Boss emerged, the whorehouse woman close beside him. She smiled up into his face as if they were lovers, and patted his hand when he thanked her. Disgusted, Soomey turned away. She had no desire to watch Boss make such a fool of himself.

"Soomey?"

She inspected the new sign on the saloon across the street. It hung crooked against the front of the tent, the letters staggering as drunkenly across its face as miners did when emerging from the saloon.

Boss caught her shoulder in a gentle grip and turned her to face him. "Here," he said, holding out a pair of scuffed boots. "These ought to fit you. And the socks are pretty thick, so if they're a little big, it won't matter."

They looked awkward and stiff. "I do not need these," she said. "I have shoes."

"The hell you do. I looked at them last night. You've got newspaper stuffed inside and it's damn thin. A couple more miles and you'd be walking on your bare feet."

"I have walked on bare feet before," she told him, remembering that it had only been when she was taken to the city where Captain Slye had purchased her that she had been given her first pair of shoes. "It will not harm me."

"Soomey, damn it, put the boots on and don't argue with

me."

She shook her head. The boots had come from the whorehouse. She would not wear them.

His eyes narrowed. "You want to keep workin' for me?" he said, in the soft voice she had learned to heed.

Soomey nodded.

"Then put on the boots."

She glared.

He glared back, holding out the boots.

Soomey flung herself onto the porch. "Give them to me," she said. "I will wear the damn things, but only because you force me to."

"Don't swear," he told her, his voice again gentle and mild. "It's not ladylike."

Soomey resisted the urge to kick him, even after she had the boots on her feet.

The trail to Centerville, in the next drainage west, was well used. Once again Silas marveled at the number of hopefuls who had already come to this isolated basin since gold had been discovered in August. It was almost as if word of the strike had been carried on the chill autumn wind.

They climbed most of the morning, up the gulch west of Bannock City, along a well-worn path of crumbled yellow granite, sparkling in the low November sun. Soomey followed silently a few paces behind him.

At last he could stand it no more. "The trail's wide enough for two. Come on up here and talk to me," he called over his shoulder.

"I have nothing to say."

He slowed just enough that she almost caught up with him. "Soomey, you told me you're a woman, not a child. I didn't—don't—believe you, and you're not doing anything to convince me."

She looked up at him and he almost winced at the fire in

her glance. "You go to whorehouse, after I tell you there is no need."

"I went to see if Tilly or one of her girls had boots for you."

"I did not need boots."

Pulling one of her shoes from the saddlebag where he'd stuffed them, he shook it, upside down. Shreds of newspaper fluttered to the ground. He looked at her through the sole of the shoe. "You didn't, huh?"

She lowered her chin and refused to look at him. "They hurt my feet. I do not like them."

"Sit down." He pushed her gently to one of the rocks beside the trail. In a moment he had the boots off her feet. "No wonder they hurt."

She had crammed the boots over the heavy wool socks, with no regard for how they fit. The socks were bunched up and wrinkled. Her feet were marked with red creases and blisters were forming on both heels.

Silas fetched the tin of goose grease he never went anywhere without. When he began to rub it onto her heels, Soomey did her best to wriggle out of his grasp. "Hold still!" he commanded.

Once both feet were well greased, he put the socks back on her, careful to smooth them out. Their heels came halfway up her ankles, but high enough that the extra fabric wouldn't rub. Then he carefully pushed her feet into the boots, making sure the socks were unwrinkled. He laced the boots fairly tight, testing their fit before tying the rawhide into a loose but unslippable knot. "Stand up."

She stood.

"Walk around. See if they hurt." He'd learned the trick of greasing his feet well on a trek into the jungle in the East Indies. He hadn't had a blister since.

"They feel odd," Soomey told him after a few tentative steps, "as if my feet are sliding in slick mud." She walked a little way up the trail. "It is very unpleasant."

"But do they hurt?"

She shook her head. "It is strange. There is no pain, but I still do not like the boots."

Silas gave her queue a tug. "They'll protect your feet, and keep 'em warm."

Her sigh was long suffering, but he took it as capitulation. "And Soomey?"

"Yes, Boss." Definitely a victim of injustice.

"I only went to the whorehouse. I didn't...ah, use it." Why was he explaining? It wasn't any of her business. But he couldn't bear her silent disapproval.

Her smile was sufficient reward. "That is good." She almost skipped as she stepped onto the trail beside him. "The boots are very warm, Boss."

It was probably as close to an apology as he was going to get.

The trail wound down into a narrow gulch with a dry streambed at the bottom. Soomey slipped twice, her leather boot soles having little purchase on the loose sand. The second time, her feet went out from under her.

Boss turned around and said, "Are you all right?"

Just then several boulders came rolling into the trail ahead of them. Before she could get to her feet, Boss had caught her by the quilted jacket and pushed her against the side of the hill. In a continuation of the same sweep, he pulled the horses around and forced them against the hillside, too. Soomey shrank back, not trusting their big, iron-shod feet to avoid her.

"Catch," Boss said, in a hoarse whisper. He pulled Tao Ni from the saddle and almost dropped him into her arms. She wondered what he would have done if she hadn't caught the boy.

At the same time, there was a shout from the hillside above them. Soomey didn't understand the words, but she heard the threat. Carefully she stood up and dug into the nearest saddlebag, hoping it was the one holding her bundle.

Boss drew the rifle from its scabbard and held it at hip level. She watched him scan the hillside above them, barely lifting his head over the horse's back.

"Boss?"

"Quiet," he snapped. "Sit down and don't move!"

Gravel and sand cascaded into the trail. Soomey pulled her bundle from the saddlebag. She sat. Soon she heard the rustling of brush over her head.

"Step back from that there hoss, mister, and nobody gets hurt." The voice was harsh, threatening.

And familiar. She hoped its owner was not holding a gun on Boss, for he sounded savage enough to shoot with little provocation.

Boss stepped back into the middle of the trail.

Soomey reached into her bundle.

A masked man appeared from the downhill side of the trail, holding a shotgun aimed directly at Boss. He gestured with his head, directing Boss to step farther away from the horse. "Drop the gun," he said. His words came out high-pitched and quavery, far more frightening to Soomey. A frightened man was dangerous and unpredictable.

She had seen a man hit by a shotgun blast at close range, once. If only Boss would not resist.

Boss dropped his rifle.

"Take off your coat."

Boss complied. Soomey wondered how she could tell him to step aside, for he was standing directly between her and the man with the shotgun. Then it was almost as if he had read her mind, for when he dropped his coat to the ground, he stepped sidewards. "I've little money," he said, "and no gold. I just got here."

"Don't give me that bullshit," growled the robber Soomey could not see. "I was in the store the other day when you paid with some fancy coins, and I saw the size of your poke. Now hand it over."

As Boss reached toward his pocket with his left hand, the robber said, "Do it slow, and don't try any tricks, or my friend there will shoot the kids."

Boss shrugged. Soomey fired.

Boss's knife flew past her head at the same instant as the bullet from her pistol struck the masked man's thigh.

"Boss!" she called. When he looked at her, she tossed him the other pistol.

He caught it handily, held it on the uphill man. "Get down here," he commanded.

Soomey peeked above the top of the cut bank. The robber lay among broken shrubs, Boss's knife still quivering high in his shoulder. Blood darkened the heavy wool of his coat.

"I can't move," he whined.

"The hell you can't. You've got five seconds."

The man rolled and slid down the rocky hillside, tumbling the last few feet to land in a tangle beside his companion. "You ain't a'gonna kill me, are you?" He no longer sounded threatening or dangerous.

Boss raised an eyebrow. "Give me one good reason why I shouldn't kill you both." He leaned over and pulled his knife free, wiping it on the robber's filthy pants. The man cried out in pain, and then fell to cursing Boss in a low, monotonous tone.

The man Soomey had shot pulled the bandanna from his lower face. She recognized him as another of those who often loitered at the front of the Golden Eagle Saloon.

"I never done nothin' to you. It was all Wilf's idea. He saw you had a fat purse and he said you'd be easy pickin's, what with them kids and all. He was gonna give me twenty dollars."

The bullet hole in his leg still bled sluggishly, but Soomey doubted he was badly hurt. Next time she would shoot straighter.

"That'd about pay for your coffin, wouldn't it?" Boss looked across the horse's back at Soomey. "What do you say? Shall I kill them?"

"Yes! They would have shot you." The very thought made her stomach clench.

"Bloodthirsty, aren't you? On the other hand, if I turn them loose, maybe they'll pass the word that I don't take kindly to folks trying to rob me."

"Oh, God, Mister, I will surely do that," the shot man promised. "Just let us go, and I'll tell ever'body I see that you're hell on wheels."

"Take that bandana and tie up your friend's shoulder. "

He rolled over and struggled to his knees. When he eased the coat from his companion's shoulder, the man on the ground grimaced, face white behind the filthy, tobacco-stained beard and mustache.

"I'm bleeding to death," he whimpered.

"You'll live to hang," Boss told him.

Soomey almost smiled at the fear on their faces. She wanted to see them grovel in the dirt at Boss's feet. They deserved to be stepped upon like the lowly worms they were.

But all Boss did was pick up his rifle and hand the pistol back to Soomey. "Here. If either of 'em blinks, shoot him in the knee."

She smiled, hoping one of them would move. But they did not.

Both men shook like leaves about to fall as Boss searched them. One carried a folding knife that made Boss sneer, and a revolver. The other had only a belt knife, similar to the one Boss carried. Boss tied the shotgun onto the saddle behind Tao Ni and stuffed the knives and the handgun into a saddlebag.

Then Boss walked all around the two would-be robbers, like a buyer inspecting likely slaves. He indicated the one Soomey had shot. "This one's not too big, but he's got a little fat on him, Soomey. Think he needs that coat as much as you do?"

As the dirty coat looked to be made of heavy wool, Soomey frankly coveted it. She shook her head.

"It's yours, then. Take off your boots and britches, too," he ordered the cringing man.

"But, I'll freeze—"

"So?"

The coat and pants came off. Under them was dirty, stained underwear.

"You, too," Boss told the other man. He gestured with the rifle. "Strip."

Soomey stifled a giggle when the big man, he of bluster and bravado, removed his pants and revealed a union suit, faded to pale pink by many washings.

"You got a horse?"

"It's tied down the hill." He shivered. "What are you aimin' to do to us, Dewitt?"

Boss ignored his question. "Soomey?"

"I go, Boss." She found the tethered horse easily. It tried to bite her when she untied its reins. Soomey dodged back, hoping it would not decide she was food. She did not like horses. They were so big!

The horse followed her willingly, and they reached the trail without her being bitten.

Both robbers stood shivering in their long underwear, their clothes tied on top of the packs. The big one's bare toes curled against the sandy soil and his legs shook. The bandage about his shoulder was wet with blood.

Soomey almost felt sorry for him, until she recalled that he had intended to rob them, had threatened to kill them.

Boss used his big knife to cut the stirrups from their saddle. "Mount," ordered.

The one with the wounded shoulder scrambled into the saddle awkwardly, while Boss held the reins. Then Boss laid his rifle aside and helped the other to mount behind the saddle. He was not particularly gentle, Soomey noticed.

"Now, I'm letting you go, but if I ever see hide or hair of you again, I will kill you," Boss told them. "Understand?"

Both men nodded.

"And pass the word, back at Bannock City. I'm a peaceable man, most of the time. But I don't take kindly to those who bother me and mine."

"Yeah. Yeah, mister, we'll tell 'em."

"Then git!" He swatted the horse on the rump and it took off back toward Bannock City. They both seemed about to fall off.

Soomey watched them out of sight. "You should have killed them, Boss," she said.

"This'll get the word out better," was all he replied.

The lights of Centerville gleamed in the early twilight. As around Bannock City, the valley bottom had been ravaged. Spoils piles marked the course of a winding creek. Before they reached the outskirts of the town, Silas turned up a narrow gulch to the east of the creek.

Soomey helped him string a line between two trees, over which he draped the tarpaulin. The night was overcast and warm. There would be snow soon, but not tonight. With a fire, they would be comfortable enough. Tao Ni's fever seemed to have subsided, so he shouldn't suffer from one night in the open.

Tomorrow Silas would find a place they could settle while he explored this valley.

"I want you and Tao Ni to stay here while I look around in the morning," he told Soomey. She was scouring her two pots with sand from the narrow creek that trickled along one wall of the gulch. "He needs to rest, and I don't want him left alone."

"You will find place to pitch tent?"

"I'll do my best. But first...Soomey, how long have you been around here?"

She counted on her fingers. "We come thirty-three days ago."

"That's all?" Silas had thought, from her familiarity with Bannock City, that she'd been there a long time.

But nobody had been in Bannock City a long time, come

to think on it.

"You came from Portland?"

"No. Li Ching change his mind when he heard of gold strike. Our ship had cargo for Bandon. Li Ching made us get off there, travel overland to Canyon City. He said we would be there faster than if we go to Portland. Then he heard of gold strike at the Salmon River." She sniffed. "I do not think this is much river."

Chuckling, Silas told her, "If you came directly to Bannock City, you never even came close to the Salmon River. It's up north of here."

"North?"

Silas smoothed the ground between his feet. With a twig, he drew lines. "The Snake. The Salmon. The Boise. And the Payette." He pointed to a spot between the Boise and the Payette. "We're about here. It's a long way from the Salmon, although if you floated a stick down that creek back there—" He pointed in the direction they had come. "And if it didn't get hung up on something, sooner or later, it would get to the Salmon River."

"Where is Portland?"

Shifting his foot, Silas drew in the Columbia. "Clear over here. A long ways." He remembered how it had taken him and Emmet more than two weeks to reach the old Hudson's Bay Fort near where Portland now stood. Of course, they hadn't hurried.

Her shoulders slumped. "I knew this, I think. Li Ching promised me that he would take me to Portland in the spring. Now I know he will not. It is too far."

"Soomey, when this is all over—when I do what I came here to do—I'll see you get to Portland." He couldn't understand why she was so determined. Her crazy idea of masquerading as a houseboy would never work. "Or wherever you want to go."

He wasn't prepared for the sense of loss that swept through him as he made the promise to her. In the little time he'd known Soomey, she had wormed her way into his heart. It was hard to imagine life without her.

Perhaps she would settle for Boise City. It wasn't much of a place yet, but it would grow. When Hattie and Emmet moved down there, surely there would be room in their household for one small, extremely stubborn Chinese girl.

Silas went for a short walk into the woods before retiring. He saw the pile of blankets as soon as he returned. "What's this?"

He had told her to make two beds, one for him and Tao Ni, one for herself. Instead, Soomey had piled all the blankets on the ground sheet she'd spread between the hillside and the fire.

"A bed."

"Soomey, I told you to make your bed over there."

She continued to arrange the blankets. "This is better for Tao Ni."

"Soomey—"

"Boss, I will not tempt you. Tao Ni will sleep between us. Very warm."

His eyebrow lifted. He did his best to prevent his mouth from twitching. "You will not tempt me? You promise?"

"I am honorable woman, Boss. I promise you I will not tempt you. Tonight."

"You're a scamp," he said, allowing the smile to show itself.

She tempted him, just by being near him. Her smile, her slim, lithe body, her expressive eyes. And her mouth. How could he forget the feel of it on his bare skin, hot and hungry?

She was a child, he reminded himself. A child!

And she was right, about Tao Ni being warmer between two bodies, damn it.

When she had the bed made, Silas scooped the drowsing boy into his arms and laid him carefully down. Tao Ni had been quiet all evening, probably because of the willow bark Soomey had poured into him at every opportunity. Tomorrow, she'd said, she would give him less. The swelling in his arm was reduced, and his bruises were starting to change from black to various shades of livid purple, blue and green.

All Silas took off that night was boots, hat and jacket. Be damned if he was going to climb into bed with her clad only in his long johns. That would be asking for trouble.

If only he didn't remember how easy it was to slip a willing Chinese girl out of her loose black trousers.

It was going to be a long night.

Chapter Eight

"WHAT A PASSEL OF FOOLS!" VESTER SET A BOTTLE OF WHISKEY and glasses on the bar, and turned his back. 'Twouldn't do for Wilf to see the grin he couldn't hide. The man's temper was always on a short fuse, and right now it was about ready to blow.

"Don't either of ye have any gumption?" he demanded of the two half-dressed men who'd just slunk into the saloon. "A ambush! Christ! What was ye thinking on?"

Henry hung his head. "Hell, Vester, Wilf said that seein' two of us with guns, Dewitt would back right down."

"That b-big Chinee kid, he was the one w-w-with the handguns." Wilf's teeth were chattering so bad he couldn't hardly talk, no one being willing to lend him a coat. He'd found some britches somewhere, but they was too short and too tight around the middle. The bandage on his shoulder was dark with dried blood and he moved as if his arm pained him.

"You knew he was a scrapper," Vester said, with no attempt to hide the scorn he felt. "You should'a kept your eye on him."

"Yeah, well, how was I to know?" Wilf protested. "Hell, I couldn't even see the brat. I was up on the hill. Henry was the one with the shotgun."

"Ahuh! And that's another thing. You boys would've been better off to let Dewitt be," Vester said, as he set steaming cups of coffee on the bar in front of the two shivering idjits "Long as we don't rile him, he won't bother us none."

Joe DiCastro tipped his chair back and blew a smoke ring. "I think," he said, examining his cigarillo, "that it'd take moren' a couple of fools to rile Dewitt."

"Who you callin' a fool?"

"Close your yap, Henry," Wilf snarled. "Ain't nobody can get away with what Dewitt did to me."

"Next time he ought to be shot dead, Wilf. Yesirree." Eli Jenkins squeezed in beside Wilf. "That's the ticket. Next time don't give him a chance to fight back. Just shoot him dead."

"Hell, Eli, don't be talking on things that ain't none of your business. I'll be deciding what's to happen next."

"Aw, Wilf I was just tryin'—" Eli whined.

"Well, don't you go trying anything, you hear, Eli? You leave all that up to me. Got that?"

"I do, Wilf. Yessiree! I surely do."

Vester was getting purely tired of Wilf. The man might be strong as an ox and bold as brass, but he had a head too big for his hat, and a mean-spirited nature that made him downright dangerous. Sooner or later he'd pull something that decent folks took notice of, and that wouldn't suit Vester's plans atall. "You want to keep on working for me, Wilf, you'll leave Dewitt alone."

Wilf glowered but didn't argue.

"It jest don't seem right, that Chinee brat getting' away with shootin' Henry. Why, if we was to—"

"Shuddap Eli!" Wilf snarled.

Vester stifled his laughter. Why not a one of these lackwits was a match for Dewitt. Not in a fair fight, anyhow.

He had to respect Dewitt—or anybody could get the best of Wilf.

Silas's immediate thought, upon awakening, was that he'd had the most delicious dream. But it was gone in an instant, while he fought his way clear of sleep's last foggy tendrils.

His second thought was that he held an armful of warm, soft woman. Her bottom was wedged against his painfully swollen shaft, her head on his outstretched arm.

She smelled of jasmine, sweet and enticing. He discovered the weight of a soft breast in the palm of his hand, teased an already budded nipple into full flowering. Her hair was a silk curtain flowing around him as he nuzzled the back of her neck. He couldn't remember her name, but there was no doubt about his wanting her. "Good morning, darlin'," he whispered against her nape.

She moved, dislodging the blanket that covered her shoulders. Revealing the sweet curve of her cheek.

Silas came entirely awake. Rolling away from her, he sat up. Across the fire, which he was feeding with shreds of bark, Tao Ni grinned. "Fire, Boss." His bruised face was grotesque, still swollen and even more colorful than yesterday, but pride shone from him like a beacon.

"Well, hell!" Silas reached for his boots. Soomey slept on, her breathing deep and even. Angry as he was, he had to absolve her of tempting him. He had a hunch that he'd done his share of getting her into his arms. He was still hard. Half turning away from Tao Ni, he reached into his pants and rearranged himself.

He'd planned to reconnoiter today, before finding them a tent site. The weather remained clear and cold, and he wanted to take advantage of it. But instead he would get the damn tent set up, so Soomey could have her own bed, as far from his as possible. If he could arrange it, he'd string some sort of a curtain so she could have a little privacy.

So he wouldn't be tempted to invite her back into his bed, to sample once more that sweet breast, those round hips.

Silas cursed viciously.

Tao Ni scrambled back, face showing his fear. "It's all right, boy," Silas told him, voice soothing. "I was cussin' myself, not you. Come over here and let's take a look at that cut." He gestured.

Slowly Tao Ni came to him, still cautious. Silas inspected the stitched cut across his forehead. It was clean, no sign of infection. Perhaps Soomey had been right not to bandage it. It was healing well. Without thinking, Silas pulled Tao Ni against him for a quick hug. "You'll be fine, soon as those bruises fade."

After an initial stiffening, the boy relaxed against him, almost clung. Silas wondered if he had ever been hugged before. Damn it! He didn't want these kids to need him. He had work to do this winter, a life to get back to come spring. What would he do with them then?

"Good morning, Boss." Soomey's words were blurred with sleep, but her gentle, husky voice sent a thrill of desire through him. Again Silas cursed, but this time under his breath.

"Morning, Soomey," was all he said, as he released Tao Ni and rose to his feet. In a moment he was striding down the gulch. The water in the creek should be cold enough to cool his ardor.

She was his responsibility, damn it! He owed her his protection, even from himself.

What an unspeakable lecher he was!

Soomey quickly bathed her face and hands before starting coffee. Boss was disturbed about something, and she knew from experience that men deprived of their morning coffee were easily angered. And it was her fault, for she had slept far too late. Oh, but she had been dreaming of a life free of fear, free of the need to hide.

Free.

"Why is Boss angry?" Tao Ni asked when she returned with water. "He was gentle with me, but then you spoke and he became so furious."

She hung the coffeepot from its hook and set her small pot beside the fire to heat for tea. "I do not know, Tao Ni, but you must not be concerned. His is a volatile nature, I believe, and easily aroused. When he returns, he will be calm again, and will speak softly." She believed what she said, but hoped he would not speak in those certain soft tones that carried a great threat. "He has promised to care for you, remember, and he will certainly keep that promise."

"But what about you, Elder Sister? Will he also care for you?"

"I am a woman grown, not a child. It is not necessary that I be cared for."

"Perhaps he will marry you," he said, and accepted a cold rice ball from her. "Then the two of you could care for me, and I would work hard for you." Nodding and smiling, he seemed to require no answer.

"I do not choose to marry," Soomey said, but not so loud that Tao Ni could hear. He was too young to understand that marriage was only another sort of slavery, with no chance of escape, for any woman. He was a male, so perhaps he could not understand.

Boss returned just as Soomey turned the coffeepot away from the fire. She poured his cup and handed it to him without a word. His face had that tight, still look to it that contained his anger.

After breakfast, she sent Tao Ni to seek firewood. She replenished Boss's coffee and sat before him, head bowed. "You are angry with me." Better to ask than to wait for him to scold her.

He did not answer, so after a long while she peeked up at him. He seemed to be studying the tree trunk that stood just outside the shelter. His mouth was still thin and tight, but his eyes held a contemplative glow.

"Boss?"

He looked down at her as if he'd forgotten she was sitting there. One hand wiped across his chin, and she heard the rasp of his beard against the hard skin of his palm. After a moment, he spoke. "Where did you get the guns, Soomey?"

Since she had been expecting him to chasten her for some misdemeanor, Soomey could find no words at first. "Guns?"

"The pistols. Two silver chased derringers, to be exact. Nice guns. Expensive guns." He hooked a finger under her chin and forced her head up, forced her to meet his gaze. "Where did you get them, Soomey?"

"They were my master's," she said. The absolute truth.

"And he just gave them to you?"

"He died. I took them." She pulled back, lowered her head again. His eyes demanded the entire truth and she could not tell him all.

"You took them. I see. And what else did you take?"

"Nothing that was not mine to take. My clothing." She shrugged, hoping he would ask no more.

"And when was this? Where?"

Soomey counted back. Captain Watkins had taught her the American calendar, but she still could not remember all the months. "In March, I think. Or perhaps the month after. Aproo?"

"April. And where were you?" Boss was watching her intently. She could see other questions hovering on the edge of his tongue. If only he would not ask them. Not yet.

"It was at San Francisco. My mas— Captain Watkins was killed in a saloon brawl. When I learned he was dead, I took the...the guns and my clothing and I ran away." And if she had not, she would now be the property of Kaspar Pfaltzgraff, first mate of the *Gilded Gull*. If she were alive at all. Taking a deep breath, to conquer the fear that even now overcame her at thought of Pfaltzgraff's viciousness, she went on, "I went to Chinese community in San Francisco and found Li Ching. He was contracting for laborers and servants in Portland, and agreed to take me."

She saw no need to tell him she had gone first to a saloon she knew the captain had frequented. He had once introduced her to the saloonkeeper's woman, Chinese like Soomey. Although terrified that they would be discovered, Jing Fei had hidden her and had obtained the black laborer's garb in exchange for her silks and velvets. When Soomey emerged, she was no longer the dainty Chinese concubine of a wealthy American captain, but a silent, nondescript boy fit for nothing but manual labor.

Shaving her scalp had been the most painful part of the process, but no boy old enough to work lacked a queue.

Boss was silent until Soomey looked up again, hoping to see his thoughts written across his face. But she saw nothing, not a hint.

At last he said, "Damned if I don't believe you."

Soomey breathed a deep sigh of relief, until—

"At least I believe you've told the truth about the guns. But I want to know more about this 'master.' Were you a slave? Did he own you?"

Soomey's throat closed, until she could not swallow. She still remembered the night Captain Slye had bought her from the old woman who collected and sold useless girl children. She had not understood his gloating words then, but he had repeated them many times afterward. They were graven on her mind.

"You're my slave. Mine to do with as I please. To hurt if I want to. Or to kill." And he had hurt her. Oh, yes, he had, many times and in many different, degrading ways.

"Yes," she said, forcing the words out past the tightness, "I was a slave."

For the second time that morning, Boss cursed, long and viciously.

Centerville was smaller than Bannock City and not as well developed. But it had a saloon and a general store, and a corral at the edge of town that served as a livery stable. Silas glanced inside the store before heading for the saloon.

"Beer," he told the bartender, knowing he'd get far more information if he was a paying customer. He sipped it when the chipped glass mug was slid along the bar to him. Not bad. He'd drunk worse, many times.

After the usual exchange on the weather—unseasonably

mild—the chances of finding a decent claim—gettin' poorer every day—and the lack of whores in a growing town—'cept for a couple of ladies old enough to retire and set up a boarding house—Silas asked about the chances of buying or otherwise acquiring a mined-out claim.

"Wal, I don't know much about mined-out, but there's a fair number that jest ain't what they seemed to be. Seems like I see a feller or two in here every day, talkin' about headin' back where he come from. Most of 'em jest walks off and leaves things sittin'."

"I'm looking for one up from the creek," Silas said, having given the subject some thought, "to set up a tent on. I don't want to mine it, for I've seen that a man can make a sight more selling to the miners than he can grubbing in the dirt."

"You got that right, mister, yessiree, you do! And stay a sight cleaner in the bargain." The bartender, no doubt impressed with the gold coin Silas had tossed on the bar, drew another mug of beer. "What might you be sellin'?"

And as simply as that, Silas became a merchant once more. "Oh, tack, tools, hardware of all sorts. I looked in at Appledore's, and he doesn't seem to stock much of that sort of thing."

"Nope, he mostly stocks foodstuffs." Swiping a filthy cloth across the wet rings Silas's mug had left, the bartender confided, "I hear tell he was a grocer back in Ohio. He showed up here a while back with a couple of wagonloads of canned goods and his woman. Took one look around and settled in. His was the first wood building in town."

"Good site, too, on that little rise." Now that he had made up his mind, Silas was eager to begin. "Well, I'll be looking around for a place to set up shop." He drained the last of his beer.

Tomorrow or the next day he'd go back to Bannock City and see if he could pick up some stock to tide him over, maybe send to Lewiston for whatever was available. Or he could send a message to his agent in San Francisco. He'd set up the tent here in town, use it for both store and living quarters until he was established.

Soomey could work in the store, leaving him free to do what he came here for. It would keep her out of mischief.

Instead of looking for abandoned claims, Silas walked down the narrow, muddy gash that served as Centerville's only street. Yes, a hardware store would indeed serve him well. And when he left, perhaps he might even turn a profit by selling it.

A few inquiries were enough to give him the information he needed to find a site. The town had not been platted yet, Appledore told him, although there was some talk about doing so. So Silas was free to choose a site to suit himself. "But don't go setting up too close to the creek," Appledore warned. "You'll find yourself having to move if someone files a claim on your land."

"What if I do just that? File a claim on my land?"

"Land sakes, man, why would you want to? There's no need. Matter of fact, there ain't no law yet."

Silas, who had never owned land in his life, could not explain. But he found out what was required and that morning he staked a claim, two hundred by two hundred feet, up at the end of town, where the street petered out. It gave him a great feeling of satisfaction.

If it weren't for Tao Ni, she would simply disappear. Soomey shoved another pine branch into place. But she could not leave a small Chinese boy alone in Centerville. He would be more safe here, in the narrow gulch outside town, where they'd camped before Boss staked his claim.

She tugged savagely on a thick twig, forcing it into place, hating the delay before she could follow Boss. He need never know that she had deserted Tao Ni for a day and a night.

She had hired on to be his eyes and ears. Boss had said so himself. Then she had been so stupid as to reveal her sex, and suddenly she was incapable of doing anything but cook his meals and wash his clothes.

Cook! She was not a servant. There were other ways to earn two dollars a week than to cook for a man who didn't even like rice.

Bah!

She'd prepared rice for several meals. Her small pot held enough willow bark tea to last many days, in case Tao Ni's arm pained him. She was leaving him both heavy blankets Boss had purchased. Everything else was still in the tent in town.

"Promise me you will remain here for two days. If I am not returned by then, I will not. Then you can go back to Boss's tent and wait for him."

Tao Ni nodded. "You will take care, Elder Sister?"

"I will take care. Nothing will happen to me, and I will return before Boss, so he will never know I have followed him."

"Watch over him," Tao Ni said, his chin quivering. "He is a good man."

"He is indeed." Soomey hugged Tao Ni, and quickly slipped out of the shelter. She must hurry, or Boss would be too far ahead of her.

She ran, faster than she had ever run before. Boss had departed more than two hours ago, and he was riding. The boots slowed her a little, for they were heavier than her shoes, and stiffer. But also better, for they did not slip from her feet if she stepped wrong, and their soles protected hers from the rocks and pebbles of the trail. She had become used to them, and no longer found her feet slipping from under her.

Several times she left the trail and hid herself in the trees, when parties of miners approached. Despite the cold, every day brought more into the area, most of them honest, decent, hardworking men. It was the others, they who wanted riches without the need to labor for them, that she feared. Still, it would be better if no one saw her, a lone Chinese laborer. Too many hated the Chinese simply because they were foreigners.

She caught up with Boss just over the summit, but did

not let him see her. Instead she followed him, picking a path through the trees when possible, lagging out of sight—but not out of hearing—when the hillsides above and below the trail were too steep. When he finally reached the edge of Bannock City unmolested, she turned aside and went to what was already being called Chinatown.

Boss had given her all the silver coins in his purse before he departed. They were equal to many dollars, she thought, although most of the coins she did not recognize. That night she slept safely in a shed behind the Chinese store. It cost her only one small silver coin.

In the morning she went into the store. "I seek a person who is a good watcher," she told the storekeeper, and laid another silver coin on the table. "He must follow my boss to Centerville, perhaps beyond. He must be brave and invisible."

The storekeeper nodded, but did not touch her coin. "There is perhaps one who might do these things. Do you know my nephew, Feng Ji Rong?"

"The one with the crooked leg?"

"Aye, that one. He finds little work, for all he is strong as any man. But with his uneven gait, these Americans will not believe he can work the placers."

"He is trustworthy?"

"I would trust him with my store, were he able to keep accounts. But alas, his eyes see only far away objects clearly."

When Soomey nodded, he picked up her coin.

She hired Feng Ji Rong for one month. He was grateful for the work, and promised to guard Boss with his life.

"I will carry your bundle back to Centerville," Soomey told him. "It would slow you when you follow Boss on the trail."

"There is not a horse alive that can walk faster than I," he boasted. When Soomey raised one eyebrow, he admitted, "But I cannot run so fast as one trots."

"I do not expect the impossible. Just watch over him, and if anyone follows, warn him."

"I shall do this," Ji Rong vowed.

With an easier mind, Soomey donned her pack. It was heavy, with all of Ji Rong's belongings as well as the supplies she had purchased. Against her better judgment, she walked along Bannock City's Main Street—there were now signs naming it so, as well as two new wooden buildings. In just four days! Such energy, these Americans.

The red-bearded man was lounging against the wall of the Golden Eagle Saloon, picking his teeth. He watched Soomey—she felt his gaze like a hot brand—but made no move toward her. For once he was alone, without the crowd of toadies that usually surrounded him. She hoped he would not challenge Boss, for Ji Rong would be no match for such a bear of a man.

Boss was nowhere in sight. Soomey resisted the temptation to peer into the windows of Tilly's whorehouse. Instead she turned her steps toward the trail. The moon was new, so she would have to walk carefully. It would take her most of the night to return to Centerville.

Were there bears in the woods? She shivered, and not just because of the light drizzle that had begun at sundown.

Dewitt! Now what's he doing back in Bannock City? And where's his Chinee brats?

Eli peered around the corner of a tent and watched as Dewitt led three mules and a packhorse into the livery stable. None of 'em carried a load, so he must'a come after something.

They'd only been gone a couple of days, so they couldn't have gone far. Vester had said maybe they was headin' out to the trail down the Payette, but Wilf hadn't thought so. 'Course, bad as Wilf wanted another chance at Dewitt, he wouldn't have wanted to believe the man was pullin' out.

Neither did Eli. Not 'til he found whatever it was he was lookin' for.

He watched until Dewitt came out and walked up to the freight office. The log walls was too thick for him to hear what was said inside, so he hunkered down and waited. Before he went to Wilf with the news, he wanted to see what Dewitt was up to.

He was almost asleep when the door opened.

"I'll stay in town for a couple of days, just in case that shipment gets here as scheduled," Dewitt was sayin' as he stepped outside. "But if there's any delay, I'll have to get back to Centerville."

"Jed's not one to let grass grow on the trail," the agent said. "I'd bet a dollar he'll be on time."

Dewitt laughed. "I won't take that bet." He shook the agent's hand. "I'll be staying at Tilly's. You can leave messages there for me."

Eli watched him until he turned in at the whorehouse, debating about whether he should tell Wilf, or let him find out on his own.

He laughed to himself, thinkin' of the look on Wilf's face, was he to come on Dewitt unawares.

Maybe they'd be a fight.

Maybe Wilf would do what he'd said and kill Dewitt.

And them Chinee brats of his, too.

Chapter Nine

"Hurry, Tao Ni. Boss could be here any moment!" Soomey snatched the tarpaulin from the branches that supported it, folded it well enough for him to carry.

Tao Ni scrambled after her, as she almost ran down the path.

How could she have slept all day? Tired as she had been when she crept into the shelter just before dawn, she should have awakened Tao Ni and taken him back to town. What if Boss had already returned?

They kept to the shadows as they approached Centerville. Once among the tents and shanties that made up the town, she took a circuitous route to Boss's tent. As far as she knew, no one saw them enter it.

There was no sign that anyone had been here in the two days it had been empty. Soomey breathed a sigh of relief. Her greatest fear had been that they would have been robbed. Well, not her greatest fear. That had been that something would happen to Boss without her and Tao Ni to guard his back.

They ate cold rice in the gathering darkness and crawled into their blankets. Boss had warned them to show no light at night, for fear someone would notice that there were only two children alone. Again she wished that she had not slept the day away. Now she would lie awake through the long winter night. Worrying about Boss.

Lights flickered across the tent wall. Miners outside, coming and going. To pass the time, she whispered a story to Tao Ni, a made-up tale of a battle between evil pirates and brave, honest sailors. As she spoke, the captain of the good ship *Valor* took on more and more of the appearance of Boss in her mind. He had been to sea, she knew, and in the Orient. Had he been a captain?

Had he kept a Chinese concubine, as Captain Wilkins had?

As she spun the tale, adding more and more thrilling action, she pictured Boss at the helm of a tall ship, golden against the sails, his fair hair blowing in the wind, his eyes narrowed against the sun. When Tao Ni's even breathing told her he was asleep, she was almost disappointed to end the story before the pirates were finally vanquished. Surely Boss would have won the fierce battle and killed all the evil ones.

And he would have freed their female slaves and returned them to China, giving each a dowry so that she could make an honorable marriage.

But one slave would not marry even though she had a dowry. Instead she would ask to be brought to America and she would set herself up in a shop in Portland, selling finely embroidered garments of silk and the sheerest linen. Just as Soomey had planned to do, once she had amassed enough by working as a houseboy. As she would do, when Boss no longer needed her.

Would he really take her to Portland, as he had promised?

Of course he would. Boss was an honorable man.

Silas leaned against the bar at the White Top Saloon in Bannock City and sipped his beer. He wondered how Soomey and Tao Ni were doing. He hated like the devil to leave them alone for so long. No telling what mischief they could get into.

The freight shipment should be here tomorrow. With any luck, it would contain unconsigned hardware and tack, enough to stock his store until the goods he had ordered from Portland could arrive. In the meantime, he was at loose ends.

A poker game was forming at a back table. Pushing himself away from the bar, Silas sauntered that way. He wasn't much of a gambler, but he'd always been lucky. Perhaps he could win the cost of tomorrow's purchases.

Before he reached the table, he was caught by a hand on his sleeve. Silas looked into the face of its owner, eyes narrowed. The swarthy visage was familiar, and after a moment's hesitation, he remembered. One of Vester's ruffians. "You want something?" he said, keeping his voice neutral.

"You back in town for good?" the man said softly. He didn't look like a miner. His coat was good wool, his face was clean-shaven. The black clothing he wore gave him a menacing aspect, as did the two black pistols, tied low.

Silas wondered if he was as dangerous as he looked. "Shouldn't I be?"

"Makes no difference to me. But it might to some folks."

"Ahuh! I reckon I know who."

"Not Vester, if he's who you're thinking. He's decided to let you be, long as you don't stick your nose in where it isn't wanted."

Letting his amusement show, Silas said, "Good of him. Anything else?"

"Just one. That was a damfool thing you did, facing down that mob. You could've got yourself kilt."

"I couldn't stand by and see the boys tormented." Silas wondered where this man had been that afternoon.

"Folks hereabouts don't trust the Celestials. There's a lot of talk against them here in town. Sooner or later there's going to be trouble. And some of Vester's boys will be right in the middle of it, feeling the way they do about foreigners."

"I don't give a damn how Vester and his boys feel," Silas snapped. "Anybody raises a hand against me or mine, I'll do what I must to make things right."

"I didn't say anything about Vester. Just some of his boys. You remember that, when the time comes."

Puzzled, Silas watched as the ruffian walked to the bar. Now why had the man warned him? And of what, exactly?

Well, it made no difference anyhow. He'd been on his guard ever since riding into the basin.

"Join you?" he said to the men around the poker table.

"Always room for new gold," the dealer said.

"Haven't seen you around town for a couple of days," one of the other players said. "You been out prospectin'?"

Silas tapped the table, requesting two cards. "Nope. I have a mind to leave the gold digging to folks who like being out in the weather. I'm opening a hardware store over in Centerville." He studied his hand, the cards showing around the table, pushed five chips into the center of the table. "You need any kind of gear, you come on over. I'll make you a good deal."

Two players tossed in their hands, a third raised. Another player tossed his chips out and looked at Silas, who did a mental tally of what he'd seen. "I'll see you, and raise five," he said.

When the hand was over, he was richer by nearly two hundred dollars. The dealer took the loss philosophically, but another player, glared at Silas and muttered under his breath.

Silas heard something that sounded like "Chink-lover," but didn't make an issue of it. Losing a fair portion of his poke was enough to make a man cranky.

The game went on, although few of the pots were as rich as the one Silas won. He listened to the talk around the table, picking up bits and pieces of local gossip.

"I hear a fellow up More's Creek found a nugget as big as the end of his thumb."

"Black Rufus, down at the livery stable, was over to Auburn afore he come here. Accordin' to him, there was ten thousand miners in there already."

"Tilly's thinkin' of openin' up a branch over in Placerville. She's gonna send Maudie and Clarice over in a day or two."

The Duchess of Ophir Creek

"You watch that daytime bartender over to the Eagle. He's slicker'n a whistle at lickin' his finger and pickin' up a bit of dust for hisself whilst he weighs it out."

"There's talk Vester's thinking of opening a saloon over in Centerville."

"I been thinking I'd head over there to Auburn, myself. If we don't have us a wet winter, we're goin' to be rockin' dry gravel come spring."

And so on. Silas heard a few things that interested him. He played carefully, but with less than his full concentration. Right now information was more important than gold.

Everyone around the table had yawned at least once when Silas took off his hat and slid his chips into it. "Guess I'll call it a night. Thanks for the game, gentlemen." He rose and bowed slightly. "Good night."

A chorus of replies followed him as he went to the bar to cash in his chips. Not bad. He had better than a hundred dollars more than he'd started with. Not a big profit, but certainly worth the three hours he'd spent playing.

He waved as he walked out the door. So Tilly was sending two of her girls to Placerville. He'd talk to her in the morning, warn her to send a guard with her girls. Just in case Vester's boys hadn't learned their lesson.

Boss had not arrived by the fifth morning. Each day Soomey had grown even more worried. If he was not here by this evening, she would go back to Bannock City. In the meantime, she reassured Tao Ni that they had not been abandoned.

She was tired of nothing but rice and dried fish to eat, and Tao Ni refused to even taste the corn dodgers Boss loved so well. Crawling through a gap they'd dug between ground and canvas in the back of the tent, she and Tao Ni crept unseen along the tent wall and made it to the woods without being observed. Thus they observed Boss's orders to stay concealed in the tent in spirit.

They found enough mushrooms to fill Soomey's big cooking pot, and later a stand of cattail, growing in a muddy pool up a narrow gulch. Following the tiny stream uphill, they discovered a pond, fed by a spring. It contained watercress, pungent and crisp. Soomey wrapped the mushrooms in her kerchief and filled the pot with as much watercress as it would hold. Boss would be so pleased to have something different with his rice.

Returning to the tent sometime after noon, they heard voices just outside it. Soomey gestured Tao Ni to hide behind the woodpile. She slipped inside and crept to the front of the tent.

"You're sure this is Silas Dewitt's tent?" The deep male voice was unfamiliar. "I called and nobody answered."

"Reckon he's not back from Bannock City yet." Another voice, one Soomey recognized as the grocer's. "He was plannin' to be here night before last, but if there was freight comin', he might'a waited for it. Could be a day or two 'fore he shows up."

"I'll wait," the man with the deep voice said. "He won't mind."

"Suit yourself," Appledore said. "But I'd be mighty sure of my welcome, was I you. Silas Dewitt don't strike me as a man who'd take kindly to trespassers."

"He'll be glad to see me. Honest." And just like that, the tent flap was being untied.

Quickly Soomey scooted back, hiding behind the pile of packs and saddles that Boss hadn't sorted yet. She peered around the end of the pile, watching the doorway.

A silhouette appeared in the entrance, a dark figure surrounded by the pale winter sunlight. Then he stepped inside, holding the tent flap open behind him. Soomey could see him clearly.

He was tall, much taller than Boss, and reed slim. His hair curled in a golden cloud around his face, but his chin was clean. Leather clothing such as she had never seen covered his body. It was creamy white, fringed at shoulder, chest, and along the sides of his arms and legs. He held a long gun, far longer than any she'd ever seen. A knife every bit as big as the one Boss wore hung from his wide belt.

Soomey ducked back as he looked around the tent. She waited, hardly daring to breathe.

"I saw you," he said softly. "You might as well come out."

She cowered down, telling herself he was lying.

"You. Behind the packs. Out. Now!" His deep voice went up an octave with the last word. Perhaps he was as frightened as she was.

Instead Soomey threw herself toward the bolthole.

She almost made it.

Almost. He caught her foot—her boot that she could not shed as easily as her worn shoes—and held fast. She kicked at his hand, dug her fingers into the hard-packed dirt floor, but he slowly dragged her back inside.

Tao Ni must have heard the sounds of her struggle, for he was there and pulling on her arms. For a moment she felt as if she were being pulled in half, and then the man grabbed her other leg and gave a great tug.

Before Soomey was entirely inside the tent, he released her and grabbed Tao Ni's wrist. A stake pulled loose, opening the gap even farther as he pulled the kicking, flailing boy inside.

Tao Ni struck the intruder with his splinted arm. The sound made a sharp crack over their rasping, panting breaths. It must have hurt Tao Ni, for he grew pale, although he did not cease his struggles.

While the man was fighting Tao Ni, Soomey dived for her pack. Her pistols were right on top. She grabbed one.

"Stop." She cried. "You stop fight or I shoot!"

Tao Ni stilled immediately. The man quickly caught him by one arm.

"You let go Tao Ni. I am very good shot." She held the gun with both hands, arms extended, the way Captain Watkins had taught her. "Let him go, now!"

Slowly the man released Tao Ni. He turned to face Soomey, arms held far out from his body.

Again she wondered at his clothing. Why did it have all that fringe on it? In her experience, only women wore fringed clothing.

"Who are you?" he demanded. "What are you doing in Silas's tent?"

"My turn ask questions. Who are you?"

"That ain't any of your business. Now you just put that gun down and get yourself out of here. I won't tell Silas you was trying to rob him."

"I rob nobody. You robber. You come in Boss's tent, Boss not here."

"Boss? Who's this Boss? I was told this tent belongs to Silas Dewitt."

"That Boss name. Why you here?"

"Told you it ain't none of your business. When's Silas due back?"

"Not tell you. Get out!"

"Now lookee here—"

Soomey gestured with the gun. "You not tell me name, you not stay in Boss's tent. Go!"

"You ain't gonna shoot me. Not a little kid like you. Why, I'll bet that gun ain't even loaded." He took one step toward her.

Soomey lowered the pistol slightly and fired. The bullet narrowly missed his right foot. The man jumped back, his face pasty white, even in the dim light inside the tent.

"What the hell!"

"Tao Ni, give me the other pistol," she said in Cantonese. "Quickly." When she had it in her hand, she gestured again. "Get out."

"Hey, look, kid, Silas ain't gonna like it if you chase me away. He's my uncle."

"Your uncle?" She stared at the man. "He not tell me he

has nephew."

"Yeah, well, he probably didn't expect me to show up." His voice trembled slightly. "Pa sent me down with cattle for old man Appledore, so I figured I'd come see Silas whilst I was here." Wiping his forehead, he said, "Look, is it okay if I sit down? Nobody's ever shot at me before."

Soomey realized that he was young, not yet a man. No wonder he was so slim. No wonder his voice cracked now and then.

"Sit." She lowered the pistol, but still held it. "You say Boss your uncle. Prove it to me."

"Well, he ain't rightly my uncle," he said, settling himself on the floor, his legs crossed before him. "Least ways not by blood."

He wiped his face. His hand shook.

"My ma, she always says Silas was like a brother to her, so I always thought of him as my uncle, seein' as how I never had any, for real."

She eyed him. He looked as if he told the truth, but more than once Soomey had seen innocent expressions hiding the worst sort of villainy. "Boss say nothing to me about family."

"If he's your boss, it probably ain't none of your business. Like I said before."

"Boss business my business." At least she hoped it was. Perhaps this young man really was of Boss's family. Would Boss be angry that she had shot at him? "Tell me your name."

He frowned. "Buff...Buffalo Lachlan." His voice was sullen. "Mostly folks call me 'Young Buff.'" He turned to look at Tao Ni. "Hey, I'm real sorry you hurt your arm. Is it broke?"

Tao Ni nodded.

"My Pa's got a broken leg. That's why I brought the cattle down, 'cause he can't ride so well yet." He grinned. "First time I been to a real town."

"Centerville is not real town," Soomey said, scornfully.

"'Tis to me. There's more folks here than I ever seen at one time, 'cept at a Pow Wow."

"Pow Wow? What is that?"

"It's a really big party. Folks come from all over to get together, dance, trade, find wives, stuff like that. We used to go to 'em all the time when I was a kid, but lately the Nez Perce ain't having 'em. Too much trouble with the whites."

"I do not understand."

Shortly Soomey knew far more than she wanted of the problems the Indians in the area were having with gold seekers. She listened as Buffalo told her of growing up in an isolated valley.

"Pa took me down to the trading post on the Snake once, when I was real young, but I don't remember much about it. Mostly we traded with the Bannock and Nez Perce and didn't go nowhere. Pa said he was tired of travelin', and Ma said she'd walked just about as far as she was gonna. She come out here from New York, back in '45."

Gradually Soomey's distrust of the boy subsided. He seemed harmless. Certainly he was friendly enough. She slipped the loaded pistol back into her pack, loaded the one she had fired.

"Where'd you meet up with Silas?" Buffalo asked. "Did you come from Honolulu with him?"

"No, I did not." By now Soomey had relaxed enough that she did not feel it necessary to sound like she understood little English. "Boss hired us to be his eyes and ears. He does not wish to be followed."

"Well, I should say not. Why Pa was sayin' that it'd be a real shame if somebody found that cave before Silas did. All that..."

"Good evening. You must be Young Buff."

"Boss!" Soomey hadn't seen him enter. "Are you well? You are very late!"

"I brought some folks across with me. They couldn't travel fast." He looked at Buffalo. "Well?"

Soomey bit her lip. Boss was very angry. She could tell

because his voice had that quiet tone to it.

"Uh, yessir. I am. Buffalo Lachlan. That's me."

"I see. And do you make a habit of talking about subjects that are better left unmentioned?"

"Well, nossir, but I thought..."

"A word of advice, Young Buff. Don't." Boss shed his coat and Tao Ni took it to hang it carefully on the centerpole.

"Sir?"

"Don't think. Not about things you don't understand. Is that clear?"

Soomey almost laughed aloud. Buffalo was standing very straight. He looked even more frightened than when she had shot at him.

"Yessir. Not a word. I promise." His voice cracked at every word.

"Good. What's for supper Soomey?" Boss tousled Tao Ni's hair. "I could eat a bear."

"Very good rice with dried fish and fresh green vegetable," she said, not knowing the English word for watercress. "It will be ready in two shakes."

"Good. I need to see to the horses. Be back in a while. C'mon, Young Buff. You can help me unload."

Shortly Soomey had a fire burning before the tent, and water coming to a boil over it. Tao Ni was bringing more wood, in case Boss wanted a larger fire later.

"The youngsters don't know anything about the cave," Silas told Young Buff as they led the unloaded horses to the corral outside town. "Let's just keep it that way. The less they know, the less they can talk about."

"I'm right sorry I let my mouth run on like that. Why if Pa was here, he'd tan my hide, sure enough."

"Just don't let it happen again. Now, what are your plans? Are you headin' back to Cherry Vale tomorrow?"

Young Buff grinned, clear across his face. "Nossir. I ain't. Pa allowed as how I'm big enough to see how the world works.

He told me that if you was here, I could stay with you for as long as I could be of help."

Silas peered at him through the dusk. "Of help to me?"

"Well, yessir, you know. Help you haul out the—"

"Hardware," Silas interrupted, frowning in warning. "Yes, I reckon you can help me set up the hardware for my store." Great God, what was Emmet thinking of, sending him this eager, talkative lad? As if Silas didn't have enough youngsters to worry about.

"And if you don't have work for me all the time, I'd like to take a look see at the town," Young Buff said. "Never saw a saloon in my whole life, and that store, I reckon it's got about anything a fella could want in the way of groceries. Why I saw some chocolate candy in there, and some licorice." His voice cracked again. "I had licorice once, when Pa took me down to Fort Boise."

Shaking his head, Silas gave in. "You can stay as long as you want, lad. Just watch what you say."

"I surely will, Silas. And I'll be a real help to you, you'll see."

"There's just one thing," Silas said, hating the necessity to say it, but knowing he must before they returned to the tent.

"Yessir."

"You mind what Soomey tells you. She's been in these camps even longer than I have and she knows her way around."

"Yessir, I...she?"

"Yep," Silas said, enjoying the stunned expression on Young Buff's face. "She."

Chapter Ten

SILAS WOKE THE NEXT MORNING, FEELING CROWDED. WHEN he'd bought the tent, he'd expected that Soomey and Tao Ni would share it with him, along with what gear he'd brought and their few possessions. Now it was piled high with the stock for his store, three snoring youngsters, and himself.

How the hell had he gotten himself in this predicament?

He rolled over and out of his blankets. Pulling his pants and boots on, he gathered up his jacket and belt and tiptoed past Young Buff and Tao Ni, both curled-up shapes under their blankets.

Make that two children in the tent. Soomey's pallet was empty, the blanket spread up neatly. Before he could become alarmed, he stepped outside and saw her, crouching beside a small fire where his coffeepot was already steaming. She was bundled in the wool coat he'd taken from the ambusher. Its sleeves were ragged where she'd cut them off, but it was clean, for she'd refused to wear it with the wide bloodstain. Her breath made small clouds that glowed briefly in the flickering light.

Damn! He must be gettin' old. How had she snuck out without him knowing? "Mornin'." He picked up his cup and shook a spider out of it.

"Rice will be ready soon."

He sure wished there was some way he could go down to the cook tent without hurting her feelings. He'd heard a man could get a decent breakfast for two bits. "Remind me to teach you to make biscuits. I'm getting mighty tired of rice," was all he said.

"I make biscuits when you give me flour. But rice better for you."

"There's flour in the big gunny sack. And saleratus. I got more bacon, too."

"You are good provider, Boss. We will eat well."

The first cup of coffee was gradually soaking into his system, making the world a brighter place, for all it was still dark as the inside of a pasha's oubliette. Silas thought about all he had to do today. And swore under his breath.

At this rate, it'd be spring before he had a chance to search for the cave again.

He shivered in the morning damp, hoping the cookstove would get here on the first load of freight. He'd paid a premium for it, but he didn't regret the cost. Maybe some folks liked camping out, but he'd spent far too many years in the open. Nobody appreciated a good Majestic range better than him.

In the meantime, he had the whores to deal with—how the devil had he ended up with that responsibility? One minute he'd been telling Tilly about his ambush, the next he was promising to see Clarice and Maudie all the way to Placerville.

"I'm going to be gone all day," he told Soomey. "Got to take some merchandise over to Placerville."

"Good. I will go with you. There is Chinese store in Placerville. They maybe will have medicines I did not have when Tao Ni was hurt."

Oh, hell! "No...um...well, you see, I need you to stay here, get the merchandise ready, set up the store. That's it. I want to open tomorrow, and I need you stay here and get ready."

She looked at him suspiciously, but nodded and went back to her cooking. "Tao Ni and Buffalo will help."

"Good!" he said, far too heartily. "That's good. You three should be able to get it all done." He rubbed his hands together. "Now, as soon as I've finished breakfast, I'll just go out to the corral and saddle up, get on the trail before it gets too late."

She looked at him, her expression neutral.

"Should be back before sundown, if I hurry."

Soomey nodded again, still watching him.

"I ordered some goods to be shipped in. It'll be a couple of weeks before they get here. There should be some yard goods in the order, for you and Tao Ni. Can you sew?"

"I sew."

"Good. Good." Again he rubbed his hands together, although they weren't all that cold. "Breakfast about ready?"

Silently she handed him his plate, piled with rice and crumbled bacon. Silas sighed.

"Biscuits tomorrow, Boss," she said, her mouth twitching. "Steak tonight."

"I should be back around sundown," he repeated, before forcing a forkfull of rice into his mouth. God! He hated rice!

Later Soomey awakened Tao Ni and Buffalo and told them what Boss expected them to do. Then she followed Boss. He was up to something. Luckily he was still saddling up when she hid behind a spoils pile near the corral. But three riding horses? And a pack mule?

Yes, Boss was definitely up to something, and he didn't want her to know what it was.

Sometimes he was very stupid. How did he expect Soomey to do what he had hired her to do if he never told her of his plans? And if she always had to stay behind and do woman's work?

Bah!

She did wish she had put her boots on this morning, though. The trail to Placerville would be muddy from yesterday's rain, as well as rocky. Her canvas slippers would only slow her down. With a sigh, she removed them. Hadn't she boasted to Boss of having walked barefoot many times? But she would keep her wool socks on until they fell off. Her feet were not as callused as they had been in her childhood.

Ji Rong had made himself a snug camp in the trees uphill from the corral. She approached in a wide circle so Boss would not see her, called softly as she approached the camp. "You are tired from yesterday," she told him when he emerged from hiding. "I will follow Boss today and you will guard our tent. Let no one enter. Tao Ni and Buffalo are alone and they are children."

While she had spoken to Ji Rong, Boss had mounted and gone. He was leading the pack mule and the two horses along the street. Soomey caught up with him at one of the town's three log cabins. Within a very short time, two women emerged. They waved at another who stood in the doorway, and walked out to meet Boss.

Soomey snorted. Now she knew why he had not wanted her with him.

The woman with the brass-colored hair had been lounging at a window at the whorehouse in Bannock City the day she followed Boss there. And the other, from her beaded and ruffled clothing, was of the same sort.

Soomey did her best to ignore the empty feeling in her middle as she flitted along behind Boss and the two whores, taking advantage of shrubs and trees along the side of the trail. Boss had hired her to watch his back. If that was the only use he had for her, she would do it, and she would do it faithfully.

She must, for she was still certain someone had been following him now and again.

When he finally turned his horse's head back toward Centerville, Silas felt like he'd been pulled through a wringer. Clarice hadn't been so bad, but Maudie—Godalmighty! She hadn't stopped talking from the minute she was on her horse this morning until she finally waved goodbye from the doorway of the elaborate tent that would be Placerville's leading whorehouse until a sawed-plank building could be constructed.

His ears were still ringing.

A flutter of motion beside the trail ahead caught his eye. He loosened the rifle in its scabbard, touched the Bowie knife on his hip. There was little gold in his purse today, but a thief wouldn't know that.

When he reached the place where he'd seen the motion, Silas peered closely into the woods, but saw nothing. A bird? He watched a moment. Just a bird.

The trail was all but empty. He met one party near the Ophir Creek crossing, three young fellows wearing inadequate clothing and carrying packs too light to contain anything useful. Like so many who came west, he thought, they would suffer and perhaps die. This mountainous land required more than enthusiasm and dreams.

Only the strong prospered here. Like Buffalo's parents.

Like Soomey.

He smiled. What a stubborn, funny, determined little thing she was. When she grew up, she'd be a real menace, with those dimples and that quick intelligence. And he'd see to it that she had an education. A Chinese woman would never be received in San Francisco or Portland, he knew. But in Honolulu, or Singapore, with an education and a generous dowry, she could marry well and have the good life she deserved.

Yes, that's what he'd do. Send her to a good school, set up a trust fund for her. Help her find a decent man to marry.

But first he had a promise to keep and supper waiting. He nudged his horse back into a trot.

Silas was dozing in the saddle when he heard the scream.

Soomey found a shaded rock outcrop upon which she could sit and have a full view of the street through the middle of Placerville. Boss and the two whores were just then entering town.

They rode about halfway up the street and stopped their horses in front of a fine new tent, much larger than Boss's big one. Soomey shivered as she watched him help the two women from their mounts. As they entered the tent, he unloaded the several bundles from the pack mule. A big, dark-skinned man emerged to help Boss, and soon they had everything moved inside.

She wrapped her arms around her knees, wishing she had worn the heavy wool coat. It was far warmer than her quilted jacket, but so loose that it made her clumsy. She tried to ignore the pain in her feet, since there was nothing she could do about it. The soles of both stockings were worn through and the remaining wool hung around her ankles in gray wrinkles. She would indeed walk many miles on bare feet today.

Boss soon emerged and remounted his horse. He led the other two back toward her and turned off close to the bottom of the street. She lost sight of him and wondered if she should move. *No,* she decided. *He will come this way when he returns to Centerville.*

When he did reappear leading two riderless horses and the pack mule, it surprised her. She had not expected him so soon. Jumping to her feet she ran to the trail, waiting on the hillside above it until he passed out of sight. Then she scrambled down and followed, keeping him barely in sight on the straight sections, catching up when there were curves enough to conceal her.

The trail went up and down, across several creeks deep in narrow gulches, bending sharply back and forth so that the climb was not steep. Soomey was halfway down into the last gulch before Centerville when she heard voices above her.

She broke into a trot, wincing at the pain it caused. There was no place to hide, for a fire had swept across this slope recently and only blackened trunks remained. Her only choice was to run as fast as she could to the concealing brush along the creek.

Rapid hoofbeats told her that the travelers were approaching very quickly. She tried to go even faster. Then she tripped.

"Lookee here! It's one of them Chinee devils!"

Soomey buried her face in her arms, knowing that any escape effort she made would be futile. Biting her lip against the new pain in her toes, she willed the tears not to fall.

Several horses approached, halted. Men's voices, three or four of them, grew louder as they dismounted and came to stand beside her. One grabbed her queue and jerked her head back, sending shooting pains across her jaw and down into her shoulder.

She screamed before she could stop herself.

The scream still echoed among the hills when Silas wheeled his horse and sent it scrambling straight uphill. Jerking his rifle from its scabbard, he fired into the air. Sometimes a show of force was all it took.

Ash billowed about him as the horse scrambled up the steep slope, stumbled, regained its feet. Through the clouds he saw two struggling figures. One, small and wiry and kicking wildly, seemed be attached to the larger's wrist. Two other men were hightailing it back up the trail, followed by a third horse, riderless. He fired three shots after them, aiming just above their heads.

"Hold it!" he yelled at the combatants, not quite aiming his carbine at them. "Break it up!"

That was when he realized that the small person was Soomey. And that she really did have her teeth firmly locked in the man's right wrist.

He was off his horse in an instant. Tossing the carbine aside, he grabbed the man's collar and jerked him backwards. The point of his Bowie knife gently nudged a kidney. "Let go, Soomey. I've got him." It was all he could do not to gut the bastard.

She growled, her hands pummeling whatever part of her captive they could reach.

"Soomey!"

A couple more punches, and she loosened her jaw. Dropping to her knees, she wiped her mouth and spat. "Hey, Boss, you come just in time." Her smile looked forced. "Too many for me to fight." Her breath was coming in pants, and her voice shook.

The man—Silas recognized him as one of Vester McGonigle's ruffians—hugged his bleeding wrist against his chest and cringed away from the knife.

Whooeee! What a little fighter she was. "What happened? Did they attack you?" If they had...

"I trip, fall down. Before I could get up, they were here. I could not run."

Her face was white, her eyes clouded with pain. A scratch marred one cheek. "What the hell were you doing this far from town?"

In a faint voice, she said, "You hire me to be eyes and ears. I was watching and listening."

"I told you to get the store ready."

"Tao Ni and Buffalo can do that. You tell me to watch your back trail. I was doing this."

"Damn it, Soomey...!"

"We didn't hurt him none," Silas's captive whined. "We was just tryin' to find out why he was layin' in the trail, like he was dead."

Soomey spat a stream of words in Chinese. Silas didn't know what she said, but he was pretty sure it wasn't compliments. He released the ruffian, who scuttled a good distance away.

"Hold it right there," Silas warned. "Did you recognize either of the others?" he asked Soomey.

Her eyes closed for a moment and she swayed. Then she spoke, her voice almost a whisper. "One carried the shotgun when we were ambushed. And the other was the crooked man. He who watched the trail before, when Tao Ni was beaten. He is evil, I think."

Damn. Seemed like every time he turned around, he was getting into a set-to with one of Vester's crowd.

Slipping his knife back into its sheath, Silas studied the man, whose wrist still bled sluggishly. Soomey had hurt him good. "I ought to skin you alive, for what you did to h...to Soomey. But I won't." He hooked a thumb back in the direction of Placerville. "Git," he said. "And stay out of my sight. You hear?"

"I hear you." Slowly the man pulled himself to his feet and started up the trail.

Silas watched for a moment. "Faster," he called, picking up his carbine. When the fellow didn't increase his speed, Silas shot over his head.

The man departed at a shambling run, still cradling his bitten wrist.

Silas turned to Soomey. "And now, young lady, I want to hear again why you're here. And don't give me that bilge about eyes and ears."

She glared up at him, chin set obstinately. "I was...I follow...I—" And she keeled over, flopping bonelessly at his feet.

Silas knelt beside her, checking her pulse. She was warm, breathing evenly. Her face was still pale. There was another deep scratch on one hand. Otherwise she appeared unharmed. Then he saw her feet. They were bare, with shreds of gray wool still clinging to her ankles. What the devil?

Carefully he removed the remnants of her socks, inspected her bloody soles. It looked like she'd run her shoes off, and then her socks. She'd been well on the way to wearing through her skin.

He had nothing to doctor her with but his goose grease. Silas spread it over the raw flesh and bound her feet with his pocket handkerchief and the ripped-off tail of his shirt.

She stirred while he was tying the last bandage. "Boss?"

"Yeah. Hold still." He finished the knot. They weren't the best bandages in the world, but they'd keep her feet protected until he could do better.

Her eyes were open, dark and pain-shadowed. She stared at him, lower lip caught between her teeth. "You mad with me, Boss?"

Just like that, he was. Foot-stomping, wall-pounding, dog-kicking furious. "What in hell were you thinking? You're a girl, damn it! A god-damned girl! And you follow me fifteen miles, get yourself taken by a pack of ruffians who'd have killed you in a minute—"

"I forgot my gun," she said, her voice still faint and quavery.

"One fucking bullet! I suppose they would have lined up in a row so you could shot them all at once? Tarnation, Soomey—"

Tears ran down her pale cheeks. "You should not have come back. They could have killed you. I am only a female, but you are powerful, important man."

"Oh, for...!" He slammed his fist into the ground, welcoming the pain. It lessened the headache she gave him. Had he won an argument with Soomey yet? He didn't think so. Taking a deep, calming breath, he picked her up. She weighed less than his pack, he'd swear.

Once he had her settled in his saddle, he led the horse down the steep trail to where the others, and the mule, cropped winter-dry grass beside it. "Suppose you tell me what happened to your shoes," he said, when he was mounted behind her in the saddle.

"They had holes in them," she said, "so I took them off. Please, Boss, can we go home? It is late and I must cook supper."

Keeping the horse to a walk, he aimed it toward Centerville. "I'll cook." He did his best to ignore the weight of her round bottom against his groin. *Damn!* He was some kind of depraved bastard himself, hungering after a child the way he did.

Although, his memory reminded him, she had breasts, and in some places that made her a woman grown.

Chapter Eleven

SOOMEY WAS AWAKE WHEN SILAS SLIPPED BEHIND THE HANGING blanket. He'd kept her dosed with laudanum all day yesterday, knowing the pain from her torn feet would be horrendous. But he didn't want to give her any more. Her soles were better this morning, but still raw and oozing. "A couple of these cuts look a little red," he told her. "I'll heat up some water and you can soak 'em."

She pushed herself almost upright, resting on her elbows. A bruise darkened the scratched cheek, but she insisted she had run into a thick branch in the woods. Her lower lip was swollen from being chewed as he'd cleaned her abused soles. But she hadn't made a squeak, even when he pulled stuck bandages free. "I have Chinese medicine, Boss. I will care for my feet. You do not need..."

"Lay down!" he roared.

She lowered her shoulders and looked up at him from enormous eyes.

"Just this once, I want you to do as I say, and no arguing. You can put your damn Chinese medicine on later. Right now you're going to soak these feet in hot salt water and not give me any trouble. You hear?"

She nodded.

"And while you're soaking, you're going to tell me just what possessed you to follow me to Placerville."

Another nod.

"And then when you're through with that, you're going to promise me that you will never, never do a fool thing like that again." He waited.

"Aren't you?"

And waited.

He made his voice soft and threatening. "Soomey?"

"I cannot promise a thing I will not do," she said, her voice low, her steady gaze meeting his defiantly. "If I believe you are in danger, I will guard your back. You are Boss, and this is my duty."

"Dammit, girl! You're fired!"

"You do not want me?"

Her hesitant, soft question cooled his anger like her defiance never could. Want her? God, yes! He wanted her, and the very thought made him sick.

She had been asleep when he'd carried her into the tent and tucked her into bed, a soft burden fitting into his arms like no woman ever had. He had worried, until he laid his fingers across her sweet mouth and felt the even in-and-out of her breath. A pulse beat delicately at the base of her throat, and he'd watched it for long moments, wondering how he could have ever taken her for a boy child.

Her face was a perfect oval, the pale ivory of so many Chinese women. Her eyes, almond-oval, were large and lustrous, and her hair, free from her queue, was a river of shining black silk. Although her hands were callused, they were well-shaped, with long, slim fingers. Her feet had never been bound—thank God!—and were high-arched and narrow, when they were not swollen and abused.

In short, she was the most beautiful woman Silas had ever seen.

And one he wanted, as he'd never hungered for a woman

before.

Woman?

Child! That's how you have to think of her, you damned Lothario. You want a woman, there's plenty of 'em, big enough and willing enough, over at Tilly's.

"Boss?" Her voice trembled.

Silas started, aware that he'd been lost in self-disgust. "What?"

"I say I will go away as soon as I can walk." She struggled to her knees, bowed her head before him. "You have been very good boss. I am sorry I have been unworthy servant. Please, will you keep Tao Ni? He is a good boy and will work hard."

"You're not going anywhere!" Scooping her off her knees, he settled her into her blankets again, holding her down when she struggled. "Lay still, dammit!"

She stilled immediately. But her chin was set in that stubborn way, and her glare was enough to scorch his hide off.

"You're not going anywhere," he repeated, in a reasonable tone. "I'm firing you, yes, but only because I don't want you thinking you've got an obligation to watch over me. Hell, Soomey, I'm a man grown and you're just a kid—"

"I am woman!"

"Be silent!" He covered her mouth with a gentle hand. "Listen to me. I've been taking care of myself for a sight of years, girl, and I reckon I can keep doing it. All I meant for you and Tao Ni to do was keep an eye on my back trail and make sure I knew if somebody was following. And to listen around town to see if folk were talking about me and my business."

She grabbed his wrist and lifted his hand. "I was doing that," she said. "What if those men followed you?"

"If that happens, you tell me. Don't try to save my bacon."

"I care nothing for your bacon. If you are in danger, should I let them kill you?"

Silas drew a deep, calming breath. He seemed to do a lot of that when he was arguing with Soomey. "No, but you tell me. Don't go running in and try to lick 'em all." He touched her poor, bruised cheek. "Look at you. Little wildcat. You gave as good as you got, didn't you?"

"I did not wish to bite anyone, Boss." She wiped her mouth. "That crooked man. He is very sly, all the time skulking and sneaking. He wishes you great harm, I think."

"Eli Jenkins? That coward? He'll not bother us again."

"If you say so, Boss."

But he could see she didn't agree. "Soomey, you're doing your best to change the subject. Will you promise not to follow me any more?"

She shook her head.

Swiping a hand across his beard, Silas wondered if she was his punishment for loose living and easy spending. "Well, then, will you at least promise me not to get into any more fights."

"I cannot promise that either, Boss. If a person fights with me, I fight too."

"Well, hell! Okay, let's do it this way. You promise me you'll do your best to stay out of trouble. And you promise me that you'll always take either Tao Ni or Young Buff with you, no matter where you go."

"Everywhere, Boss?"

"Soomey!"

She giggled behind her hand. "Yes, Boss, I will make this promise. But only if you will make me a promise also."

Silas closed his eyes a moment. How come she was always about a mile ahead of him? "What's that?"

"Promise me you will not go to whorehouse again."

"Soomey, I can't promise—" He saw her face crumple. Cursing beneath his breath, he gathered her into his lap, telling his body once again that she was a child and in need of comfort.

He held her close until he was sure she would lie quietly and listen. "Soomey, I need Tilly's help. And I owe her."

She made a sound somewhere between a snort and a laugh.

"No, listen. I'm telling you the truth."

"You lie to me before, Boss."

"I've never lied to you, Soomey. I have not used Tilly's...ah, facilities. Never. Yesterday all I did was take Maudie and Clarice to Placerville. They're opening a new house there for Tilly."

"What did Tilly do for you, that you owe her?"

"Noth— Look, Soomey, it's a long story, and not particularly interesting—"

"I am interested."

"Well, I'm not. I was a fool, and a madam—Tilly reminds me of her—helped me out. O.K.?"

Shrugging, she settled back against his chest, her small backside warm and solid against an equally warm and much more solid part of him. Silas counted, silently, to one hundred. In Hindi. Then he started again in Spanish. All the time she rested quietly in his lap, seemingly content to remain silent. Every breath he took brought him the faint scent of jasmine.

"You go to Tilly's many times," she said at last, as if she didn't really care whether he answered or not.

Silas knew better. "I will go there many more times, too. She's holding money and papers for me, in her safe. And she's getting my mail, because I'm still not sure where I'll be from one week to the next." He noticed that she was rubbing her scarred wrist. She always did when she argued with him.

"We do not stay here? What of your store?"

Shrugging, he said, "It's movable. I might go back to Bannock City, or I might decide to move over to Placerville. It all depends."

Her disapproval was obvious. "That is not way to make much money."

"I don't need to make much money, Soomey. Look, I came here to do a favor for friends, not to get rich. I've got plenty of money now."

"So why do you not do your favor and go? There is danger for you here. I feel it." She touched her chest. "My heart tells me that if you stay in this place, you will be hurt very much, or you will be killed. So you must do your favor quickly, and go away. Soon."

"It's not that simple," he said, wondering how much he should tell her. He wasn't worrying about her revealing his purpose, only that knowing might put her into danger too. Deciding in favor of discretion, he said, "I'm looking for a cave, Soomey, but I can't remember where it is."

"What is in this cave?"

"Nothing that you need to worry about. It belongs to my friend—Young Buff's pa." Well, that was the truth—twenty percent of the truth, anyhow.

She moved, reminding him again that he held a lapful of warm, soft female. "Here," he said, "you slide on over there on your bed. I'll go set the water to heat. Then I'll tell you the rest."

Silas thought quickly as he built up the fire and hung the cooking pot on its hook. The cast iron hook had been high on his list of important needs. Trying to boil water or coffee by setting the pot on a couple of rocks over a fire was courting disaster. He remembered a child on the wagon train coming west, scalded so badly he'd screamed for hours, just from a tipped over coffeepot. He didn't even want to think of Soomey or Tao Ni, burned as that child had been.

The sun was shining, a pale, winter light, but with an almost reluctant warmth. He decided to bring Soomey outside, rather than leaving her in the dark tent. Besides, in a little while, he should start getting some customers. The handbills Tao Ni and Young Buff had tacked up all over town should bear almost immediate fruit.

Once she was settled, Silas poured a handful of salt into the Dutch oven which had been standing by the fire, and stirred in hot water. He tested it with his hand, finding it almost the perfect temperature. "Ease your feet into that," he told her. "Careful! Take it slow."

A few hisses and some gritted teeth later, Soomey's feet were immersed.

The Duchess of Ophir Creek

Silas replenished the water in the pot and poked the fire up again. "I hid something in a cave in one of these valleys a long time ago," he said, staring off into space as he recalled that difficult, frightening time. As he remembered, he packed his pipe, lit it.

After a while he went on, "When I hid it, I was scared, and worried, and not too wise. Then later I should have come back for it, I suppose. I told Emmet where the cave was, but I didn't make a map or anything." He paused to test the water. It was almost hot enough, so he swung the hook a little aside, leaving the pot just enough over the fire to keep it warm.

"We figured we would come back in a little while, but we got busy, and then it was almost winter, and we went...well, we went away." He'd been young then, so young and full of dreams. Emmet had been restless and, Silas suspected, reluctant to take on the responsibility of a woman and child. The two of them had traveled west, intending to find a ship going anywhere at all, as long as it was far away.

"Emmet changed his mind. He came back, but he didn't need the...the contents of the cave, so he pretty much forgot about it, I guess. So did I, for I believed he'd taken what was there. Then last spring I got a letter, from Emmet's wife, Hattie."

"The mother of Buffalo," Soomey said, as if she'd just now put two and two together.

"That's right." He drew again on his pipe, only to discover it had gone out. "They're getting older now, and their children are growing up. They want to move to town, and to do that they need...the contents of the cave. But he doesn't remember where it is, so I came home to see if I could find it."

"God, Soomey! When I saw Bannock City, I couldn't believe it. Sixteen years ago the only other people who knew about this place were my friends and a few Indians. And now—" He gestured. "Well, just look around. Nothing looks the same. I don't remember which of these three valleys the cave was in, let alone what hillside it was on."

Soomey watched him silently as he wiped her foot. When the other one was soaking, she said, "Does Buffalo know what is in the cave?"

"Yes, but it's not his secret to tell, so don't you go bedeviling him, you hear?"

"I would not do that, Boss. But why can he not help you search? Tao Ni, too. And me."

"I'll do the searching. You can mind the store."

"Bah! All the time you tell me to do safe, easy things. I am strong. I have lived through much that you cannot even imagine. Why do you always think I am weak and easily frightened?"

"Soomey, Soomey, I do not think you are weak. My god, girl, I don't know many men who would have walked all the way to Placerville and back in one day."

"I did not walk."

"Huh?"

"I ran. Your horse goes much faster than I can walk."

"Great God! What am I going to do with you, child?"

"And that is one thing more. You will not call me child. I tell you again, I am woman." She poked her finger into his upper arm. "Buffalo is child." Another poke. "Tao Ni is child." Three quick pokes. "I am not. When will you believe this?"

"Woman, huh? How old are you?" He'd bet on fourteen, fifteen at the most. Maybe where she came from, that was a woman, but not in his book, no matter what his treacherous body thought.

Half his age.

"I was born in year of Tiger. I do not know what that is in your American years, but I will go to Chinese store in Bannock City and ask."

"You're not going anywhere!"

Soomey smiled sweetly. "Boss, I will take Tao Ni with me. He will like to go there. And maybe Buffalo, too. He told me he wishes to see, ah, what were his words? 'Bright lights, poker games, and pretty women.' I will take him so that he may do this thing."

"Soomey," he began, ready to put his foot down.

"Boss, I am good worker, but I am not slave. I have day off. You cannot tell me what to do on day off. We will go then." She pulled her foot out of the Dutch oven. "This water is cool. Now, I will put medicine on my feet. Then you will help me cover them, so I can go inside. Soon customers will come. I can take money, even if I do not walk."

When Boss stalked off a little while later, Soomey smiled behind her hand. He was a good man, but so firm in his belief that she was a child, to be protected and cherished. Stubborn!

Within minutes, Ji Rong stuck his head inside the tent. "He is at the grocer's. They are drinking coffee, so he should be safe for a short while."

"Come in, quickly. As you can see, I have injured my feet. So it will be your duty to watch Boss doubly well."

He squatted beside her. "Last night I watched until very late. He went to the corral to care for his horses, and then he strolled along the street, from one end to the other. He did not seem to have a purpose. When he came back, I watched the tent, but alas, I fell asleep. I am unworthy."

Soomey smiled. "I do not expect you to guard him day and night. I will set Buffalo to watching at night, and perhaps Tao Ni will help you sometimes."

Ji Rong bowed his head briefly. "You are generous."

"Have you found a better place to sleep?" Soomey said, remembering the frost that still lay on the ground in shaded places this morning.

"Thank you, yes. I have made a comfortable little nest under a fallen tree. It is not far from here, up the hill." He pointed.

The hill he'd indicated overlooked the tent in which they sat, and Soomey thought it gave a good view of the street, as well. The next time she was outside, she would look, to make sure. "You must go now. It is time for the store to open, and I would have to sell you something, if you were seen here."

Ji Rong took his leave, promising to be as boss's shadow until dark. Soomey was not entirely confident that Buffalo would be able to do as good a job at night as Ji Rong was in daylight. She sighed. If only Boss were a reasonable man, she thought. Then he would simply allow someone to go everywhere with him, and Soomey would not have to worry.

Buffalo and Tao Ni arrived soon after Ji Rong's departure. They were full of news.

"Somebody picked up a nugget that weighed near a pound up Ophir Creek yesterday," Buffalo told her. "Half the folks in town are headin' up that way today."

"The red-bearded man has come. He talks of building a log saloon," Tao Ni said. "And the crooked man is with him." His thin face showed fear. "I do not like them, Elder Sister."

"You must speak English, little brother. How else can you learn?"

"I reckon he was tellin' you about the new saloon," Buffalo said. "Must be eight or ten men out in the woods cutting timber for it."

Soomey's stomach knotted. She had not thought there were so many of Vester's ruffians. How could two children and two cripples protect Boss from such a troop? Her feet would not heal quickly.

"You must be very careful when Vester's men are about," she warned Buffalo. "I believe one of them injured Tao Ni. Perhaps the crooked one—his name is Jenkins. I think he means Boss great harm."

"Wouldn't surprise me none. That's a bad bunch, Soomey. My Pa warned me about fellas like that, said I was to stay a goodly distance away from 'em." He looked disgusted. "'Course, my Pa still thinks I'm a little kid, sometimes."

Soomey refrained from saying that height and a mostly baritone voice did not make a man. She could not conceal her smile as she said, "I think we must all stay our distance from them, Buffalo. Unless, of course, Boss is in danger."

"Yeah, that reminds me...Tony thinks someone's out to get Silas. You really think so?"

Wondering how Buffalo had understood so much of Tao Ni's heavily accented English, she nodded. "We are to watch his back, yes. But I think it is because of what he does. I do not think Boss fears anyone."

"Me, neither," Buffalo agreed. "He's one savvy he-coon, as Pa would say." He poked among the bundles that held their supplies. "You got any food around here? I'm hungry enough to eat a skinned polecat."

Soomey found him some cold biscuits, left from breakfast. Boss, she'd discovered, was a very good cook. Last night he'd almost made cornmeal edible.

Almost.

Most of the people who came into Dewitt's Hardware Emporium the first few days after it opened were just looking. Soomey sold a lantern, two coils of rope, a tarpaulin, and a pound of nails. She took orders too, proud that she knew how to read and write. Mostly she smiled at people and answered their questions.

"Yes, Boss have more stock soon. Maybe one week."

"I learn speak English long time past. Other bosses also Americans."

"Boss says I not bargain for merchandise. His prices fixed. Very cheap!"

That last answer was difficult for her to give. Boss would never be rich if he did not learn to set high prices and allow his customers to bargain him down on those items which were not in great demand. She did not know what he had paid for most of his stock, but she did know that she could sell the lanterns and the rope for far more than their set prices. And lamp oil, too, if she had any. But Appledore sold lamp oil, so Boss said he would not.

Sometimes she questioned Boss's intelligence.

Soomey felt like royalty, sitting on her throne—a chair borrowed from Appledore. Tao Ni and Buffalo served as her feet, and Boss carried her to the canvas-walled necessary which he had constructed at the back of his claim. Lookers and customers alike were polite, and some were even friendly.

She wondered if they would be thus if Boss were not looking in occasionally, asking how she was doing.

By the third day almost every resident of Centerville had visited the store. The tent was nearly empty and the remaining stock disordered. As she had every afternoon, Soomey tested her feet, carefully and gradually putting her full weight on them.

They hurt still, she admitted, drawing a quick breath through set teeth. She sank back onto her chair. "You must make everything tidy, Tao Ni. I cannot walk yet."

"Damn right, you can't," Boss said, coming through the doorway and letting the flap down behind him. "Buff, you get the fire started for supper. I put out the closed sign, so we won't have any more customers today." He knelt to pick up a coil of rope that had slipped behind the others and become unwound.

After supper Boss and Buffalo went to the livery corral to check on the horses. A light, icy rain had fallen in the afternoon and now the wind whistled through the trees, making the walls of the tent seem to breathe like a living thing. Soomey wrapped herself in her blanket and curled up on her pallet, Tao Ni sitting at her feet.

"I saw one on the hillside this afternoon, elder sister," he said softly in Cantonese. "He seemed to be watching this tent."

"Speak English. You must practice, so you can learn to phrase your thoughts in the language."

"It is very difficult," he said, carefully. "My tongue does not like the taste of the words."

"They will become familiar to you, until one day you will not notice their taste." She reached out to run a hand over his forehead. "You will have a scar, but it will not be ugly. It heals well."

"It itches," he said in Chinese, and pulled away.

"English, Tao Ni. Always English," she reminded him.

He grimaced. "Then you say my name Toe-nee, like Buffalo do...does."

Frowning, Soomey studied him. He was so young to lose his Chinese identity. If he became Toe-nee, would he someday forget his lineage?

China held nothing for him, no more than it did for her. Neither knew of family, neither had a place to go back to. She took his chin in her hand and made him look into her eyes. "Be Toe-nee to Buffalo, then, if you wish it, but never forget you were Chinese first. It is a thing to be proud of, as I shall continue to remind you."

He nodded soberly, but Soomey wondered if he understood what she had asked of him. She sighed, wondering if his children and his children's children would care that their ancestor came from an ancient and honorable heritage.

She embraced him briefly. "Now, tell me of your adventures today." He often wandered in the woods, for he was far better than she at finding the mushrooms Boss was so fond of.

"I see feets...ah, no, track..." Tao Ni shook his head in frustration.

Soomey relented. "In Cantonese then, this one time."

His smile thanked her. "There were footprints on the hillside. They led to town, but they wandered far that way first," he pointed to the east. "There is a tree where one rested for a while, maybe more than one time. I sat there and looked at what the one saw." He paused, his eyes big and frightened. "He could see this tent and all who came to it. Only this tent."

"We must tell Boss." Soomey tossed the blanket aside and struggled to her knees. "Come."

He resisted. "Wait, Elder Sister. We do not know if the one was Ji Rong. He does not always sit by the store. Sometimes he goes elsewhere."

Sinking back, she agreed. "I will ask Ji Rong if it was he

tomorrow. If it was not, you will go and see if the one returns after the next snowfall. His tracks will be easily seen."

Chapter Twelve

VESTER SET HIS BEER STEIN DOWN AND LOOKED TOWARD THE door as it blew open. A stranger entered, snow thick on the shoulders of his heavy wool coat. The way the wind was howling, this was going to be a real hell-raiser of a storm. His boys had come in from their work early and now were drinking up Billy Watson's whiskey instead of his.

Hellfire! If the storm had just held off two more days, I'd have been in business. His new saloon only lacked its roof.

"Won't be long before them damned yellow bastards are as thick hereabouts as they was in Bannock City," the stranger said, after he'd wetted his whistle. He leaned back against the bar and addressed the room. "Yessiree-bob. Jest comin' down the last switchback, I passed a whole passel of 'em headin' thisaway. They was carryin' big loads on them shoulder sticks o' theirs. Looked like they was movin' in for good."

Billy said something back, but it was too soft for Vester to hear.

"I come out from Kaintuck, aim to git myself a stake and go back and marry my gal," the new man told Billy. "Her pa can't argue with a rich man, now can he?"

"Git yourself over there, Eli," Vester said, "and see what he's got to say. Find out about them Chinee."

"Aw, Vester—"

"Git, I said."

Eli took his beer and stumped over to the bar and spoke to the new man.

A little later, Eli returned to Vester's table. "He don't know nothin' much, Vester. Just that they went up into that gulch behind Dewitt's when they got to town. Leastways that's where it seems like they was goin', 'cause they ain't nowheres else up there with water."

Vester shook his head. He'd hoped it would be a while before the Celestials made their way over here. That was another reason he'd picked Centerville for his saloon, instead of Placerville. He didn't want all those little yellow devils mindin' his business for him.

Now his boys would have to step right lively when word got around that a claim was going to be abandoned. If they didn't there'd be a half-dozen Celestials on it by morning, like ants on spilled sugar.

"That Dewitt. He's got a hand in this, sure as shootin'. Damn Chinee lover," Henry grumbled.

"Somebody ought'a show him the error of his ways, shouldn't they Vester?"

"You think you're a big enough man to do that, Eli?" Vester said. He looked around the table, wondering if any of his boys had enough starch to face down Dewitt. The man was gettin' to be a nuisance.

Eli was staring into his beer glass. Wilf chewed his moustache, and Henry's face got real red before he looked away quickly. None of the rest of 'em would look him in the eye, neither.

Boss's tent seemed smaller each day. Outside the wind roared and whistled, now bringing heavy, wet snow, now driving icy rain before it. Drifts acquired a crystalline crust and branches sagged and sometimes broke with their glistening burden of ice.

Soomey learned to knit while it snowed, using wool Boss had bought from Mrs. Appledore. The grocer's wife had brought a dried apple pie to them the first day of the storm, but had pretended that only Boss and Buffalo were in the tent. Soomey and Tao Ni might have been invisible, so well had she ignored them.

The pie had been delicious. Somehow she must learn to make the flaky crust that enclosed the spicy apples. Soomey could think of nothing she liked the taste of better than cooked dried apples.

Later, after they had eaten all but the pan, Boss had returned it, shiny and clean as Soomey could make it with fine sand from the creek. He had brought back the yarn and four precious steel needles, telling her she needed new stockings. And he had shown her how to make them.

"I learned to knit from Hattie. One winter she taught me to make stockings. Since I'd practically memorized every book in the house—we only had three—she said I might as well acquire a useful skill."

She giggled softly behind her hand. "It is women's work, Boss."

"When your feet are cold, it doesn't matter who does the knitting, if the result keeps 'em warm," he said, his hand over hers, guiding it. "See, now you stick the needle in here and wrap the yarn around it..."

Soomey found it difficult to follow his instructions. She was distracted by the soothing tone of his voice, the warmth of his body close to hers. The smell of him—tobacco and woodsmoke.

She had finished the first sock and was almost to the toe of the second when the snow finally stopped swirling about the tent. At the first sign of clearing, she insisted on walking to the necessary alone. Her feet still hurt, but the sense of release made the small ache seem unimportant. How she hated closed-in, dark places.

Eli settled himself where the snow had blown away from the base of a big, old pine tree. Now that the storm had died, folks would be out and about again. He could see a corner of Dewitt's tent through the lower branches, but he was altogether hid from folks lookin' uphill. He did wish there was better cover lower down. From up here faces was just blurs. With folks all bundled up in the cold, it was hard to see who was who.

He didn't guess it mattered, though. Sooner or later Dewitt or one of the Chinee brats would be comin' or goin' all by hisself. Or maybe that tall, curly-headed kid that was livin' with 'em.

He didn't care about them, except that one or t'other usually followed Dewitt. He'd almost got caught yesterday, when the big Chinee came on him unawares. Have to keep a better eye out from now on.

His belly itched, and he stuck a finger inside his long johns to scratch. Maybe he oughta' have himself a bath one of these days. He'd seen a sign down at the Watson House. Trouble was, they wanted two bits a bucket for the hot water.

Highway robbery, that's what it was!

His ma had taught him that cleanliness was next to godliness, but he wasn't too sure about that. Seemed to him that if God had intended folks to be clean, he wouldn't have made so much dirt.

A hardware store! Dewitt couldn't even dig his own gold. He must'a seen how much work it was to find a good claim and made up his mind to get rich off those who toiled by the sweat of their brows.

Folks started drifting in to the hardware store. Appledore was one of the first, standing out because of his fancy black bowler hat. A couple of miners went in and came out a little later, one of 'em carrying something. Rope, it looked like. The black-headed whore came by, but didn't go in. She waited by the door until Dewitt returned and stood there, talking to him, for quite a spell.

The Duchess of Ophir Creek

After a while Eli noticed a stove-up Chinee squatting by a tree a ways from Dewitt's tent. The miserable devils surely had moved in, curse their slanty eyes. Pretty soon they'd be working all the good claims, just like they was doing over in Bannock City.

Was it up to him, they'd get what they deserved, and it wouldn't be worked-out claims.

He dozed, feeling the meager warmth of pale sunlight on his legs. As shadows lengthened he woke, cold and stiff. Without leaving his hidey hole, he stretched his arms and waggled his fingers, easing out the stiffness. Almost closin' time now. Two miners emerged from the tent, each carrying a shiny new shovel. Pretty soon after that Dewitt came to shut the tent flaps, a sure sign he wasn't going anywheres tonight.

A few minutes later, the gimpy Chinee limped away up the street.

Eli stood up.

Time to go.

The tent wall beside Soomey shook violently, as something struck it with great force. An instant later, three quick shots echoed across the valley.

Buffalo fell to the floor.

Before she could move, Boss grabbed her and threw her down behind a pile of merchandise. Tao Ni landed on top of her.

"Stay down!" Boss snapped.

Soomey wormed free of Tao Ni's body, untangled his clutching hands from her shirt. But she could see nothing in the dark tent. She tried to raise her head.

"Soomey, if you want to get your fool head shot off, go outside to do it," Boss said in his low, dangerous voice. "I don't want blood all over my tent floor."

She cowered against the ground, with one arm around Tao Ni. He was sobbing quietly, his small body shaking. She soothed him with gentle touches and whispered, "Do not fear, small brother. Boss will protect us." She waited, almost without breathing, for a fourth shot.

Sliding sounds and murmurs came from across the pile. In a moment, Boss spoke. His voice was too low for her to hear words. Another voice answered.

Buffalo was not dead!

If only she knew how badly he was hurt. But she could see nothing with her face pressed into the dirt floor of the tent.

It became lighter for an instant. Had someone entered?

There was no sound inside the tent. Should she not be able to hear Buffalo breathing?

Where was Boss?

"Buffalo?" she called, finally, after waiting a very long time. She kept her voice low.

"Yo."

"Are you hurt?"

"Nope. Are you?"

"We are well. Is Boss there?"

"He went out the back, movin' low and real fast."

"He will be killed!"

"Not Silas. He'll do just fine."

"I am frightened," she admitted. Somehow this was far worse than looking into the eyes of Captain Slye as he claimed she was his to kill, if he chose. Perhaps it was because she did not know who had fired the shots.

"I ain't scared now," Buffalo said, "but when I felt that bullet whizzin' by my head I felt mighty anxious." There was the barest quiver to his voice. "My Pa told me once the best thing a man can do when somebody's shootin' at him is drop like a rock. Makes you harder to hit, I guess."

"I will remember," she promised. "Tao Ni, do you hear what Buffalo says?"

The boy nodded. He had stopped sobbing and now lay quietly, cradling his splinted arm. It must have hurt when Boss threw him to safety.

"Can you see?" she asked Buffalo.

"Not a thing. Silas said to stay right here and keep an eye on things, and that's what I plan to do," he said. "I got my rifle, so nobody better try to come through that door without singin' out first."

Soomey smiled at his brave boast. She knew he would protect her and Tao Ni with his life.

They waited a long time, whispering together, afraid to raise their voices. Buffalo crawled to join Soomey and Tao Ni, making a narrow opening between two crates for his rifle. When footsteps sounded at the front of the tent, he raised it, held the barrel steady.

The flap lifted. Soomey tensed.

"It's me," Boss said.

Soomey's expelled breath was echoed by both boys.

Boss entered, a dark shadow in the darker tent. "Light a candle, Buff. But keep it in there among the crates."

A few minutes later the four of them crouched in a small pool of light, surrounded and protected by boxes and bundles of merchandise. Boss tossed three spent shells onto the floor. "I found where he shot from, but it was too dark to trail him." He cursed, using words that even Soomey, who had heard the best sailors had to offer, had never heard before. "But they weren't stray shots. Whoever did the shooting was aiming right at this tent."

Looking across the tent, Soomey found she could see the bullet holes, three of them, tiny points of pink, sunset sky shining against the gray canvas. They were scattered, not clustered. And one was perilously close to where her chair still sat, undisturbed.

"Buff, Tao Ni, get your gear. Sit still, Soomey. They'll get yours, too. We're getting out of here." He started rolling up their beds.

An hour later, Silas had them back in the gulch south of town, poorly sheltered by a couple of stretched tarps. All of them were shivering in the cold, clear night.

"Build a fire, Buff. Not too big—we don't want to be seen from the trail. Soomey, soon as you can get water hot, you make some tea. There's some jerky in my pack. Maybe you can shred it into hot water. Anything quick, so we can get this fire out."

"I fix food, Boss. You go to town, find who shot at us."

Grateful for her quick understanding, he tousled her hair. "I'm going to do just that, kid. You should be safe here. Buff, you stand watch, soon as you've had your supper."

"I'll take care of them, Silas. Don't you worry."

He looked into the boy's eyes, and saw a familiar determination looking back. "Yeah, I believe you will." Clapping him on the shoulder, he said, "I'll be back quick as I can."

He went back to his tent the way they'd come, along the backside of the cabins and tents, staying in shadows. When they'd left the hardware store, most folks had been at supper. With any luck, their flight had been unobserved.

Silas stepped across to the front of his tent and stood, just like a man who'd come outside for a smoke after supper. Down at the other end of town, light streamed from the door of the Watson House—pretentious name for a tent housing a bar that was nothing more than two planks laid over a couple of sawhorses, with some sawn logs serving as seats. A couple of men were standing in line at the whorehouse, but most of those he could see were on their way to or from the saloons. In his opinion, the men on the street at this hour were rowdies and bully boys. The family men and serious miners stayed at home at night, resting up for another day of lugging gravel to the creek.

He'd heard a miner say today that they needed more snow this winter to keep the creeks full next summer. Silas believed him. Right now there was the barest trickle flowing in the bigger creeks and the small ones were all but dry.

If the snow that fell didn't start sticking, there wouldn't even be that much water in the creeks come spring, he thought. More than one miner was talking of trying out a dry rocker.

Silas, never having done mining more strenuous than picking gold nuggets out of clear water, had no idea what that entailed. It sounded like work, though.

A sound from the side of the tent caught his attention. He tiptoed along the canvas wall and peered around. Huddled against the tent was a Chinese—obvious by the round hat on his head, white socks on his feet. He looked up at Silas and grinned a gap-toothed grin.

"Hey Boss, how you do?" He sounded drunk.

Silas tossed him two bits. "Get yourself a blanket," he said. "You'll freeze out here."

"You bet, Boss. Thanky ver' much." He scuttled around the back of the tent, his stride uneven.

Shaking his head in pity, Silas returned to the street.

He strode down toward the Watson House and entered, stopping just inside the double canvas that served as a door.

Two miners were huddled next to the pot-bellied stove, and another was talking to Billy Watson, sitting with one haunch on the bar. Towards the back, Vester and half a dozen of his bully boys were gathered around a table. They all turned to stare at him, but no one moved. No one else paid much attention. The music and conversation continued unabated.

"Evenin', Silas," Billy said. "What'll you have?"

"I'm looking for someone carrying a rifle," he said, his voice cutting across the saloon sounds. "A repeater."

Feet moved on the rough wooden floor, and chairs scraped. A few throats got cleared.

"Heard some shots earlier," one man said after a moment of dead silence. "You looking for who fired 'em?"

"I am. Whoever he was, he seemed to think my tent was a target."

A surge of denials washed around the room.

Silas looked at each man there, letting his gaze rest a little longer on the faces of the men at Vester's table. "Whoever the shooter was, I'd like to teach him to be a little more careful about where he aims," he said, forcing his voice to mildness.

Again a long moment of silence.

"Well, I hope you do, Dewitt," Billy Watson said. "We can't have folks shootin' careless-like around town. Why they could hit somebody, sure as anything." Billy reached for a bottle. "You got time for a drink? I've been wantin' to talk with you."

Silas ignored him. "Vester, you told me once you had a finger in most pies. You know anything about this?"

For just a moment Silas thought Vester was going to answer his challenge. Then he leaned back in his chair and swung his head slowly from side to side.

"Not a thing, Dewitt. I and my boys got no reason to be shootin' at your tent." He looked around the circle of men at his table. "Do we boys?"

A chorus of denials answered him. Only one man neither spoke nor shook his head. Not a stranger, but not someone whose face Silas could place either. Tall, swarthy, lithe, he carried himself well, moving with an unconscious, catlike grace. His clothing was black, his hat trimmed with silver conchos. And he wore two guns, both slung low on his hips.

The stranger turned and light from the hanging lantern showed his features plainly. It was the fellow from the poker game back in Bannock City.

DiCastro, that was his name. Joe DiCastro. And he'd taken up with Vester McGonigle.

Was he the shooter?

Silas doubted it. He was the sort who'd face a man down, who'd want to do his killing out in the open, so folks would admire or fear him.

But he knew something about who'd done it. Silas would bet his shirt on that.

He walked toward Vester's table, deliberately bumped into the back of Eli Jenkins' chair.

The man started to object, but shut up at Vester's sharp command.

The big, red-bearded man leaned forward, spread his hands on the table. "Join us for a drink, Dewitt?" Again his body was tense. Waiting.

"I don't drink with ruffians," Silas said softly. "I came over to give you a warning. Pass it on."

"And who might I be passin' it on to?"

Silas shrugged. "He carries a repeating rifle, wears boots with run down heels, and chews."

Once more Vester seemed to relax. He chuckled. "That ain't much to go on. What makes you think I know anybody like that?"

"Because, Vester, you know every cowardly, back-shooting, grave-robbing son of a bitch in these hills," Silas told him, smiling. "And while you're at it, you can tell your bully boys something for me, too." He dropped his left hand to the handle of his Bowie knife. "Tell 'em that the next time they lay hand on either of my Chinese kids, he'll be the last thing they hold."

"Why you—"

"Just tell them, Vester. Or be prepared to pay for their funerals." He let fly with his right sleeve knife. It thunked into the table, not six inches from a hand hovering too close to a belt gun.

Once more the saloon was filled with silence.

Silas reached across the table and pulled his knife free. Beer dripped to the dirt floor and was quickly absorbed. He cleaned the blade on Wilf's pantleg, and then turned and walked to the doorway, his back prickling in expectation of a bullet. Safely there, he turned, saying, "Make sure they understand, Vester, or I might have to kill them."

He touched the brim of his hat and faded quickly into the night.

Damn, that had felt good! Nothing like running a good bluff.

"You make much money today, Boss," Soomey said when

he returned to the shelter. She had counted it, as best she could in the dim light of a lantern turned low. Using the little hand scales, she had weighed the gold dust carefully and figured it at twenty dollars an ounce. Of course, it would assay out to less than that, because of impurities, but not much. The gold here was unusually clean and pure. "Three hundred forty-seven dollars, ten cents."

He removed his coat and hung it from a stout branch on one of the concealing shrubs. "Ten cents?"

"Tao Ni sold one handful of cornmeal. He did not know he was not meant to."

She thought Boss snorted, but his head was turned, so she could not be certain.

When Boss had removed his boots and was sprawled against his saddle, she handed him a cup of tea. All through the snowstorm she had been thinking and still had not discovered an answer to her dilemma. Was there a way she could use tonight's events to her advantage?

It was time for Boss to admit her to his bed. He was restless at night, now, and each morning awoke hard and ready for pleasure. A man should not suffer so, not when he had a willing woman.

At first she had wanted to do so only because she believed that he would be more kind, more caring of her and Tao Ni if she satisfied him. Men were very strange. Even Captain Slye, when she had done as he wished and brought him to his peculiar completion, had been less cruel, if only for a few hours.

The skin of those who called themselves white had always repelled her, pallid like the underside of a fish, yet hairy like a beast. Boss's skin was pale, yes, but it had a warm tone to it, a hint of the very color of those tiny grains she'd weighed so carefully today. A golden man with silver-gilt hair—that was Boss. So beautiful!

A kind man. A noble man. She believed he would be gentle in his use of a woman, causing no deliberate pain when he took his pleasure on her.

She shivered, despite a wave of heat through her body that should have made her warm. Perhaps the infection in her feet had worsened, although she had been careful to keep them dry and warm.

"Soomey?"

Ah, she had all but ignored him, so lost had she been in her thoughts. "Yes, Boss?"

"I want you three to get out of town tomorrow. Go to Placerville, or Bannock City. Take the horses. Stay away until I send for you."

Her purpose was just, Soomey told herself, as she drew a deep breath. "Good. I wish to visit the Chinese store in Bannock City. Tao Ni and I will stay with Li Ching."

He frowned. "You can go to the store if you want. But you'll sleep at Tilly's."

For a moment she had no words. "Boss!"

"You heard me. She's got a room she'll rent you. It'll be crowded, but the three of you can share it."

"No, Boss. I will not sleep in a whorehouse!"

His arms crossed over his chest and his brows lowered. "Then you're not going."

Outraged, she stared at him a moment. He looked rock solid. "I am not slave. I go where I wish."

He grabbed her and pulled her nose to nose with him, shaking her a little. "The hell you will!"

Soomey felt the heat of his body, wished he would hold her with gentleness, not anger. "Boss, I am not whore. I will not sleep in whorehouse."

"Listen to me, you obnoxious brat. Tilly's place is about the cleanest boarding house in Bannock City. If my sister came to town, that's where I'd put her. She'd be a hell of a lot safer there, than in that canvas-walled dump of a hotel, or either of the other boarding houses."

"You have a sister?"

"No, I don't have a sister, but if I did...Never mind. You're staying at Tilly's."

"I can sleep in house of Li Ching."

"Yeah? And where's Young Buff gonna stay?"

Covering her mouth with a hand, Soomey stared at him. No Chinese would welcome Buffalo into his house, no matter how Soomey praised him.

"Boss, there is no need for Buffa—"

"Give over, Soomey," he said, setting her back into place. "If you want to go to Bannock City, you can go. But Buff will go with you and you'll stay at Tilly's. Got that?"

She sighed. "Yes Boss. It will be as you say."

When I come back and prove to you I am not a child, then you will sing from the other side of your mouth, she thought at him.

Just wait.

Chapter Thirteen

"Buff, come on over here a minute." Silas beckoned the boy to join him where he was saddling the horses, several yards down the gulch from the canvas shelter where they'd slept. It was only a little after dawn, with long, horizontal sunbeams fighting their way through wisps of thin fog. A good day for travel.

Buff picked up one of the packs as he passed. "Yessir?"

Moving around so the horse stood between him and the shelter, Silas spoke quietly, "Can you handle my carbine?"

The outrage on the boy's face was almost funny. "Only reason I brought the long rifle was 'cause I wanted Pa to keep his new Winchester. It's a treat, Silas. Why he can put seven bullets in—"

"Your Pa's a fine shot. None better. But the reason I asked you is that you need more protection than that single-shot gun. Your job is to watch over those kids, not let any harm come to them. Can you do that?"

"I'll guard 'em with my life." Buff's face glowed with pride and determination.

"Your gun and a sharp eye will be enough. I don't want you risking your life either." God! What was he doing, sending a boy off to guard two little kids? While he went haring around the hills after a treasure he wasn't even sure he could find.

"I won't let anything happen to 'em, Silas. Honest."

"Soomey's going to want to go to the Chinese store, and I doubt you'll be welcome there. But you go everywhere else with them, you hear?" He kneed the mare, tightened the cinch before she could swell up again. "And don't let her talk you out of staying at Tilly's. She's dead set against it."

Was the kid blushing? "Yessir. We'll stay at Tilly's if I have to hogtie her." He dipped his head, wouldn't meet Silas's eye. "Uh, Silas?"

"Yeah?"

His voice was low, hesitant. "Do I have to stay in the same room as them?"

Surprised speechless, Silas stepped back and looked at Young Buff. Really looked.

The boy had several inches on him, was at least as tall as his pa. And there was a definite line of darker hair across his upper lip, although his cheeks were still peach-fuzz smooth. His shoulders were wide and his hands showed evidence of a man's labor. He had brought a small herd of cattle over a trail that would whiten the hair of many older, wiser men. Emmet and Hattie had given him permission to stay in the town, certainly knowing all the pitfalls and temptations of civilization.

Silas pulled out his purse and poured half its contents into Young Buff's—no, just Buff, for he was handling a man's responsibilities—into his hand. "You can take any room Tilly's willing to rent you," he said, smiling.

"Gee whillikers, Silas, you don't need...Pa gave me money... oh, heck, I don't know what to say."

"You better be thinking of what you're going to tell Soomey. She has a real strong dislike of whores." Silas handed Buff his carbine. "And stay out of poker games."

"Yessir, I...well, gee, yessir."

The journey to Bannock City seemed to take twice as

long as before. It was more comfortable, though, Soomey acknowledged, as she nodded in the saddle. While she was absent, Boss would be well guarded by Ji Rong and his cousins. Although their vigilance would cost her as much as she earned from Boss in five weeks, she did not begrudge them a penny, if they would keep Boss safe from his enemies.

With the heat of the sun on her head and Tao Ni's body warming her back, she was entirely content.

No, that was not right. She would not be entirely content until Boss acknowledged her womanhood.

Such a stubborn man! This morning he had told them they must not return until four days from now. "I've things to do," he'd said, "and I don't want to be worrying about you three while I do them."

She knew what he had to do. Find his 'secret,' whatever it was.

Well, she understood obligation, and could not complain. But someday she would learn why he was beholden to Buffalo's father. And to Tilly.

Boss was a complex man. At first she had taken him to be simply another of the adventurers who came to the gold fields, albeit a finer man than most.

She had learned much from other mention he had made of events in his past. He had been to China and other ports in the East. He had been a merchant—a good one, she imagined, for he had much money. And he had been in this place many years ago.

That was the most interesting of all. Why had he been here? And when? She had overheard enough since arriving in Bannock City to know that the basin, with its three almost parallel, gold-rich valleys, was newly discovered. "Never been anybody hereabouts but a bunch of red Injuns," was the way someone had put it.

Boss must have been a child when he was here last, for he was still a young man, not many years older than herself. She smiled at that thought. How surprised he would be when she presented him with proof of her age.

Proof. Could she obtain it? All she knew was that she had been born on the first day of the Year of the Tiger. But how long ago was that?

More than once she had attempted to determine how old she was, but only recently had she gained some idea of her people's way of calculating age. So young when first sold, she had not been taught those things that most Chinese children learned very early. In the intervening years, she had had little contact with others of her countrymen, only the occasional deckhand, for whom she often had to translate.

Although she read English very well, she could barely read her native language. Just enough to understand signs and to make her chop.

Perhaps Li Ching could tell her. He must be well educated, for she had seen him reading while they were on the trail, squinting at the fine calligraphy in the firelight. And if he could not, he would know who in Bannock City could calculate her age.

At last they topped the last hill and descended into the valley. They had only been away one month and already the town had grown greatly. "Look," she said to Tao Ni, who was awake now, "there are three streets, where there was only one."

Buffalo reined in, so that her horse caught up with his. "I never did see anything so excitin'. Why I'll bet there's five thousand people all in that one little town."

Remembering the first time she had seen Canton, Soomey smiled. "Many people, not all good. You be careful with your purse. Some people have very nimble fingers, so you never feel them take it."

He grinned back at her. "Yeah. Pa warned me about pickpockets. And shell games, and shaved cards. And I don't know what else. It took him near an hour just to tell me all the things I was to be careful of."

"And your mother, what did she warn you of?"

At this Buffalo laughed heartily. "To mind my manners, mostly. She started in to caution me against women and whiskey, but Pa said I was man-high and ready to learn the ways of the world."

"Well, I will warn you of women and whiskey, then. You must be very careful. There are those who drug their whiskey, to make stealing a purse more easy. And not just in saloons. Women do this too."

"Tarnation, Soomey, you sound just like my Ma, and you just a kid."

"I am not 'kid,' Buffalo, no matter what Boss says. I am many years older than you and far wiser in way of world." Furious, she kicked the mare into a trot. She would warn him no more. If he found himself with empty pockets and an aching head, she would laugh. That is what she would do. And she would not fetch him coffee for his hangover or warm, moist compresses for his head, or any of the comforts Captain Wilkins used to demand of her.

She would let him suffer.

Soomey led the way, guiding the mare toward Chinatown. She would find Li Ching first of all. After that she would purchase the medicines and herbs she needed.

And she would not sleep at the whorehouse tonight.

Once the youngsters were on the trail, Silas struck camp, hauling everything back to his tent in town. Since he was afoot, it took several trips, but he didn't care. He wanted folks to see that he was about, wanted to give the impression he wasn't spooked by the gunshots yesterday.

He stopped by Appledore's and begged paint and the use of a small brush. It was only a few moments' work to letter "Hours 9 a.m. to noon" on the slab of bark that served as his OPEN FOR BUSINESS sign. Many of the stores in the Boise Basin were open only part time, the owners spending the rest of their days working their claims.

Then he sat in the doorway of his tent and awaited trade. He begrudged the time to keep the store open, but felt it a worthwhile diversion for anyone watching him.

Idleness was the devil's own workshop. Hadn't someone told him that back when he was just a youngster himself? He sure believed it now, the way his thoughts kept returning to Soomey whenever he had an unoccupied minute. He forced them away from memories of her slim body, golden in the firelight, although not before his body reacted. God! He was as randy as a youth.

Silas chuckled. About as randy as Buffalo probably was, thinking of Tilly's, he'd bet.

Hattie and Emmet could be proud of their son. He was a decent, brave lad, watchful of those younger than him, as a man should be. Emmet must have known he would be eager to sample all the fruits of civilization as soon as he was shut of the cattle. It spoke well of Buffalo that he'd thought more of being a help to Silas than of his own pleasures.

Well, now he was headed for...what was it Soomey had said he wanted to see? Bright lights and loud music and fancy women.

Or something.

Closing his eyes in remembrance, Silas thought of his own first experience of that sort. He'd been around the same age as Buff was now. His ship had docked in Honolulu after a stormy voyage from the Columbia, near where Portland stood now. Silas had been awed, having seen little of America's eastern cities, although he had passed through St. Louis and Independence on his way west.

He'd never seen the likes of Honolulu, back in '47. Or of its women. He'd missed his sailing, and had almost lost his stake. As it was, by the time he departed, his purse was a sight thinner than when he'd arrived.

It was not memories of the girls in Hawaii that filled his

mind, however. Silas saw only one girl—Soomey.

Small, delicate Soomey, who had more strength of will in her slight body than many men larger than Silas.

A girl who insisted she was a woman. Whose body was woman round and woman sweet.

A girl who trusted him, who depended on him. And who had no idea what she asked when she demanded that he use her instead of Tilly's whores.

The winter sun reached its zenith, low in the southern sky. With great relief Silas took down the sign and tied the flap closed. Counting the day's take took him only a few minutes. Nowhere near as good as yesterday, but respectable enough. With a wry grin, he opined he could probably get far richer in business than he ever would as a miner. And he knew a sight more about how to go about it, too.

After depositing his cash box with Appledore—Silas wouldn't be surprised if the man hadn't ambitions to be Centerville's first banker—he strode up the hill behind the general store. It was as good a place to start his search as any.

"I will take you to Feng Jiao Yan," the labor contractor told Soomey when she explained her quest. "He is a scholar of sorts, and one who frequently casts horoscopes. Perhaps he can be of assistance."

She bowed her head, politely. "I thank you, honored one. It is of great importance to me that I discover my birth date."

"Do you wish him to know your sex?" Li Ching asked. "He will be discreet."

After a moment's consideration she said, "Perhaps it would be best, although I do not like it. A secret shared is a secret revealed."

They went through the Chinese store and down a narrow passage behind it. Soomey saw a shack with familiar ideograms painted beside its curtained doorway. A crib, although this one was not locked and barred as those in San Francisco. Its occupant was within of her own choice.

Soomey wished her well, but wondered why any woman would willingly choose such a life.

Feng Jiao Yan was old, too old for working the rockers or hauling gravel. He sat in a darkened room, scrolls piled untidily about him. The strong scent of incense permeated the still air.

She bowed when introduced to the elderly scholar. After an exchange of pleasantries, Soomey knelt before him and explained her quest.

"You have no memory of your birth date?"

Twisting her fingers together on her knees, she said, "I only remember someone telling me I was born on the first day of the year of the Tiger. Do you know when that might have been?"

In a frail voice that reminded Soomey of the rasp of sharkskin against wood, Jiao Yan proceeded to question her. Did she remember where she was born?

"Somewhere in Guangdong Province, I am certain," she told him. "We traveled only a few days after I was sold by my father." And she had wept most of those days, not understanding why her mother had turned her face to the wall and shaken her head when father had caught Soomey and tied her wrists together. Nor why her father, that stern, unsmiling man, had tossed her into a cart with other girls, as if she was no more than a pig being sent to market. And had walked away without looking back.

Later she realized it was because she was a female, and there were older, more useful females in the house. She was unnecessary.

Jiao Yan consulted his scrolls, halting occasionally to ask her another question. At last, he smiled. "I have your age now. You are forty-five years old. A great age."

"I cannot be," Soomey protested. "I am not a child, but neither am I old enough to be a grandmother. Look at me!"

He peered at her a long time. Shaking his head, he turned back to his scrolls. His lips moved silently.

"What do you remember of great happenings in your childhood?" he said eventually. "Floods? Locust swarms?"

"Little of importance. And when I was sold to...to my first master, I was confined for a long time on a ship." A polite way of describing her circumstances, she supposed. "Wait. Was there not a great battle, when British ships attacked Canton? I remember something..."

How could she have forgotten? Their ship had almost been caught in port. For years after, Captain Wilkins, her master then, had cursed the British for losing him most of a valuable cargo.

"Good, Good." His balding head bobbed on his scrawny neck like a hungry bird's. "And were you a child, then, or a woman?"

"A child," Soomey said, hearing her voice tremble. For some reason she had been convinced that if something happened to Captain Wilkins, she would be sent back to Captain Slye. That had frightened her far more than the great noise and the fires that had engulfed the city. "I was still a child, but on the cusp of womanhood."

She had been a child in years. But ancient in experience of evil. She had no idea how long she had been held on Captain Slye's ship, the *Abner's Revenge*, but it had seemed forever.

Again Jiao Yan studied his scrolls. He picked up a brush and wrote, his hand steady. When he finished, he laid the scroll aside and said to her, "You are indeed fortunate to have remembered so momentous an occasion. I myself was among the survivors of that terrible siege, so I am certain of when it occurred."

"And...?"

Holding one hand up, he said, "Patience, granddaughter." He clapped.

A middle-aged man pushed his head through the curtain at the back of the tiny room. "You wish, grandfather?"

"Bring wine. We have a cause for celebration."

Soomey squirmed impatiently. She had never really learned Chinese manners, but she had spent enough time in the labor company to know that Jiao Yan was most honored in this house and his every whim must be indulged.

A dusty bottle and two ceramic dishes sat on the red enamel tray the man brought in a few minutes later. Jiao Yan poured a tiny portion of wine into each dish. "Now, granddaughter, I give you good wishes, for you are twenty-one years and nine months of age." He held up the dish and sipped from it.

Soomey did the same. "You are certain?"

He puffed his narrow chest out. "Entirely. You were born in the year of Water Tiger, an inauspicious beginning, but one you have apparently overcome."

"But what is that in American years, grandfather? I cannot tell..." She drew a calming breath. "I beg your pardon. It is extremely important that I be able to prove my age in American years."

The old man finished his wine and eyed Soomey's dish questioningly. She gladly handed it to him.

"You are kind and generous." He drained it. "Now, then. It is very simple. I shall calculate your age in American years." He consulted a scroll, then a second, then yet another.

"Hah!"

Soomey jumped.

"Yes. You are exactly twenty-one years, ten months of age in American years."

"How can I prove it?"

"Prove it? You do not need to 'prove it.' I have told you it is so."

Sighing, she said, "Yes, grandfather, but it is necessary that I prove my age to my boss. Is there not some way I can do that?"

He sighed as well. "Look here," he said. "This is how I calculated your age." And he showed her how the Chinese calendar followed cycles of twelve and of sixty. "If you were truly born in the year of the Tiger, as you believe, then you must have been born nine, twenty-one, thirty-three, or forty-five years ago. Do you understand."

Soomey nodded.

"So! It is simple. You cannot be nine years of age, nor forty-five. So you must be either twenty-one or thirty-three. You may choose one age. It will not matter to an American."

Yes, it would. It certainly would matter to one American, she thought.

Smiling, Soomey pressed one of her ten-dollar gold pieces into Jiao Yan's gnarled hand. "Thank you, grandfather. You have lightened my heart very much."

The old man beamed. "I am gratified to have brought happiness to such a pretty face. Come and visit me again, child."

"I am not..." Pausing, Soomey realized that to Jiao Yan, she was still a child. She bowed. "I will come again if I can," she promised.

It was almost dark when she emerged. Tao Ni was waiting outside Li Ching's shanty. He had eaten the midday meal with Feng Min Bao, who kept the store, and spent the afternoon with several of the merchant's many nephews.

Before they departed, Soomey bowed to Li Ching. He may have failed to take her to Portland, but he had been helpful today. She supposed she must not carry a grudge. "My thanks to you, uncle. It is a momentous feeling to know one's age. Please celebrate for me, tonight." She pressed a silver dollar into his hand.

Returning her bow, Li Ching smiled. "May good fortune smile on you, Sung Su Mei. You are a strong woman and will achieve your goal someday." He also bowed, and they parted in mutual good will.

Soomey held out her hand. "Come, Tao Ni. Let us discover what mischief Buffalo has managed to entangle himself in, shall we?"

"Do not speak thus of Buffalo, Elder Sister. He is a good man. Did Boss not entrust our safety to him?"

Ah, so Tao Ni had a new hero. A tiny demon of jealousy nipped at Soomey's spirit. She had been the center of his world for so long that part of her was unwilling to share his respect with anyone else. "So, then, we will see what business he has engaged in, and be vastly impressed."

The boy skipped beside her, for once carefree and acting his age.

They found Buffalo waiting outside the livery stable, as agreed. "Took you long enough," he said when they arrived.

"It was necessary," Soomey told him. "Feng Jiao Yan is an old man and his mind works slowly. He spent much time with his calculations."

"Calculations? You mean like arithmetic? He had to use arithmetic to figure out how old you are?"

"In a way." She wished she'd never told Buffalo why she was going into Chinatown. He was sure to ask questions she did not wish to answer. "He had to calculate my age in American years from my age in Chinese years"

"Is that hard?"

Shrugging, she said, "I do not think so, but perhaps there is more to it than I saw."

"So? How old are you? Thirteen? Fourteen?"

"I am more than twenty-one years old. Much older than you."

He stopped right in the middle of the street and stared at her. "Bullfeathers! You're too little to be that old."

Stopping and turning, she frowned at him. "And you are too big to be so foolish. Size does not indicate age. Boss is less tall than you, but he is much older."

Buffalo kicked at a rock. "Well, I'll bet that Chinese man didn't know anything about American years. You can't be that old."

"It is not something to be argued about. Come." She started walking again. "We must find a place to sleep tonight."

"No need. We've already got rooms at Tilly's."

"I have told you. I do not sleep at Tilly's."

"Yes ma'am, you do. Silas said so." Without another word,

he tucked her up under his long arm and strode up the street.

For a moment, Soomey was too astonished to struggle. When she remembered to, it did her no good at all.

Chapter Fourteen

"Tarnation, Soomey, you've tore my shirt." Buff kept a firm grip on her wrist, no matter how she twisted and pulled.

She glared at him. "I told you I will not sleep in this place."

"Silas said to stay here and that's what we're gonna do."

"Boss says many things. He is not always right."

"This time he is. Now you just settle down." He tapped loudly on the counter. "Wonder where everybody is."

Soomey aimed a kick at his shin, but he was quick, pulling it out of her reach. To make matters worse, Tao Ni giggled behind his hand.

The curtain behind the counter was swept aside and a woman entered. She was dressed in purple satin and cream lace, her red hair held in intricate swirls atop her head by glittering combs. For a moment, Soomey regretted the loss of her own beautiful clothes. She had loved her red velvet gown.

She transferred her glare to the woman.

Tilly.

Boss's friend. Perhaps more.

"She ain't too pleased about bein' here," Buffalo said, "but Silas said I had to bring her. You sure she can't get the window open, ma'am?"

"No! You will not lock me in a room!" Soomey struggled all the harder. She knew Boss was concerned about her safety, but being locked up frightened her more than any imagined threat. "Please."

One eyebrow raised, Buffalo said, "If I don't, what'll you do?"

"I will go," she admitted. "There is a place for me with Li Ching. I will be safe there."

"Hold on a minute." Tilly stepped back and looked her up and down. "I can see how you fooled 'em, honey. That's not to say you'd have fooled me, not for long, but men, they don't always see what's right under their noses."

Buffalo started. "Hey—"

"Hush, lad. I'm not insulting you." She smiled at Tao Ni. "Why don't you and the youngster here—he's a boy, ain't he?— go into the kitchen? Mrs. Daintry's been baking cookies all day."

Soomey started to back away. When Tilly turned her back...

A soft but surprisingly strong hand clamped around her wrist and pulled. She found herself following the woman through a curtained doorway into a parlor of wondrous magnificence. Buffalo and Tao Ni disappeared through a door opposite, but she was pulled to the left and into a small, plain room. All it held was two chairs, a huge desk and a black and gold safe.

"Sit," Tilly said, gesturing at the straight chair.

Soomey stood, glaring at her.

Shrugging, Tilly said, "Suit yourself." She seated herself in the other chair, a leather-padded one, and Soomey saw that it swiveled from side to side.

"You cannot make me stay here," Soomey blurted, when Tilly said nothing.

"That's right, honey. I can't. I won't even try."

"You won't?"

"Nope. But I hope you'll decide to stay."

"Why? So you can make me whore like you?" Tilly's expression hardened, causing Soomey to regret her angry words.

She sat, unsure of herself.

After a moment, Tilly said softly, "I've thrown men out of the place for insults milder than that."

"You will not sell me? You promise this?"

"I don't sell my girls. Every girl in my house is here because she chose to be." Her soft fingers tapped on the desk surface. "And let me tell you, honey, they're a sight better off than in a factory or caterin' to some fat old lady with more money than heart."

Soomey stared at her, seeing truth in her face. Perhaps even in America, women had few choices, beyond marriage. If Tilly's girls had truly chosen their way of life, perhaps they were worthy of her respect, not her scorn.

Had she not made her choice, when Captain Wilkins died?

"Look, honey, why do you suppose Silas wanted you to stay here?"

"Because..." Soomey found she had no answer. Boss would not want her to become whore, would he? No, for he insisted on thinking of her as a child, too young for sex. Sighing, she admitted, "I do not know."

Picking up a sheet of paper from her desk, Tilly read, "... don't know if the shooter was after me or the kids, but I want them out of range anyhow. Soomey's a girl, but you may not want to tell anybody else. Right now she's probably safer if everybody sees her as just another Chinese boy. And watch her. She's got a real talent for stirring up trouble, especially if she thinks she's protecting me or the boys. She's a fine girl and I've grown attached to her."

"Well?"

"I do not make trouble for Boss. He makes his own trouble!"

Chuckling, Tilly nodded. "Child, I believe you, from what I've seen of him. But he's worried about you and thinks you'll be safer here than anywhere else. Can't you stay, just to please him?"

"You will not lock me in?"

"Not if you promise to stay. I will ask you to keep out of sight as much as you can, unless you want the girls to see through your disguise. Like I said, you wouldn't have fooled me for long, and I'd rather they thought you a lad."

Soomey considered. If Boss wanted her to stay here so he would not worry, she would do it, however reluctantly. "Will you give me key to door?"

"Your promise?"

"I will stay. But only this one time."

"Then here's your key." Dropping it into Soomey's hand, Tilly rose. "Let's go see if those boys have left us any cookies for supper." She swept from the room, her satin skirts rustling sensuously.

Once more Soomey regretted the loss of her fine clothes.

Silas was beginning to wonder if the cave full of gold was just a dream, conceived by his fevered mind during a bout of malaria. God knew, anything was possible.

Like visions of Soomey.

Last night he'd slept poorly, waking often from dreams in which he held her, kissed her, caressed her. Made love to her, her legs locked about him as he drove deeply inside her.

He'd heard her humming, that barest of musical sounds she made when busy or thinking. And awakened to silence.

He'd smelled her, jasmine underlain with a tangy hint of perspiration, an odor uniquely hers. And opened his eyes to pine-scented dawn.

Tossing the dregs of his coffee on the fire, he straightened and looked about him. Centerville was just waking, with smoke from cooking fires and the town's few chimneys lying in long, silvery streamers in the morning light. Silas stretched. He had a couple of hours before his posted opening time, so he'd check out that narrow gulch up behind Appledore's store. He didn't remember the cave being in terrain like that, but at this point he'd better consider every possibility.

God! How could he have been so stupid as to not draw a map?

Two frustrating hours later, he returned, annoyed and uneasy. There had been something—someone?—in the woods, moving when he did, always dodging out of sight whenever he turned to look. He hadn't gotten a real look at it—him?—not more than a quick glimpse of motion from the corner of his eye.

There had been tracks, although they were mere scuff marks in the forest duff. Man or animal? He couldn't be sure, although he couldn't imagine an animal that would stalk him like that.

Once, long ago, Silas had been stalked by a panther. For years afterward, he'd dreamt of it, always just out of sight, but never leaving his trail. Until the fresh carcass of a dead moose had tempted it away.

His shadow was not a big cat. Nor a bear. Of that he was certain.

Which left only one choice. A man.

As he reached the edge of town, Silas saw someone dodge behind a tent ahead of him. Without thinking, he gave chase, but the fellow was too quick. Somewhere in the maze of tents and shanties, he disappeared. But Silas had gotten a good look at his back. He'd been wearing dark pants and coat, a fur cap.

Now who had he seen lately wearing a fur cap?

The young Chinese man sat in his usual place, against the side wall of Appledore's store. Silas wondered where he slept, what he did for food. He wasn't a beggar, although he'd not refuse a coin tossed his way.

Perhaps he lived in the night, when darkness concealed his activities. Many men did, most of them dishonest.

The four hours Silas minded his store passed slowly, only occasionally enlivened by a customer. Most wanted to visit as much as buy, although he did sell a couple of tarpaulins and some harness straps. He wondered what the miner was going to use them for. There wasn't a buggy in Centerville.

He sure hoped the rest of his freight order would get here soon. Not many goods left. Except canvas.

Then there was another afternoon of searching. This time Silas watched his back, but he saw no sign of this morning's shadow.

He didn't find his cave, either.

Wilf shifted his legs, wiggling cold toes inside his boots. He sure wished he'd found a better place to watch from. His behind was about froze.

He'd give a pretty penny to know what Dewitt was looking for. Every day he was out traipsing about the hills, poking into piles of rock, digging here and there.

Just him lately, though. The Chinee brats and that tall kid wasn't anywhere to be seen. Wilf wondered what had become of 'em. Nary a sight of any of 'em the last couple of days.

Not since the shooting.

That shooting surely had been a job of work. Too bad none of 'em had been kilt. He'd bet anything they'd been real scairt, though. Now they'd gone to ground, like a rabbit with a bobcat on its trail.

Trouble was, Dewitt hadn't stayed scairt. He'd put the fear of God into some of the boys down to the Watson House that selfsame night.

Not him, though. Wilf Turner feared no storekeeper.

Not that he wanted to be caught following Dewitt. A man had to be mindful of what he did when he was stalking game, so's to keep his quarry walking easy and loose.

"Have to watch my step," Wilf muttered, remembering how he'd almost been spied this morning.

Maybe he'd back off some. Head back over the ridge tomorrow morning, stay in Bannock City 'til after Christmas. Now that there was a church over there, folks would be attending services. That'd give him a chance to see what they had hid in their tents and shanties, maybe work the trail right outside of town. And it'd let Dewitt relax and stop jumping at shadows.

He surely didn't understand Vester's always going on about his boys not fouling their own nest. What difference would it make if a greenhorn or two got robbed? They was always more coming up the trail.

Once he had some gold jingling in his pants, maybe he'd pay a visit to that new whorehouse. It wasn't as fancy as Tilly's, but he'd bet the gals wasn't as particular, neither. Thoughts of what he could do with a willing whore made him forget his cold arse, until he saw Dewitt close up his store.

He waited another quarter-hour, maybe a little more. And sure enough, there went Dewitt, heading upstream this afternoon. Wilf got to his feet, stiff from the long watch. He stretched, making sure his legs was working. Then he took off along the same path.

After a supper of bread and a strange, sharp cheese, Soomey slept surprisingly well on the hard bed that was all the tiny room held. She and Tao Ni had huddled together, grateful for the thick comforter, because the night had turned bitterly cold. Even before they'd retired, there had been ice on the inside of the room's small window.

She had expected the night to be noisy. But their room faced the edge of town, with only a few shacks and tents between it and the denuded hillside. The sounds of the miners' frolic seemed far away.

Most important of all, no one came to the door.

The gaunt woman who'd cooked their supper knocked late the next morning, about the time Soomey had decided to emerge in search of food. "You there, Miss Tilly says you can come to the dinin' room for breakfast."

Surprised and a little uncertain, Soomey smoothed Tao Ni's queue one more time. "Be humble," she told him. "Say nothing unless you are spoken to." Would there be customers at the table? "And do not eat with your fingers."

Soomey had tried to teach Tao Ni to eat with a fork, but he had resisted her efforts. Would their table manners disgrace her in Tilly's eyes? Although she still distrusted the madam, there was a certain obligation on Soomey's part, requiring that she show respect to her hostess.

Tilly and one other woman sat at the table, sipping from dainty, flower-decorated cups. A bureau held several silver dishes with small flames heating them. Soomey could smell bacon and cooked apples, among a medley of unfamiliar but tempting odors. Her mouth watered. Boss had promised dried apples, but had forgotten them when he bought supplies.

She bowed to the women, nudged Tao Ni to do the same. "You honor us by sharing your home with us," she said in Chinese. In English, she said, "Very nice you give bed, food. Thanky very much."

The golden-haired whore giggled, but Tilly smiled and winked. "Well, now that sounded mighty polite, whatever it was you said." She looked older this morning, but still impressive.

"Now fill your plates and sit down. Both of you are so skinny you look like the first breeze would blow you away." She gestured. "This here's Mabel. The other girls aren't up yet."

First Soomey filled a plate for Tao Ni, careful to choose only foods that he could eat with a spoon. It was just as well he did not care overly much for bacon. By the time she had filled her own plate, she was more at ease. Tilly and Mabel spoke together of ordinary things—a grease spot on a garment that had not washed out, the high cost of tobacco, a new strike up on Granite Creek.

She ate a small taste of everything provided, savoring unfamiliar flavors along with the sweet applesauce. If she was going to live in America, she must become accustomed to its food and its customs. All the while, she kept a careful eye on the boy, but he managed his spoon nicely, and kept his eyes politely on his plate.

"Soomey? Is that a Chinese name?" Tilly said to her, once her plate was clean. "I thought they were all funny sounding, like Ah Foo or Chin Chin."

Soomey wondered if Tilly knew how peculiar her name sounded to Chinese ears. "Is my name for many years," she admitted, "but is said better 'Su Mei.'"

"That don't sound any different to me," Mabel said.

"I can hear a little different sound." Tilly attempted to change her pronunciation. "Soo-mee. Sa-mee. Sa-may." She grinned. "Hell, kid, it is all right if we just keep on calling you Soomey?"

"I not mind."

Another woman entered, this one very young and slim. Her dark hair was a like a billowing cloud, almost obscuring her face. She yawned as she sat at the table.

"Long night?" Mabel said.

"Great night," the newcomer said. Another yawn. "Gawd, I'm plumb wore out." She pushed back her hair and peered at Soomey from eyes as green as the sea. "Hey, you're that Chinese kid. You come in with Buff, didn't you? Man alive, what a cocksman!"

Soomey stared at her. Had she misunderstood? Or was this whore truly speaking of Buffalo, who was still a beardless boy?

Mabel raised an eyebrow. "That good, huh?"

"Never better."

"Girls!" Tilly clapped her hands. "They're just children. Watch your language." She rose and gestured for Soomey and Tao Ni to follow her. They went into the small office off the ornately decorated parlor. As she passed, Soomey eyed a monstrous wooden box sitting against the wall. It had teeth! Many of them, both black and white.

"Now then," Tilly said, as Soomey perched on the edge of a chair, "what are we going to do with you?"

"I do not understand?"

The madam's cheeks turned almost as red as they had been the night before, but now Soomey realized she had been wearing paint. "Well, honey, it's this way. Your young, ah, escort, has discovered women. It could be days before he's ready to come up for air, if past experience is any sign. And as long as he isn't around to keep an eye on you, I can't let you out of the house. Silas wouldn't like it."

Conquering the tears that threatened to choke her, Soomey said, "Then I will stay in the room, since Boss wishes it. Tao Ni will stay with me." Why did she wish to weep over Buffalo's behavior? He was nothing to her. He owed her nothing.

But he was so young. He had been so innocent.

"You will?"

"I promise you I will not go out of your house without Buffalo for two more days. Then it will be time to return to Boss."

Soomey and Tao Ni were playing a child's game with twigs and stones that evening when they heard loud voices from downstairs. She went to the door and opened it a crack, fighting the key that wanted to stick in the lock. Listened.

All was confusion below. After a moment she heard a high shrill voice cry, "Buff! They'll kill him!"

"Stay here," she told Tao Ni. "Lock the door." She grabbed her pouch, and ran down the hall.

In the parlor, Celeste, she of the green eyes and black hair, clad only in a filmy robe, wept in the arms of a bearded miner. He was clumsily patting her back. Soomey grabbed the whore's arm. "Where is Buffalo?" she demanded.

"He's down at the Eagle and he's in trouble!" Celeste's voice rose into a wail, and again she collapsed against the miner's chest.

Soomey wanted to slap her, but instead she ran outside and turned toward the Golden Eagle Saloon. The crowd outside its doors was open and shifting, so she eeled between shouting miners until she reached a cleared area.

Slipping and sliding in the slushy mud of the street, Buffalo and three others were trading blows and kicks. Soomey watched for a moment. The four were evenly matched. The fight was not many against one, but many against many. Buffalo, if he fought as well as she believed him able, should be in no danger. Except to his fine leather clothing. And perhaps his pride.

Buffalo landed a solid blow to one man's nose and blood spurted. But even as Buffalo grinned at his opponent, a second man tackled him, and both went tumbling to the ground. The man with the bloody nose stumbled away. But the fourth man stepped forward and began to kick at the two rolling on the ground.

Immediately they left off their fighting and leapt to their feet to face him. He was a big man, wide and far heavier than the slim boy, or his short opponent. The short man backed away when he got sight of his attacker, but Buffalo stood firm.

They circled, then Buffalo struck out, clipping the big man on the chin. The blow had no more effect than a mosquito bite. The big man slapped at Buffalo, sending him reeling backward. Two of the bystanders caught him and pushed him back into the open space.

Buffalo lowered his head and charged, catching the big man around the waist, sending him backward two steps. But the boy's slight weight was not enough to overpower his enormous opponent. The big man grabbed Buffalo's shirt and pulled him up onto his toes. Despite Buffalo's struggles, he was held and struck once, twice in the belly, then released. The meaty sound of the blows made Soomey's stomach tighten.

Buffalo staggered a moment, then straightened. He stepped in close and struck repeatedly at the big man's belly and chin, only to be caught in long arms the size of small logs.

Fingers jabbed at Buffalo's eyes and Soomey squinted in response. But Buffalo was quick. He ducked his head and clipped the bigger man on the chin. The click of teeth was so loud that Soomey heard it over the shouts. Buffalo wrenched himself free.

Only for an instant. Soomey's breath caught as she saw the huge arms tighten again around Buffalo's slim body. But suddenly one of Buffalo's legs was wrapped around his opponent's, and immediately both men were on the ground, rolling. Buffalo's wiry strength almost countered his opponent's bulk. Soomey saw the big man again try to dig at Buffalo's eyes, and hoped he could somehow manage to escape before he was seriously hurt. She slipped her hand into her pouch, grasped the butt of her gun.

The short man rejoined the fight, attacking Buffalo.

The miners were no better pleased than Soomey. "Leave' em alone!" someone just behind her called.

"Fair fight! Fair fight!" from another.

"Git outta there!"

"Two agin one ain't in the rules!"

"They ain't no rules."

"They air too!"

In a moment those two miners were trading blows and the crowd's attention shifted to the new dispute. Soomey saw the glint of a knife in the short man's hand.

She fired from within her pouch, aiming at the ground beside him.

The shot brought silence, except for the grunts and pants of the still-fighting miners. Even Buffalo and his opponent ceased their struggles and drew apart.

Quickly, before the crowd could discover who had fired, Soomey darted forward and grabbed Buffalo's wrist. "Come. Now!" She tugged, but he simply stared blankly. His opponent did the same.

"Buffalo! Please, you come. Now. Quick!" She tugged and slowly he struggled to his knees, then his feet.

"Hey, ain't that one of Dewitt's Chinee?" someone said.

"I reckon it is," she heard another reply. "I don't want no

trouble with him."

"Me neither."

She stifled a smile. Boss already had a reputation of strength. She had made the right decision to trust her fate to him. Now that they knew Buffalo belonged to Boss, no one would bother him again.

Buffalo leaned heavily on Soomey as she led him through the crowd. No one attempted to stop them, although not every man moved readily from their path. The man Wilf, who had been vanquished by Boss twice, blocked their way just before the door to Tilly's.

"You ain't always a'gonna have Dewitt to save your bacon," he said in a low, rough voice. "Sooner or later someone'll catch you alone and show you what folks think of you Chinee scum."

Soomey ignored him, hearing the bluster in his voice. She guided Buffalo around him and toward the back of Tilly's. Once in the kitchen, she poured warm water into a basin and found a clean cloth to sponge the blood and dirt from his face.

"Le'me 'lone," he muttered, fighting her touch.

Soomey ignored him and kept washing until she was certain he had no cuts that needed stitching. "You are very foolish boy. Tomorrow you will hurt very much," she told him, dabbing once more at the split in his lower lip.

The door burst open. "Buffalo! Are you hurt?"

He looked up and tried to smile at the green-eyed whore. "'Course not," he said. "There was only three of 'em."

Celeste knelt beside Soomey and framed Buffalo's face in her dainty white hands. "Oh, you poor boy! Look how they marked you."

"You ought to see them," he boasted. "It was a real whing-dinger of a fight!"

His lip must have hurt to smile so widely, but Soomey knew he would never admit it. Disgusted, she tossed the cloth back into the basin. "You will live," she said, knowing he could not hear her words while the pretty whore made much of his deeds.

Perhaps the woman would keep him so occupied that he would find no more trouble until they were ready to return to Centerville. She hoped so.

Two days later they were on their way home.

Buffalo's curly hair was stringy and lank, his eyes bloodshot, his body slumped in the saddle. And his fine leather garments were dirty and torn.

"You are a very stupid boy," she told him, once they had maneuvered their horses through the congestion at the edge of town and were relatively alone on the trail. "What will your mother say to you?"

He muttered something. Soomey did not think it was polite.

"I was ashamed for you, when the whores talked of you at meals."

"Damn it, Soomey, shut up!"

"I will not. You look as if you have been drunk for a week."

"Haven't had a drink since last night."

"That is good. But this morning that Celeste whore, she tells us that you drank a whole bottle of French champagne out of her shoe. How could you?"

Another mutter, this one less belligerent. The smile on his face spoke of treasured memories.

"And another thing—you gambled. I will not believe you won."

"Did too."

"Ah, but how much? Do you have more money than when you began?"

"Hell no, but what's that got to do with anything? Tarnation, Soomey, a man's gotta celebrate sometimes. And celebratin' don't come cheap." He groaned and rubbed a hand across his face. "Do you have to talk so much? And so loud?"

"Bah! Perhaps you are a man. A boy would not be so foolish."

"You are cruel, Elder Sister," Tao Ni said softly from

behind her. "Buffalo is in pain. You should not shout at him."

"I am not—" Soomey realized she was indeed shouting. "Do all males defend the stupidity of one another?" she said, but not loud enough for anyone to hear.

Chapter Fifteen

Four days. That's what he'd told Young Buff. Come back in four days.

Silas looked once again at the sun, low in the sky now. In another hour it would be behind the hills, and the winter night would quickly follow.

Are they here yet?

Maybe Buff had counted wrong. Or one of those bastards that hung around the Golden Eagle had given him some trouble. Or Soomey had got herself into mischief. God knew, she had a knack for it.

He told himself to stop worrying. It was at least a six-hour ride from Bannock City under the best of conditions. As cold as it had been last night, Buff probably wouldn't have wanted to start until the frost was off the trail. Silas slipped and slid down the talus below the outcropping he'd just investigated and made his way to the bottom of the slope.

He'd be glad to see them. It wasn't just Soomey he'd missed, but all three of the children. That's what he'd told himself each night as he laid alone in his tent and listened for the sound of her breathing. There had been no faint scent of jasmine, and he'd not eaten a bite of rice for four days. Sure had been quiet, too, without Soomey and Buff drilling Tao Ni on his grammar.

The boy was picking English up real fast. He still didn't say much, but Silas knew he understood almost everything he was told. Once more Silas wished he could pick up a new language as quickly. His ineptitude had often worked to his disadvantage in trading.

He peered through the fading light. The trail stretched, pale and empty, back into the forest. If they weren't at the tent when he reached it, he'd just have to head up the trail and look for them.

Even if he had to go all the way to Bannock City.

"Boss is not there," Tao Ni said as they passed Appledore's store. "His tent is dark."

"Likely he's out in the woods," Buff said, "lookin'." He dismounted and reached up to take Tao Ni from behind Soomey, then turned to help her down.

But she had slid off the horse and stood beside it, waiting for life to return to her legs. How she hated riding the great beasts. They were so tall and so wide. She much preferred the dainty little donkey Li Ching had allowed her to ride once on the way to Bannock City.

"Fetch water, Tao Ni, and I will start our meal. Boss will be hungry after a day of searching."

The boys went their separate ways while Soomey read the note she found pinned to the tent flap. 'Don't unpack,' it said it a bold, black hand. 'We're moving on tomorrow. I'll be in about sundown.' The signature was a scrawl that seemed to combine Boss's initials, but she could not be perfectly sure.

So. They would move again. Had something happened, or was Boss simply convinced that his treasure—his mysterious, secret treasure—was not to be found in the hills surrounding Centerville?

She would certainly like to know what it was he sought. Meanwhile, she should begin preparing supper. When Boss returned, he would be hungry.

The Duchess of Ophir Creek

"Where the hell were you? Did you have trouble on the trail?"

Soomey almost dropped her cooking pot. She spun around to see Boss standing, fists on hips, glaring at her. "What you mean, where were we? We were coming from Bannock City. Where else?"

"You should have been here hours ago!"

Measuring rice into the pot, she deliberately did not look at him. He would see in her face, in her eyes, how much she had longed for his presence. And that would not do, for it would make him feel far too important. "We did not start until late, so we did not arrive until now."

"What delayed you?"

"Buffalo felt ill—perhaps something he ate—so we allowed him to rest until the sun was high and the frost had gone." What, she wondered, would Boss say if he knew that Buffalo had been ill from the effects of overindulgence—in all the dissolute pleasures Bannock City had to offer?

He would probably approve. Yes, as a man who undoubtedly had himself indulged in such dissipation, Boss would approve, or at least sympathize.

She had long ago decided that males were very strange. They condemned behavior in females that in other males they encouraged and even admired.

Just then Buffalo returned from taking the horses to the livery corral. Boss met him outside and spoke sharply to him although Soomey could not hear words. They walked away from the tent, but only so far that their voices could be heard as an indistinct murmur. When Boss laughed, using that singular tone that males always used when speaking of pleasure, she knew she had been right.

As they ate, Soomey listened while Boss told Buffalo of his plans.

"We'll find someone to mind the store, but I want you all with me, so that means we move, bag and baggage. Tomorrow if possible, even though it's Christmas. I'm still hoping to find the cave before the snow gets too deep. Building the cabin's going to slow me down some."

"Ma sets a right store by Christmas," Buffalo said slowly. "Maybe I should'a gone home."

"Oh hell, Buff, I didn't even think..."

"Ma will understand. If I had gone off and left you, she'd be real put out with me. She said I was to keep you out of trouble."

Silas rather thought she'd told Buff to keep himself out of trouble, but he contained his smile. Christmas! He wondered if Soomey and Tao Ni even knew what it was. Well, they had that haunch of venison and those carrots Mrs. Appledore had given him. Maybe Tao Ni could find some mushrooms. He'd not say anything for now. They could celebrate up at the cabin site.

"I doubt there's much snow in the high country yet," Buffalo said. "If this keeps up I'll be able to get home whenever I want. I disremember a winter when we didn't have a couple feet of snow on the ground by now."

Chuckling, Boss said, "It's a far cry from the winter I went up to Lapwai. I was stuck in a snow cave for ten days, halfway there. And that was earlier in the year than this."

"I never heard about that. What'd you go to Lapwai for?"

"Emmet sent me to fetch Flower." He turned to Soomey, who seemed enthralled. "Buff was named after her father—a real old he-coon. She was supposed to be at the Whitman Mission, but she wasn't so I kept going."

Soomey listened as he told of a weeks-long trek over mountains and through blizzards. Boss made it sound simple, but she wondered if it had been. Her experience of snow made her doubt it. Snow was bitterly cold and difficult to travel in.

"We got back to the cabin down on the Boise just in time. Your sister was born the next day. Having another woman about made a real difference to Hattie. Buffalo, he'd died a month back and Emmet didn't know anything about birthing." Boss chewed on his pipe stem a moment. "I reckon I was about the age you are now—fourteen or so—although I've never known exactly. Hattie and me, we tried to find out when I was born, but nobody seemed to know."

"I turned fifteen last month," Buffalo said, as if insulted at being thought younger than he was.

Soomey looked at Boss with new respect. He was truly a courageous man. Few grown men would have had the perseverance to complete such a mission, and he had been little more than a child. At the same time she regretted knowing how strong and brave he had been. How could such a one understand her weakness, her submission to Captain Slye?

"...anyone who might be looking for work?"

Soomey had missed Boss's first few words. She listened more carefully as she gathered the empty plates to be washed.

"I don't know all that many folks hereabouts," Buffalo said. "Have you asked at Appledore's?"

"Posted a notice there yesterday." Silas leaned through the tent flap to light a splinter at the fire. He held it to his pipe and drew several times to get it going.

Even with her eyes closed, Soomey would know Boss was nearby. His tobacco had a sweet odor, one that clung to his clothing and his hair. She drew a deep breath, smelling woodsmoke and fresh air and sweat—smelling Boss. No one else smelled just like he did.

She chewed her lip for a moment, considering. Ji Rong had caught her on her way back from the necessary. He was certain no one had followed Boss for at least three days. In his opinion, the watcher was more interested in her and Tao Ni than in Boss.

Soomey was not so certain, but once they no longer lived in town, she and Buffalo and Tao Ni could watch Boss. "There is one who might work for you," she said.

With spectacles, Ji Rong would be able to see well enough. Her purchase of them had been an afterthought, made only when she'd seen them on a shelf in Min Bao's store. She would give them to him in the morning.

Boss looked at her, surprise written on his face. "You know somebody? Who?"

"There is a young person, his leg is twisted, but he is honest and diligent."

"You mean the Celestial with the limp? I don't want a beggar working here."

"Feng Ji Rong is not beggar. He works—" No, she did not wish to tell Boss what she had done to protect him. Not yet, at least. "His work is no more. He is seeking other."

Boss looked at her, as if suspecting she was telling him less than he wished to hear. "Tell him to come see me, then, tomorrow."

"I can find him tonight." She started to rise.

"Sit down. Morning's soon enough."

She obeyed. Her legs still ached from being stretched astride the horse's back. When they moved tomorrow, she would insist on walking. Did she not have excellent, strong boots?

"Here." Silas looked about him. The steep hillside leveled into a bench a couple of hundred feet above the valley floor. There was a good view of the Ophir Creek drainage, although Centerville was out of sight around the shoulder of the hill. It was a little over an hour's walk to town. "We'll build here."

He'd taken a good saw, shovels and a couple of axes from the stock in his store, borrowed pack mules from Hiram. As soon as the next shipment of freight came, they'd have a few comforts. Life hadn't seemed this uncomfortable when he'd come across from Pennsylvania with Hattie. Or had age and experience taught him to hate sleeping wet and waking up cold?

He assigned chores as soon as they'd unloaded the horses and the pack mules. "Buff, you and Tao Ni scout out some trees—nothing bigger than two hands' breadth. I want to be able to handle them. And Soomey, you dig the foundation trenches."

With his heel, Silas marked the approximate dimensions of

the cabin on the ground. It would be nothing fancy, but it would have a loft for him and the boys, and a corner to curtain off for Soomey's bedroom. Later he'd add a room for her.

He wanted to be as far from her at night as he could. It was getting more and more difficult to ignore the soft sounds of her breathing and the rustling of her blanket as she turned. Last night he'd lain awake for a long time, half aroused, images of her drifting across his mind.

Damn! He hadn't been this constantly horny since he was Buff's age.

A haunch of venison roasted as they worked, getting turned on its spit whenever anyone thought to do so. After she had finished the first trench, Soomey set soaked beans to simmer beside the fire, flavoring them with the last of the bacon and some of the bittersweet syrup Boss called blackstrap. Tao Ni was seeking mushrooms in the woods, and had said he would go to the spring where watercress grew. Perhaps some had survived the cold weather.

If only she had thought to dig cat-tail when she was in Bannock City. She had harvested all she'd found near Centerville. "Ah, well," she said as she wiped sand from the carrots, "I will only cook these a little bit, so they will be crisp." With her cleaver, she chopped them into thick circles.

She wondered about this holiday, Christmas. Neither Captain Slye nor Captain Wilkins had spoken of it, so she knew little about it. Buffalo said it celebrated the birth of a wise man, and Boss said it was also a time of gift giving.

She would like to give Boss fine, fragrant tobacco. He had complained that what he had left in his pouch was dry and harsh. For Buffalo, she could have sewed a shirt of bright calico, and for Tao Ni, as well. Alas, she had not known, so there were no gifts.

At the end of the day, she had both foundation trenches dug and blisters on her hands. She was washing them carefully when Boss and Buffalo came from the woods.

"You tell me I will not have to dig for you," she teased, smiling up at him. "What is this I have done today?"

He took her hands, smoothed his thumbs over the blisters. "Hell, Soomey, I'm sorry. You should have used my gloves."

She looked at his hands, then at hers and giggled. "I would be so busy keeping them on that I would never dig." She pulled her hands free, although she would rather have left them clasped in his. "If you will wait one minute, I have water hot for washing. Then we will eat."

"Sounds good," Buffalo said. "My belly's been talkin' for the last hour."

They sat in the tent to eat, she and Tao Ni on thick layers of canvas, Boss and Buffalo on short, fat sections of log cut from one of the trees they had dragged into the clearing. The candle lanterns hanging from the tent poles gave little light, but she did not need it to see their faces. Soomey was not surprised when the only sounds as they ate were the scraping of forks on tin plates. They had all worked very hard that day.

Eventually Boss finished and set his plate aside. "That was mighty tasty, Soomey. You're a good cook."

A glow of pleasure spread through her.

"I don't know what you did to those carrots, but they was almost edible," Buffalo said. "Ma, she's tried cooking them every which way from Sunday, and I just can't learn to like them, except fresh out of the garden."

Her face as warm as her heart, Soomey gathered up the plates.

"Leave 'em," Boss said. "Buff and Tao Ni can do 'em later."

She saw Buffalo frown, but he said nothing. He did not like doing women's work, but had told her how his mother had made him learn to cook and sew right along with his sisters. She wondered if his father had taught them to hunt and plow.

"Now," Boss said, when she had sat again, "I guess it's up to me to play Santy Claus."

"What is that?" Tao Ni whispered to her.

The Duchess of Ophir Creek

"Hush," she murmured. "I do not know but Boss will surely tell us."

Reaching behind him, Boss pulled out three small packages, all wrapped in clean brown paper and tied with bows of satin ribbon. He handed them around. "Merry Christmas."

She looked at the odd-shaped package curiously. The ribbon was scarlet, almost exactly the color of her favorite dress. Her callused fingertip caught on it, then slipped along its bright curl.

Buffalo was ripping the paper from his package. Tossing it aside, he held up a wooden case, opened it. "Aw, gee, Silas. This is...well, it's just about the greatest present I ever got." Delicately, between thumb and forefinger, he lifted a shiny razor, much like the one Captain Wilkins had used.

"I'll show you how to strop it tomorrow," Boss said. "Glad you like it."

"I do. Heck. Well, gee. I...thank you kindly."

Boss laughed. "You're welcome." He turned to Tao Ni. "Aren't you going to open yours?"

"This is for me?" Soomey heard wonder in his voice.

A nod.

Carefully Tao Ni untied the ribbon—bright green—and unfolded the paper with hands that trembled. Soomey wanted to tell him to hurry, for she was as excited as he.

It was wrapped well, with several layers of paper. Tao Ni smoothed each one before removing the next. But at last he held in his hand a folding knife. He looked up at Boss. "For me?" he said again.

"For you. Just mind you don't cut a finger off with it. I made sure it was real sharp."

"I be ver' careful," Tao Ni vowed. He clasped the knife to his chest, apparently unaware of the tears running down each cheek. "I thank you."

Buffalo reached out and pulled the younger boy close. "Let's see what you've got there, Tony. How many blades does it have?"

Soomey felt close to tears herself, a different sort of tears than she had ever shed. "You are good man, Boss," she said softly.

"Open your present," he told her.

"I have nothing for you."

"You don't need to. Hattie always said that giving gifts was way more fun than getting 'em. I see now what she meant."

Removing the ribbon, Soomey put it carefully aside. She would keep it forever. The paper folded back to reveal a small hand mirror, framed in honey-colored wood. Even in the dim room, she could see how fine it was. Her face looked back at her without distortion. "Oh, Boss...!"

"You like it?"

She set the mirror down and leaned across to take his hand. So strong. She raised it to her mouth, kissed his knuckles. "Thank you. How did you know I have always wanted mirror?"

"Hey, that ain't no way to thank a fella," Buffalo said. "You got to kiss him right."

Flustered, Soomey sat back down. "What you mean?"

"Well, my sisters always kiss me on the cheek, but Ma, she kisses Pa right on the mouth after she opens her presents."

Soomey looked at Boss, wondering if she dared.

He looked back, his expression forbidding. After a moment, he tapped his cheek. "This'll do."

She went to him, kissed his cheek. It was cool and smooth, and his beard tickled her chin.

So strange a longing. She had never before liked kissing.

They labored the next two days. Silas went down to his store early each afternoon to see how Ji Rong was doing. The second time, he dropped in at Appledore's afterward.

"Set awhile, won't you?" The grocer waved Silas toward a seat made from half a barrel. "You'll be wantin' to hear the latest news."

"I saw a couple of new tents, but didn't get down to see what they were. More saloons, I imagine?"

"Just one. The other's a hotel, leastways that's what it's meant to be. But it's got no beds, and no outhouse. Too close to the creek."

His pipe started, Silas leaned back, making himself comfortable. "Is he going to move?"

"That's what he says, but he ain't shown any sign of when. So far he's not had many lodgers, either, considerin' he's charging four bits a night to sleep on the ground." Appledore used a crate as a step so he could seat himself on the counter. "That Chinaman you got working for you. I reckon you know he's brought in his family, too. They're camped up the draw behind your store, along with all them that came last week."

"I think they're all related. It was Soomey's idea for them to camp up there. They'll keep the riffraff from sneaking in the back."

The grocer shook his head. "I don't cotton to them myself. Always gabbling to themselves in that outlandish tongue, so a body don't know what they're sayin'. Let 'em learn to talk English, if they want to do business with me."

Knowing how common Hiram's prejudices were among the miners, Silas simply shrugged. "I see Vester's almost done building his saloon."

"Well, now that's another problem. Leastways, I see it so. Too bad there ain't a way to keep ruffians like that out of town." He lowered himself from the counter, went to add another log to the fat stove standing in the center of the store. Over his shoulder, he said, "Now I'm in favor of puttin' up buildin's, same as the next fellow, but I'd just as soon they were stores and boarding houses, not saloons."

In Silas' experience, saloons always came before anything else. He'd been surprised to see a grocery store as the first permanent building in Centerville. "I take it you don't think much of the saloon keeper."

"It ain't him so much as his gang," Hiram said. "I've no quarrel with Vester. Oh, he's a bully, but he ain't one to bother honest folks, but some of them fellows works for him are something else again. I declare, there's one looks like one of them Texas gunfighters, with silver doodads on his hat and fancy spurs. Carries two handguns, too."

"Hey Eli, where you been?" Wilf crowded in beside Henry and shouldered Eli off his stool.

Eli knew better than to complain. "Nowhere."

Wilf motioned to the barkeep, somebody Eli'd never seen before. 'Course, they was a lot of fellas he'd never seen before. And more comin' up the trail ever' day. He dragged another stool up to the table and edged in beside Wilf.

"You've been somewheres, Eli," Henry said. "I ain't seen you for nigh a week."

"I tell you I ain't been nowhere," Eli said. "You jest didn't see me, that's all."

Wilf half emptied his beer mug. "Well, I was over there in Bannock City," he said, wiping his moustache. "It don't look like the same place. There's a bunch of new buildings, and tents a'springin' up everywhere."

"We got new buildings here, too, Wilf. And somebody said there was close to a hundred tents now."

"Shaddup, Eli. I was talkin' about Bannock City."

He turned away, and started talking to Henry. Eli waved again at the bartender, but as usual, he was ignored.

Goddam it. I've jest about had enough. Why there ain't a one of 'em as good as me, but to see 'em carry on, you'd think I was dirt under their boots.

If Wilf only knew, wouldn't he be surprised! *Someday they'll all know, then they'll be sorry.*

Joe DiCastro sat down across the table and lit one of his long, thin cigarillos. "Too bad you weren't here yesterday, Wilf," he said, a shit-eatin' grin on his face. "Pete Johnson pulled up stakes and moved over to Placerville. Said his claim was playin' out and not worth keeping."

"Consarn you, Eli!" Wilf said, slapping the table. "How come you never told me?"

"I didn't know—"

"Well, you knew I had my eye on that there claim." He shoved back from the table, nearly knocking Eli off his stool. "Let's go."

"I ain't drank my beer yet, Wilf."

"I said, let's go. I want to git down to Pete's claim afore anybody else does."

Before Eli could answer, DiCastro spoke up. "Too late. Half a dozen Celestials are already workin' it."

Wilf's curses fell about Eli's ears like Missouri hailstones, each one hard and hurtin'. He ducked away from the swat Wilf aimed his way and hurried out into the dark street.

Jest you wait, Wilf Turner, he thought. One of these days I'll show you. You and ever'body else. You'll be sorry you didn't show me some respect. Soon's you all find out what I been up to.

Soomey woke with the soft patter of rain on canvas. She wondered where Boss had found this tent. It was even more ragged than the one Li Ching had provided on the journey from the ship. So far, though, it had not leaked. She stared into the darkness.

Thinking.

Boss was still in need of a woman. She had seen the telltale swelling in his trousers the day they had returned. And tonight, after supper, he had stood and turned his back to her, but not before she had seen the physical evidence of his hunger.

Was that why he slept on the other side of the clearing, beyond the almost-cabin? There was enough space in this shabby tent for him, if he hadn't insisted that she have one side all to herself. Instead he had strung a tarpaulin between two trees and spread his blankets under it.

Was he cold? Although warmer weather had come with the clouds, it was still close to freezing outside. He had only one blanket to cover him, just a thin pad of canvas between himself and the cold ground. He had insisted she and Tao Ni each take one of the warm Hudson's Bay blankets, although they could have shared one and been just as comfortable.

Did he lie awake and dream of having a woman? And if he did, who was the woman he desired?

Foolish man. Had she not told him many times she was his if he wanted her?

Soomey chewed her lip. Americans had such strange ideas. They called their wives 'good women' and kept concubines to satisfy their animal appetites. Captain Slye had forbidden Soomey to speak of his wife, although she accompanied him on every voyage—a dried-up, sickly hag who did little, in Soomey's opinion, to earn respect. She had never seemed to suspect the sort of brute he was, nor had she appeared to care that her husband kept a slave chained in the tiny cabin next to hers.

How had he explained the screams?

Rubbing her wrist, which had healed many years ago, Soomey debated with herself. Boss was honorable, so he would not abandon her and Tao Ni under ordinary circumstances. Still, she would feel more secure if she could bind him with ropes of desire. If he needed her, he would consider more deeply before giving her up.

Besides, she assured herself, Tao Ni needed a man to look up to.

Decision made, she crept out of her bed and slipped through the tent flaps. The night was dark, with heavy clouds dripping gentle rain. On bare feet she stole across the clearing, detouring around the cabin with its half-built walls.

Boss's tarpaulin made a blacker shadow in the night. She slipped beneath it and knelt beside his bed. Her eyes were accustomed to the dark, but even so his face was simply a pale shape in the gloom.

He breathed deeply and evenly. Carefully Soomey turned back the blanket. He was clad in his underwear, soft, smooth wool that clung to his skin and smelled of him. She eased her hand upon his chest, froze into absolute stillness when he moved.

He had only been shifting in his sleep. After a moment she inched her fingers lower, scarcely touching the soft wool of his longjohns. She found buttons and carefully undid them. Her hand was warm, but his skin was hot against it.

Again Boss shifted, this time with a sigh. Patience, she told herself. If he wakes, he will send you away.

She had brought Captain Wilkins to release this way often, but he had been awake. Soomey had always preferred it, for without his fat belly crushing her against the bed, she could remain detached and think of other things.

She moved her hand to his belly, following a line of crisp, silky hair. Her fingers encountered a staff of enormous size, which pushed eagerly against her palm. She clasped it gently, feeling its power and promise. Boss's spear was indeed prepared for battle!

Again Boss moved, thrusting his hips upward. He moaned, but his eyes remained closed.

Still moving carefully, Soomey pushed the blanket completely from his body. She would not straddle him, for to do so would surely wake him. It would be better if Boss believed he had had a particularly passionate dream.

Using both hands now, she stroked her fingers across the tip of his shaft, feeling his body tense under her touch. She clasped him and moved her hand, slowly at first, responding to his urgent thrusts. Within seconds, there was no need for her to do more than hold him, for he moved faster and faster.

She became aware that she too was gulping air with rapid gasps. A hot tightness grew in her belly, until she felt heavy, almost aching. Her heart pounded. She clenched her hand tightly about his shaft, drawing an even stronger response from him.

His back arched as, with a shout, he erupted, hot fluid spreading over her hand in wave after wave. When his body fell back on to the pallet, she lay across him, knowing that something very strange and wonderful had happened to her.

And then two hands were on her like manacles, lifting her and shoving her away. She fell to the ground beside him.

"What the hell—" Boss rolled to his knees, buttoned his union suit, and sat back on the pallet.

She heard him fumble, then a match flared. "All right, young lady, suppose you tell me just what in hell you thought you were doing."

Boss must be truly angry, for his voice was soft and deceptively gentle. "I was...you were in need. I tell you, no reason for you to be without woman. I wanted to...I—"

"Enough!" He blew the match out just as the flame reached his fingers. Then he pulled her from the floor and forced her to sit before him.

She heard him take several deep breaths before he said, "Soomey, I told you once that my sexual needs are not your responsibility."

"You did not say exactly that."

"Close enough. Now suppose you tell me what made you think I wanted you to...to..." He gestured at his belly. "Hell, Soomey, I feel almost like I've been raped."

Immediately angered, she said, "You do not know what rape is! I was gentle with you."

"But you did it to me without my consent, didn't you?"

That was a concept she had not even considered. Soomey nodded. But she still did not believe he could understand what rape was.

He drew her close and held her gently and without desire. "Soomey, you're too young to understand, but what happens between a man and a woman should be mutually desired and mutually pleasurable. Anything else is no better than rape."

"I am sorry, Boss. I do not understand these things." Perhaps he was different from the captains. They had not thought that taking her against her wishes was anything but their due. Had they not owned her? Or were slaves somehow different?

And pleasure? How could there be pleasure for a woman in such a humiliating act?

Yet the feelings she had experienced, when Boss was in the throes of passion, had been pleasurable, in a way.

Again she said, "I am sorry. I did not mean to distress you."

He hugged her briefly, then set her away from him. "It's over. We won't worry about it anymore. Now, hadn't you better be heading for bed?"

She did not move. Finally she blurted out the words that had hovered at the tip of her tongue for days. "In Bannock City, I learn my true age."

"You did, huh? And how did you do that?"

"I speak to Feng Jiao Yan, a very wise man, and he helps me to discover it."

Boss picked up his shirt and pulled it on, then reached for his trousers. As he pulled them onto his legs, he said, "Let me guess. You're thirteen. No, make that fourteen." His grin flashed white. "Very grown-up indeed."

Restraining herself from giving the kick he had earned, Soomey said, "I am twenty-one years old. At the New Year, I will be twenty-two."

"The hell you are!" He stood, towering over her. "Look, Soomey, you don't have to try to pretend to be a woman for me. I told you I wouldn't go to the whorehouse. I've lived without a woman before this, and it's not going to hurt me to do it now."

"I do not lie!"

"Call it stretching the truth, then." Squatting again, he placed both hands on her shoulders. "Look, darlin', just because you're a girl instead of a boy doesn't mean I'm going to abandon you. When I hired you, I took responsibility for you. Both of you. Do you remember what I promised Tao Ni?"

"You tell him you will take care of him. You are good man."

"That promise was to both of you. I'll take care of you 'til you're grown, and then I'll see you get a stake to build on. Emmet did that for me, and I mean to pass the favor on."

"I am grown, Boss. Only Tao Ni needs caring for."

"Tarnation, Soomey! You make a man tired just arguing with you." He released her and stood, staring down at her.

Noticing that it was growing lighter, Soomey met his gaze with resolve. He did not believe her now, but she would find a way to convince him that she was woman grown.

He needed her, even if he did not admit his need.

After a long moment, Boss said, almost to himself, "I'd give a pretty penny to know why you're so determined to get into my bed." He shook his head. "It's almost time to be getting up. You go ahead and start coffee."

Soomey watched him disappear into the woods. She could tell him why she wished to be his concubine, but she doubted he would understand. Americans were either selfish and greedy—like Captain Slye, and sometimes Captain Wilkins—or they were extraordinarily honorable, like Boss.

Of the two, the dishonorable were the easier to deal with, for they were predictable and easily fooled.

She went back to the roofless cabin and rooted around in the pile of supplies. Perhaps she should cook cornbread for Boss again today. He had complained about rice again at supper.

Chapter Sixteen

BOSS WAS STILL ANGRY WITH HER. HE HAD BEEN GONE ALL DAY, seeking his cave, and now he sat on a sawed-off log beyond the fire, staring into the night, his back to everyone. He had spoken little at supper and then only sparingly.

Soomey went to her bed as soon as she had cleaned the pots and plates. She was tired, for she had worked hard all day, and had thought much.

She wished she understood Boss's anger. How could a mere woman force a man such as Boss to submit to her will? Although she still refused to allow memories of the years with Captain Slye into her mind—to do so was to make her almost blind with rage—she had been helpless, while Boss was not.

She had been Captain Slye's possession, with no say in her fate. Boss could have pushed her away before she gave him pleasure, and he had not.

Yet if he truly felt raped, how could he not be angry?

Soomey forced her thoughts into a more calming path. Buffalo had said he would be going home soon, and had invited her and Tao Ni to go with him. He had assured her that they would be welcome at his father's house.

"Ma likes havin' folks come visit" he'd assured her. "She says the worst thing about Cherry Vale is that it's so far from anywhere else."

What would it be like to go to Buffalo's home? She could scarcely remember her own, so young had she been when she was sold. There had been women in the dark little hut, but she no longer remembered their faces. Nor could she remember feeling as if she belonged.

Buffalo had assured her of a welcome in Cherry Vale, but she was not so confident. Americans did not like those who looked or spoke or believed different from them. This she had learned soon after she became an American's slave.

No, she did not believe she would go to Buffalo's home. But she would send Tao Ni, for he needed a place where he could eat well and be warm, and be a child again. Surely Buffalo would see that Tao Ni was treated kindly.

In the spring, he could come back to Centerville and they would...Her thoughts faded and she felt herself drifting into sleep.

It began, as it always did, in the hut. Smoky, dim, drafty, smelling of the dung they burned and the sweat of its occupants. Soomey spent as little time inside as possible, preferring the musty odor of the few goats the family owned, now that she was old enough to watch them as they browsed.

She sat in her usual place, a dark corner as far from the fire as it was possible to be, tired from a long day of chasing goats on too little food. It seemed as if her belly was always at the edge of hunger, never satisfied.

When her father entered, she shrank back even farther, for he was uneven of temper and swift with punishment. But this time it did her no good, for he stretched out a long arm and dragged her into the light.

His words had frightened her, although they were now indistinct in her memory. When he looped the rope about her neck, she'd tried to break free, but it had choked her.

Images flashed across her mind, of being bounced about in a cart tangled with others, of bright lights and the sounds of many voices. She shivered in cold air as her clothing was taken from her, struggled as impersonal hands spread her legs and probed within her.

His question had been spoken softly. "You're certain she's a virgin?"

An obsequious voice answered, "I swear on my mother's grave, Boss."

"You'll share your mother's grave if she's not." Hard fingers had gripped her chin, turned her face this way and that. "She's young enough, and decent looking. I'll give you ten pieces of gold."

"Alas, I cannot. She cost me thrice that."

"Fifteen."

The bargaining continued, meaning little to Soomey, but familiar in its pattern and rhythm. Only when it was done did she realize that she had been the merchandise they'd bargained for.

More confusion, and then she was carried aboard a ship, a heavy, graceless vessel with an ugly carved beast at its prow. Rough hands fitted her left wrist with an iron bracelet that was to encircle it for a very long time. A toothless old woman washed and perfumed her, dressed her in a shapeless, faded shirt that reached almost to her knees.

Once more she relived the terror and the pain and the rage when Captain Slye taught her what he wanted from her.

His thick fingers probed and pinched, his hard palms slapped against her buttocks, his teeth left marks around her flat nipples. She was one shivering mass of agony when he mounted her as a dog mounts a bitch. Then he taught her what true pain could be, as his great rod hammered its way into her, tearing and ripping until she felt split asunder.

Soomey screamed. And screamed, as she found herself held against a hard chest. She struggled, knowing it was futile.

A deep voice soothed. "It's all right. Hush. A dream. That's all. Just a dream."

She fought blindly. She would die first, before again submitting to his cruel demands.

"Soomey! Wake up!"

Still she struggled.

"Soomey. Hush now. Hush. Hush, darlin'. Hush."

The words became a lullaby as she was held in a warm embrace and rocked back and forth.

No! Captain Slye was not here. Captain Slye was dead. He had been caught by pirates soon after selling her to Captain Wilkins. Once he had described how they tortured their victims, promising it would be her fate unless she showed more enthusiasm in giving him pleasure. She hoped he had suffered them all—and slowly.

She ceased her struggles and forced her eyes open. In the light from the dying fire, she stared up at the man who held her, his hair a gilded halo about his noble head, his pale eyes catching an errant beam of moonlight. "Boss?"

"I heard you screaming," he said, his voice still low and soothing. "Bad dream?"

Striving for composure, Soomey drew a deep, shuddering breath. As always, the images from the past were in the forefront of her mind, as if they had happened only yesterday, instead of long ago.

She nodded. "I sometimes remember...remember events I would rather forget," she told him. "They were not pleasant."

"Sounds to me like they were downright terrifying," he said, easing her from his lap and back onto her pallet. "Want to talk about them?"

Soomey rubbed her wrist. It always hurt more after one of her dreams, as if she still wore the manacle. "No." Forcing the residual memories back, far back into her memories, she said, "It does me no good to remember. Better I think about what I am to do today and tomorrow than about what was yesterday."

His fingers stroked her cheek lightly. "Sometimes it helps to talk out your troubles."

She shivered, but not from cold. "And sometimes it does not." Shaking her head, she said, "If I speak of the dreams, they become stronger and then I dream more often. I do not like to do this."

Boss plucked the blanket from her pallet and wrapped her in it. Before she could protest, he carried her outside, setting her down next to the fire ring. Little warmth came from within it, but there was almost always a tiny ember smoldering in the deep, flaky ash. Soomey watched as Boss made a careful pile of pine needles and blew upon it. Tongues of flame fed upon the needles and licked at the twigs he offered them. Soon the kindling was burning well, and Boss added split logs.

Why couldn't she learn to do that? Her fires caught reluctantly, needing much persuasion.

Boss kicked a sawed-off log closer beside her and sat on it. He said nothing for a long time, but she was aware that he watched her. Suddenly his hand caught her wrist, pulled it away from her massaging fingers. He raised it close to his eyes, ran his fingers around the low, uneven ridge of flesh that was an indelible reminder of her slavery. "This is old—long healed." He did not ask.

"Yes," she admitted. "You knew I was slave."

His fingers rubbed at the ridge, absently, as if he did not know what he did. "You said you escaped in March or April," he said at last.

"I have not been chained for many years, I think." Shrugging, she said, "For so long I had no way to know. Time passed, one day and then another, all the same."

"Who chained you?" His voice was hard, sharp.

"His name was Captain Slye. He is dead."

"Ahuh! And you're not sorry, are you?"

Soomey shook her head.

"Did you kill him?"

"I would have, if I could. He was an evil man."

She felt his hand, gentle on her head. His fingers stroked

lightly down behind her ear, sending ripples of heat before them. For a moment, Soomey was tempted to lean into the touch, like a cat seeking a caress.

Until she remembered. Boss did not want her as a man wants a woman. Not her. Not Soomey, who had been a slave and a whore.

She sat straight, staring into the fire. The tarpaulin above them rattled in the wind. Soomey looked out into the dark and saw that it was snowing, the white flakes forming and reforming ghostly shapes as they blew. She shivered, even though the blanket was warm and the fire now burned brightly.

As if her tongue could not restrain itself, she said, "I think some men cannot find pleasure with a woman. They turn to other men, or, like Captain Slye, to children." Biting her lip, she forced the tears back. "Perhaps they can only find pleasure in giving pain."

"What did he do to you?"

Soomey was almost sorry Captain Slye was dead. Boss's voice held fearsome threat. "I do not wish to speak of it." She could imagine his disgust if she told him of the ways in which she had given Captain Slye pleasure.

"Soomey, what did he do to you?"

She closed her eyes and bowed her head. "Please," she whispered, "do not make me—"

Again his fingers stroked across her cheek. "He raped you, didn't he?"

She nodded.

"What else? Did he beat you?"

Again she nodded, not raising her head high enough that she would have to meet his eyes. "And other things. Please, do not make me tell you."

"Shit! How long..." He paused to clear his throat. "How long were you with him?"

Shaking her head, Soomey said, "I do not know. There was snow, once, when we sailed to Beijing, and another time we were in a port when storms came. He called them 'monsoons.'" She shrugged. "I was very young when he bought me, perhaps of an age with Tao Ni. He sold me when I grew breasts."

"To another filthy pervert?"

"Oh, no. Captain Wilkins was very kind. He clothed me in silks and fed me well. He did not even chain me, and sometimes he took me ashore." Had he not, she would never have met Jing Fei and would have had no place to go when the captain was killed. "When he died, I did not want to belong to another man," she said, hoping he would understand. "Not all are as kind as Captain Wilkins." *Or you,* she added, silently.

"So you hired on with me and tried to get into my bed. Tell me, Soomey, why didn't you simply set up as a prostitute and be done with it?"

"I will not be whore! They have no choice. Any man who gives them money is welcome in their beds."

He stretched his feet out to the fire and Soomey saw that he wore nothing on them but heavy wool socks. "Seems to me what you were doing is a sight worse than selling yourself."

"You do not understand."

"I think I do. You figured that if you kept my bed warm and cozy, I'd take better care of you."

Since this was exactly what she had first planned, Soomey said nothing. How could she explain that there was more now to her wanting to be Boss's concubine as well as his servant? She wanted him to value her for her industry and talents as well as for the pleasure she could give him.

Sighing, she told herself that she was fortunate indeed that he had not driven her away after last night. He had been very angry. She peeked at him from under her lashes. He was staring into the fire, even though he had told her and Tao Ni never to do it. One could not see danger approaching, he said, if one's eyes were blinded by the light.

"Boss?"

"Yeah." He did not turn to look at her.

"I will make you promise not to tempt you if you will make me promise always to care for Tao Ni."

He turned his head, but his face was in shadow, so she could not read his expression. "What about you?"

"I can care for myself. He cannot. He is young, but he is also shy and...and...I do not know the word. He has no shield to protect him from the small cruelties."

"He's vulnerable. Is that what you're trying to say? He doesn't have your toughness." There was an edge to his voice that frightened her.

"Ah, yes. That is what I was trying to say. Thank you, Boss."

"I promised you that once, Soomey. I don't break my word. Not to you. Not to anyone." Leaning forward, he pushed the almost-consumed logs closer together. "Let's get some sleep."

She had angered him again. Soomey lowered her head almost to her knees. "Yes, Boss."

She watched him as he strode into the blowing snow toward his bed, without speaking again.

Portland no longer seemed to be such a wonderful place for her to go. Even if the streets were paved with gold, it would hold no joy.

Boss would not be there.

"I purely don't like that Dewitt," Wilf told the boys gathered around the table. Vester and DiCastro had gone over to Bannock City for a couple of days. 'Twas the first chance he'd had a chance to speak his mind for a long time. "And them I don't like, I squash."

"Yessiree, Wilf. You surely do."

"Shaddup, Eli. When I want to hear from you, I'll let you know."

Jenkins nodded, lowered his chin, but not so soon that Wilf didn't see the spite in his eyes. The puke didn't have the brains of a turkey cock, but he was useful. Mighty useful.

"Now, boys," he said to the group crowded around his table

at the New Eagle, "we're gonna squash him and we're gonna do it good."

A chorus of agreement drowned out the sound of the fiddle and banjo that kept time for the dancing miners.

"I'm lookin' for suggestions. Anybody know for sure where he built that cabin of his?"

"Out towards Ophir Creek, I heard tell," Henry said.

"That's right, Wilf. He's got him a bolt hole up somewheres west of here. I saw him headin' in from that way this mornin'."

"Damn it, Eli, I knew that. But I rode that there trail yesterday, all the way to Placerville and back. I never saw any cabin."

"Tomorrow I'll go up and look—"

Wilf slapped his hand down on the table, slopping beer from half the glasses setting there. "Shit, Eli! How many times I got to tell you not to take off and do things on your own. You never know what I got in mind, and more'n once you've messed up my plans."

"Sorry, Wilf. I jest wanted to help. I knowed you'd be wantin' to get even with Dewitt, and I just thought..."

"Well, don't you go thinkin' any more, you hear, Eli? That's what I do—the thinkin'. Got that?"

"I do, Wilf. Yessiree! I surely do."

"See that you remember." He took a deep draught of his beer. Thinkin' was thirsty work. "Now, boys, like I said, We're a'gonna take care of Dewitt. Then we're a'gonna do something about them slanty-eyed little shits he favors. Now you all listen to me."

The men leaned closer, giving Wilf a feeling of power and importance. If it wasn't for Vester, he'd be boss of this here town. These boys listened to him and did what he said.

"Fine cabin," Hiram Appledore said, as he replaced his hand tools in the leather satchel. "You'll be a sight warmer than in that tent."

"I'm hoping so," Silas agreed, "and drier." He wrapped a framing chisel in soft canvas and handed it to the grocer.

Billy Watson slapped him on the shoulder. "Y'know, now I've got the hotel built, I think I'll build myself a cabin too, seeing how snug yours is. Maybe you'd give me a hand with the fireplace?"

"Be glad to," Silas said, silently thanking Emmett for showing him the trick of assuring a good draw. Some skills you just never forgot. "As long as Hiram does the finishing work. He's a pleasure to watch."

Appledore closed the satchel. "My pa was a cooper, made the best barrels in Gallia County. He taught all us boys which end of a tool to take hold of."

Everyone else had gone back to town. These two had stayed to give Silas, who was going down to check the hardware store, a ride in. They stepped back when he did, to look at the cabin. The surface of the roof was thick plates of yellowpine bark, laid on like shingles. It wasn't as sturdy as cedar, but it was what they had. Silas couldn't complain. "I thank you," he said to the other two men. "We couldn't have done it without your help."

Again Billy slapped him on the shoulder. "Neighbors helps neighbors," he said. "C'mon, let's get to town before it's too dark to see."

"Hey, Buff," Silas called.

The boy stuck his head out the cabin door. "Yo?"

"We're off to town."

Buffalo emerged, carrying the carbine. "See you later, then." He would stay alert until Silas returned.

Silas climbed into the bed of Appledore's wagon, thinking that no matter how late it was when he came home, he'd have good moonlight for the journey.

Kneeling before the fireplace, Soomey enjoyed the warmth. She would warm the food left from dinner later, but now she was heating water. For a bath.

She had bathed at Tilly's, but it had not been the same. The little shed at the back of the whorehouse was well known to all the town. She knew, for she had seen them, that many men liked to stand outside and watch the women come and go in their light kimonos and underclothing. So she had carried a bucket of warm water to the cold little room she and Tao Ni shared and washed herself a piece at a time, shivering as she did so.

Tonight she was going to remove everything and be warm while she used the last of her perfumed soap to clean her body and her hair. With Buffalo standing guard outside, she could take as long as she wished.

And when she was done, she would make Tao Ni bathe as well. Buffalo would help her catch him.

Silas walked out away from town with a feeling of freedom. His order of freight had finally arrived. Ji Rong's numerous cousins had spent the last two days unloading and stowing it, piling the big wooden crates high all along the back wall of the tent. The cabin was finished, all but a little fixing up inside, and Soomey would work on that. He'd been so busy that he'd had no time to brood on what Soomey had told him.

What courage she had! As a child she'd lived through experiences that would have destroyed many adults, and had not just survived, but had grown into a strong, competent woman.

Woman? How could he doubt it any longer? He still questioned her age, but he didn't doubt she was more than the thirteen or so he'd first estimated. That scar on her wrist had been healed a long time, and it sounded like she'd been with her second owner for a couple of years, at least.

Yes, she was a woman. His body quickened at the thought. She was willing. She was available. So why did his conscience still balk at taking what she offered?

What she'd tried to force on him.

Settling his pack more firmly, he picked up his carbine. They were low on meat, so instead of looking for that damned cave, today he was going hunting. What he needed was time to think, time to consider Soomey as a woman.

Time to contain the rage that still smoldered under scant control.

The world of the Orient trader was a small one, despite the distances involved. He'd met Moses Slye once, in Canton. That must have been six, maybe eight years back. They'd both been at a banquet hosted by the powerful merchant who'd controlled most of the foreign trade in that city.

God! Had Soomey been a prisoner on his ship even then? Or another child, equally helpless?

"Boss! Boss! Wait! I come!"

He turned at the shrill voice. Tao Ni was running up the game trail behind him. "What are you doing here?" he snapped when the boy, panting, caught up.

"I watch for you, Boss. Buffalo goes for firewood, Soomey helps Ji Rong in store."

"Well, you just go on back down to town and help Ji Rong too. I'm doing fine alone."

Shaking his head, Tao Ni said, "No can do, Boss. Soomey say watch, I watch."

"Damn it, kid! Nobody's going to bother me today. I'm just going hunting." It had been days since he'd sensed anyone spying on him. And the new snow would make it damn near impossible for someone to trail him in secret.

"Soomey and Buffalo say you go nowhere alone. I come with you."

"Soomey and Buff have no say in the matter. Go home, Tao Ni. Now."

The boy sat in the middle of the trail. "I cannot. I will wait here a while, then follow behind you."

Silas scratched his chin, discovering in his beard tiny icicles caused by his moist breath. "You've followed me before, haven't you?"

"Not for many days, Boss. This is first time since bad man catch me."

The boy sounded as if he was telling the truth. But something was going on here that he was going to get to the bottom of. "Then why, all of a sudden, did Soomey decide you needed to?"

"Not sudden. Soomey follow you all the time. Or Buffalo. Sometimes Ji Rong. We watch your back, like you tell us. All the time, from Bannock City to now."

"Well hell!"

Tao Ni cowered back.

Silas smiled. "I'm not mad at you. Just surprised." Though he shouldn't be. In the time he'd known Soomey, he didn't think he'd ever won an argument or gotten the best of her. She'd decided it was her job to protect him, and she was damn well going to do it.

Silas held out his hand. "C'mon, then. Let's see if we can find a deer stupid enough to stay this close to town."

"Better we find bear," Tao Ni said, skipping along beside him. "Eating meat of bear gives power and potency."

"Yeah, well, I'll settle for a deer, today," Silas said, remembering one day when he and a big old silvertip had vied for right-of-way on a trail. He'd yielded with no regret.

He was here to remember the occasion, wasn't he?

Chapter Seventeen

"Boss, there!"

Silas looked where Tao Ni pointed. Sure enough, the trail of blood led into the thicket of young pines. He spat a word he would have given the boy hell for using. New snow, which had only threatened when they started out this morning, had changed to freezing rain as the day lengthened. Every one of those feathery branches would drip on them as they pushed through.

He'd been careless, firing at the doe as it slipped through the brush, rather than being patient and waiting for a clear shot.

Before Silas could stop him, Tao Ni disappeared into the thicket. In a moment he called, "In here, Boss. It is fallen."

Silas followed. He dispatched the doe quickly, mercifully. He'd never taken the pleasure in hunting that some did. It was simply something he did out of necessity.

Once the carcass was hanging from a nearby tree, Silas looked around, noting landmarks so that he could return for the rest of the meat. One haunch was all he would carry back today.

Something familiar...A tall, lightning-struck snag towered above the thicket, huge, rounded granite boulders at its base. Young trees grew all around the rocks, where the top of the pine had fallen after being shattered by the lightning bolt.

Forgetting the deer, he pushed his way back into the thicket. A huckleberry bush grew between two of the boulders. Silas grabbed it, pulled.

"What you doing, Boss?"

Releasing the tough stems, he stepped back. "How fast can you get to the cabin and back?" he said. "I need a shovel."

The boy was off, running.

"And a pick," Silas called after him.

While he waited, Silas moved the smaller stones aside. He'd finally found his cave.

When the huckleberry stems became too large to bend aside, he cut down one of the saplings and started skinning its branches away. He could use the trunk as a lever.

Tao Ni was back in less time than Silas expected. He'd brought two shovels as well as the pick, tied together with leather thongs. With his still-splinted arm, it must have been quite a load.

"You find gold, Boss?"

"Maybe," Silas told him. "Maybe I did."

The huckleberry bush grew deep in the soil, holding smaller stones in place with its strong roots. When Silas finally uprooted it, he was able to roll the rocks behind it aside, until a small opening was exposed at the base of the granddaddy of all boulders.

He lodged the sapling under it and pushed. The wooden pole creaked and bent, and the rock stayed where it was. Silas shifted his lever, tried again. This time the boulder shifted. It rolled slightly to one side, making the opening a little bigger.

Silas reset the lever. The boulder moved again. "Tao Ni, can you hold this while I reach inside?"

The boy took hold of the sapling while Silas eased off. But there came a point where one small boy wasn't enough. The rock threatened to roll back. "Wait a minute," Silas said, letting it. "Let's dig."

He used the pick and Tao Ni scraped soil aside with the

smaller shovel until the boulder seemed about to break free.

"Stand back," Silas warned the boy. He braced his feet against the rock and pushed. With a sound like massive doors opening, the boulder pulled free of its bed and rolled. It gained momentum, lumbering down the hillside faster than a man could walk, careening off trees and other boulders, until it finally came to rest three hundred yards away, caught by another outcrop.

They looked at the hole it had concealed. It was small, too small for Silas's wide shoulders. Yet it looked the same as it had, sixteen years ago. He had been a slender boy then; now he was a man.

"Can you crawl in there?"

"You bet." Tao Ni wriggled into the hole without difficulty. In a moment he scooted back out. "Is dark, Boss. But I see sacks. Many sacks. Feel like leather. Piled high." He held one hand up higher than his head. "These are what you seek?"

"They sure are." Silas stepped back, looking at the cave mouth. How the hell was he going to conceal it while he removed the gold? Even if all the leather bags were intact, it would take him many trips to get everything out. And after this long, he'd not trust the bags. Not to support that much weight in gold.

Tao Ni was kicking the debris on the forest floor outside the thicket. As Silas watched, he picked up a short, straight stick. "What are you doing?"

"You find gold, Boss. File claim. That way nobody take it from you." He continued to search.

"Good idea." Silas helped him, until they had enough sticks of the appropriate size. Together they paced off about twenty acres centered on the cave, setting stakes at each corner and along each side at fifty-foot intervals. Silas took a notebook from his pocket. On a sheet of paper torn from it, he wrote his name, the date, the approximate dimensions of the claim, and a description of the landmarks by which he'd identified the corners. Folding it carefully, he buried it under a rock by one corner stake. As soon as he could, he'd come back with a tin can to put it in. And he'd record his claim at the mining office that had opened in Bannock City. There was still no law here, but California's mining laws had been generally accepted in the interim.

Soomey was at the store all day, helping Ji Rong. So many new miners had arrived in town that business was very good.

As she prepared to depart that afternoon, he said, "Perhaps Boss should have more than two people in the store. There are some who tire of waiting. And some who bear watching."

"There are always those," Soomey said, "but I will tell Boss. He will not be pleased if he thinks he is being robbed."

The young man shrugged. "I cannot say it has occurred yet, although I cannot account for some small things. Perhaps I forgot that I sold a hammer and a pan."

"Perhaps," Soomey agreed, although she doubted it. Ji Rong had an impressive memory. She rather thought he knew the location and number of each item the store held. "I will speak to Boss."

"There is talk in the town," he said. "Some resent us."

"Enough to cause trouble?"

He walked to the door with her. "I do not think so. Not yet, at least. But that Vester, he does not like the Chinese."

Remembering the time he had calmly watched the mob torment her and Tao Ni, Soomey nodded. "Watch your back," she told Ji Rong. "Walk carefully and never go about town alone."

"I do not. Even now my cousin watches." He gestured toward the back of Boss's land, where a dozen of their countrymen were camped. In response to Ji Rong's gesture, a hand waved from behind a tree.

"Good. I will see you tomorrow. Take care." Soomey picked up the pack, with its load of groceries. She was amused. As long as she cooked for Boss, Appledore, who clearly did not like Chinese, was polite to her. He even stocked rice, now.

When she reached the cabin, it was apparent that something exciting had occurred. Tao Ni was chattering to Buffalo, and Boss was smiling as he had not for many days. She listened to the boys. But could not understand what they spoke of. Caves and mining claims and...the treasure?

"Boss?"

He nodded, pausing in the stoking of his pipe. "Yeah. We found it." His smile was wide and his eyes laughed.

Her heart all but stopped. Boss had come here to find his treasure. Only for that. It was obvious to her that his hardware store was of little interest to him. He merely had the habit of buying and selling. It had been a convenient means of hiding his real purpose in the gold towns.

Quickly she controlled herself. Pretending interest, she looked around. "Where is it?"

Boss chuckled. "Still where it's been for sixteen years. Tao Ni covered it up again."

"But how...?"

"We'll bring it down later. I figure it's safer up there for now. We'll pretend to be running a prospect hole, bring out a little at a time. Buff's going home to Cherry Vale soon, so he'll take a load, make like it's supplies." He smiled, clearly very pleased with himself.

It was an effort for Soomey to smile and joke with the boys that evening. All she could think of was that Boss would be leaving soon. He had said, once, that he would provide for her when he went, but she put little faith in a promise so lightly made. Once he had his treasure and was gone, she would be only a fading memory.

Besides, she could take care of herself. But how empty her life would be without Boss.

Later that evening, when Boss went to make his nightly patrol, she seated herself beside Buffalo, who was whittling a spoon for her. "So you go to your home soon."

"Soon's we can get me a load of gold." He tossed the half-completed spoon and his knife onto the table. "Godalmighty, Soomey, you know, I never really believed in that cave. It's like one of those fairy tales, you know?"

She had heard stories of treasure. "Be careful that you do not find sorrow in your new fortune," she said, remembering how many of them had ended unhappily for those who found riches beyond imagination.

"It's not my fortune. It's my Ma's and Pa's. But now they'll be able to move into town—Portland, or maybe Boise City. And Ellen can find herself a husband." Picking up the knife again, he used its point to score lightly in the rough tabletop.

"Ellen? She is your sister, is she not?"

"Sure is. Ma says she's uncommon beautiful, but to me she's just right pretty." He blushed. "Compared to Celeste."

So pretty Ellen was seeking a husband. Boss was a good catch—handsome, successful, unattached. Why had she not guessed before?

And why did she feel so desolate?

Forcing herself to smile, she said, "Your sister is indeed fortunate. May she find a husband who will be good to her." The words burned her tongue as she spoke them. Quickly, she added, "I have a favor to ask of you."

His knife point moved carefully across the table, forming letters. "Sure. Anything."

"I ask you to take Tao Ni to your home. He is a good boy and will work hard. Perhaps your mother can take him with her when she goes to city. He will make a good houseboy."

"Houseboy? You think my Ma would use Tony like a servant?"

She did not understand. "Why not? He is diligent, honest, strong. He would serve her well."

"Soomey, he's like my brother."

"So? You think your mother will think of him as another son?" She laughed, harshly, although it was not a joke. "A Chinese boy with no family?"

Buffalo stood up, towering over her. "Why not? What's so strange about that?"

"But he is Chinese," she said, wondering why he did not understand.

Buffalo looked at her, his expression pitying. "You've never seen my family, Soomey," he said. "My godfather's black as coal and my godmother's part Nez Perce."

Well, Dewitt, you've got yourself caught in a real cleft stick this time, don't you? Now that he had the gold, would he do as he'd planned—haul it up to Cherry Vale, take his share of it, and go back to his trading empire? Or would he stay here and build a new empire, starting with one ill-stocked hardware store in a tent? And two hundred pounds of raw gold.

Silas leaned against a tree and stared out over the valley below. Moonlight glittered on ice-clad branches, cast eerie shadows in the folds and wrinkles of the hills. Below him, along Ophir Creek, orange points of light and broad patches of pale ground marked where miners, like giant badgers, were turning the earth inside out in their search for gold.

Common sense said he should go back to the business he'd built from practically nothing, with five ships plying the trade routes in the Pacific and Indian Oceans.

Anticipation tempted him to stay here and see what the future brought. He hadn't been this enthusiastic about a venture since his first small investment in a cargo.

Maybe it was time for a change. For a long time he'd been feeling as if life held no more excitement. For a long time before coming back here, that is. He certainly hadn't suffered from boredom since he first walked down the main street of Bannock City.

Not since he'd found Soomey.

Child-woman.

Stubborn. Tempting. Protective. Lovely.

Desirable.

And what was he to do with her?

"Boss?"

He turned, wondering if she'd sensed his thoughts.

She stood there, all but invisible in her black pajamas and the wool jacket he'd taken from the ambusher. Her hands were tucked up the cut-off sleeves, her shoulders hunched against the cold. A cloud formed before her face with every breath she took.

Silas removed his pipe and tapped it against the tree. He hadn't even noticed when it went out. "You'll freeze," he said, holding out his arm. "Come here."

She came into his embrace but stood stiff instead of leaning into his warmth. "When do you leave here?" she said, after a few moments of uncomfortable silence.

"Leave? I wasn't planning on going anywhere."

"You came for your treasure. Now you have it. When it is taken away to your friends, there will be no more reason for you to stay in this place."

Looking for the right words, he laid his hands on her shoulders. She was so tiny, more than a head shorter than he, and seemed so fragile that he often wondered where her incredible endurance came from. "I haven't decided," he said, finally. "Why?"

"Because I must make plans," she said. "It is winter and travel will be difficult. I must find a place to stay until spring."

Involuntarily, his hands clamped on her shoulders, the bones feeling like delicate sticks in his grasp. "Damn it, Soomey, I said I'd take care of you!"

She jerked free of his hold, spun around. "You will not!" she spat. "I need no man to care for me. I care for myself! I am not child!"

"Hold it!" He held his hands up between them. "Don't get so huffy. I promised I'd see you to Portland when I leave here, and I will." If I go, he added to himself. The thought that if he stayed so would she, swept across his mind like a comet—bright and fiery. Again, unbidden, the image of her slim, naked torso sailed across the turbulence of his mind, heating his blood. Bringing an ache to his groin.

Silas set his hands back on her shoulders, turning her, pulling her, resisting, but not quite refusing, back against him. Wrapping his arms about her, he said, "We don't have to decide anything tonight. Let's just enjoy it. Look out there."

The moon had come up behind the hill against which the cabin nestled. It was full. Or very close to it, in a sky so deeply black, so diamond-dusted, that it took his breath away. No fires gleamed in the valley now, but icy branches sparkled until it seemed as if the two of them floated above a forest of glass, close enough to touch.

She was quiet in his arms, yet he sensed a stiffness, a withdrawal. This might be the last time he held her, he realized. Everything would change, now that he had the gold. Buffalo would go home, he would have to find a way to get his share to Portland or San Francisco, and Soomey...well, Soomey would do what she chose, and he might as well resign himself to the fact.

"I never told you about how the gold got into the cave, did I?" He spoke almost as much to himself as to her, wanting to reach back to the frightened boy who'd buried it.

She shook her head.

"Remember I said I'd gone up to the Nez Perce settlement at Lapwai to get Flower, Buffalo Jones' daughter, so Hattie would have a woman with her when Ellen was born?"

Soomey nodded, her hair, loosened from its queue, sliding with an almost inaudible hiss across his chest.

"Well, before Old Buff died, he'd told Hattie about this basin, said it was a place 'whar gold jest lay on the ground for the takin.' Apparently he'd had no use for it, but he wanted his girl to have it. And Hattie, who'd nursed him in his dying. He gave her a map and charged her with seeing that Flower got her share."

"He trusted her?" Soomey could not imagine a man giving a woman such riches. This Hattie. No one was as perfect as everyone thought her.

"He didn't have much choice, but yes, he trusted her." Boss told how they'd loaded supplies and tools on Hattie's oxen and followed the creeks to the place on the old man's map. Boss and the one he called William and the Flower woman had stayed in one valley, Hattie and her man, Emmet, had taken her baby and gone over a ridge to another.

"They were gone a week, and they almost didn't get back in time. The renegades came a couple of days before they returned." Releasing Soomey, he stuffed his pipe with tobacco, even though he'd already had his night's smoke. Perhaps some things needed help in the telling. "We'd gathered oh, maybe six hundred pounds of gold nuggets, pea-sized and above. Hattie and Emmet picked up maybe half again that much."

Boss laughed. "Hell, there was so much gold in the creeks that they sparkled in the sun. So much that we didn't even bother with the fine stuff, just what we could pick up in our hands. Then the renegades showed up." He lit the pipe, took several minutes to get it going well.

Soomey heard pain in his voice, and wanted to tell him to say no more. She could not bear to hear of his being hurt. Yet she must know. "Renegades? Those are bad men?"

"Those were just about the baddest men ever lived, darlin'. Four white, two Indians. They came on us unawares. First thing we knew, they had me and William cornered. We fought them off at first, but they finally took us. And Flower."

From his tone, she knew what he must say next.

"We could close our eyes, but we couldn't close our ears." His voice was flat, filled with bitterness. "For near three days they used her, while William and I lay there, tied hand and foot. They kicked us whenever they thought of it, told us they were going to sell us to the Blackfeet.

"Slaves. And William, he'd been a slave once, already.

"We could hear the water in the creek, but they didn't give us any. They killed one of the oxen, roasted it. God! I can still smell it cooking. But I wanted water even more. We could have died of thirst, but one night it rained."

"How did you escape?"

"Emmet came." He related how Emmet had cut them free, how he had crept silently through the renegades' camp, slitting throats. "William and I finally got to where we could walk. It took a while, but we found Hattie and we took off. Emmet stayed behind, took care of two, maybe three before getting shot, and Flower killed the one who'd caught her. But one of the filthy bastards yelled before he died and all hell broke loose. Pyzen Joe and one other, they were still alive when Emmet and Flower hightailed it out of there.

"Flower caught up with us later, practically dragging Emmet. He was hurt real bad." He turned and faced north, gesturing to where the mountains rose steep and high. "We went up there, across a pass so steep that I thought we'd slide down the other side."

Soomey wanted to take him in her arms, to comfort him, for it was plain that he still felt some of the rage and fear of that time. "You were a child, then, were you not?"

"A little younger than what Buff is now," he said in a voice not quite steady.

"You were very brave, Boss." She wondered if she could have been as brave as the Flower woman had been. Surely being used by many men at one time was far worse than anything she had ever suffered. And now she understood why Boss had been so sensitive about rape. He had seen it, understood how horrible it was for a woman.

"When did you come to this Cherry Vale?" She knew that was where Buffalo had lived all his life.

"We found it on the third day, or maybe the fourth. Actually, William found it. Emmet was hurt too bad to go any farther, so we stayed. We didn't know if Emmet was going to live or not."

Boss was silent a long time, and Soomey knew he was remembering much he had not told her. Sometimes it was best to keep memories to one's self.

"I came back here after a week or so. We needed the supplies—flour, coffee, beans. None of us cared much about the gold then. But it was there, still in those heavy deerhide sacks Hattie'd made to carry it in. Forty, maybe fifty of them, about so big." He stretched his hands apart a distance equal to that from her shoulder to her fingertips. "And half that wide. All full of gold."

She had seen small pokes filled with gold dust and a few tiny nuggets. What he described was unimaginable.

"I'd only brought two oxen with me, to carry the supplies. A couple of the renegades' horses were still hanging around, so I caught them and loaded them with as much gold as they could carry. It wasn't much, because I didn't have the wherewithal to make pack saddles for them. Maybe a hundred pounds or so."

"A hundred pounds of gold!" Soomey found she could not comprehend such riches.

"I wasn't about to leave the rest layin' about, since I didn't know when I'd get back for it. So I hid it in a cave. Took me a while to find the cave, then haul it all up the hill. Then I piled as many rocks as I could over the entrance, and rolled some more down from higher up."

"And no one came back for it?"

"Emmet said he'd looked for it once when he was hereabouts, but hadn't found it. I'd meant to make a map, but never got around to it. I guess my directions weren't too clear. Or maybe he forgot exactly what I'd told him." Boss shrugged. "Hattie told me in a letter once that there wasn't anything they wanted that a cave full of gold could buy."

"But now there is?"

"Emmet's been feeling poorly the past couple of years, especially in winter. Hattie thinks if she can get him to town, where he won't work so hard and where the winters are milder, he'd feel better. And I think she wants the kids to see what the world's like. None of 'em has ever been to a real town."

"So Buffalo said. This Cherry Vale sounds like a very lonely place." She could not imagine living where there were no other people except family.

But Buffalo's family was very different from the one she'd known. Perhaps loving each other made a great difference.

"What happened to the one called Flower?" What a strange name. In Chinese it would sound natural, but in English, it sounded most peculiar.

"She took off. One of the renegades survived the landslide, and came after us. He caught the women alone. Flower killed him. Then she left."

"Truly a fierce woman. I admire her very much," Soomey said, thinking how cowardly she had been, not to do the same to Captain Slye.

Now she knew why Boss did not want her. What contempt he must have for her weakness in yielding her body and her freedom without a fight.

Chapter Eighteen

Well hell! Pulling the door shut behind him, Silas paused on the steps of Appledore's store and looked down the rutted main street of Centerville. Few miners were about, for the day was clear and almost springlike. He reckoned most everyone was working down at the creek, taking advantage of the break in the weather.

The town looked peaceful enough, although it would come to life in an hour or so, when the sun dropped behind the ridge. If tonight was like other nights, there would be a fight or two, some harsh words, and maybe even a few shots fired. Nothing to worry about. Mostly Centerville was quiet, compared to Bannock City. A good place to live and work.

For how long?

Even in Bannock City, most of the violence was the sort you expected in a gold camp. Theft and claim jumping were common. Few nights passed unbroken by gunfire. Men settled disagreements with their fists or with knives. Hot tempers and gold-hunger stripped away the trappings of civilization and brought out the barbarian in most men.

But what Hiram had told him was worse than barbarous. It was bestial.

Making up his mind, he descended to the street and strode

rapidly to his store. Soomey should still be there.

She was. He helped her count the day's till and sent Ji Rong and Tao Ni over to Appledore's with it. "Sit down," he told her, hating what he was going to have to say.

"I have only this one little thing to do," she said, making notes on a piece of paper. "We are almost out of coal oil and I must—"

"Sit!" He paused, forcing himself to lower his voice. "Sit down, Soomey. I want to talk to you before they come back."

She looked trustingly at him.

"I'm sending Buff home. He'll take as much of the gold as we can load onto Hiram's mules."

"Good," she said, nodding. "It is not safe to leave it in cave now. There are too many miners coming to this place."

"You and Tao Ni are going with him." There. He'd said it. And every word had been bitter on his tongue.

She jumped to her feet. "No."

"Day after tomorrow. I'll tell Buff tonight when we get home."

Her eyes seemed to spark in the dim light. "Did you not hear me, Boss? I say I will not go."

"I'm still your boss," he reminded her. Maybe he'd met a person more stubborn than Soomey, but he couldn't remember when. But this was one argument he had to win.

"And I am still one who was hired to watch for those who would harm you. I cannot do this if I am far away." She turned her back and began sorting through a pile of leather scraps. "Do not send me away. Please, Boss."

Was that a quaver in her voice? Silas laid his hands on her shoulders, marveling once again how so much determination and courage could reside in so slight a body. "Soomey, the feelings against your people are getting worse. There's talk in Bannock City of taxing the Chinese." With any luck, she'd listen to him, and he wouldn't have to tell her the real reason he wanted her gone.

She spun around. "All the time you Americans torment China people. Why? We do not steal from you. We work hard."

Shrugging, Silas shook his head. "Maybe that's why. Your people work harder than anyone else. Maybe it shames us." He thought of those who were most clamorous in their outcry against the Celestials. Saloon loiterers. Most of them had more calluses on their butts than they did on their hands. But because of the noise they made, they were also the most listened to.

Folks were suspicious of the Chinese anyway. Now that the belief had spread that they were all getting rich, gleaning supposedly played-out claims, they were more than ever the focus of anger and persecution.

"No one will harm me. All know you are my Boss and they respect you greatly."

"Listen to me, you little fool. Yesterday a couple of hunters found a body in the woods outside of town. A Celestial. He'd been tortured. He died slow. And hard—" Silas could not go on. Just saying the words made him sick with fear for her.

"You're going," he said, hearing the harshness in his voice. "Don't argue with me." He turned away, before he could take her into his arms and swear he'd never let her go.

"I do not wish to leave you," Soomey said again, as she tied her pack behind the saddle. She truly dreaded spending three days astride this enormous horse, but Buffalo refused to allow her to walk.

Boss handed her a gunnysack containing smaller bags of flour, cornmeal and rice. "It's just not safe for you to stay here. Ji Rong and I can handle the store, and now that I've found the cave, I don't have much else to do."

"Ji Rong cannot guard you and watch the store."

"Soomey, when are you going to figure out that I don't need a keeper? The only reason I wanted you and Tao Ni to watch who was on my back trail was in case somebody followed me while I was looking for the cave."

She tested the knot that held her bedroll and tarpaulin. "You were not looking for cave when those men ambushed us."

"They'd have ambushed anybody coming along that trail."

Soomey sighed. She would not win this argument today any more than she had won it yesterday or the day before.

It took the efforts of both Boss and Buffalo to load the bags of gold onto three mules. The animals had had little exercise this winter, and were disinclined to be put to work again. They were rangy beasts, with big yellow teeth and wicked expressions.

Soomey disliked them on sight.

At last they were ready to depart. Tao Ni was perched among bags and bundles on Boss's pack horse, while Soomey rode his big black gelding. Buffalo's mount was a pretty red mare with a red-spotted white rump. He'd told her that Indians living to the north had bred them for the color pattern.

Boss lifted Soomey into the saddle. In the brief moment she was in his arms, she wanted to cling to him, to cry that she could not leave him. "Must I go?" was all she said.

"You'll be safer up in Cherry Vale. We're just lucky that the pass is still open."

She wished it had snowed many feet. Then she could have stayed with Boss all winter. Reaching out, she touched her fingers to his cheek. "You are a good man," she said, softly, "but a very stubborn one."

He laughed. "I'm stubborn? Hell, Soomey, you could give a mule lessons." He swatted her horse's rump. "Take care of yourself. I'll see you come spring."

Soomey's horse followed Buffalo's without urging, and she held her face rigidly forward.

Silas went into the cabin, not wanting to watch them out of sight. Saying goodbye to Soomey had been just about the most painful thing he'd ever done. He'd miss them. All three of them, but Soomey most of all.

He'd lost count of the times he'd told himself it was best to get her out of here before his hunger overcame his good sense.

Every day he had found it more difficult to keep his hands off her.

Just having her in the cabin was like dangling a tender fawn in front of a hungry panther. Irresistible.

She would be safe in Cherry Vale. Feeling against the Chinese was growing in Centerville too, especially among the miners who'd been here a while. The ground had been frozen most of the last month, and the creeks were all but dry. Often unable to work, they lived on what little money they'd arrived with, or on credit from Appledore and the other merchants in the basin. Many of them spent far too much time in the saloons and gathered around the stoves in the stores, complaining, looking for someone to blame for their predicament.

He didn't want Soomey and Tao Ni to be the ones they took their frustration out upon again.

Now that Vester's saloon was open, it seemed like there was a lot more of the undesirable element in Centerville. Loiterers in city garb instead of the heavy denim and canvas clothing favored by the miners. Troublemakers like Joe DiCastro, too, men who carried handguns openly and always seemed to have plenty of gold.

And maybe a murderer.

He and Hiram Appledore had spoken together just yesterday, wondering if it wasn't time to take charge in Centerville. It was either that or let the ruffians do so. That was the single most important reason why he wanted Soomey and the boys out of town. Tonight was the town meeting Hiram had called, and Silas was afraid there'd be a ruckus.

Before he left the cabin, he made sure the hearthstones were swept clean, then dusted with ash. Last night all four of them had worked to conceal the hole in which they'd buried the rest of the gold. With any luck, it would be safe until he could take it to Cherry Vale in the spring.

He headed for town, carrying all of his knives and a pocketful of ammunition for his carbine. Trouble and Silas

Dewitt were old friends.

The farther they traveled, the more reluctant Soomey was to continue. Danger was ahead for Boss. She felt it in her belly.

They rode through the morning and the short winter afternoon, following a winding trail that clung to the steep slope above a narrow creek.

"So far down," she said once, wishing the horse would not walk so close to the edge.

"I came over a different way when I brought the cattle," Buffalo said. "This trail doesn't get so high. We're not as apt to run into snow."

Soomey shivered. "How high must we climb?"

"I don't know. Up a ways." He pointed ahead of them. "Over that ridge. We'll camp this side of it tonight, since we got such a late start."

It was almost dark when Buffalo turned from the trail. He led them through tall pines for a short distance, until they were concealed from other travelers. As soon as they had eaten, they crawled into their bedrolls for warmth. The fire died down as they talked, Buffalo telling of his childhood. Soomey listened with only half her attention. She kept thinking of Boss, alone and unguarded. Her worries were not banished by sleep, and in the morning she woke unrested and troubled.

The mules were packed and they were tying their bedrolls on the horses when she made up her mind. "This is not good," she announced. "Tao Ni, you will go with Buffalo. I must return to Boss."

"But Soomey—"

"You say he will be welcome, so I ask you to take him, Buffalo. A mining town is no place for one so young, but until now he had no other place to go."

Tao Ni came to her and clung. "I want to stay with you, Elder Sister. Do not send me away."

She loosened his hold on her waist. Tipping his face up,

she smiled. "I will come for you when the leaves appear on the willows. We will go to Portland, as we planned," she told him in Chinese. "I ask you to do this so I may be certain you are safe. Then I will be free to give all my attention to protecting Boss."

"But—"

"Please, small brother, do as I ask. Buffalo promises that his mother and father will treat you as one of their own. You will be happy there, and well-fed."

"I am happy with you."

Her heart was touched. "And I with you. But I have a debt to Boss, and it is time to pay it. We cannot leave while I owe him for our lives."

Buffalo stood waiting. "You sure you know what you're doing, Soomey?"

"I am sure that I must do this, Buffalo. Please care for Tao Ni. He is as a brother to me." Pausing, she smiled at him. "And you, as well," she added.

"Well, none of my sisters ever gave me so much grief as you have, but I reckon I'm right fond of you, too." He lifted Tao Ni to his perch on the pack horse. "I don't like this, but I know better than to argue with you. Not where Silas is concerned."

He gathered up his reins. "You got enough food to get you back?"

Soomey nodded, not trusting her voice. She really did not want to part from them.

"And you got those little guns of yours where you can get at 'em easy?"

Again she nodded. "Please do not worry, Buffalo. I will travel safely."

"I sure hope so." He tossed her into the saddle. "Tarnation! I really don't like this." With one hand holding her bridle, he stared up at her. "If anything happens to Silas, you come to us. Follow this trail up and over the ridge. Then just go along the creek on the other side, down to the river. You'll have to swim across it, but once you get there, you can find your way to our place. The trail's well worn."

"Nothing will happen to Boss," she said, wishing she was as certain as she had made herself sound. "Perhaps I will see you in the spring." Throat tight, she turned the gelding and guided him back in the direction they had come.

Centerville was like a powder-keg with a hung fuse. Silas felt the tension when he reached town close to sundown and wished he knew the source of it. Somebody was stirring things up, but who? And why?

He picked up the day's receipts from Ji Rong and deposited them in Hiram's safe. Doing so reminded him that Tilly still held his pocketbook. Next time he was over to Bannock City, he should retrieve it. He accepted Mrs. Appledore's invitation to supper, not wanting to be alone with his thoughts. All the while he kept looking over his shoulder for Soomey.

The town meeting in Appledore's store that evening was well attended. Hiram had posted handbills all over town. A young man who'd just arrived with a wagonload of ready-made pants and shirts sat in the front row, beside the one-legged hostler. The proprietors of all the boarding houses, cook tents, and sleeping quarters were present. Twenty-odd miners, most of them older men, crowded into the big room, sitting on barrels or full gunnysacks, standing against the log walls. A woman who made her living selling home baked bread from the tail of a rickety wagon was the only female there. None of the Chinese had attended.

Conspicuous by their absence were two of the saloonkeepers and the several gamblers who worked the saloons. Nor were any of the young rowdies present, those who kept the streets of Centerville ringing through each night.

Everyone agreed that the nightly brawls and public drunkenness had gotten out of hand. Law and order was needed. The woman stood up and spoke against the whorehouse that now held five girls. The men looked at each other silently.

A miner complained about the crooked games at two of the saloons. Another advocated closing them down. The crowd booed. At the end, nothing was resolved.

Billy Watson and Silas remained when everyone else departed into the cold night.

"Well, it looks like if we're gonna do anything, we've gotta do it our ownselves," Hiram observed, pouring applejack into three cups. "None of 'em wants any responsibility."

"Are you surprised?" Silas was no stranger to lawless situations.

"Well, yes, I am," Hiram answered. "Back in Ohio, when something was needed to be done, folks just naturally pitched in and did it."

Billy sipped the strong liquor. "Whoo-ee, that's good applejack, Hiram! It must'a been froze almost solid to get this strong." He sipped again, set the cup down. "Was a pack of toughs come into town, back in Tennessee when I was a boy. They tried to take over. After a day or two, my pa and all the other men got together and run 'em out."

Silas tried the applejack. God! There wasn't much apple left—just jack. It burned like pure grain alcohol. "Just like that?"

"Well, they was a few fights, and a couple of 'em took a quick trip to the Pearly Gates, but yeah, mostly it was just like that. Pretty soon them boys saw the error of their ways and rode on."

"Any of your men hurt?"

"Not too bad," Billy said. "My Pa, he took a knife in the arm, and one of the other men got creased across the arse, but that was all. Them toughs didn't realize that a boy in Tennessee learns to shoot right after he learns to walk."

"So far," Hiram pointed out, "all we've had is fights among the saloon crowd, a few crooked card games, and some watered whiskey. Maybe what it's gonna take is for somebody to get killed right out there in the street."

"It ain't going to make much difference," Vester said. "Long as we mind our manners in town, nobody's likely to give a damn what we do anywheres else."

"What about the claims? There was some talk of havin' all the miners register their claims, so's to stop claim-jumpin'."

"Hell, it ain't all that hard to git a bill of sale," Wilf said, patting the sheath holding his favorite knife. Not many of these chicken-hearted greenhorns would say no when they saw the color of raw steel.

"That's right, Vester. Wilf, he never had no trouble getting' folks to sign over their claims to him."

Wilf glared at Eli, but decided to let him be. He'd been doin' a right good job following Dewitt lately.

Trouble was, Dewitt seemed to have given up poking around the woods, like he'd maybe found what he was looking for. He'd been in his store damn near every day lately.

"Do whatever you figure you can get away with. Jest remember, if you get caught, it's your arse in the crack." Rising, Vester looked around the table. "Some of you have been ignoring my rules, and look where it's got us. If you'd done like I said, there wouldn't be any of this law and order talk."

"Aw, hell, Vester, it's wintertime. Goin' five miles down the trail before we robs anybody—that jest don't make any sense," Henry complained.

"No, it don't!"

"There's plenty of places right here in Centerville we could knock over," Wilf said, disgusted with Vester's rules and no longer caring if the saloonkeeper knew. Why the man was turnin' purely honest, now that he had a business of his own. "Dewitt's, for instance."

"Yeah, that's right," Eli said. "Why there's crates of shovels and picks jest a'sittin' along the back—"

"Shaddup, Eli," Wilf told him. He looked across the table. "I reckon you're makin' a big mistake, Vester. Seems to me it's time to show them shopkeepers who's boss in this here town.

And it ain't them."

Vester looked back at him silently for a while. To Wilf it seemed like everybody around the table was holding his breath.

"You go right ahead, Wilf. I don't reckon it's worth it to fight a battle I can't win." He glanced around the table again. "There's a sight of gold still to be taken out of this here creek, and I figure to get my share of it. That means staying around, staying alive. I seen what vigilantes can do, down in Californy. I don't aim to give Dewitt and them an excuse to start no Vigilance Committee hereabouts."

Most of the boys around the table looked mighty thoughtful for a bit. Wilf watched, not sayin' anything, while he let 'em chew on Vester's words for a minute or two. Then he shoved his chair back.

"I'll take care of Dewitt. Who's with me?"

Henry ducked his head and stared into his empty beer mug. DiCastro studied his cigarillo. The rest of them avoided lookin' at him.

Then Eli jumped to his feet. "I'm with ye, Wilf! We'll take care of him, that's for certain sure!"

"Shaddup, Eli," Wilf growled. He jerked his chin toward the door. "Let's go. We got plans to make."

To hell with the rest of 'em!

The next morning Silas sat on the log before his store, nursing an aching head. Hiram's applejack was potent, far stronger than the beer he usually drank. He should have stopped at the second cup.

It was early yet, but already he could see a lot of coming and going from the three saloons. Especially Vester's place. He chewed on his pipe, nowhere near as relaxed as he forced himself to appear. He could smell that fuse smoldering.

Ji Rong arrived for work. Silas heard him moving around inside, restocking shelves. A screech of tortured wood spoke of his opening a crate to replenish the depleted shovel stock.

If Silas had priced them half again as high, he could still have sold them.

For a few minutes he heard nothing, then Ji Rong came to the door.

"Boss," he said, "robbers have been here."

"What?" Silas laid his pipe on the ground beside him and stood.

"There is a place where one has come in and out many times," Ji Rong told him as they walked through the store. "The boxes are broken and much is missing."

Together they inspected the plundered crates. Four had been opened, all next to the back corner of the tent. It appeared as if about a quarter of the contents of each had been taken. The tent wall had been pulled free of its pegs for about four feet and the seam Soomey had restitched had been opened just enough to let someone enter.

"Get some boards and fix 'em," Silas told Ji Rong, nodding at the damaged crates. "And see if one of your relatives can fix that hole. I'll be back in a while."

He cursed under his breath. The cost of the stolen items was not high, but he had never taken kindly to being cheated or robbed.

The gap where someone had worked to enlarge the opening was well-concealed, just around the corner and out of sight of the Chinese camp. Someone walking by could have seen the intruder, but only from a short stretch of the trail, perhaps seven or eight feet in length. Silas bet himself the theft had been done in the dark, when all honest folks were at home and in bed.

When he and the boys had been busy cleaning out the cave.

He found where some of his goods had been stacked outside before being taken away. But any trace of the intruder was lost as soon as he reached the well-worn path.

Not for a minute did he believe the Celestials had robbed him.

He crossed the street to tell Hiram what had happened.

"I don't reckon you can identify what was took," Hiram said.

"No, but I'm going to keep my eyes open for shiny new shovels, and that's a fact." Silas stood for a few minutes, just looking down the street. He'd come here to Centerville—when? Five weeks ago? And found two log buildings, seven big tents, and a pole corral. Plus dozens of smaller tents, a handful of shanties, and even a few canvas shelters open to the weather.

Now there were more than two dozen finished buildings, including Vester's saloon. Hiram's bank was under construction. He should follow their example, Silas told himself. Only a fool would keep valuable trade goods in a canvas tent now that Centerville was bursting at its seams.

He started back toward his store, thinking about what kind of structure might suit him best.

Angry shouts erupted from the other end of the street. Silas turned, and saw a noisy, milling crowd of men gathering in the street near the saloons.

Hiram came out onto his stoop and shaded his eyes, looking toward the melee. "What's goin' on?"

"Damned if I know," Silas told him, "but it might be a good idea if I checked it out."

"Want me to come with you?"

The grocer was not a young man, nor was he as fast on his feet as he might be. "You stay here, back me up if I need it."

Hiram reached inside the door for his shotgun. "You want this?"

"Nope. You keep an eye out, use it if you need to." He started down the street.

The miners crowded together in a circle centered on Vester McGonigle and a young man who was getting the worst of the saloonkeeper's meaty fists. From shouted comments, Silas gathered that Vester had been accused of doctoring his whiskey.

Silas wondered where the youngster had learned to drink, if he didn't know that all saloonkeepers stretched their rotgut as far as they could. He decided not to interfere unless Vester seemed to be doing permanent damage to the lad.

As brawls always did, this one spread, until a dozen or more men were exchanging blows in the street. Silas moved back when the brawl tumbled his way. Then he was shoved from behind, bumped into the middle of the fight. He was trapped, unable to take a full stride in any direction. An elbow hit him in the gut, a booted foot trod on his.

"Watch it, Dewitt," a hoarse voice said behind him, as he was pushed hard. Silas came up against the back of a big man, who turned and swung. No stranger to brawls, Silas blocked the blow and delivered one of his own into the miner's gut. Punching right and left, he worked his way out of the heart of the fight, making good headway until a body careened into him, knocking him off balance.

He managed to stay on his feet, although he caught a wild blow to the upper arm, another to the ear, hard enough to make his head ring. With another great thrust, he broke free of the combatants, only to find himself face to face with Joe DiCastro.

The gunman nodded, unsmiling. "Dewitt."

"DiCastro," Silas acknowledged. "What started this?"

"Vester got tired of the young pup's big mouth and went to toss him out. Guess he wasn't as drunk as he looked."

"I'd be obliged if you'd help me break it up," Silas said, looking DiCastro straight in the eye. "It's gone on long enough."

"You're askin' me to help you keep the peace?"

"You seem like a likely candidate," Silas told him. "I reckon these boys will listen to you better than to me."

DiCastro stared at him for a long moment. Then he drew his guns and aimed them both to the sky. They boomed, one after another, and the crowd went immediately silent.

Silas heard the third shot at the same instant he felt a savage blow to his back. It sent him stumbling, just as another bullet tore through his thigh.

Hitting the ground, he felt caught in cold molasses. His

sleeve knife was in his hand, yet he was unable to throw it. A shotgun blasted and he tried to roll away, but he could not move.

His grip on consciousness weakened. Colors shifted about him, sometimes coalescing into figures, then flowing and merging into crimson waves of pain. With every breath he took the agony grew, and he fought to find the words, to tell the voices that they must loosen the bands that wrapped his chest until he could only gasp for each new breath.

Instead the colors grew dimmer, softer, and the voices calmed into a murmur.

When someone stabbed a red hot poker into his thigh, he woke, fighting. A face—round and red-nosed, bearded and familiar—hovered above him. "Hold still, boy, while we get that bleeding stopped," it ordered.

He tried to fight the bonds that held him, but without breath he had no strength.

The agony in his thigh peaked, then receded—ever so slowly. He almost recognized the face this time, almost understood the voices.

Then he heard a wail, and suddenly he was awake.

"You stupid Boss. I tell you stay out of trouble."

Chapter Nineteen

"You're a damn fool," Appledore told Boss. Soomey silently agreed, but had given up arguing.

"I'll do just as well up in the cabin, with Soomey to do for me," Boss said. His voice was low, hoarse. But far stronger than it had been yesterday.

"You go bending that there knee, you'll tear yourself up and never walk good again," Ollie Jones, the peg-leg hostler, said. At first Soomey had not wanted him tending Boss, until she saw that he doctored people as carefully as he did animals.

"He will not bend knee," she promised. "If he try, I tie him to bed."

The men laughed, but Soomey had never been more serious. Boss believed she could help him heal, and she was determined to do so. She did not blame him for wanting to move from Appledore's. The grocer and his wife had given him their bedroom and were sleeping in the store. She vowed never again to think unkindly of them.

Uncle Wu had given her a packet of clean spiderwebs to put on the horrible wound in Boss's thigh and packets of herbs to soak it with. Once they were in Boss's cabin, she could apply them. Surely they were far better than the black, tarry substance that the hostler had smeared on the bandage. She had far more faith in Uncle Wu's nostrums than in the hostler's, no matter how gentle his hands.

They laid Boss in the back of Appledore's wagon, with sacks of beans all around him so that he would not roll about. Soomey rode with him, doing her best to avoid watching his white face as he fought the wagon's motion. Had there been any other way of taking him to the cabin, she would have insisted on it.

"Only a little farther, Boss," she murmured, in response to a particularly lurid curse. She wished he had taken the laudanum the Appledore lady had offered, but Boss had refused. "Gives me the green and yellow godawfuls," he'd said.

Soomey wondered if they were anything like Chinese devils. She had been in their clutches once.

They turned off of the main trail onto the rough track leading to the cabin. The wagon swayed and bounced. Soomey had to grab the side to keep from being thrown on top of Boss, who had gone silent. She wanted to see if he was unconscious, but she did not dare release her hold.

At last they arrived. Appledore and Watson lifted the makeshift stretcher from the wagon and carried it into the cabin. She had spent yesterday building a cot from saplings laced together with rawhide. The men helped Boss roll from the stretcher onto the pile of blankets that covered it. He lay face down because of the terrible bruise on his back.

Again Boss cursed. Soomey saw his face was white as snow and beads of sweat stood on his forehead. After tucking a blanket around him, she touched his brow. It was cool, though filmed with sweat. Good! He had not taken a fever from the journey.

Still, he would be better for some of the medicinal tea. She laid sticks on the coals in the fireplace and swung the pot of water over them. Blowing, she made certain that the new wood caught. While she worked with the fire, the men brought in supplies.

"You're sure you can take care of him, youngster?" Appledore asked, when everything had been unloaded.

She nodded vigorously. "I take good care Boss. Have many times tended sick."

"The boy will do fine, Hiram," Boss said, his voice faint.

"I don't like leavin' him here with only a Chinese kid to take care of him," Watson said, as Appledore hesitated.

Appledore frowned, "He's bound to do as good a job as Ollie Jones. The hostler may know how to set a bone, but I sure didn't like him doctorin' that hole in Silas's leg." He stared at Soomey a long time. "You promise to let us know if you need help?"

She nodded. "Ji Rong will come each day, tell you how Boss feel."

As they walked to the wagon, Soomey heard Watson say, "Hiram, it jest don't seem decent to leave him up here alone with a heathen."

Appledore's reply was inaudible.

Boss moved on the cot, causing it to creak. "They gone?"

"Yes. And now you will do as I say." She tested the water. Still not hot enough for tea.

He reared up, only to fall face down, cursing again. At last he turned his head and she could see how his back pained him. "If only Uncle Wu had some leeches," she began.

"Nobody's putting a blood-sucking worm on my back," Boss gasped. "I don't care how bad it looks. It'll heal eventually."

"It will heal more quickly if you rest," she told him, "and your head will not hurt so."

"My head doesn't ache any more." His smile seemed like an effort, but it pleased Soomey to see it. "I reckon it's about the only thing that doesn't."

He seemed to doze then, and Soomey prepared tea—a bitter herbal brew Uncle Wu said would hasten the healing of his leg, as well as relaxing him, helping him rest. For herself she brewed a small cup of fragrant Keemun, from precious leaves that Boss had ordered from San Francisco.

She would see that he healed quickly and well, for she believed he was in great danger. As much determination as Soomey had, she knew she could not protect him if he was helpless.

How she wished Buffalo was still here! Or his father, Emmet Lachlan, surely a great warrior. Boss had once told her that Emmet had taught him knife throwing and dirty fighting. Soomey rather thought she knew what the latter entailed although she had never heard the term before.

But they were not here, so it was her obligation to protect Boss while his wounds healed.

He moved again, restlessly.

"You are in pain?"

"No more than usual," he said. "Damn, I've never had a bruise hurt so bad. It's worse than the leg."

"The wound in your leg is only a hole and it will heal. Uncle Wu said that your very bones were bruised when the bullet hit your knife."

With a quiet chuckle, Boss agreed. "That's what it feels like, all right. I oughtn't complain, though. If the knife hadn't been in the way, I reckon I'd have been breathing through the hole it made."

"You must not think it funny! You could have died!"

"Darlin' I'm all too aware of that. But I sure do hate to see the shape it's in. I liked that knife."

Soomey thought of the heavy steel blade, bent and distorted by the bullet that had hit it a glancing blow, then gone on to tear a long, shallow furrow in Boss's shoulder. He had a perfect imprint of the knife in the skin of his back, with frightful black and purple bruises from shoulder to shoulder, and down almost to his waist.

Compared to his back, the clean hole through his upper thigh was an insignificant wound. Except for its location.

Had it been three fingers' width higher, Boss would never

father children.

She cajoled him into drinking the bitter infusion of Chinese herbs, wondering what the mixture contained. The names Uncle Wu had used meant nothing to her, for she remembered none of the plants growing in her homeland.

That day and the next, Soomey did little but care for Boss and cook, tempting him with sweets and tender cuts of beef and pork. He complained about trying to eat while lying on his belly, but agreed that turning over would be worse.

Soomey had had far more disagreeable patients, but few more impatient. The second day she asked Ji Rong to request the loan of books from Appledore. When he returned from town, he carried but one tattered volume.

"Appledore had only this one," Ji Rong told them, as Soomey leafed through it. "I will bring others if he finds them."

"This'll do," Boss said. "I've read it before and wouldn't mind hearing it again."

Ji Rong left then, and Soomey laid the book aside. It looked difficult and uninteresting. But that night Boss asked her to read to him, so she picked it up and seated herself on the stump beside his bed.

"This is a strange book." She leafed through it again. "The words do not fill the pages. Such a waste of paper."

Boss chuckled. "That's called poetry, Soomey. It's like stories, only it rhymes."

"Rhymes? What is that?"

He shook his head. "The lines end in words that sound alike." He raised an eyebrow. "Like 'Soomey' and 'gloomy.'"

"That is not funny."

"No, it's not, is it? Never mind. Just read."

Shrugging, she turned back to the first page. "'In Old Colony days, in Plymouth, the land of the Pilgrims...' What is a Pilgrim, Boss? And where is this Plymouth?"

"I'll explain later. Read."

She did, for several lines. Then she said, " Boss, where are these words that sound alike?"

Boss lowered his head into his hands and lay there, still, for long moments. "Soomey, have you ever read for pure pleasure?" he said at last, his words muffled.

"Reading is to entertain. I never have pleasure from it."

"To entertain? And you don't enjoy being entertained?"

"Boss, I entertain Captain Wilkins. He liked to be read to at night, before bed. So he taught me, and I read to him." She gestured with her open hands, showing her puzzlement. "Most of it I did not understand—all about places I did not know and people who seemed to do little but fight and pray."

"And you never asked him to explain?"

She shook her head. "Oh, no. I never ask questions, except how to say a word. He would have beat me."

"Bloody bastard!"

"Captain Wilkins was a kind master, Boss. He only beat me sometimes, and never very hard. And he gave me pretty gowns. Red and green and blue. Silk. Even velvet." Once more she regretted leaving them behind, but the gold from their sale had helped pay Li Ching for her passage.

"Soomey—"

"Yes, Boss?"

He sighed. "Never mind. Just read, and save all your questions for later."

From the tone of his voice, she knew he was angry, but she had no idea why.

What an innocent she was! Silas shifted on his cot, attempting to find a position that didn't hurt. Calling a man who only beat her sometimes a good master!

Well, he supposed Wilkins had been, compared to the son of a bitch who'd first owned her. Just thinking about what she had suffered at Slye's hands sickened him. He could not imagine the twisted soul of a man who would find pleasure in harming a child.

He turned his head and watched as Soomey puttered about

the hearth, checking the cornbread she had baking, turning the Dutch oven in which a stew bubbled aromatically. She had left off the tight band she usually wore to conceal her breasts. They rose plainly under her loose blue calico shirt, high and firm.

They were small, but sweetly round—about the right size to fill the palm of his hand. He clenched his fists against the imagined sensation. Closing his eyes, he cast his mind back to the night she had tried to seduce him, all warm and delicious woman, with knowing hands and an eager mouth.

"Supper ready soon, Boss," she said, smiling over her shoulder.

Silas edged his arm under him, lifted, despite the deep ache that intensified as he moved. Slowly, carefully, he forced himself to a sitting position, swinging his legs carefully over the edge of the cot. The wound in his thigh pulled painfully, so he shifted until he could rest that foot on the stump that served them as chair, footstool, and bedside table.

He was damned tired of lying on his belly, not even able to drink without slopping on his bedclothes.

After supper and another cup of the bitter tea, she settled him for the night. For some reason the very sound of her voice added to his irritation. He closed his eyes and willed himself to sleep.

So of course he was wide awake.

He wanted to yell at her to settle down and stop keeping him awake. When she went outside, he pulled the blankets up about his head and did his best not to wait for her return. Then he listened as she poured water, moved pots, scoured the tin plates and forks, and added wood to the fire.

God! Was she never going to settle?

All was quiet for a while, until a soft rustling caught his attention. Easing the blanket down an inch or so, he opened his eyes.

Soomey stood between him and the fire, a slim figure backlit by the dancing flames. She wore not a stitch, her lithe, strong body burnished by the restless light. As she unbraided her long queue, she turned, so that he could see her breasts, crowned by dark nipples, pebbled with the cold.

Her loosened hair slid across her shoulders and clad her in a shifting, almost molten gown, reaching below her buttocks. When she bent over the bucket, letting that black silk dip into the steaming water, his hands tingled, as if it flowed over them, each glossy strand clinging for an instant, like an insubstantial kiss. Chest tight, hands clenched, he watched her as she washed and rinsed the dark mass. When at last she wrapped it in a length of linen toweling, he found that he was starved for air, as if he had been holding his breath.

For a moment she paused, turning her head in his direction. He kept his eyes barely slitted open, hoping she would not notice he was awake. He should tell her he was, but if he did she would clothe herself. No one could expect him to be that noble. She bent, dipping a cloth into the bucket at her feet.

Silas swallowed, his throat tight.

With slow, sensuous movements, Soomey washed herself. He felt as if he were watching a dance, a particularly erotic, seductive one. He felt called to join her, as she swept the damp cloth across her breasts, between her thighs. His body tightened, until he forgot the ubiquitous ache of his shoulders.

Yet he could not move, for if he did, she would take fright, like a shy doe chance met in the forest.

When she bent to wash her narrow feet, he wanted his hands to pull the cloth between her toes, to smooth it over the slim arch. The ache in his groin intensified, until be felt as if his passionate eruption was imminent. Yet he forced himself to be still, and watch.

She dried her feet, bending away from him. Silas had a momentary vision of going to her, of easing himself into that dark cleft between her buttocks, of finding the hot, wet sanctuary his body sought. Involuntarily he groaned.

She went instantly still. At last she said, in a near-whisper,

"You are awake."

"Yes."

"You have been awake long?"

"I never slept."

"Ah." She picked up her shirt and slipped into it. "I am sorry Boss, but I had not bathed for so long." Her voice trembled. "Please do not be angry."

"Damn it, Soomey! I'm not angry. This is your home too. If you want to take a bath, that's fine. Just next time tell me, and I'll go outdoors."

"I have promised not to tempt you." She pulled on her trousers.

He saw the moue of distaste she made as she did so. "Soomey, are those all the britches you have?" He'd never seen her wear anything but her black trousers, which meant that she couldn't have washed them in the two months he'd known her. God! No wonder she didn't want to put them back on.

She hesitated, then shook her head. "I have one other garment. But it...it is not something you would like."

"To hell with what I like. Go get it!"

Again the hesitation.

"Do it!"

"Yes, Boss." She went into the curtained-off corner where she slept.

In a few moments she emerged, and Silas stopped breathing entirely. "My God!"

She had removed the towel from her head and her hair flowed across her shoulders. But it was not the silken curtain that caused his chest to constrict and blood to pound in his cock.

Her 'other garment' was a red silk kimono, much like he'd seen high-priced Chinese whores wear in Canton. It clung to her every curve, made her ivory skin glow, brought out highlights like blued-steel in her long hair.

Nervously, her hands twisting at her waist, she looked up at him. "It is most unsuitable garment."

His mouth was dry, his tongue immobile. Silas swallowed several times. "It is...Soomey, you're lovely!"

Her head came up. "I am who I was one hour ago. Only the clothing is different. I am still Soomey."

"Come here." He held out his hand. "Help me sit up."

She did, stepping back as soon as he was propped against the wall behind his bed. "Does your back not hurt you?"

"Never mind my back." He gestured at the stump. "Sit."

She sat, huddled inside the curtain of hair, ruining the effect of the kimono. Now all he saw was a red and black bundle of misery.

"I didn't mean you were different. It's just that...well, hell!" Silas finally admitted that further denial was useless. "I've been doing my best to convince myself you were lying when you..."

"I do not lie to you!"

He held up a hand. "Hush!...to convince myself that you were lying when you claimed to be twenty-one. But it wasn't working, and what I saw tonight proved it never will work." He sighed. Crow had a bitter taste, that was for sure. "You're a woman, Soomey, and I know it."

"I tell you so!" Her eyes flashed in the dim light. "Many times."

"Yeah, and I denied it just as many." Silas shifted, trying and failing to find a more comfortable position. "You see, I was doing my best to deny that I wanted you. As long as I told myself you were just a kid, I had to be a gentleman."

"What does it matter? I was willing to pleasure you."

He struggled to find the words to make her understand. "Soomey, have you ever...well, have you had a...Soomey, do you enjoy making love?"

"I do not know making love. I know how to give you pleasure. It is not a thing I enjoy, but it does not distress me, if you do not try to hurt."

Clearing his throat, Silas said, "What about kissing? Do you enjoy that?"

"No. It seems most strange that having tongue poked in one's mouth should be something to enjoy."

"Doesn't it seem unfair to you that men enjoy doing that and you don't?"

Shrugging, she said, "I think it is a male thing. Women are useless creatures except for giving pleasure and bearing sons. We are not meant to take pleasure."

Silas had not wept since he was very small, but at this moment he wanted to. What a terrible thing had been done to her, wicked far beyond the sexual abuse inflicted on her. "Oh, Soomey, yes you are. You are meant to take pleasure, as well as give it."

He studied her, wondering if all that she had suffered had made it impossible for her to know sexual fulfillment. He had heard of women who hated men so thoroughly that they were frozen inside, of others who had been so abused that only other women could arouse them.

She looked back at him, her expression trusting and totally centered on him. "If this is so, will you teach me?" she said, in a breathless whisper.

Would he? Great God, even now he was hard and throbbing, almost sick from need. How could he teach her that sexual congress could be a pleasure when all he wanted to do was bury himself in her until he was drained and exhausted?

He could, because he must. He owed it to her.

"If that's what you want," he said, despite desiring her with a hunger so great he felt he could die of it. And because he was basically an honest man, Silas Dewitt added, "It will be my very great pleasure."

Chapter Twenty

Soomey loosened the sash of her kimono and removed it, shivering in the cool air. Boss was probably too sore yet to lie on his back, but she knew how to pleasure him in almost any position. She reached for the blanket that covered his legs.

He caught her hand. "What the hell do you think you're doing?"

She looked at him, surprised. "You say you will teach me to know pleasure. I will give you pleasure, and you will teach me."

He released her. "Put your robe back on," he said, his voice low and smooth as it always was when he was angry.

She did, not understanding. Biting her lip, she sat, waiting for his next words. Sometimes she wished he would beat her, for his stillness frightened her far more than if he were to rage and shout at her.

"Where'd you get that?" His voice was mild once more, as if he'd never been angry.

"My kimono?"

"You didn't have it back in Bannock City, did you?"

She shook her head, wondering if she should tell the truth. Perhaps she could tell only part of it. "When I was at Tilly's, I had much time to sew. The silk was not costly." He did not need to know that she had made the kimono in hopes that it would make him see she was old enough for him.

"Soomey, I don't give a damn how much it cost. I was just curious why you didn't buy something a little more practical. This—" He reached out and fingered the silk, "doesn't look like it's meant to keep you warm." His fingers lingered, then moved to touch her hand where it lay on her knee.

His fingers stroked gently, moving in a circle.

Soomey shivered again.

"Your skin is softer than the silk," he said, his voice lowering and becoming almost a whisper. His fingers wrapped around her hand, turned it over, and drew circles on her palms. "Yet you're not soft, are you?"

She saw his teeth flash as his smile came and went quickly.

"No, you're not soft at all, not inside, where it matters. If you were, you wouldn't be here now." Clasping her hand, he pulled, and she moved across to sit beside him on the cot.

He tilted her chin up and studied her face. "You still look so damn young," he said.

Closer and closer he leaned, his face approaching hers so very slowly. When she felt his breath on her mouth, she opened her mouth to receive his tongue, as she had been taught. Instead his lips moved against her cheek, softly, a bare whisper of touch. His beard was soft and prickly together, tickling across her face, sending tiny darts of sensation all through her.

Confused, Soomey reached out to him again, but he caught and held her hands. His mouth continued to brush her skin, eyebrows, temples, the shell of her ear. His tongue left a wet trail down her throat, below her ear, and then she felt the nip of his teeth, tiny, delicate nips that were both painful and delicious.

"Soomey?"

"Yes Boss?" That could not be her voice, breathless and weak.

"I want you to clasp your hands together and don't let go until I tell you."

"But Boss—"

He touched a finger to her lips.

"Do it," he said softly, "to please me."

She obeyed, tucking the interlaced hands between her knees, lest she forget.

Boss traced a line with his finger from her mouth across her chin and down her throat. When he came to the hollow at its base, he paused, lowered his head, and touched his lips to her pounding pulse.

He drew back then, and she saw that his brows were drawn together.

"I'm not the man I should be, for this," he said, a half-smile on his face. "Can you stand up? Between my knees? I seem to be having trouble bending."

Uncertain what he wanted, she stood. That he could move his head and arms at all was remarkable, given the bruising on his back and shoulders.

She stood as Boss traced the edges of her kimono, again sending the shivers all through her. His touch was light, so that she could almost be imagining it, yet it left a trace like a fiery brand on her skin.

His face was lit by the flickering firelight, looking fierce and strong, yet curiously gentle. Longer now than when she'd first seen him, his hair fell almost into his eyes, but even indoors it seemed to catch light and reflect it back in a golden shimmer. Although his beard was lighter, it held glints of the same metallic shade, despite the scattered threads of silver among its curls. How she wanted to touch his face, to feel the springiness of his beard, the shimmery silk of his hair between her fingers. She wanted to lay her fingers across his mouth and trace the shape of his lips, almost hidden in the beard.

And then she forgot to think, for his fingers were circling her nipples, not quite touching, tightening them to hard, throbbing points.

He nuzzled into the deep Vee of her kimono, between her breasts, his mouth wet against her, while his hands still circled and teased—but never quite touched—her nipples.

She burned wherever his fingers stroked, wherever his mouth left its moist trail. Soomey had never experienced sensations like this before, and was not certain she liked them.

But she didn't want them to go away. It was as if she was caught in a fire, melting like butter in a skillet, and it hurt! The pain came from within, from deep in her belly, yet the pain was also pleasure. She moaned.

Boss pulled back. "Did I hurt you?"

"No...yes. Oh! I do not know these feelings. It hurts, yet it does not." She unclasped her hands and spread them across her belly. "Here!" Wrapping her arms around herself, over breasts that still throbbed, she said, "And here. Oh, Boss, it feels so strange!"

His smile was strained, yet it also showed he was pleased. "I reckon I've sat up about as long as I should," he said, "much as I'd like to continue your education." Releasing her, he eased himself down onto the bed, supporting himself with one elbow so that he faced her.

Instantly she was concerned. "Where does it hurt? Lie back and I will..."

"Soomey, I'm fine. Just a little stiff and achy. And tired."

"You must sleep now. I will prepare more tea for you."

He made a face, but did not object. And when she bought the bitter infusion to him, he drank with only a small grimace. She helped him settle in for the night, and when she was done, he smiled up at her.

"Did you enjoy your lesson, darlin'?" he said.

Soomey looked back at him, not returning his smile. "I do not know," she admitted. "I must think about it."

She did not sleep at all well that night. Her body seemed to ache for something, yet she did not know what it was.

Leaning idly against a support for the overhang at the front of Vester's Saloon, Wilf watched the busy street. He'd heard there was already more than thirty wood buildings here, with more going up every day. Someone in the restaurant the other night had claimed they'd counted more than a thousand souls in Centerville just last week.

This long spell of dry weather had brought folks out to work, to shop, and to seek sport in the saloons. Many were working their claims, hauling gravel down to the creek's edge in anticipation of the spring runoff, or sinking pits to bedrock, panning as they went. Some were making upwards of fifty dollars a day, he'd heard tell.

He knew ways to make much more, and would use them.

What a fool Vester was, worrying about keeping on the good side of Dewitt and Appledore. A strong man could be the boss of this whole town, if he had half a mind to. Most of these miners had come straight off the farm. Meek little pissants who'd knuckle under to anybody stronger than them.

Vester wasn't strong anymore. He was getting old.

Wilf wasn't.

He shifted the toothpick to the other side of his mouth, watching two of the accursed Chinee walk down the street, one the cripple who kept Dewitt's store. There was more of them in the basin every day, streaming in like so many locusts to a cornfield.

That damned Dewitt! He'd brought the first two Chinee to Centerville, and more had soon followed. It was a right pity those shots hadn't been a little more on target.

A man like Dewitt, with his Chinee catamites, wasn't fit to walk the same streets with decent folks. He wondered if Dewitt did it to the two of them together, or just to the big one.

If keeping his hands off her had been nigh impossible when he'd been doing his best to convince himself she was a child, doing it now was pure hell, Silas thought, watching Soomey flit around the cabin clad in her red silk kimono.

She'd washed her black trousers early, before he woke. Now

they were hanging by the fire, almost dry. It couldn't happen too soon for him.

Without thinking, he started to turn onto his back. He made it, eventually, discovering that the ache when he put weight on his shoulders was bearable today. Now if the damn leg would heal!

Flexing his knee experimentally, he was surprised to find that his wound pulled only a little in the groin. The muscles were tight, but it was nothing like the hot spear of discomfort he'd felt the first day they'd been in the cabin.

That was two days ago? Or three? He wasn't sure. When there was nothing to tie them to, the days all seemed the same.

"You are awake? Good." Soomey poured coffee into his cup and brought it to him. "Today I wish to go to town. We have little coffee and there is no more bacon."

"Didn't you tell Ji Rong when he was up here yesterday?"

"No, for I wanted to go to Appledore's myself. Ji Rong does not know good coffee."

"Well, you're not going anywhere, so make a list for Ji Rong and we'll just go without bacon until tomorrow." He didn't want her anywhere near town until he was there to keep an eye on her. "If we run out of coffee, I'll drink your tea."

Her eyes flashed. "I wish to go to town. You cannot keep me here!"

"I can't?" Lazily he caught her wrist. "C'mere." He pulled until she had to sit on the edge of the cot or fall across him. Cupping her cheek, he rubbed his thumb back and forth across her parted lips. "What if I promise to give you more lessons? Will you stay?"

The fire in her eyes darkened to smoldering desire. "If you wish," she said, and her voice wasn't quite steady. "You are Boss."

He gave her a gentle swat across her round little bottom. "See that you remember that, next time you get a hankering to go to town."

The glare was back. "You are beast!"

"Oh, no, darlin'. I'm just a man."

"That is what I said." She turned away and went to the fireplace.

Silas chuckled, wondering if he would ever have the last word with Soomey, if they lived a hundred years. And sobered instantly, when he realized what his thought implied.

What would a lifetime with Soomey be like? Exciting, for sure. Lively, for she would never let him grow indifferent or become bored.

Difficult, if he decided to stop his wandering. He was a sociable man, not like Emmet, and he would want to live in town, not out back of beyond.

She was willing to be his concubine. She had said so, more than once. He could have a proper American wife to bear his children and do the pretty with the neighbors, while he kept Soomey in comfort—and for comfort—across town.

The thought disgusted him.

He said little when Soomey brought him his breakfast, or after. Instead he watched her as she worked, never stopping between one task and the next. She had bread rising, his shirts soaking in a tub, a tray of mushrooms drying, and beside the hearth there was a pile of darning that she worked on in between. The last he appreciated, for he was about through the heels of his socks. And a pot of something meaty simmered on the hearth.

Ji Rong came—with two more books—and went—with Soomey's shopping list. Silas leafed through a thick volume of Shakespeare and a thin one by a writer he'd never heard of. *Walden* it was called, and it looked like heavy going. He laid both aside, not being in the mood for either philosophy or drama.

He'd rather watch Soomey.

She had changed back into her black pajamas before Ji Rong arrived. They had to be just about the ugliest garments he'd ever seen. They yellowed her pure ivory skin, concealed her slim curves—thank God for that!—and gave her an anonymity that was probably for the best. But he didn't have to enjoy seeing her like this when they were alone.

He sat a while after dinner, his leg stretched out onto the stump, reading *The Tempest*. Although it was his favorite, he found little in it to please him. Yet he could think of nothing else to occupy his time.

How many more days until he could walk?

Soomey had brought in another short length of log, and she sat on it, darning by the pale afternoon light from the window. She seemed to have nothing to say, for her answers to his occasional comments were short and invited no further conversation. At last Silas had had enough. He laid the book aside, not bothering to mark his place.

"You about done with that sock?"

She looked up. "Only a little while more." Then she peered closer at him. "What is matter, Boss? Do you hurt?"

"Hell, yes, I hurt!" Shifting, he winced as the rawhide lashing on the cot squealed in protest. "But that's nothing new. It's too damn quiet in here, that's what's the matter." But it wasn't, for no amount of noise would ease the ache of a cock that had been standing at attention since his first sight of her this morning.

"I will read to you." She reached across him to pick up the Thoreau, but he caught her and tumbled her onto his lap instead.

"I've got a better idea." He slipped his hand under her shirt. As he'd figured, she wore nothing else.

She was immediately still. Silas stroked across the cool skin of her back, feeling muscle and bone under its satiny surface. Her hip nestled into his groin and he bucked gently against her.

Soomey pushed back with both hands on his chest. "You wish to have pleasure?"

It was like a bucket of cold water right in the face. "Damn it, woman! Will you stop worrying about me having 'pleasure'? When I want to fuck, I'll let you know. All right?" He all but threw her from him.

She stumbled, then caught herself. Her eyes were enormous and fear was written across her face as clearly as if the letters were painted there. Never looking away, she sank onto her knees and clasped her hands on her thighs. Lowering her head, she said, "I understand, Boss. I did not wish to displease you."

"Stand up!"

He might as well have struck her, given the way she winced. But she pulled her ugly clothing around her and curled back into her subservient crouch.

He wanted to tell her to undress, to put the red kimono on again. *Well hell!* Gentling his voice, Silas said, "Soomey? Look at me."

She shook her head, not raising it.

"Damn it woman, look at me!"

If anything she shrank even more into herself.

"Oh, for—" Hoping his leg was up to it, Silas hooked his foot around her butt and jerked her forward. As she tumbled, he caught her by the upper arms and pulled her back into his lap. She struggled, but he held her firmly, one hand at the back of her head, the other arm wrapped tightly around her waist. Her hands scrabbled and tore at him, but all he did was close his eyes. Her fingernails were damn sharp!

"Let me go!" A fist caught him in the mouth and he tasted blood. "Let me go! I am not your slave! You cannot force me to..."

Since gentleness was not going to make an impression, Silas grabbed her by the queue and pulled her head back. It stopped her long enough to let him catch both wrists in his other hand and lay his good leg over hers. She struggled a moment more, then lay quiet, glaring up at him.

"You done for a while?"

She spat.

"That wasn't ladylike, darlin'," was all he said, as he wiped his wet cheek across his shoulder.

"I am not lady!"

"No, you're a little hellion and nobody'd ever mistake that." Shifting his grip on her hair, he tipped her head. As he'd been longing to do all morning, he took her mouth in a long, leisurely kiss, sliding his tongue along her plump lower lip.

She bit him.

"That does it," he growled. "Sit!"

"No, I..."

"Sit!"

Almost instantly she was back in the servile position at his feet. He let her stay there for several minutes while he pulled his frayed temper together.

"You said I can't force you to do anything, that you're not my slave." When she didn't respond, he prompted, "Soomey? Isn't that what you said?"

"I say that," she agreed without lifting her head.

"Then I can't force you to 'pleasure' me, either, can I? And if I want you to, and you don't want to, then it's your choice, isn't it?"

"That is different thing."

"Ahuh! Suppose you tell me why."

She spread her hands. "I do not know. It just is."

"Then let me tell you what I think, darlin'. I think you've been told for so long that what you want doesn't matter that you've forgot how to fight for it. Isn't that so?"

"No, it is not. When Captain Wilkins die, I took his go..." She clapped her hands over her mouth and her eyes grew even rounder.

"Yeah," he chuckled. "I sort of figured you'd taken his gold as well as yours. You probably earned it, servicing the old reprobate for how long? Six or seven years?" He waited but she didn't answer. "Never mind. That may have been the first independent thing you ever did. And then what? You said you'd got help from a friend in 'Frisco?"

"I hide for many days, while my friend finds Li Ching. He

agreed to take me to Portland, but when we dock at Coquille River, he heard of gold rush, so that was where we went. I had no choice," she said, a plea for understanding in her eyes. "If I had not gone with him, I would have had no other one to guide me to Portland. I could not take passage on ship alone."

"No, I guess you couldn't. But what made you think you'd have any sort of life as a houseboy? And what would you have done when someone found out you were female?"

"They would not have discovered this," she said. "I wanted to be houseboy because all of them I know have easy life, days off, work indoors where it is warm." She shivered.

Silas doubted it was due to the drafts in the cabin. "And what of marriage. Children?" The way she took care of Tao Ni and had mothered Buffalo, she'd be a wonderful mother.

"I did not believe I would have children. Marriage is only one more kind of slavery."

"Only if you let it be."

"Boss, I do not like to call you liar, but you do not know Chinese marriage. Husband is master. Wife is slave. I tell you this because I know it is true. And I will not be slave again. I will die first."

"You don't have to marry a Chinese man. What about an American?"

"Bah! You see how Americans treat Chinese. We are nothing. Fit only to wash clothes or collect night soil. Or be whores." She looked him straight in the eye and her voice was steady and strong when she said. "I am not...I will not be whore!"

Silas bit back the words he wanted to speak. It was too soon. He needed time to think. Holding out his hand, he said, "No, I believe you'll never be a whore, Soomey. You're too strong a woman for that."

She rose and stood before him. "You say I have a choice. I will believe you, that you give me a choice, even though I do not believe that many men would. And so I ask you, Boss. Will you let me pleasure you? Please?"

Well hell!

As he hesitated, she went on, "And will you teach me more of how I can enjoy pleasure, too?"

He reached for her. "Ah, Soomey, you'll be the death of me yet," he said, as he lowered his mouth to hers.

"Now, the first lesson is how to kiss..."

Chapter Twenty-one

HIS MOUTH MOVED OVER HER FACE, HER THROAT, HER SHOULDERS. Soomey was quickly lost in a sensual haze. Boss did not tell her how to kiss. He showed her.

She had been touched many times, many ways, but never like this. Sometimes his mouth was wet, leaving a trail across which his breath wafted with a sudden chill. Other times it was sharp, as he nipped and nibbled between her breasts, along her hipbones, and at the tips of her fingers.

But always it was hot, setting her aflame from within, burning her wherever it touched, until a last tiny, sensible part of her mind wondered if she was not branded for life with the imprint of his lips.

Not once did he plunge his tongue into her mouth, although he many times touched her lips with its tip, often stroked it across her swollen, throbbing nipples, occasionally dipped it into her navel, sending strange, hot spasms through her.

Always he held her wrists, his long fingers like familiar manacles, but now bonds she willingly, gladly accepted.

She writhed under his touch, as with his free hand he stroked from her head to her feet, his fingers splayed across her body or wrapped loosely around an arm or leg. He spoke to her in a low, harsh tone, telling her of what he would do to her, his words sometimes sweet, sometimes crude and graphic, yet always exciting.

Telling her how she would enjoy what he did.

And Soomey believed him, for not once did Boss cause her pain, not once did he curse her or demand pleasure of her. Never did he treat her like a toy that he could break and toss aside if he chose.

"I want to taste you again. So sweet. Like raspberries and honey. I've never felt skin like yours, soft as a baby's. And you smell like flowers and snow." He buried his face between her breasts. "Oh, God, Soomey, I want to be inside you, to feel you come around me. I want to..." His voice faded as he guided her hand to his mouth and flicked his tongue against her palm.

One by one he suckled her fingers, and she felt the tug all the way to her toes. She tried to catch his beard, but he reared back and she was left grasping at the air. "Please," she gasped, not knowing what she begged for, knowing only that she must have it. Now.

"Oh, now!" she said, her voice sounding weak in her own ears, "please, Boss. Now!"

"What do you want, darlin'? Tell me."

"I want...I want...I do not know. But it hurts. Oh, it hurts, and I want you to make it stop!"

He pulled her into the shelter of his arms, holding her close against his chest. Kissing her fingertips, he said, "You don't like it?"

"No! Yes! Oh! I do not know. I have never felt this way before. It is most strange. Yet...yet it is not a bad feeling."

He nuzzled her ear, breath hot as it wafted across her skin. "But you want it to stop?"

Did she? Soomey felt as if each tiny hair on her body was standing on end. If touched they would chime like a thousand silver bells. She felt as if she was high on a mast, about to leap into the air and fly. She felt as if she could weep with heartbreak and shout for joy.

"I do not know. It is most unsettling."

Boss slid his hand slowly down, across her belly, to cup her mound. For a moment he did nothing, then one finger moved, parting her.

He touched her in a way that she had never known. His finger moved lightly, stroking as one would rub behind a cat's ears.

Heat flooded her face, spread downward across her breasts and belly. And within her something shattered, sending her soul flying into a thousand pieces.

A long time later she heard Boss say, "Is that better?" His voice was tender, yet strained.

Soomey had only enough strength to nod.

He pulled her snugly against his chest, so that she felt its movement, sensed the strong, steady beat of his heart. His beard tickled the side of her face, and she turned to bury her nose in it, breathing deeply of his distinctive odor.

His manhood was hard against her bottom. Although he did not thrust it against her as Captain Wilkins would have done, she knew her duty.

"I will give you pleasure now," she said, wondering if she had strength enough to do so.

Instead of answering, he picked up a blanket from the foot of his cot. "No," he said, and eased her from his lap. "You'll go to bed, and so will I." He held the blanket out to her.

"But—"

Laying his fingers across her lips, he silenced her. "Go to bed, darlin'. That's about all the lessons I can manage for one night."

She obeyed, looking back just before slipping into her curtained-off corner.

Boss smiled at her, his teeth flashing white in the light from the fire. "Sweet dreams, Soomey."

She dropped the curtain. Tonight she would have no nightmares.

Silas hadn't had a bout of malaria for close to three years, and he'd just about decided he'd conquered the malady. So when he woke the next morning aching and fevered, he assumed it was a result of his injuries.

"Next time you will listen to me," Soomey told him, as she laid a damp cloth across his forehead. "You try to do too much too soon."

"Damn it, Soomey," he muttered, and tried to push her hand away, "just leave me alone."

"You are so hot! It is not good." She stroked the cloth across his face and neck, pushed the blanket back and dabbed at his chest.

It felt like a block of ice rubbing on him. Instantly Silas was overwhelmed with shivers. His teeth chattered until they hurt, and his body felt as if it would shake apart.

With his last vestige of intelligence, he said, "Brown bottle, my pack. Quinine. Read label..."

He remembered the cold. More than the hidey-hole under the church porch, where wind blew through the gaping boards, but rain didn't seep in. More than being hungry, more than loneliness. He hated the cold.

He never knew how old he'd been when his ma died, how long he lived on the streets, through an icy upstate New York winter. Yet when the Pastor finally caught him, he'd fought for his freedom, for Pastor Boeck had uttered that dread word, "workhouse."

Silas was a strong boy, for all he was only eight, and he was quickly taken as a bondservant. It was the best thing that had ever happened to him. Life on the Rommel farm had been far better than he'd expected.

Karl Rommel's wife died in childbirth a few months after Silas went to work for him. There had been no time for mourning, for the baby had needed a mother. His new wife had been Hattie, little more than a child herself. She had needed a brother as much as Silas had needed a sister. She made him part of her family.

But he'd never completely forgotten what it was to be alone and without hope.

A soft touch to his cheek. "Boss. Please Boss, you must wake now."

He pushed the touch away, wanting to enjoy the comfort of being just warm enough, just cool enough. Of not hurting.

"If you do not open your eyes, I will pour cold water on your face."

Memory returned. "Damn it, Soomey, I was sleeping real well." Reluctantly Silas opened his eyes.

She sat before him, holding a dish of rice. "You are starving. I can count your ribs. It is time to wake and eat."

"Not rice."

"Rice is very good. It is easy to digest and it is not spicy or greasy."

"I want meat." He struggled to sit up, but her hand on his chest was enough to keep him horizontal.

"You are too weak for meat. The rice will strengthen you. If it sets well on your stomach, you can have some soup."

"Soup!" He put all the scorn he could into the word.

"It is meat soup," she told him. Holding a spoonful of rice before his mouth. "Very good soup. Now open."

Silas opened.

In a million years, he'd never admit that the rice tasted almost good.

Uphill from the cabin, Eli crouched at the base of a pine, cold and uncomfortable, yet watching its door real close. A little while ago he'd seen through the single window that somebody was movin' inside. Now he was watchin' to see who would come out.

Today might be just what he'd had been waitin' for. Last night he'd been in the store when Appledore told somebody that Dewitt was getting around on a crutch now. He was likely to be ridin' in to town today or tomorrow. With any luck, he'd leave the Chinee brat alone in the cabin.

There! No, it was the Chinee, heading out to the open shed where Dewitt's big bay was kept. In a few minutes, he led the saddled horse to the door of the cabin.

Yes! Here came Dewitt, hobbling pretty slow on that crutch. As he watched, the Chinee helped him mount, then scrambled up behind him.

Damn! He watched them out of sight before moving. Then he rose stiffly to his feet. "Gettin' colder," he mused aloud. "Smells like snow."

He hoped not. Wilf said he had to stay up here and watch the cabin. If it snowed he'd be powerful cold.

He slipped and slid down the steep hillside and went to the door of the cabin. Knocking, he waited, just in case there was somebody in there that he hadn't counted on.

No answer.

He pulled the latchstring and the door swung open. The window was shuttered now, and the interior of the cabin was dark. Stepping aside from the doorway, he looked around until he spied a lamp hanging by a rawhide thong from a rafter. He lit it and looked around the single large room.

There wasn't much furniture. A cot against one wall, piled with blankets, shelves mounted along another. In the corner between, a threadbare blanket hung. Eli pushed it aside. "Wal, lookee here!"

Beside the bedroll was a small, tidy stack of folded cloth—a couple of calico shirts, some yardgoods. He pawed through the stack, smiling when his fingers rasped against silk.

So! Dewitt had fancy tastes. Holding up the silken garment, he frowned. It was shameful enough that took his pleasure with boys, but dressing them up like fancy women was purely unnatural.

Refolding the kimono carefully, he put the stack back to the way it had been, near as he could remember. Nothing under the bedroll, and there warn't no other hiding places in this corner.

He was fingering through the contents of the shelves when he found the pie. Apple. He dipped a finger into the syrup on the bottom of the plate. "I swan, that's tasty!" With his knife, he cut a narrow slice and lifted it to his mouth. Carefully he spread the syrup across the pan. No need to let 'em know he'd been here.

Nothing more interesting turned up, even though he poked into every nook and cranny. He even tapped along the hearthstones, makin' certain there warn't a hole hidden under the flat rocks. He once heard of a fella put his life savings under a brick in the hearth.

Frustrated, he let himself out. He'd hoped to discover a clue to where the tall, yaller-headed kid and the other Chinee had got to. Nobody could remember seeing 'em since before Dewitt got hisself shot.

Wilf wasn't a'gonna be happy. He'd told Eli to find out where Dewitt hid all the money he made at the hardware store. Now it looked like must'a done like some of the other storekeepers and put it in that big safe of Appledore's.

With Soomey snuggled against his back, Silas could almost forget about the dull ache in his leg as they rode up the trail from town. He'd overdone it, today, but it sure felt good to be out and about. That cabin had started to feel like a prison cell.

The snow that had threatened all day had arrived, but it didn't look like much of a storm. Cold enough, though. The wind went right through his wool coat. Soomey must be about frozen. He wasn't, but he'd be glad enough to get to the cabin and put his leg up.

And he'd be glad to be where he didn't feel her body soft against his back, reminding him of delights in store.

Tarnation! Just thinking about it had him hard as an ax handle. It was the waiting that was bad. And he'd been waiting too long—way too long.

If his malaria hadn't flared up, he'd have had her by now. They both wanted it, and he'd overcome his scruples at last. But now she was determined not to allow him his 'pleasures' until she was sure he was healthy again.

The cabin appeared out of the storm and he felt a vast relief at finally being there. *Damn!* He was as tired as if he'd hauled an anchor single-handed. When Soomey helped him alight, he had a moment's wonder if he was going to make it inside. But he did, hobbling slowly, while she stabled the gelding. By the time she came in, he even had the fire built up, although he wasn't sure he'd be able to get to his feet.

"You do too much today, Boss, just like I tell you. Now you are too tired to eat, too tired to read. You will go to bed." She helped him to his feet, her slight body surprisingly strong.

"No, I—"

"Be quiet! I say you will go to bed. Now. Sit down and I will take off your boots." She guided him to the cot and practically shoved him down. She had his boots off almost before he could protest. "Foolish man. You are not yet well and you must prove how big and strong you are. Ji Rong takes good care of the store."

All the time her fingers were unbuttoning his shirt. "He wonders if you trust him." She pulled it from his arms. "Even Appledore says you are in town too soon," she continued as she pushed him onto his back and lifted his legs to the cot. "He says he and Watson can take care of rowdies, no need for you to trouble yourself." Now she was unbuttoning his pants and tugging them down over his hips. When his legs were free, she carefully lifted the flap she had cut in the leg of his long johns over the bullet hole and pulled the bandage aside.

Her fingers were cold on his leg and he flinched.

"Good. There is no redness. You have not harmed yourself. Now, sit up. I must see your back."

He obeyed, half smiling as she peeked inside his underwear

and traced the healing gouge with a gentle finger.

"It heals well. But it will leave an ugly scar." Replacing his underwear, she pushed him back down. "You stay there while I make more soup. There are carrots and turnips and potatoes." Her twisted mouth showed how poor a substitute for rice she thought potatoes were.

"Yes ma'am." He grinned when she turned quickly to look at him. "You're the boss."

"No. You are Boss, but I am your nurse, and that means you must obey me." She peeled vegetables and dropped them in the cauldron that was suspended over the fire. Then she reached for the lamp, stretching up on her tiptoes to raise its glass.

And paused, her hand around its base.

"Boss? Did you have light this morning, while I saddled?"

Silas frowned. "I don't think...no. No, Soomey, I didn't. After you closed the window, I just lay here, figuring I'd better rest up for the trip to town," he said, hating the weakness that still restricted full use of his leg.

"Then someone has been here," she said. "This morning, while you were eating, I filled the lamp until a little oil ran out, it was so full. I thought we might not be here before dark, and I wanted it to be ready." She lowered the glass, twitched the wick so that the flame burned steadily. "There is not so much oil in it now."

"Are you sure?"

Nodding, she said, "I am certain. Remember I say we need more oil? Well, that was because I put all we had in the lamp this morning. So I am sure it was full. And now, listen." She shook it gently.

Silas heard the faint gurgle that told of empty space above the oil. "Damn!" He struggled to his feet, reaching for the crutch that she had set beside the cot. "Look around. See if anything's missing." At the fireplace, he moved the big black rock that formed one corner of the narrow mantel. Reaching into the space behind it, he brought out the soft leather bag she kept her earnings in and poured its contents into his hand. "Looks like it's all here." He returned the bag to its hiding place. "And nobody's disturbed the hearth."

"One searched my belongings, Boss," came Soomey's voice from behind her curtain. "They are not as I left them."

Silas found his legs undependable. He sat back down on the cot. "You see anything else?"

She emerged and looked carefully around the cabin. "Perhaps some of these are moved," she said, lightly touching the few eating utensils lying on the shelf. "And I think perhaps there is not so much pie as before."

Silas laughed. "There's your reason, then. Someone came in here looking for food and couldn't resist your pie." It wasn't uncommon for travelers to take shelter in cabins along the trail, and no one begrudged them a bite or two of food. "Whoever was here probably lost the trail in the snow and decided to rest a while. I don't think we need to worry."

Soomey looked unconvinced. "If you say so, Boss," she said. "But I do not like it."

Neither did Silas, but there wasn't much he could do about it. There was no evidence the intruder had even looked for the gold. He forced himself to relax back onto the cot while Soomey puttered at the hearth. Once he woke from a light doze to sniff appreciatively at the rich smell of meat and vegetables permeating the cabin.

God, but he was tired! The fever had finished what his wounds had begun and he felt like he'd been dragged through a knothole backwards.

"Boss?"

He opened his eyes. "Yeah?"

"Here is soup. I will help you sit so you can eat."

Silas elbowed himself to a sitting position. "I can do it," he said, more sharply than he'd intended. "I'm not sick. Just tired."

"And foolish," he thought she murmured, but when he asked her to repeat it, she shook her head.

She left him alone after supper. Silas didn't care. He drifted in and out of sleep, often watching her through half-opened eyes, not always sure whether he was awake or sleeping. At last she put her knitting aside and extinguished the lamp. In the dim light from the fire, he watched her remove the ugly black cotton shirt and trousers, unwind her breast band. She approached and bent over him. He smelled her, jasmine and woodsmoke.

She kissed him. Lightly, softly, on the mouth.

Instantly awake, instantly aroused, Silas reached for her and tumbled her down across his chest. She struggled, but he held her firmly.

"Let me go," she cried, trying to pry his fingers from her wrist. "You are too sick to do this! You need your rest."

"I need this a hell of a lot more than rest," he growled, swallowing her protests as he delved deep with his tongue, tasting the flavors and nuances of her mouth.

Her hands stilled, then clutched at him. She clung, as Silas plundered her mouth, taking all she could give, wanting more.

He pulled her across him. "Straddle me," he commanded.

Soomey hesitated, then moved so that one leg was on either side of his hips. "I am not hurting you?"

"You are not hurting me," he assured her. He felt ridges where the wool band had been tightly wound around her torso. "Doesn't that itch?"

"It itches most fiercely," she said, rubbing her fingers along her ribs, "but it is necessary." She crossed her arms over her breasts, then smiled and lowered them. "You look at me so... so hungry, Boss. You like what you see?" Her wiggle was pure seduction.

Silas took her breasts in his hands, palming the turgid nipples. He rubbed lightly, letting his fingertips touch, his palms, the heels of his hand, but not holding, not clasping.

She shuddered and leaned into his touch. "You are...you must...oh, please!"

"Tell me what you want," he whispered hoarsely. "Tell me,

Soomey." Letting his hands barely skim her body, he traced the lines of her shoulders, along her arms, to her waist, where he clasped and marveled at how nearly he could encircle her there.

She looked at him from under lowered lashes. A smile flowered on her mouth, a sweet, tempting smile. "I want to pleasure you, Boss."

"Damn it, Soomey, I told you—"

"No. Wait!" She held up a hand. "I do not wish to pleasure you as I did the captains," she said. "I do not know the words. You must help me." She bit her lip.

"If I can."

"You must tell me the words. I want to do for you what you did for me. To pleasure you, yes, but first I want to make you burn for me, to make you wild with wanting, as you did me."

Even her words drove him close to the edge. "Darlin', you do that just by being yourself."

Her eyebrow twitched skeptically. "Perhaps. But always you know what you are doing, what you want. I wish to make you forget, as you did me. What do you call this?"

Silas pulled her down to him, covering her mouth again. When he'd drunk deeply and completely of her, he whispered, "I call it heaven. But I reckon most folks call it making love."

Chapter Twenty-two

Boss was gentle. He was fierce. He showed her sensations she never dreamed of, feelings she had not known of.

When Soomey lay exhausted across him, he touched her, just so, and she found new heights of passion. And later, when he held her against his warm body and pulled the blanket across them both, she kissed his chin and marveled again how delightful kissing could be.

He slept, at last, as worn out as she, but Soomey did not. She had much thinking to do.

Somehow it seemed disloyal to Boss to compare him to the captains, but she found herself unable to leave off doing it. Perhaps it was because so much of her life had been centered on giving men pleasure. Since the day her father sold her, she had had no other function, no other use.

A slave is whatever her master decides she will be.

She had paid little attention to the books she read to Captain Wilkins, for they were generally dry and uninteresting. But once he had brought a book to her that, he said, was very popular, even if it was written by a woman. She had begun reading, until the captain stopped her in disgust. "Nonsense. The woman's a dam' fool. Why, civilization couldn't endure without slaves!"

He grabbed her by the hair then, and forced her to look

at his smugly smiling face. "If it weren't for me, Soomey, you'd be selling yourself in some filthy whorehouse in Macao, riddled with disease. Or starving in a hovel, with a passel of slanty-eyed brats. If you weren't dead. So be grateful that you're a slave, you hear." And he had ripped the book in two and tossed it to the floor.

Soomey had nodded submissively, but his anger had spurred her thoughts. She had salvaged the book, to read more, but she had been afraid to keep it. Now all she remembered was one line: "So long as the law considers all these human beings, with beating hearts and living affections, only as so many things belonging to the master..."

Was she a thing? No, she was a person, although one of very little importance, and at the mercy of her owner. But what if she were not a slave? What would happen to her then?

When Captain Wilkins died, she made up her mind to be free.

But was she? Oh, yes, she could leave Boss if she chose, find work with a miner or a storekeeper. She could even go on to Portland in the spring, as she had planned, and become a houseboy to some rich family. No one need ever know she was woman, for all Chinese looked alike to Americans.

Or open a shop to sell fine silks. Boss had told her he would give her a dowry. With enough money, she would not have to pretend to be a man. She and Tao Ni could have a house of their own, not belong to any man.

No! A life without Boss was impossible for her to imagine.

So perhaps in a certain way, she was still a slave. To be free, she must leave her heart behind her.

He stirred then, and his arms tightened about her. Soomey snuggled closer. How different he was from the captains! He was gentle with her. Her pleasure was as important to him as his own. And he allowed her to have opinions that were not his.

She thought back to some of the arguments they had had, realizing that if she had spoken so to Captain Slye, he would have tortured her long and painfully, perhaps even killed her. And Captain Wilkins, a far kinder man, would have beaten her soundly.

Often Boss had shaken his head in exasperation, sometimes he had grown silently angry, but he had never raised a hand to her, and his occasional curses had never been directed at her.

Yet he was not an easy man. Boss was strong and stubborn, just and honest. She had seen how other men respected him. And other women.

Tilly thought highly of him. "Silas Dewitt's one of the few men in this town I'd give the time of day to," she'd said one morning when they were all at breakfast, "and I wouldn't charge him a dime."

"I thought you said never to give anything away," Mabel, the golden-haired whore, remarked as she sleepily stirred her coffee.

"There's always exceptions," Tilly said. "Dewitt's the kind of man who'll treat a whore as good as a queen. If he was down to his last dollar, he'd share it with a friend."

"There ain't a man alive that good," Mrs. Daintry, the housekeeper, protested. "They're all sinners born."

Tilly smiled. "Oh, Silas ain't no saint. In fact, I've a feeling he could be right dangerous. But he's decent, and that's a fact."

The conversation had veered to the shortcomings of some of the customers then, and Soomey had stopped listening. But she had not stopped thinking.

Her opinion of men was gradually changing, now that she had seen that not all were like those she had known. Appledore was polite to her, even kind, although she knew he disliked all Chinese and distrusted most. The dour miner for whom she and Tao Ni had worked before Boss had been cold and strange, for all he was soft spoken. He had frequently quoted from the Americans' sacred writings, prophecies of death and destruction to those who did not share his beliefs. Even the crooked man, Jenkins, seemed less menacing than Captain Slye had been. She believed he would hurt, even kill those weaker than he, if given a chance, but he had shown no desire to enslave them.

Again Boss's arm tightened and she became aware that his breathing was not that of a sleeping man. "Are you well?" He was warm, but not hot as he had been when stricken with the fever. She reached to touch the bandage on his leg.

He caught her hand and guided it to his manhood, swollen and hard. "I hurt," he said, hoarsely, "and only you can make it stop."

Soomey did her best.

The rest of that day Boss instructed her in all the ways a man could pleasure a woman. Soomey discovered in herself an insatiable hunger, satisfied only by Boss's caresses.

Yet she was not easy in her mind. Her life had taught her to expect the worst, and she did. It could not last, this happiness. Eventually Boss would tire of her.

He was a very important man, a powerful man. She had listened as he spoke of his travels in the East, of his ships and his warehouses in Singapore, Honolulu, and San Francisco. Only loyalty to his friends had brought him to the gold fields, for he was rich beyond her imagination.

Eventually he would go back to his ships and leave her behind.

With only her memories.

Silas woke to sunlight. Soomey stood in the open doorway, letting a shaft of golden light slice across the room.

"It is like springtime," she said, without turning. "Yet there is still snow." She took one step outside, then backed up. "And mud." Grimacing, she scraped her bare foot against the doorsill.

Listening, he could hear water trickling under the snow, dripping into the rainbarrel. She was right, he thought, drawing a deep breath. It was like springtime. "Let's go to town," he said, and cautiously rolled to his feet.

The aches and pains were gone, aside from a slight stiffness in his shoulders. His leg felt strong, with no soreness, although the bullet hole still itched sometimes.

Nothing like a day in bed to cure what ailed a man. Especially if he wasn't alone.

Smiling, he watched as she leaned out of the doorway, looking all around. Her hair was loose, cascading over her shoulders like liquid silk, and the red kimono clung lovingly to her slim body. When she turned to smile at him, his heart beat faster.

"Must we?" Her smile told him what she would rather do.

"We're out of bacon, coffee and beans. You may be able to live on rice, but I want something that'll stick to my ribs."

"Rice is good for you," she shot back. "Beans, bah! They take long time to cook, have little taste, and fill the belly with air." She made a little puffing noise with her lips. It was all Silas could do to keep a straight face.

He pulled his long johns on, shivering slightly in the draft. They were warm from drying before the fire, and they were clean—better than his pants. He made up his mind to see if any of Ji Rong's relatives would take in laundry. Bannock City was too far to send his wash. And Soomey had more interesting things to occupy her time.

The ride to town showed just how well recovered he was. Nevertheless, he discovered his leg wasn't up to a day's standing. Another freight shipment had come in, so Silas busied himself with correspondence, sitting at his makeshift desk while Ji Rong dealt with customers. His agent in San Francisco was trustworthy, but there were some things Silas didn't delegate.

Both Hiram and Billy Watson came by, but neither stayed long. The better weather had brought another influx of hopeful miners, and both men were busy as old maids with new gossip to spread.

Along about midafternoon, Soomey came back from her shopping expedition with two large bundles swinging from a shoulder pole. She looked like just another coolie.

His body stirred, reminding him that he knew better. "I wish I could kiss you," he said, too low for anyone to overhear.

Her smile showed that she shared his wish. "Are you ready to go home?" was all she said.

"Hell! I wish I were. But there's a mixup somewhere here and I've got to figure it out before I do. Somehow we got two dozen ladies' linen drawers instead of two dozen drawknives." He held up one of the offending articles, lace and all. "You want one?"

Soomey reached out to touch it, giggling. "I do not know drawknives, but I am certain that is not one," she said. "The lace is very fine." She drew her hand back, shook her head. "I have no need for such a garment."

"I'll send 'em over to Tilly and her girls. In the meantime, I've got to see if they made any other mistakes in this shipment. The wagon-master will carry the replacement order back tomorrow, so I've got to get it together."

"Then I will go to the cabin and prepare supper," she said. "I have bought many good things to eat, but some of them will take time to cook."

Soomey sorted her purchases and filled her pack with the ones she needed immediately. Ji Rong would tie the rest behind the gelding's saddle for Boss to take to the cabin. Before she left, Silas drew her back into the piles of crates and, making sure they could not be seen, kissed her long and well.

"For shame, Boss," she said softly. "If one saw you, he would think you very wicked, to be kissing a Chinese boy."

He kissed her again, then released her. "Hurry home," he told her. "I don't want you on the trail in the dark."

He followed her to the door and watched her until she was out of sight.

What was he going to do with her?

Waiting by the side of the trail, Eli saw the Chinee brat trudging toward him. Alone.

The Duchess of Ophir Creek

For a few minutes he watched, unable to believe he'd got so lucky. He'd figured he'd have to connive and contrive in order to get the kid alone. But here he was, comin' up the trail jest like he had a right to be here.

Eli slipped among the trees alongside the trail. Halfway up the next hill there was a good place to make his move, a narrow passage between two rocks, barely wide enough for a wagon. He ran ahead and waited.

As the Chinee approached, he stepped onto the trail. The boy came between the two rocks and saw him. "Hey, there, boy," he said, smiling. "That's quite a load you're carryin'."

The brat looked at him, eyes narrowed. He didn't stop walkin'.

"I'm headed for Placerville. We might as well go along together," he said, falling into step with the boy. "Less lonesome that way."

"I do not go to Placerville."

Eli pretended to look closer. "Hey, you're that Chinee lives with Dewitt. Don't he have a cabin up here, somewheres?"

"Somewhere, yes."

Trudging along, Eli wondered how far it was to the place he'd marked. He doubted he could keep talking much longer, unless the Chinee talked back. "Dewitt got himself a mine hereabouts? That why he built so far from town?"

"Boss is not miner. He has store." The Chinee stopped and looked suspiciously at him. "How you not know this?"

He shrugged, smiling. "I guess I figured he had a mine too. So, you're goin' up to his cabin? You live there?"

"I carry food to Boss's cabin," he said, walking even faster.

"Hold up there. No need to run away." The little bastard was practically trotting. "I'm jest bein' neighborly."

"I not your neighbor. No need to talk to you."

At last! There was the rock marker he'd piled up earlier. "I want to show you something. There." Eli pointed toward the woods. "Just a little ways in."

"I go to Boss's cabin. No time to see anything."

"Oh, but you're gonna see it, you little catamite." He drew his belt knife, pressed its tip against the Chinee's ribs. "Just step lively and I won't hurt you." He gestured uphill, where a faint game trail led into the woods. "That way."

"Boss will kill you."

"Your boss won't have a chance. I saw him, limpin' out to the outhouse the other day. He's as lame as can be, and probably weak in the bargain." He gave another poke, reminding the brat he still held the knife. "We figure to take him tomorrow, once we've done with you."

Soomey forced herself to obey him without question, though it galled her to be so passive. Perhaps by not resisting, she could lull him into complacency. But as long as the big knife was so close to her body, she must be patient.

If only her guns were in her pack, instead of at the cabin. What could bare hands do against a knife? No! She must not despair. If an opportunity came to escape, she must be ready to seize it.

Why had he taken her captive? Did he know of Boss's gold and want to trade her for it?

She hoped Boss would refuse. She was only a female, not worth much gold. Fear nibbled at her belly, like a small rodent in a granary. This man was vicious. She had sensed the evil in him from the first. Why had she not made Boss see it?

For a long time he forced her along a game trail, until Soomey was certain that even Boss would not be able to find them. Her captor muttered under his breath, as if he were repeating plans to himself. Or orders.

The faint trace led across a boulder-strewn draw. He stumbled slightly, and the knife sliced into her side. She gasped at the stinging pain.

"Shaddup. I ain't hurt you none," he snarled, pushing her so that she fell to her knees.

Before she could rise, his boot slammed into her shoulder.

"Git up!" He kicked at her again.

Soomey rolled so that the kick was a mere nudge, but before she could scramble out of his reach, he caught her pack and threw her to the ground.

"Take off that damn pack," he ordered. "Toss it over there under them bushes."

For the first time she looked into his eyes. What she saw frightened her as she had never been frightened before.

Slipping her arms from the pack's straps, Soomey tossed it, hoping that he would not make her hide it well. If Boss came looking for her, the pack would tell him she had come this way. Not for a moment did she doubt that he would come for her.

And then she was pushing it deeper into the shrubs, concealing it as best she could. If Boss followed, he must not find her. If he did, he would be captured as well. That must not happen.

The pack well hidden, she bolted, running uphill, scrambling among loose rocks and drifts of wet snow. Terror and desperation lent her strength.

He was right behind her, as quick as she, his boots rasping on the sandy soil. His curses filled her ears, making her run even faster. Dodging between two boulders, Soomey found her way blocked by a third. Frantically she scrabbled at its face, found a handhold.

He caught her by the collar, jerked her off her feet. Before she could roll away, he kicked her again. His heavy boots knocked the breath from her.

"Slippery little shit. Filthy catamite." Kick. "Slanty-eyed bastard." Kick. "Cock-suckin' heathen." A final kick caught her behind the ear. The world turned black.

She remained conscious, but she could not move. His words came to her from far away, and his face wavered before her as he bent over her.

"Worthless varmit." He picked her up and slung her across his shoulder. Hanging face down, she felt blood pounding in her head, saw the ground reel past, and then she saw nothing more, heard nothing more.

Until she opened her eyes to a peach-and-flame sunset.

She was lying on her back, her hands bound before her, feet tied together and pulled back under her buttocks, bending her knees so sharply that they ached.

Along with every other part of her body. She tried to move, and discovered that a rope went from her feet to her throat. If she struggled, she would choke herself. She lay still for a moment, then managed to roll partly to one side, so that her feet no longer bore the weight of her body.

There was no sound in the forest. She was in a hollow of some kind, lying in the folds of a foul-smelling blanket, damp and slick with mildew. On the uphill side, two falling trees had ripped away soil, leaving a deep pit fully two man-lengths high. The surfaces of the enormous root balls were covered with torn roots and crumbling dirt.

Soomey had no idea of how long she lay there, for the sky became overcast before the stars appeared. The pain in her shoulders and knees crested with her every move, until she found she dreaded the need to breathe.

It had been full dark for what felt like a long time when her captor returned. He threw another blanket across her. "Can't have you freezin' to death," he said. "Not before Wilf gets here."

He moved about the hollow for a few minutes until finally he lit a lantern. She saw that he had stretched a tarpaulin across the far end between two overhanging branches. In combination with the upended root balls, it effectively confined the lantern's light inside.

He came to her then, leaning over so that his patchy, yellowed beard was close to hers. She smelled the foulness of rotted teeth, the faint, sour odor of onions. He swept the blanket from her.

"You're a pretty little thing. I never noticed that. No wonder Dewitt decided to use you like a woman." His hand stroked along her body, lingering on her chest, feeling the thickness of the breast band, then brushed across her belly and to her crotch.

He frowned. Prodded between her legs. Eyes narrowed, he looked closely at her.

Soomey spat into his face.

He slapped her, hard. "Lay still."

A knife gleamed in his hand. Soomey felt its cold edge as he slid it under her trousers. She closed her eyes, not wanting her last sight to be his face.

And opened them again as she felt the cold air on her belly.

"So Dewitt ain't a sodomite after all," he said, holding up scraps of black cotton. He prodded her belly with the knife, making Soomey draw in her breath with a gasp. "But I'll warrant he buggers you, don't he gal? And you like it too, you little whore." Slowly he slit the legs of her trousers. He touched her only with his knife, yet Soomey felt defiled.

His knife moved to her throat. Its point bit into her, but quickly retreated. She felt a hot trickle of blood along the side of her neck at the same time as cold air moved across her chest. She hardly breathed as his knife worked under her breast band.

Almost paralyzed with fear, she swallowed the scream hovering in her throat. She did not fear rape—how could she? But her imagination drew on years of experience, showing her all the other things a man could do to her. Could she endure again?

She tasted blood and forced herself to stop biting her lip. Breathing slowly, she held herself completely still as the knife pricked and sliced across her breasts and belly. Warm blood seeped over her body. Only a little, but she knew there would be more.

Her clothing in ribbons about her, Soomey lay naked and shivering under the darkening sky. The knife blade was cold against her bare breast.

Chapter Twenty-three

SILAS STARTED UP THE TRAIL TO HIS CABIN WELL AFTER DARK. The night was overcast and there was no moon behind the clouds. He kept the gelding at a slow walk, letting it pick its own way along the rocky, uneven path.

There was no light in the cabin. He smiled. So Soomey was planning to surprise him. She had said something about an elaborate dinner. Maybe she planned to serve herself up as an appetizer.

Soomey on silk? As he unsaddled the horse, he envisioned her, pale skin gleaming in the light of one candle, sinuous strands of shining black hair defining breasts and belly. Her eyes deep and mysterious. Inviting.

And she would be sweet, sweeter than any wine he'd ever tasted, more piquant than any spice he'd carried on his ships.

He could have left off brushing the gelding down—five miles was not a strenuous ride—but instead he prolonged it, savoring the anticipation. He hadn't approached silently. She must know he was here. If he delayed long enough, maybe she'd come looking for him.

And that would be good, too.

When he had delayed nearly a quarter-hour, he decided she must be asleep. He hung the tack on the shed wall and grabbed his saddlebags. Time enough to unpack tomorrow.

Tonight he wanted Soomey.

The latchstring was out. Clever! He opened the door. "Wake up sleepyhead!"

Silence. And cold.

Stomach knotted, Silas dropped the saddlebags and fumbled to light the lantern. In its flickering glow he looked around the single room, swept the curtain still hiding her corner aside.

The cabin was empty.

"Soomey!" He stepped back to the still-open door. There was one other place she could be hiding. He stalked around the cabin and jerked open the outhouse door. As empty as the cabin.

"Soomey, damn it, where are you?" Cupping his hands around his mouth, he called again, louder.

And again. Only faint echoes answered.

He kept calling until he was hoarse. And listening.

At last he gave up and went back inside. The lamp still flickered, so he adjusted the wick. Carefully he looked around the cabin. There was no sign she had been here after this morning. No pack. No coat.

Nothing.

Silas had watched her start up the trail, unable to take his eyes from her slim figure. She had definitely left town. But had she possibly returned later?

And if so, why?

Outside again, he stared into the night. The air still held that springlike warmth Soomey had commented on this morning. Although it was so dark he could hardly see his hand before his face, he would be able to make it back to town if he must.

Or should he stay here?

She must be lying hurt along the trail. If she were badly injured, she wouldn't have been able to call for help. God knows, he could have missed seeing her in the dark.

Silas took the lantern from its hook and made sure it was

full. If he didn't find her between here and town, he'd get help to mount a search come daybreak.

Not for a moment did he believe she might have left him.

Soomey tried again to stretch far enough to reach her wrist with her teeth. She was alone, but she knew she would not be for long. Her captor was not going to let her die of cold or starvation. She knew this, for she had looked into his heart through the mad windows of his eyes.

At least he had retied her before disappearing into his crude shelter. Her position now brought bitter memories, but it allowed her to move a little.

Not enough, though. Her arms were stretched out to her sides, held just far enough apart that she could not chew the ropes that wrapped her wrists. Her ankles were each tied to a stake set in the soft ground of the hollow.

Not soft enough. She had tried many times in the night to pull them free and had failed. During her last attempt, she had thrashed violently enough to dislodge the blanket Jenkins had wrapped her in, and now she lay almost completely naked under a cloudy sky. Only one leg was still covered.

She was only a little bit cold, for the weather was mild. Like springtime, she'd told Boss. *Yesterday?*

Yesterday.

That meant today marked the Chinese New Year. She was twenty-two years old.

A very great age, she had told Buffalo. But too young an age to die.

As if her thoughts had set them off, she heard, faintly, the long crackle of a string of firecrackers exploding. Her countrymen were beginning their celebration.

Soomey could not remember a Chinese New Year celebration. She had heard of them, but in the small village where she'd been born, few households had been prosperous enough to afford fireworks. Her companions on the journey from San Francisco had told her of colorful dragons roaming the streets and great feasts that lasted all day and all night. Some of those in the labor company had carried their own store of fireworks, in anticipation of celebrations in the mining towns.

Only yesterday Ji Rong had told her of the ceremonies and feasts planned by his family. He had invited her and Boss to attend.

And with the thought of Boss, she could no longer hold her fear at bay.

Her captor had told her, in loving detail how he would kill her, slowly and painfully.

Soomey, who had not wept since she was a child, felt tears flowing across her cheeks. A great knot of sorrow grew inside her when she thought of all the happiness she and Boss might have had. She could have convinced him to keep her as a concubine, wherever he went. She would have grown old with him, this man who had taught her of love.

For many years she had seen death as something inevitable and almost inviting. Surely it would be no worse than what she had suffered at the hands of Captain Slye.

But not now! "Oh, please," she sobbed, "not yet!"

Eli heard Wilf before he saw him, a little before sunrise. The man wasn't much good at walkin' quiet-like, particularly along a trail Eli had strewn with pine cones and whatnot so he'd hear whoever come along. He waited under the tarpaulin. Let Wilf come to him for a change.

"You catch 'im?" Wilf said, once he'd scrambled down into the hollow.

Eli jerked his chin toward the Chinee. "See for yourself." He continued honing his knife, but watched from the corner of his eye.

Eli knew the minute Wilf saw the Chinee was a woman. His whole body stiffened, and he stopped in his tracks. Turned around. "He's a girl!"

"Yup."

"Goddam you, Eli. What'd you go and snatch a girl for? Now all hell's a'gonna break loose."

Standing, Eli said, "I don't see why. Nobody knows but Dewitt, and he ain't likely to tell folks."

"Nobody—that's right!" He stood looking down at her, scratching his beard. Finally he said, "You had her yet?"

Eli didn't answer.

"Dammit, Eli, I asked you a question. Did you already have her?"

"We ain't got time. I laid a trail for Dewitt. He could get here most any time now."

Wilf shed his coat and reached for his suspenders.

"I told you, we ain't got time for that nonsense. Not 'til after."

"Shaddup, Eli," Wilf said, working his britches undone. "This won't take me any time atall."

Crimson rage rose in Eli's breast like vomit. "'Shaddup, Eli!' That's all you ever say. Not 'You done a good job, Eli.' Not 'Thankee, Eli.'" His hand tightened around the hilt of his knife. "I ain't your slave, Wilf. And I ain't no shiftless fool like Henry, neither." All of a sudden he was on his feet, walking toward Wilf. "If you knew...if I was to tell you some of what I've done... well, you'd be purely amazed."

Wilf's laugh was as mocking as ever. "What've you done, Eli? Tied tin cans to dogs' tails? Set barns afire, maybe? Stole old ladies' purses?" His laughter echoed around the hollow. "Oh, yeah, you're a bad 'un, Eli. You surely are."

"I've kilt more folks than you have," Eli spat, "like that Chinee last month."

"Oh, yeah, you surely did kill him," Wilf agreed, but his tone said just the opposite. "You gutted him and cut off his privates. You even scalped him."

Eli's rage colored the whole world blood red. "I'll show you!" He screamed, and lunged forward. His knife slid into

Wilf's belly just below his ribs, slicker'n a whistle.

Wilf's eyes got real wide and his mouth worked, like they was words he wanted to say but couldn't find. One hand came up, reached out, but before it touched Eli, his arms went limp and the rest of him just folded down to the ground.

When Wilf's body slid off the knife, blood spurted, then quickly died into a trickle.

"I showed you," Eli said.

A small sound made him turn his head. The Chinee whore was watching, her eyes big and round in her face, which was so pale she looked almost like a white woman.

Eli looked down at his knife, still dripping blood. Then back at her. "You're next," he promised, savoring the thought.

Her eyes closed.

She'd uncovered herself sometime during the night, baring her shameless body to the sky. No wonder Wilf had let his lust get the better of his good sense.

He wiped the knife on his britches, then slid it into its sheath. "You thirsty?" he asked.

She turned her face away from him.

He kicked her. Not too hard. She was already covered with bruises from yesterday. "I asked you if you was thirsty?"

She nodded.

"Figured." He lifted the canteen, poured a thin stream of water into her face. If she couldn't get her mouth under it, that was her problem. "You won't need any food," he told her. "You ain't a'gonna live long enough."

He grabbed her hair and jerked her head around. "Look at me, slut! I'm talkin' to you."

Her eyes stayed closed.

"Well, you can't close your ears. So let me tell you what's to happen." His voice took on a peculiar tone, as if her were reciting something he had memorized. "Dewitt's a'gonna be along any time now."

That opened her eyes.

"No," she said. "Boss will not come after me."

Giving her head another shake for good measure, he released her hair. "He won't? I reckon he will. I left him a trail, plain as day, and he'll follow it. You mark my words."

She was a brazen piece, glaring at him when she should be cringing. The more fool she, not having the common sense to be scairt.

He grabbed her hair again, using it as a handle to twist her head far to the side, until her breath came in quick, short gasps. Cords stood out in her neck, and he could see her heart pounding under her dirty hide. "Whore. Jezebel." He shook her. "Look at you, naked and shameless!"

Releasing his hold a bit, he let her hair slide through his fingers. He'd heard something once about a woman's hair—what was it called? 'A...a glory to her.'

He'd show her glory! His knife was sharp, sharp enough to shave with. She shrank back as the cold steel touched her.

A few minutes later he eyed his work with satisfaction. Now he'd like to see Dewitt find any beauty in her.

"You'd not be bleedin' so much if you'd laid still," he told her, as he stood up and looked down at her. Tears had smeared the dirt on her face, and streaks of blood trickled between the few tufts he'd missed. "I ought to cut out your tongue, bitch. Maybe I will, pretty quick."

She didn't move, didn't open her eyes.

But he heard her thoughts, stubborn, vengeful. She'd kill him if she could.

"You ain't gettin' no chance to kill nobody, and neither's Dewitt!" He'd be along soon. 'Twas light enough for him to see the signs left for him.

Eli climbed out again and began tossing the wood he'd gathered down into the hollow. Jumping back down, he arranged it in a circle around the girl.

At last everything was ready. He went to his hiding place, settled himself to wait, anticipating the satisfaction he always felt after killin' somebody.

'Twas better'n having a woman.

Silas rode the trail twice, before admitting he was wasting his time. At first light he headed out once more. If he didn't find Soomey on the way to town this time, he'd have the whole town out looking for her.

He had to believe she was only hurt. Only lying unconscious beside the trail. The thought that she might have been taken by the same bestial creature who'd butchered the Chinese man last month was intolerable.

She was alive. She had to be!

He rode slowly, watching to both sides. Several times he stopped, dismounted, and inspected the edge of the trail. Nothing but deer tracks, boot prints, and what could have been a wolf's dung. He'd topped the low divide between Ophir Creek and Grimes Creek and was a few hundred yards down the other side when he saw the mitten.

It was only a mitten. Black wool, smaller than most men would wear, but just like a thousand others in the basin.

Except that he recognized this one. He'd seen it on Soomey's hand yesterday.

Silas picked it up, held it close to his face. It smelled of wool, but perhaps there was a faint, almost illusory scent of jasmine. He tucked it inside his coat. At least he knew she'd been here.

But where was she now?

A game trail followed the contour of the hillside, neither climbing nor descending. He walked carefully, slowly, watching for sign that human feet had trod it. But the thick forest duff showed nothing. Not until a small footprint showed itself clearly in a patch of bare, wet soil. Heartened, he strode on, moving faster now. A distant crackle caught his attention. The Chinese had already begun celebrating their New Year. Was Soomey...no. Ji Rong had asked his family. No one had seen her.

As he went deeper into the forest, the undergrowth became more dense. Finally Silas stopped trying to lead his gelding. He removed its bridle and hobbled it, but left it saddled.

He almost missed the second mitten, would have if he hadn't turned to glance back whence he'd come. Its color was all but lost against the shadowed, dark red bark of the pine. Detaching it from the stub on which it had snagged, he started to put it with its mate. Then he stopped, lifted the mitten to his nose as he had the other. As he inhaled, he glanced along the faint trace he was following.

This was too easy.

Silas did not believe in coincidence.

He faded into a dense stand of young firs, forcing himself to stand still and think, instead of hurrying blindly ahead.

An ambush. Bullets fired into an occupied tent. A lamp used when no one was home. A shot in the back. And a little boy savagely beaten and tossed aside.

Suppose they were all connected. A far more likely explanation than that they were all isolated incidents.

Damn right!

Which meant that someone—some one—was behind them all. And that someone was out to get him. Or Soomey.

Or both.

He moved farther back into to the woods, slipping between the trees with a skill learned many years ago. Game trails generally went in more or less straight lines. So he'd just see what he might turn up along that direction. And if he found nothing in a reasonable time, well, he could come back here and follow the trail into whatever trap had been set.

A clearing choked with huckleberry shrubs swallowed the trail, so Silas eased from under the trees. And almost stepped on her pack.

Silently he slipped back into the shaded woods, standing close against a tree trunk, letting only his eyeballs move. After several minutes, he decided that he'd not been seen. He dropped to his knees, crawled to the edge of the clearing. With infinite care he snagged one of the pack straps and pulled it slowly toward him.

A swift examination showed him nothing. It was still cinched shut, the thongs tied crookedly, because Soomey refused to let him teach her how to make a decent knot. Savagely he repressed the thought that he might never teach her, now.

Silas left the pack behind and went even more cautiously through the woods. As he approached a tangle of fallen trees, he slowed, looked around.

They had been giants. Two of the huge yellow pines lay together, one with the characteristic splintering from a lightning blast, the other perhaps taken down as the first fell. Their root balls rose fully twenty feet above the forest floor, their branches tangled into an impenetrable mass. Long needles still clung to the branches, although they were more brown than green.

A good hiding place.

A good trap.

Now if he were waiting for his prey to walk into his trap, where would he be? Silas crept around the perimeter of the area he thought most likely to contain a hiding place, wondering if he was wasting precious time. Thus far the only reason to suspect a trap had been Soomey's possessions. He'd seen no tracks, smelled no smoke. Heard nothing. The only sounds were shrill 'chick-a-dee-dee-dees' and the far-off popping of Chinese fireworks.

Soomey had told him she was born on the first day of the Year of the Tiger. New Year's Day in China.

Her birthday.

Just ahead of him there was a shadow where there should be light. He lowered himself to his belly and wriggled forward, slipping under low branches and inching between shrubs, pushing his carbine ahead of him. At last he was close enough to see the man who sat against a tree, his face turned in the direction Silas would have approached from, had he followed the trail. Dead branches from the fallen trees littered the ground around him. No one could approach silently.

But where was Soomey?

Easing backwards, Silas concealed himself in the ground-hugging branches of a young fir. The fellow was expecting someone. If it wasn't him, Silas wanted to see who it was. He was as certain as he could be that Soomey was somewhere nearby.

The morning became a contest of patience.

Silas won.

After about an hour, the watcher stood and moved away from his tree. Silas had to give him credit. He trod lightly, avoiding contact with branches that might scratch against his clothing. But there was no way to disguise the sound of a man relieving himself.

Taking advantage of the small noise, Silas slipped past his hiding place, deeper into the tangle of fallen branches. He worked his way along a massive trunk, thinking to use the hollow left by its displaced roots to hide in.

Almost to the edge, he paused, looking back at the watcher's hiding place. *Damn!* If he had gone about two inches farther, he would have been in plain sight. He pulled back into the maze of branches and looked around. After several moments' scrutiny, he realized he was caught. Trapped as surely as if he'd followed the trail. Any motion on his part would reveal him to the watcher.

Well hell!

He checked the knife up his left sleeve, the one concealed in his belt buckle. A quick touch reassured him that the Bowie on his right hip was in place. He'd made sure his boot knife was well sheathed before sneaking up on the watcher. So all he was missing was the well-balanced blade he'd carried down his back since Emmet had taught him to throw it, almost sixteen years ago. No great loss, since he doubted that he'd be able to throw it yet, even if it hadn't been destroyed. His shoulders were still sore.

One deep, slow breath. Another. Bowie knife in left hand,

carbine in right, Silas rolled over twice and dropped into the hollow.

For too long an instant his attention was held by the spread-eagled, naked form in the center of the hollow.

"Soomey!"

"Hold it right there, Dewitt. Move and I'll put this bullet right through her."

Silas estimated his chances of getting off the first shot. Poor to none.

"Drop 'em,"

He dropped the knife and carbine, lifted his hands to shoulder height. But he dropped the knife close enough that Soomey could reach it, if she woke.

If she could wake. Her skin was pallid where it wasn't purple with bruises. He could see no movement of her chest, no flutter of her slightly parted lips.

"Turn around."

He turned. Looked up at the rim of the hollow, where a familiar, scrawny man held a rifle aimed not at him but past him. At Soomey.

"Eli Jenkins."

"Yep." He gestured with the barrel. "Now move. Over to the side. Agin' the roots."

Silas moved, still holding his hands aloft. On his left wrist the hilt of a knife was just out of reach. If he got a chance to lower his hand...

Jenkins was good. The barrel of his rifle never wavered as he dropped into the hollow. Silas stood still, knowing what a bullet of that caliber could do to the flesh of a small woman. "What do you want?" he said, when Jenkins stood at his level. "Why?"

"Whatever it is you been lookin' for," Jenkins told him, eyes flashing, "I want it."

"What makes you think I've been looking for something?"

"Goddam it, Dewitt, I ain't a fool! You been goin' out

near every day, rangin' around the hills, pokin' in piles of rock. You was lookin' for something, and I want whatever it was you found."

Silas tried to keep his voice calm, his words non-threatening. "Well, yes, I was searching, but it wasn't for anything you might want. It was a...a cave with some family things in it. A trunk full of old clothes and books, tools, things like that."

Jenkins looked at him with narrowed eyes. "Where are they?"

"I sent them to my sister."

"Bullshit! Vester's been keepin' an eye out at the freight office and you never sent nothin' nowheres." The barrel of the rifle shifted slightly, and Silas didn't have to look toward Soomey to know where it was aimed. "I reckon I could cripple her good, was I to hit a foot from this close."

"That lad who worked in my store, he's my nephew. He took them, just before I got shot."

"Huh! I knew I should'a took care of him. And the Chinee brat, too."

"You're the one who beat Tao Ni, aren't you? Why?"

"Why not? They're foreigners, no better than dogs. It don't matter what happens to 'em." Gesturing with the barrel of his rifle, Jenkins forced Silas to back up until he was against one of the giant root balls that walled the hollow. As he followed, he kicked Silas's carbine aside.

He didn't seem to see the knife that lay half-hidden under a broken pine bough. Thank God!

With his free hand, Jenkins dug in his coat pocket and pulled out a length of cord which he tossed to the ground. "Turn around."

Silas faced the wall.

"Now, tie your feet."

"The hell I will."

"Her head? Or her belly?" Jenkins' laugh was an obscene counterpoint to the shrill birdcalls that resounded through the forest. "A shot to the belly takes a long time to kill a man. I wonder if a woman dies as hard."

Silas sat in the dirt. He picked up the cord and looped it around his ankles, pulling it tight, knowing Jenkins was watching closely.

Once Silas's feet were secured, Jenkins started moving about. His feet crunched among the dry twigs scattered over the floor of the hollow, sounds that never grew so faint to indicate he was far enough away for Silas to lunge for his carbine.

Silas took a chance on turning his head. Soomey still lay as one dead, but now he could see the slight rise and fall of her chest. She lived!

Jenkins came into view, dragging a man's body by one leg, grunting with effort.

The man had to be dead. Blood soaked his coat, far too much blood for anyone to lose and survive. His arms and legs flopped like a scarecrow's, useless and slack.

As soon as the body was positioned beside Soomey, Jenkins let the leg drop. "Lookee here, Dewitt!" he called.

Silas turned his whole body, as if he hadn't been watching. "Who is it?"

Again that crazed cackle. "A friend of your'n. But he won't bother you no more."

Looking closer, Silas recognized the man. Wilf Something-or-Other. Bully and ambusher. One of Vester's gang. The one Eli Jenkins most often seemed to be bootlicking. "Why'd you kill him?"

"He asked for it!" Jenkins kicked the body, spat on it. "Shaddup, Eli! Do this, Eli. Do that, Eli. Kiss my arse, Eli." Setting the barrel of his rifle against the dead man's belly, he fired, spraying gobbets of flesh in every direction. "He never knowed what I done, never gave a damn. But I showed him, I did. He won't never laugh at me again."

Silas had known men like Jenkins, little men who hung upon the coattails of stronger men because they craved a sense of power they would never own. Dangerous men, for they were as unpredictable as the weather. They might seem loyal, even servile for years, until something set them off. Then they erupted into madness, and woe betide whoever got in their way.

Was Jenkins beyond all reason? Silas hoped not. He said, "I never laughed at you, Eli."

Jenkins considered. At last he nodded. "No, you never did. And you made a fool of Wilf, sure as shootin'." His head bobbed, like a rooster's at the watering pan. "But they laughed. Not out loud, but I could see it in their black, slanty eyes."

He gestured toward Soomey. "I already showed one the error of his ways, and now I'm a'gonna show this'n."

His mouth dry, Silas said, "Soomey never laughed at you." There was no doubt in his mind of who had tortured and killed the Celestial whose body had been found in the woods.

"The hell she didn't. I seen her, smiling at me ever' time she saw me. Her and that little brat was always with her. They mocked me."

He stepped back under the tarpaulin, and emerged carrying a metal can.

Silas recognized it. The can contained coal oil he had introduced to the basin. It had come from his store. With extreme effort, he held himself still while Jenkins poured the pungent, volatile fluid over the piles of wood around Soomey, splattered it across her naked body.

She moved as the cold liquid touched her skin. Alive, thank God! Silas saw a gleam as her eyes opened slightly. He prayed she could see the Bowie knife.

And had the strength to use it.

Chapter Twenty-four

So cold! Soomey tried to curl herself into a tight little ball, but something held her arms and legs. Again the pungent, icy liquid splashed over her, fiercely stinging each scratch and cut.

A familiar voice spoke from somewhere nearby and she turned her head. Slowly, for she seemed weak and powerless.

Boss!

He was here! And captive, or he would have untied her, wrapped her in a warm blanket. Great sorrow washed through her. If Boss was captive too, they would both die. And she wanted him, at least, to live.

She opened her eyes wider, fought the haze of pain that seemed to grow as her hold on consciousness increased. Scarcely two body-lengths from her, Boss sat against the enormous root ball, arms wrapped around his bent knees. His pale gray eyes stared into hers with a force that made her forget the great aches in her body, the cold that seemed to consume her.

His gaze shifted from her to the ground beside her, and back again.

He was trying to tell her something. What?

Again that shift of eyes, an almost imperceptible jerk of his chin.

Soomey turned her head, twisted her body as far as she could in that direction, but all she could see on the ground were the sticks and twigs that Jenkins had piled around her.

Boss's lips formed a word.

Soomey frowned, shook her head slightly, and closed her eyes as a wave of pain turned her vision red. Far off she heard a faint popping, and remembered what day it was. When she raised her eyelids, Boss was still staring, just to her left.

His mouth formed the word again, but his beard obscured his lips, and she did not understand.

Deliberately Soomey ignored the talk between the two men. She knew Boss was trying to goad Jenkins into anger, so that he might be less vigilant. She forced herself to look carefully about her, for there was something Boss wanted her to see.

The men's voices rose and fell, Boss's angry, but controlled, Jenkins's fervent and intense. Soomey had heard that note in Captain Slye's voice more than once, just before he inflicted a particularly painful perversion upon her.

No! She was supposed to be looking for something, not thinking of the past. But what?

She tightened her body, relaxed, tightened it again. During the night she had learned that doing so lessened her shivering, made her feel warmer. After a few moments, she found she was able to shift sideways so that she could look around more, see just a little above her head.

And there it was! Almost concealed by twigs, was the horn handle of the big knife Boss usually carried at his belt. It might have well been in Centerville, for all the good it would do. She knew she could not reach it.

But she must, Soomey told herself. She knew Jenkins intended to kill Boss, too, but first he would torture him.

It was her fault Boss was in such great danger. He must have come to find her. So it was her responsibility to save him. Stretching her arm to the limit of her bonds, she tried to touch the knife.

And failed.

But he had seen her attempt! His voice grew more querulous, as if he were begging for mercy. Boss would never do that, unless he wanted Jenkins's attention solely on himself.

She twisted, not minding that her shoulder shrieked in pain. Her arm tingled, but she continued to force herself to turn, until she was lying almost on her side and her forehead was only a finger's length from the knife. There was enough play in the ropes binding her arms that she could bring her hands almost halfway to her face, so she was able to move a little from her original position.

At last she could go no farther, not matter how she stretched and twisted.

Easing herself into a less painful position, Soomey looked around her. The knife lay just about two handspans beyond her fingertips. She would never be able to reach it, tied as she was. It if were only closer. Just a little bit.

She tried again, pushing against the ground with her other hand, brushing the twigs aside so she could—

The twigs! Of course! Soomey scrabbled among them, picking up as many as she could.

One was long enough that she could reach it with her mouth. She caught it firmly between her teeth. Twisting about again, she used it, and finally, after several tries, was able to touch the knife with it.

The twig slipped across the smooth carved-horn grip. But the knife had moved.

Slowly, patiently, ignoring the voices across the hollow, she used the twig to nudge it, moving it a hair at a time, but gradually bringing it closer to her hand. Her jaws ached. Each tooth in her mouth hurt.

Closer, until at last her fingers touched the blade.

Boss gasped, loudly. Jenkins laughed, sounding like one of the gulls that used to swoop about the ships—a high-pitched, insane noise.

Was he hurting Boss? Or was Boss acting?

It did not matter. She must let nothing distract her.

A few more nudges and she could grasp the knife with just the tips of two fingers. Dropping the twig, she concentrated on pulling it even closer. And found her fingers so weak that she could not hold it.

She relaxed, closing her eyes. *Boss will die if I cannot hold the knife. My fingers are only cold. They will warm—must warm, quickly.* She flexed her fingers, opened them wide, made a fist. Again and again, until they felt loose and almost strong again. Strong enough, she hoped.

This time when she curled her fingers about the knife hilt, they clung, and she was able to lift it. She bit back a sob of relief.

Boss groaned, and Soomey clenched her eyelids shut.

Several deep breaths and she was ready. Bending her hand back as far as she could, she worked the blade of Boss's knife against the rope that held her right arm extended. Back and forth. Back and forth. Doing her best to ignore Boss's groans and gasps, Jenkins's exhortations and crazy laughter.

She had to set the knife down twice to rest her hand, but at last she felt the rope give. With a little jerk, her hand was free. And she was so tired!

But she could not rest. Glancing quickly toward the two men, she saw that Jenkins had his back to her. A big knife glittered in his hand, its tip stained darkly. Blood!

Oh, Boss, I am moving as fast as I can!

Quietly, carefully, she rolled to the side and cut the rope holding her other arm, and then squirmed around and cut the one binding her feet. Sitting up was agony, but she bit her lower lip and pushed herself upright. Experimentally she flexed her arms. Took a deep breath. Prayed to every god she had heard of.

"Boss!" She threw the knife. Clumsily. But it flew through the air and landed on the ground just to Boss's right.

She had never seen anyone move so fast.

Silas had never moved so slowly. As he reached for the

Bowie with his right hand, he brought the left up and threw the small knife from his sleeve. "Run, Soomey! Get out of here!" He bent to slash through the rope around his ankles.

Jenkins squalled. Silas's thrown blade quivered in his shoulder. Jenkins pulled his own belt knife and stabbed at Silas, narrowly missing as Silas rolled to the side. Silas kicked out, catching Jenkins on the thigh, knocking him back. The man was strong for all his scrawniness though, and kept his balance. He drew Silas's knife from his shoulder and threw it. It narrowly missed, struck a stone, went skittering across the floor of the hollow.

Silas lurched to his feet, at the cost of a shallow cut across his biceps. Added to the others Jenkins had already inflicted—cuts Silas had willingly suffered in order to keep the man's attention from Soomey—Silas knew his effective fighting time was limited.

He parried another attack from Jenkins, circling, hoping to get to the middle of the clearing so he'd have more maneuvering room.

Jenkins was on him like burrs on a horse's tail, stabbing, feinting, taunting. "You ain't got a chance, Dewitt. You're bleeding like a stuck pig. Won't be long before you're too weak to lift that big knife." Jenkins reached behind his back and pulled another knife, this one long and slim.

The bastard was an accomplished knife-fighter!

Silas feinted, slicing at Jenkins's knife hand, while snatching a heavy branch from the pile around Soomey.

A movement beyond Jenkins caught Silas's eye, and in that instant of inattention he felt the fire of a long cut across his belly. He slammed the branch against Jenkins's wrist, but the man kept his grip on the dagger. His retreat, however, gave Silas time to drop the branch and draw his poniard from his boot. It was a slim, triangular blade that had saved his life more than once.

Jenkins's eyes narrowed when he saw the poniard. He

retreated slightly. They circled each other for long moments, neither attacking, each testing the other's defenses with feints and short, quick advances. There was no sound except for the scuff of their boots in the dirt and their breathing.

"Say your prayers, Jenkins," Silas taunted softly, knowing he had one chance before blood loss weakened him beyond saving. He attacked, slashing and stabbing, dodging, feinting, moving as fast as he ever had.

Jenkins fell back before the onslaught.

Silas prayed that his strength would last long enough. He drew blood once, twice. His knife bit deep, lodged for an instant between muscle and bone.

Jenkins's dagger dropped from a limp hand. But as Silas stabbed at his belly, his big knife caught Silas's and knocked it aside. "Do your own prayin', Dewitt," Jenkins panted. "There's many what figured to best me with a knife, but ain't none of 'em alive to crow about it." He struck, the tip of his blade leaving another shallow cut, this one across the knuckles of Silas's left hand. "You ain't a'gonna last too long, bleedin' like you are." A new attack, Jenkins's single knife blurring in a flurry of slashes.

Silas was hard put to defend against it, for he was tiring. It must be soon. God! Would Jenkins never tire? Never make a mistake? Silas had fought many times, occasionally against two or more opponents, but he had never encountered anyone with Jenkins's skill or strength.

He circled again, deliberately putting his own back against the wall. If he could only draw Jenkins a little closer...just a foot...closer...closer...

Again Jenkins attacked, but this time Silas was prepared. He spun aside, extending his arm as he did. The blade of his Bowie slid across Jenkins's ribs, cutting through heavy wool coat, shirt, and underwear, to leave a deep, bleeding gash in pale skin.

Not without cost, for the back of Jenkins's blade struck Silas's right arm at the elbow, numbing his forearm, taking strength from his hand. Deliberately he dropped the Bowie and attacked again, this time with the poniard. Its three edges were sharp, but not so sharp as its wickedly tapering point. As Jenkins drew back his arm for another savage slice, Silas sank the poniard into his belly, forcing it upward with all his strength.

Even so Jenkins fought him, inflicting yet another cut as Silas struggled to hold him on the point of the poniard. Blood washed across his hand. Weakening, Silas withdrew his blade and shoved Jenkins away from him, almost falling himself.

Incredibly the man stayed on his feet. But as he staggered toward Silas once more, Soomey appeared behind him, a stout branch in her hand. She swung wildly, connecting with Jenkins's shoulders.

He swayed. Tottered. And fell.

Before Silas could move, she struck Jenkins again, this time across the back of his head. The sound was like a melon cracking.

Jenkins twitched, then seemed to collapse, his lanky body shrinking and diminishing into the ground. One last breath rasped from his mouth, and he was still.

Silas looked at Soomey across the body. She was naked, covered with bruises, crusted with blood from a hundred cuts. For the first time, he realized that she was all but bald, with short tufts of hair sticking up from a scalp smeared with dirt and fresh scabs. "My god, Soomey—"

As he stepped across Jenkins toward her, she reached out to him. "I am sorry, Boss. I tried. I tri..." She swayed, then fell, bonelessly, into a heap at his feet.

Silas knelt and gathered her to him. She was so small and so frail. So cold. "Soomey. Darlin'." He tried to lift her, but he was too weak. He laid her across his knees while he slid out of his bloody, slashed coat and wrapped it around her. Then he pulled her to him and held her, rocking, murmuring. "You were wonderful, darlin'. You saved us both. I was about at the end of my rope. I don't think I could have gone for him again. If you hadn't stopped him, we'd both be dead." He crooned to her until he felt her rouse and press herself closer to him.

The sound of distant fireworks intruded on his consciousness again. The Chinese were having themselves some celebration.

He didn't blame them. He felt like celebrating himself.

"You are hurt," she said, finally. "Are you in great pain?"

He laughed. It hurt, but damn! He felt so good that they were both alive that he had to laugh. "Darlin', I hurt like hell, but likely not near as bad as you do."

Soomey bandaged his deepest cuts, using strips from the tail of his ruined shirt. "I will do better when we go home, but now this will keep your blood from flowing."

Silas still had little feeling in his left hand, but he could wiggle his fingers, and that was all that mattered. They sat in the middle of the hollow for a long time, cuddled together. Until she stopped shivering and he felt strong enough to stand again. "You'll have to get off me, Soomey. I don't think I can lift us both."

She scrambled off and did her best to help him up. Silas cursed under his breath, knowing the weakness was a residue from his earlier wounds and the bout of malaria, as well as the blood loss today. "I could probably lick a pair of three-day old kittens, but not much else." He accepted a pull from her as they struggled out of the hollow.

They paused on the rim and looked back. Jenkins's body lay nearly in the center, a shrunken, black form surrounded by scattered twigs and branches. Beside him lay what was left of Wilf. "We should have looked in their pockets," Silas said. "They may have people somewhere who should be told."

"We will tell Appledore. He can send someone. You come now." She took his hand and pulled him away.

Silas followed willingly, ashamed that getting himself through the woods was stretching his strength to the limit. He wished he could carry her, for her feet were bare and the ground must be cold. His ragged coat couldn't possibly be doing her much good, either.

The gelding was contentedly cropping the tips of huckleberry branches when they reached the clearing. Soomey removed its hobbles when Silas found he could not bend over without the world going red.

Neither could he mount, after arguing with Soomey about who needed most to ride. He won the argument and she pulled herself into the saddle. But she won the next, for the blanket Silas had tied behind the saddle was wrapped around him as he trudged up the trail, holding to the saddlehorn.

At the cabin, they got the gelding unsaddled and that was all. Enough grain remained in its feed bucket to last a while and there was water, too, Silas noted with relief. He went to the cabin, hoping Soomey had been able to light a fire.

She had not. She sat on the hearth, huddled into her blanket, her silk kimono draped over her bent head. Even from the doorway, he could see her shiver.

Silas lifted her, finding the strength somewhere within. He set her on the cot and wrapped her in the second blanket. Then he knelt before the fireplace and fed slivers of pitchy pine to the few embers that remained from last night, blowing gently to encourage them. There was water in the bucket, enough for tea, and he set it to heating.

When at last the fire burned well, he fetched Soomey. Holding her tightly against him, he waited, hoping she would absorb heat from him as well as from the fire.

Soomey woke snuggled against Boss before the fire. She was still cold, but not the bone shaking, belly-deep cold that had wracked her on the ride back to the cabin. Her small pan was full of water, boiling merrily. Carefully she eased out of Boss's arms. She must wake him, for he had many cuts that needed washing and bandaging, but first she would prepare the tea.

Her red kimono lay on the floor beside Boss. Soomey reached up and touched her head, felt the tufts of hair and the rough scabs. Her skin was raw, where Jenkins's knife had scraped it, and sore. She went into her corner and pawed through her few possessions. Yes! There was a scrap of black cloth that she had been planning to use to mend the knees of her trousers. She folded it and wrapped it around her head. Her mirror lay on a small shelf and she reached for it, then pulled her hand back.

No. She was hideous. It would do no good to see herself.

When the tea was steeped, she woke Boss. He grimaced as he pushed himself upright, but said nothing. She watched him from the corners of her eyes as she sipped, wondering how he would tell her to go. And when.

No man had use for an ugly woman, not even if she gave him great pleasure. Her face would be scarred, she was sure, for she had felt the skin over her cheekbone split when Jenkins kicked her. And perhaps some of her hair would not grow back, where he had cut deep and taken skin with hair.

Boss reached across to her and touched her face, just under the cut on her cheek. His fingers were gentle, drifting across the bruise, so lightly that they caused no pain.

"I'm sorry, Soomey. Sorrier than I can say."

She stared. "You are sorry? Why? You did nothing bad?"

"Nothing bad? My God! I let you go off alone. Let that devil take you. Torture you." He set his cup down beside him and covered his face with both hands. "I'll never forgive myself for what he did to you."

"You did nothing to hurt me, Boss. I was stupid. My guns were not in the pack, where I— My pack! Where is it?"

"To hell with your pack. I want you to tell me what he did to you. Did he...hell, did he rape you?"

"No Boss, he did not. I do not think he could have, even if he had wanted to." She shook her head, remembering how she had felt a vast, cold emptiness when Eli Jenkins had looked at her naked body. There had been no desire. Nothing. "I do not believe he was a man, not like most men."

"Thank God! At least you were spared that."

Soomey stared at him for a long time. Again he held his

cup, but without drinking, as if he needed something to cling to. She did not understand him, but she met his gaze unflinchingly, waiting. No matter how she loved Boss, she would not let him see the hurt he would do to her.

She would go when he said, without a backward glance. She owed him that.

Chapter Twenty-five

THREE CUPS OF VERY HOT TEA, A LONG TIME BEFORE THE FIRE, and Soomey no longer shivered. But inside, where no fire could reach, she was still very cold. As she washed Boss's many cuts and scratches, she treasured each touch of her fingers on his warm skin. Soon, tomorrow or the day after that, she would never see him again.

She could not believe that most of his wounds were little more than scratches. Watching the fight, she had been certain he would be killed, or severely maimed. The only cut that worried her was the one on his forearm. It seemed to have missed anything important, but still it took almost a hundred of her neat stitches to sew it shut.

Carefully she fitted two almost-flat sticks she'd cut from a piece of firewood on either side of his elbow, holding it straight. "You must wear this for at least ten days," she told him, binding it.

"Hell, Soomey, I won't be able to do a damned thing."

"You want your arm to fall off? I tell you Boss, you will keep it straight for ten days or it will heal badly."

"Nothing's going to fall off," he said. "You just don't want your fancywork to get messed up."

"Ah. You must be right," she agreed, as she tied the

wrappings and tucked the ends in. "I would be ashamed for people to say, 'Look at that terrible scar. Whoever sewed him back together must have been a very bad doctor.'"

Boss caught her hand before she could pull away from him. "Your turn now."

"My turn?"

"You doctored me. Now I'll doctor you."

She tugged, trying to pull free. "I can do this for myself."

"I will do it."

As always, when Boss spoke in that very quiet voice, she dared not defy him. She sat. "I told you, I am not badly hurt. You do not need to do this."

"Be still."

Biting her lip, she said no more. But she cringed as Boss unwrapped the kimono from her body. She had put it on in place of his coat when her shivers stopped, but now the loss of its insignificant protection made them start again.

His hands were gentle as they washed her. The many scratches and shallow cuts on her breasts and belly stung from the soap, but only a little.

"You looked cut up worse than you were. I just wish there was something I could do about those bruises."

So did she, although she would never admit that every movement was a painful effort.

He poured fresh water into the basin. "Now your face."

"No. Please. I can—"

He pointed at the stump. "Soomey, sit down. Be silent."

Soomey closed her eyes, not wanting to see his disgust as he washed her face. Blood and dirt had concealed the worst damage.

"Your lip's split, there," he said, dabbing gently. "But I don't think there'll be a scar. And those scratches—unless they turn putrid, they shouldn't show in a week or so. But this..." His fingers touched the cut across her cheekbone. "My God, Soomey! He only missed your eye by a hair. He could have blinded you!"

He touched her lightly again, his fingers tracing from her nose to her ear. "There's going to be a scar."

Miserably, she nodded.

"Darlin', do you trust me?"

Her eyes flew open. "Of course I trust you. You are Boss."

"Then go get that bottle of whiskey from the cupboard."

Did all men drink whiskey when shaken? "Boss, maybe more tea would be better."

"Never mind. I'll get it." He stood, and she did too. "Oh, no you don't. Sit."

He was back in an instant, pouring whiskey into a tin cup. He held it under her nose. "Drink up."

The fumes stung. "I do not drink whiskey."

"Yes, you do." The cup's brim nudged her lower lip. "Slowly. That's right. A little more, now."

Soomey pulled back against his hand. "Enough. It has a very bad taste." But she was aware of a warmth in her belly, fighting the coldness.

"Some people like it. Now, finish it all."

"No. I will not."

"You will, Soomey, if I have to hog-tie you and pour it down your throat. Drink!"

She drank, grimacing, in tiny sips. But under Boss's commanding gaze, she drank it all. "It does not taste so bad now," she said as she finished it. "And it has made me very warm inside." She heard herself giggle. "My nose— I cannot feel it." Opening her eyes, she tried to see if she still had a nose, but she became very dizzy. "Boss!" She groped for him, found his hand. It made her feel secure, as if she would not, after all, fly up to the ceiling.

Boss poured a little more whiskey into her cup. "You sit there and drink that while I get everything ready, O.K.?"

"Do not leave me!" Had that been her voice, that high, needy sound?

"I'm not going anywhere outside this cabin. You just sit here by the fire, and in a few minutes I'll be back."

She sat, sipping the now-delicious whiskey, conscious of Boss moving about the room. She saw him pour more water into her small pot and hang it over the fire, spread blankets on the floor, set the lantern beside them. Then he lit several candles and set them on the floor as well. "You are building an altar," she observed. "But where is the incense?"

"You'll see." He looked in the pot. "You got any more of that black thread?"

"Thread? What you need thread for? I will mend your clothes."

"Do you have any?" Again his voice held that quiet tone that must be obeyed.

"Yes. I will get it for you." But her legs were curiously weak, and she did not seem to have any feet.

"I'll get it. Where?"

With a great effort, Soomey remembered where it was. She told him. Then she closed her eyes again, for the room seemed to want to spin when they were open.

A long time later, Boss lifted her from the stump and laid her on the floor. Soomey did not care, for she was floating in the most delicious dream. "I believed that there were no good men," she told him as she patted his cheek. "But you are good man, Boss. I love you very much."

"Tell me that again in a few minutes," he said. "Now, I'm asking you again, Soomey. Do you trust me?"

"Boss, I tell you I love you. Is that not trust?"

He leaned close. "Soomey, listen to me. I'm going to sew up your cheek, and I can't have you thrashing about." Then he caught her wrist and looped rope around it.

Soomey fought, but her struggles were weak and ineffectual. She screamed, but no one heard. Her other arm was caught and held, just as Jenkins had tied her. Now she would surely die.

"Stop fighting!" He caught her chin, held it so she had to

look at him. "I knew you'd never let me tie you, so I had to take you unawares. Do you understand?"

"Let me go!"

"I will, but not yet."

"Please, Boss. Let me go. I will be good. I will give you many pleasures. I will work for you for no money. I will never feed you rice again. Anything. But please, let me go! Please. Please."

"Damn!" Silas hadn't realized how she'd react to being tied. Maybe he should have warned her before he did it, but it was too late now. Well, no help for it—she'd never be able to lie still while he sewed her up. And that cut on her cheek had been untended too long already.

He just wished he could have done this before she stitched his arm. Even without the splint, his elbow was stiff and hard to bend. *She'll kill me if I pull those stitches loose,* he thought, as he pulled the pot of hot water away from the fire. Then laughed. He'd cut the arm off himself, if doing so would save her pain.

"Soomey, I'm going to hurt you now, hurt you a lot. Do you want more whiskey?"

She didn't answer, didn't move.

Hating what he must do, Silas straddled her and washed her face again, sponging whiskey along the edges of the cut, but not into it.

He took a deep breath and reached for the needle and thread.

Through it all she never moved. If it hadn't been for her breath whistling between clenched teeth a couple of times, he'd have thought her unconscious.

His stitches weren't as neat as hers, Silas thought much later, as he untied the ropes on her wrists, but they held the edges of the gaping wound together. If they didn't pull out. If the cobwebs he'd pulled from the ceiling worked as Hattie had taught him they would. If...if..."Let her be all right," he said to the empty room. "Please, let her be all right."

As if in answer, another distant string of pops sounded.

"Now for your head." He removed the cloth she'd covered herself with. It was stuck to some of the oozing patches. Gently Silas worked it loose, wetting it with warm water when needed. As he washed her scalp, he cursed Jenkins once again.

Fortunately, he saw, most of the damage was superficial. A shaven head didn't compare to what Jenkins could have done to her. Tenderly he dried her head, then wrapped it again in one of his clean handkerchiefs. She had worried more about her baldness than her nakedness, he'd noticed.

Exhausted, he left everything as it lay. Easing himself down beside her and pulling the blanket over both of them, he sighed. If she hurt anywhere near as much as he did, she'd be grateful for the whiskey. Briefly he considered taking some himself, then decided against it. A hangover on top of everything else would be just too much.

Silas was worried. It had been two days now, since they'd escaped from Jenkins, and Soomey still lay listlessly in the cot, never speaking, only moving when nature called. He had coaxed her to take a little tea, and even a few mouthfuls of rice, but she was visibly failing. Her cheeks were sunken, her hands looked like pathetic little bird claws, and her eyes were enormous black smudges in a white face.

The cut on her cheek was healing cleanly, though, and for that he was thankful. The cobwebs must be the secret, for several of his own wounds were inflamed and ugly. He had taken a look at the deep cut on his arm, and it, at least, was healing well.

"I'm going to town," he told her, standing over her. "Will you be all right?"

She stared at him, unblinking.

"Soomey. Did you hear me?"

Her chin dipped slightly.

"Will you be all right."

Another dip.

"I'll be back as soon as I can. There's water here, and tea. And some broth. Will you try to drink them all?"

No response.

He knelt. "Damn it, woman, will you drink the water."

The chin moved again, but her eyelids drooped shut.

Silas slid his splinted arm behind her head and lifted. He picked up the tin cup of broth and held it to her lips. "Drink!"

She did, tiny sips, her throat moving convulsively as she swallowed. When the cup was empty, he let her lie back down.

"I'll be back as soon as I can," he said. "Don't leave the cabin." He waited for her response.

"Soomey. I told you to stay in the cabin. I want your word you will."

"I will." The words were as a breath of wind.

"And you'll drink the tea and the water."

"Yes."

Not once did her eyes open.

Soomey watched him go. Had she any strength at all, she would not be here when he returned. But she had none. It was as if her will had been cut away along with her hair. She knew she must leave him, must free him from any sense of obligation he felt toward her.

Boss had thought her unconscious when he had sewed her cheek. Afterward he had crooned to her, as one would to a babe. He had held her close, and had soothed her with his words and with tender kisses and touches.

With promises.

Promises that he must not be allowed to keep, for they had been made in a moment of great strain, of great exhaustion.

His words were engraved on her heart. That was enough. Someday, when the pain was only a dull ache of remembrance, she would take them out and cherish them. No one had ever told her he loved her. No one had ever said she was to be his wife.

And no one ever would, again.

Yes, she must go.

Soon. Very soon.

If only she believed she could forget Boss, could someday stop loving him.

Silas made good time to Centerville. "Will you ask your Uncle Wu if he'll go back to the cabin with me?" he asked Ji Rong. "Soomey has been hurt, and I need his advice."

"She is seriously injured?"

"Bruised and cut up a bit. I want a second opinion," he said. "I'll be back in a while. You can close up while you go to your uncle."

"I go quickly." Ji Rong followed him out the door.

Next Silas went to Appledore's. He told Hiram a little of what had happened and suggested that Wilf's and Jenkins's bodies be brought down for burial. He thanked the grocer for his concern, and assured him that he would call on him if necessary. "I think she'll be more comfortable with another Chinese doctoring her," he said.

Hiram's eyebrows climbed halfway up his forehead. "She?"

Damn! "Hell, Hiram, I wasn't going to tell you like this. But yes, Soomey's a woman. She'll be my wife as soon as I can get someone to marry us."

"Silas, are you..." Hiram stopped, licked his lips. "You're a man, Silas, and you've been about the world more than I have. I guess you know what you're doing."

"Something I should have done weeks ago," Silas said. "Now, I've got to go. If you hear a fracas, you might come running with your shotgun."

"Where are you going?"

"To ask Vester a few questions." He left, knowing Hiram was standing open-mouthed behind him.

Vester's Saloon was doing a land-office business, even though it wasn't yet noon and the sun was shining. Three poker games were in progress at as many tables. A slick-looking gambler held a faro bank. Did these men do their mining at night, Silas wondered. Or did they prey on those who worked instead of played?

The bartender told him Vester was out back. There was a well-beaten track along the side wall of the saloon. At its end was a fenced enclosure, a hefty padlock dangling on its open gate. Vester and a man in a once-white apron were inside, doing something with an open barrel. DiCastro, who was leaning against the gatepost, stood erect when he saw Silas.

"Morning, boys," Silas said. "Fine day."

"What do you want, Dewitt?"

"Why, nothing you might have, DiCastro. But I'd like a word with Vester."

The gunfighter stepped into the gateway. "He's busy."

"He'd be a sight busier if I was to go away and come back later with help." Silas eyed DiCastro. "Now I reckon I could get a knife into you about as quick as you could shoot me. But is it worth it?"

DiCastro glared, but his hand, which had been hovering, relaxed back to his side.

Silas raised his voice. "Vester!"

The big man straightened and turned. When he saw who'd called, his red beard split, showing a wide grin. "Well, now, Dewitt. What can I do for you?"

"Let's talk." Silas motioned Vester to lead the way back to the street.

"Hold up a minute," Vester said, stepping back inside the fence. "Now Ferd, you just keep on stirrin'. When it's all mixed together, you pour that bottle of quinine in. And when you're done, you can start on another barrel. You saw what I did."

"You want me to come along?" DiCastro asked.

"No, you stay here and keep your eye out. Them five barrels of whiskey are pretty invitin'." He winked at Silas. "No sense puttin' temptation in the way of weak-willed rascals, now is there, Dewitt?"

Silas conquered the urge to return Vester's grin. *Damn!* The man had a likable streak. "Let's take a walk," he said.

They walked to the edge of town and up a low hillside. High enough that they could see clear across town, Silas found a comfortable rock and they seated themselves. Both stuffed their pipes and lit them.

After a few minutes' silence Silas said, "Eli Jenkins? He followed your orders?"

"You said *followed*. Is he dead?"

"Just answer my question, Vester."

"He did a thing or two for me, now and then. Nothin' important, though. He was a strange 'un, that's for certain. He looked to be meek and mild, but I didn't trust him any further than I could throw him. Too sneaky by half. Always slinking around, prying and poking." Vester drew on his pipe, then took it out and looked at it. "Damn thing. I broke my good one, and this one jest don't seem to want to stay lit."

"So he didn't work for you?"

Vester's head turned and he gave Silas a long, measuring look. "You lookin' to blame me for something he done?"

"I'm looking to see if there was someone behind him, or if he acted on his own."

"Like I said, Dewitt, he was a strange one. More Wilf's man than mine."

Vester pulled the pipe from his mouth. Speaking to it, rather than to Silas, he said, "He made me uneasy, the way he was always watchin' folks." He shook his head. "Reminded me of a weasel. Sneaky, sly, and likely to turn on a man without warnin'."

Silas looked at Vester a moment, trying to read his face. But the thick red beard hid his mouth, and his eyes held an expression as innocent as any new-born babe's. "You have any idea who shot me?"

Vester rubbed a hand across his mouth. "I was afraid you'd ask that." He dug at his pipe, tapped it gently against the rock.

"I run a decent Hell, Dewitt. I may water my whiskey, but not too much, and nobody's ever died from drinking it." He paused.

"Not unless they drank too much, anyhow. Nobody ever walked away from a card game in my saloon with his pockets empty, either. I always give 'em the price of a meal and a bed."

"You've got DiCastro working for you. If he's not a gunfighter, I'm the King of Siam."

Vester's laugh boomed out. "Oh, yeah, he's a gunfighter, sure enough. Got his face on some wanted posters, down in New Mexico. But he's my sister's boy, and she'd never forgive me if I didn't see that he had a place to stay until the hunt dies down." This time when he faced Silas, he was serious. "I swear on my mother's grave it wasn't him who took that shot at you."

"I didn't say it was," Silas agreed. "Are you that sure about the rest of your bully boys?"

"Well, I never liked turnin' my back on Wilf, come to think of it. Or Eli neither." He shrugged. "As for the rest of 'em, I told my boys to rough up whoever came to our little fracas, just to show the town that we're not going to take kindly to too much law and order. But I don't hold with killin' unless it's needed. And they knew it."

He appeared to consider. "You made Wilf and Henry look like fools, Dewitt. They done their best to get even, and you managed to balk 'em every time. I don't reckon Henry's gonna bother you none, 'less Wilf eggs him on. He ain't got much backbone."

With his pipe stem, Vester tapped on Silas's knee. "Now when I come over here from Bannock City, I figured you and me was goin' to butt heads, sooner or later. But we ain't, so far. Maybe we won't, so long as I and my boys stay down here in our end of town, and you stay up there in yours."

Silas answered the question not quite asked. "I reckon that'll work. So long as your boys don't get too far out of line."

Again Vester spoke to his pipe. "I figured to build my saloon in Placerville, then I heard you was here in Centerville."

"Why didn't you?"

"There's some men I can lick, some I step aside for, because I know they're stronger than me." Vester's teeth flashed inside the bushy beard. "I reckon you and me, we're about even."

It wasn't quite a challenge. "So?"

"So two strong men in a town keeps things even. My boys leave the respectable folks alone, and your crowd keeps the reformers in line."

Pulling a folding knife from his pocket, Vester dug into his pipe. "After Henry and Wilf made such fools of themselves tryin' to ambush you, I told 'em to let you alone. Anything my boys did to you and yours after that, they done on their own."

"Ahuh! And I suppose you don't have any idea who broke into my store then."

"Well, now, I reckon Eli had a hand in that, and I ain't speculatin' about who helped him with it. Let's just say that I appreciate you putting me in the way of making a little profit."

Reluctantly, Silas agreed. "And it wouldn't be right for me to let you get away with it more than once, now would it, Vester?"

"You reckon you could whop me?"

"I think I could make a pretty good try at it."

Considering, Vester looked him up and down. "You ain't as big as me, but you're solid." He laughed. "Anytime you feel like tryin', you let me know. We'll have us a grand old time!"

"We'll see." Mentally he went back over what Vester had said. "So nothing that's happened to me since the ambush was your doing? What about the Chinese kids? Have any of your bully boys been after them?"

"Why the hell for? Them Chinese, they're like fleas on a dog. Everywhere, and impossible to git rid of. What's a couple of brats, more or less?"

"And you've heard nothing?"

"Nary a word." He fussed with his pipe once more. "One thing I do know, though."

"What's that?"

"Wilf had him one of them newfangled Remington repeaters. He's not the kind to shoot from ambush, but he's been lettin' Eli hole up in his cabin since that big snowstorm. I shore can't think of anybody else that might have done it. And I know most of what's goin' on in this here town."

Silas was conscious of a certain relief. He didn't like Vester, but he'd gotten the impression the man was an honest scoundrel, if that made sense.

"I'm obliged for you being frank with me," he told Vester, rising. Then he thought of something else.

"What you said about Jenkins being likely to turn on a man? You were right."

"Yeah?"

"He killed Wilf. Gutted him."

Chapter Twenty-six

Uncle Wu examined Soomey while Silas waited impatiently. At last he came outside.

"Well?" Silas demanded.

"Very sick. You go town three day. I stay."

"The hell I will!"

The old Chinese doctor, not quite five feet tall, seemed to grow. "I doctor. Say you go." He pointed down the trail toward Centerville. "Go. Come back three day. Su Mei not be sick."

Silas went.

By the time he returned to the cabin, Silas figured he'd driven away most of his customers and alienated all his friends. He'd given serious thought to picking a fight with someone like Joe DiCastro, just to let out some of his mad. He was amazed Ji Rong hadn't quit.

To save his sanity, he'd worked hard at getting the new store built. He wanted to have it ready before they were married. Soomey deserved a better home than the dark, drafty cabin.

When he saw Soomey looking as if the least breeze would pick her up like an autumn leaf, he exploded. "When was the last time you ate a decent meal?" he yelled.

Her answer was long in coming, and when it did, she sounded almost drugged. "I do not know. When I eat, it seems to make a big, hard nugget in my belly. Then no more will go in."

"Uncle Wu said your appetite had improved." *Damn!* He should have been up here, seeing that she ate right, instead of trusting the old Chinese.

"He thought I was eating, but I could not. I fooled him, hiding food in my blanket."

"Little fool!" Silas knelt beside her. "Now look, Soomey, I want you to eat something every hour or so." He hushed her protest with a gentle hand over her mouth. "Just a bite or two, that's enough. But every hour. Promise me."

She looked at him, her eyes showing her doubt. "I promise I will try, Boss."

"That's all I can ask." He'd seen a man's life saved that way once, when some frightful tropical fever had made him so sick that little would stay in his stomach. One mouthful, every hour, day and night, had been enough to keep him alive, yet not enough to cause vomiting.

He went to the shelves in the corner and chose a can of peaches. The sweet, syrupy fruit would set better than beans.

For the better part of a week he fed her. Twice he went to town because he had to get more canned fruit and check on the store, leaving her alone for three long hours at a time. The second time he came back to find her out of bed, stowing her meager belongings in her pack.

"I am well now," she said in reply to his demand for explanation. "It is time for me to go from this place."

"Damn it, Soomey, you're not going anywhere!"

She paused in her packing. What gold she had would keep her alive until she could reach Portland. It was unfortunate that some creature had chewed on her pack during the time it lay in the woods, but she had mended the hole most carefully. Sadly she set the red silk kimono aside. A young Chinese male would not have such a garment. But her pistols must go with her, as must the remaining Chinese herbs and medicines.

"I worked for you. I have quit. You cannot force me to

remain." She kept her back to Boss, knowing that if she looked into his face, her will would be weakened.

Soomey did not hear his reply, but from the tone, she suspected it was a curse. She tucked the leather bag containing her remaining gold coins into the lacquer box containing uncooked rice. They should be safe there. Finally she rolled the thin blanket she had used on the journey from San Francisco and stuffed it into the top of the pack. "I am ready."

"The hell you are." He took the pack from her and tossed it across the cabin. "Sit down," he thundered, pointing at the stump that still served as their chair.

She remained standing, still not looking at him. "I am not slave. I may go when I choose and where I choose." She heard her voice tremble and was ashamed. Such a poor, weak female!

"Then choose to stay. Please, Soomey. Don't go."

In surprise she looked up at him. "You ask me? Why?"

"Because I don't want you to go. I'd worry about you."

This morning she had finally forced herself to look in the mirror. All the black thread stitches were gone, but the scar across her cheek was still red and puckered. Her bruises had faded to faint brown patches. Soon they would be invisible, unlike the bruises on her soul.

But her hair! It was only a black stubble on her head, with small pink patches where new skin was growing. There would never be hair in those patches.

Ugly! How could Boss bear to look at her?

"There is no need for you to worry about me. Li Ching will be going to Portland as soon as the passes are clear of snow, and I will go with him. I have already paid him to take me there."

She looked at him, imprinting his face upon her mind. Eventually, she knew, the image would fade, and all she would have would be a dim memory of a man with silver-gilt hair, cool gray eyes, and a mouth that could give indescribable pleasure.

"I must go," she said at last. "If I stay with you, soon you would come to pity me. I do not want that."

Silas stared at her. "Pity? What do you mean, pity?"

"Look at me! I am ugly." Sweeping the kerchief from her head, she brushed her other hand across the stubble. "I am bald."

She reached for the closure of her too-big plaid shirt. "Shall I show you the rest? All the scars? There are many, and they will not disappear. Ugly!"

Silas swept her into his arms, feeling her fragility, though she was far more substantial than she had been. Wanting to comfort her, to love her. "Ah, Soomey, those are only on the outside. What's inside, that's what I love. I don't give a damn about a few scars, and you could be bald as a billiard ball and I wouldn't care."

She grew very still in his arms. "What you love?" she whispered after a long silence. "What do you mean?"

He sat on the stump, holding her on his lap. With one hand he tipped her chin up so she was forced to look him straight in the eye. "What do you think I mean? I love you, little tyrant. I can't imagine life without you. That's why you can't go away."

For the first time he saw fear in her face. "You say this now, but what of tomorrow? Next month? When my hair grows in patches and my face is still horrible?"

He kissed her on the tip of her nose. "We'll buy you a wig—one with long black curls and a big pink bow." The next kiss was to her forehead, to wipe out the frown lines. "And a box of fancy French face powder." This time his lips touched the slightly ridged scar on her cheek, making him wish he'd done a better job of sewing it up. "And I'll hire a stable of servants, so you won't have to lift a finger if you don't want to."

"Concubines do not have servants." Her voice was small, hesitant.

Silas pulled her against him, holding her securely, stroking her head. "Once this is grown out, the bald spots won't even show. They're all small, and none of them is more than a quarter-inch across."

"Did you hear me, Boss? I tell you concubines do not have servants."

"I hear you. I don't know why they shouldn't, but that's not important anyhow. My wife will have servants."

"Your wife?" Almost a whisper.

He held his laughter at the disbelief in her voice. "Umhmmm. There's a preacher who wandered into town the other day. He'll marry us. Ji Rong's going to Bannock City tomorrow to bring back the old Chinese scholar, and he'll invite all your friends, too."

"Your wife?" A squeak.

"We'll use the new store for the wedding. We're raising the roof tomorrow, and—" He stopped when her hand clamped firmly over his mouth.

"You shut up, Boss. My turn to talk."

Her wrist was thin, delicate skin stretched over fine bones, easily pulled away from his mouth. "There's only one thing you need to say," he told her, kissing the palm of her hand.

She shivered. "What is that?"

"Whether you want to live here or somewhere else. I'll take care of the rest."

"You are crazy man!" she sputtered. "You do not wish to marry me! Americans do not marry Chinese women. No man marries his concubine! And I am used goods—"

"Darlin'," he said, lowering his head, "be still." The rest of her protests were swallowed as he covered her mouth with his.

A long time later, she said, "To me marriage seems only another sort of slavery. But you say you hate slavery."

"Marriage is a partnership, Soomey. Or it should be."

"What is to prevent one partner from taking advantage of the other?"

"Trust. Honesty." He stared across the room at the opposite wall, brows lowered, thinking. "Some business partners have a contract, setting out what each will do."

She pondered his words. "I like that. Will you give me

contract of marriage?"

He looked at her a long time, wishing he could read her mind. With a sigh, he nodded. "If that's what you want."

"It is. Then if you decide you no longer want me—"

"That'll never happen!"

She hushed him with a hand on his lips, then jerked it back when his tongue touched her palm. "If you decide this, you can fire me. If I decide I no longer want you, I can quit." After a moment's thought, she added, "But you will not have to pay me two dollars a week anymore, Boss. I will be your wife for free."

"You will, huh?"

"Yes." She hesitated. "If you still want me."

"Soomey, I swear," he lifted his right hand, "that as soon as I can get you to a preacher, I will marry you. And if there's some kind of Chinese ceremony you want, we'll do that, too. And you'll have your contract." He cupped her face between his hands. "Is there anything else?"

She frowned. "I am Chinese. Your friends will not approve."

"Darlin', my friends will love you. Anybody else won't matter. Besides, there's all that gold. My share's considerable. Folks will probably treat you like a duchess."

"Duchess? What is this?"

"A very, very special woman," he told her, knowing he'd never spoken truer words.

Her eyes were dark with doubt as she shook her head. "I am dreaming," she said. "But I do not wish to wake up. Not ever."

Spring was scarcely a green mist on the willows along Ophir Creek when Silas came down from his cabin to meet his bride. He wanted to sing, to shout his joy to the skies. Soomey had insisted that she could not marry him until her hair was at least an inch long and her bruises had all faded. So he had waited, unwillingly, but understanding why.

While her hair grew, Soomey turned the two raw rooms

at the back of his new store building into a home. She had made curtains for the single glass window and decorated the unfinished plank walls with Chinese knickknacks—fans and delicate pictures painted on silk and a scroll that, she said, ensured them many sons. It hung over the bed.

She had also made her wedding dress, but he hadn't seen it yet. He hoped it was red.

He'd been banished from town for two days now, on orders from Soomey and Tilly, who was acting, of all things, as mother of the bride. She had arrived in Centerville in a demure gray dress, her vibrant hair covered with a dark wool shawl. He doubted anyone but him had recognized her.

Well, maybe Vester, but he'd keep his mouth shut.

Another string of firecrackers stuttered, punctuating a wild whoop. The party had already started. He prodded the gelding into a more rapid pace, eager and apprehensive all at once.

Today was his wedding day. Soomey would be his wife at last.

"I cannot!" Soomey pulled the lacy veil from her hair and threw it onto the bed. "I will not!"

"That's enough, young lady!" Tilly picked up the veil and made sure it had not been torn. She laid it carefully across the quilt and stood looking at Soomey.

Soomey looked back at her, determined to win this argument. "I will not wear a veil. My hat covers my head so that it cannot be seen. The veil does not." She had fashioned the hat from the same red silk as her gown, a rich brocade with tiny purple flowers woven into it. But even she had to admit that it was not an object of beauty, even though she had copied it as best she could from a drawing in one of the Appledore woman's fashion books. All it was good for was covering her head, no longer bald but still ugly.

"Oh, for—" Tilly's magnificent bosom swelled with the deep breath she took. "Look, honey, nobody but you cares about your hair. In fact, I think it's kinda cunning that short."

"Cunning? What is this?"

"Oh, you know. Not pretty, exactly, but not ugly either. Just, well, you know, cunning."

"Bah." Soomey picked up her hat, turning it this way and that. "This is not so bad."

"Bad? Honey, it's so bad, it's funny. Why Silas will take one look at you and bust out laughing."

"He will laugh?" Soomey turned to Tilly in horror. "Boss will laugh at me? He will think I look ridiculous?"

Tilly nodded seriously. "He'll think you look like a clown."

The red hat landed in the corner as Soomey made up her mind. "I will wear the veil," she said to Tilly, "but I will not dare move my head or it will slide off."

The woman picked up a small jar and dipped a twig into it. Before Soomey could protest, she rubbed something that smelled suspiciously like pine pitch on the top of Soomey's head. "I figured we'd have to stick it down, so I had Celeste fix this for me. You can wash it off with a little of that coal oil Silas sells."

She would leave the pitch on her head forever first, Soomey vowed silently. She never wanted to smell coal oil again, not after having it splash across her naked body, stinging and stinking. She stood still while Tilly adjusted the veil.

"Look." Tilly held up a large mirror. "Aren't you just grand?"

Soomey saw herself, yet it was not her. The woman in the mirror had shining eyes and blushing cheeks. A pale pink line underscored one of her dark eyes, and her hair was very short, but she was not at all ugly.

Her gown was everything she had hoped, a blend of Chinese and American style. Its high-collared blouse fastened with elaborate frogs, and clung to her body, flaring just below the waist in a tiny skirt that the fashion book she had borrowed called a "peplum", whatever that meant. Her skirt was slim, rather than flared, for so many yards of fabric had seemed wasteful to her. She had split the skirt to the knee on the left, so that she could walk, and now she looked down, thinking that Boss would like the glimpse of bare leg the slit allowed, for she had refused to wear the hideous black stockings Appledore's wife had tried to sell her.

The dress was beautiful. She looked again, seeing a lovely stranger. "That is me?"

"That's you, honey. Now, let's get this show on the road." She enfolded Soomey in her arms. "You're gettin' a good man."

"Oh, yes," Soomey agreed. She peered through the crack. "So many people! You must go out first."

"Uh-uh, honey. This is as far as I go. 'Twouldn't do for someone to recognize me. Why those decent women out there would be as insulted as if someone caught 'em in their shifts."

"But—"

"Git, girl. Silas is a'waitin'." Tilly swung the door wider. "Start the music, boys," she called, giving Soomey a little push.

Soomey hesitated, reached for Tilly's hand, and squeezed. "You are a very good person. Thank you."

A fiddle, a di, and a yeuquin created a peculiar harmony as Soomey stepped into the big room that would be Boss's store. Now it was decorated with fir branches, drapings of red fabric, and many candles. It was filled with men, most of them miners Soomey had seen in the store or around town. A few women were clustered near one wall, their hats like peculiar flowers against the new wood. As she stood, the crowd parted, forming a corridor. Soomey took a step, then another. Her feet were strangely leaden.

Boss stood near the opposite wall with Tao Ni and Buffalo. Behind them were a tall, very thin man in a rusty, long-skirted coat—the preacher—and Feng Jiao Yan, wearing a fine embroidered robe. Boss smiled at her, and her dismay intensified. What had she done?

What was she doing?

Soomey kept her eyes on her clasped hands as she walked the length of the room. She willed herself not to weep as the ceremony progressed. The preacher's words meant little to her, but she repeated them when told to, made promises when Boss asked for them. Jiao Yan's blessing barely penetrated her awareness. Only when Boss slipped a heavy gold ring on her finger did she look up at him.

"With this ring, I thee wed," she heard him say, and suddenly it all became real. She waited, trembling, until he had finished speaking, then flung herself into his arms. "I love you, Boss," she sobbed. "And I promise to be very good wife."

The preacher droned on, but she ignored him. "I will never serve you rice. I will never argue with you, or disobey you, or... or—"

Boss stopped her vows with a kiss. His lips barely touching hers, he said, in a very quiet voice, "Don't make promises you can't keep, darlin'."

"Oh, no, I do not, but—"

His hand covered up any more words. "Now, turn around and say hello to everyone."

Heat suffused her face as Soomey turned and saw that the entire town had heard her impassioned promises.

The music began again and Soomey found herself swung from man to man, enduring enthusiastic kisses from dozens of bewhiskered miners. When at last she was back under Boss's protective arm, she touched her stinging cheeks. "I feel as if I have been scrubbed with a very stiff brush."

"You look like it too," Boss said. "Do you want some wine?"

His hand was on her back, rubbing lightly between her shoulders and her waist. Soomey shivered, yet she was curiously hot. Looking up at him, she saw a matching heat in his eyes. "I want you," she said, emboldened by her new status. "My husband, when can we leave this place?"

His smile was both possessive and sensual. "Just as soon as

we can sneak out." He glanced to either side. "Look, you mosey over that way, like you're going after some punch, then when you get close to the door, slip out. I'll duck out the back way, and meet you at the livery stable."

"Can we not just go?"

"Not if we don't want a shivaree." He gave her a little push. "Never mind. I'll explain later. You go on and ease out."

Every person she met on her way across the room wanted to wish her well, Soomey found. But at last she was outside, shivering in the cold night air. From the front of the building, voices called, then firecrackers exploded in a long rattle. She pried the veil from her head and wadded it into a small bundle as she ran along the deserted street.

Boss was waiting, already mounted. "Where are we going?" she panted. Running in a slim skirt was very difficult.

"I borrowed a cabin." He reached down and lifted her onto a thick pad behind his saddle.

She wrapped her arms around him and snuggled close.

They rode for about a quarter-hour, over the hill behind the livery stable and up a draw. The little cabin they stopped at was barely larger than the bed it contained. Even as they arrived, more firecrackers sounded from town.

Boss cared for the horse before leading her inside. He took the veil from her hand, shook it out, and replaced it on her head. "Did I tell you today how beautiful you are?"

Soomey held him away when he bent to kiss her. "Boss, I mean what I say. I will be a good wife to you. Obedient, agreeable, submissive..."

Again he stopped her with a kiss. Soomey all but forgot what she had been saying, and she let herself enjoy the caress of his lips, the sensuous tickle of his beard. His hands roamed her body, sliding across the silk and leaving trails of heat.

He lifted her high, looking up at her, his eyes shining in the candlelight. "Beautiful," he exclaimed, letting her slide slowly along his body until her lips were at a level with his.

"Mine," he boasted, looking into her eyes. "My wife."

"My husband," she answered, framing his face between her hands. "A beautiful man." For a moment she studied him. "We will have beautiful sons. Strong sons."

"Beautiful daughters, too," he whispered, nuzzling her just under the ear. "Stubborn and independent, just like their mother."

"No. They will be properly obedient."

His laughter vibrated through her body. "Soomey, Soomey," he said, setting her back onto her feet, "whatever gave you the idea that I wanted an obedient, submissive wife?"

Surprised, she searched his face. "Is this not what all men desire? So they may be masters in their houses?"

"Maybe so," he said, his fingers busy on the frogs of her blouse, "but not this man. The woman I fell in love with is strong, brave, courageous—she would have died to save my life more than once—and as independent as they come." Hands cupping her bared breasts, he rubbed his thumbs over nipples already throbbing in anticipation. "Oh, darlin', just do your best to stay out of trouble from now on, will you?"

She would have answered if she had been able to find her voice amidst the swirling storm of emotions his teeth and tongue and lips and hands aroused in her. So instead, Soomey chose to match him caress for caress, pleasure for pleasure.

They loved for hours, until the candles guttered and the lantern flickered for want of oil. Soomey was exhausted, sated, when Boss at last collapsed atop her, his skin filmed with sweat, his breath rasping in his throat.

She held him when he would have rolled away, wanting the solid weight of him to remind her, as she drifted into sleep, that he was truly hers.

Before setting her chop upon it, Soomey had read their marriage contract carefully. It gave her the right to quit if he did not live up to his part of the agreement. But she never would, for to do so would be like dying.

He had the same right. Once again she silently vowed to be a good wife, however Boss defined the role. Were he to leave her, it would be worse than dying.

She kissed his shoulder, that being all of him she could reach with her lips. Boss moved, rolled away, then reached back to pull her tightly against his body.

"Love you," he muttered, before his breathing slowed in sleep.

To Soomey, his words were far more significant than those he had spoken before the preacher. For these he had not even been aware of speaking.

These words she believed.

Boss loved her.

THE END

Author's Note

There were towns in the Boise Basin upon which the places in this book are based and there was a gold rush there in the 1860s, but all people and events came solely from my imagination. Please forgive me for taking some liberties with topography, too. Sometimes those darned creeks and gulches just don't occur in the right places.

About the Author

AMONG HER VARIED CAREERS ARE A COUPLE JUDITH B. GLAD actually chose, rather than falling into. With her children in school, she decided it was time for her to follow her own dreams, so she went back to school and studied botany. After completing her M.S., she became a botanical consultant, and spent the next twenty-odd years picking flowers for a living. Well, it was a little more complicated than that, but she picked enough flowers to keep her happy.

Consulting is not always steady work, so one slow winter Judith decided to spend a little time at her second career choice. Now she'd done a lot of writing as a consultant, but somehow describing proposed mine sites and interpreting statistical data wasn't the kind of writing she wanted to do. So she wrote a book. And another, and... Before she knew it, she was spending more time writing than picking flowers.

Judith lives in Portland, Oregon, where her garden blooms all year 'round and the long, rainy winters give her lots of time for writing. Visit her website (www.judithbglad.com) for samples of her stories.

Judith B. Glad's
Western Historical
"Behind the Ranges" Series
The Queen of Cherry Vale
Ice Princess
The Duchess of Ophir Creek
Noble Savage
Knight in a Black Hat
The Lost Baroness
The Imperial Engineer
Undercover Cavaliere
Squire's Quest
Lord of Misrule (a Christmas novella)

And her other books:
Regency Romance:
The Anonymous Amanuensis
A Sisterly Regard
The Portrait (novella)
Contemporary Romance
Solomon's Decision
Never the Twain
Twice Victorious
A Safe and Welcome Nest
Paranormal Romance
Improbable Solution
Mainstream
A Strange Little Band

Made in the USA
Charleston, SC
23 November 2013